just don't mention it

ESTELLE MASKAME

sourcebooks
fire

Published by Sourcebooks Fire, an imprint of Sourcebooks
P.O. Box 4410, Naperville, Illinois 60567-4410
(630) 961-3900
sourcebooks.com

Originally published in 2018 in the United Kingdom by Black & White Publishing Ltd.

Library of Congress Cataloging-in-Publication data is on file with the publisher.

Printed and bound in Canada.
MBP 10 9 8 7 6 5 4 3 2 1

To all of my incredible readers, because this story is for you.

ALSO BY ESTELLE MASKAME

Did I Mention I Love You?
Did I Mention I Need You?
Did I Mention I Miss You?
Dare to Fall

1

FIVE YEARS EARLIER

MY WRIST IS STIFF as I run a hand back through my hair, damp and tousled after lying in the tub for the past hour, dipping my head below the water every once in a while to count how many seconds I can hold my breath. My record is ninety-three, but I wish it were more.

I sit down on the edge of the tub and reach for the packet of painkillers by the sink. There are only a few tablets left, so I'm hoping Mom will stock up on some more soon. I pop two of the tablets out of the package and clamp my fist around them, enclosing them in my palm as I lean over and pour myself a glass of water. I swallow the first, and then the second, then pour the remainder of the water into the sink.

My gaze falls to my shoulder. The skin is grazed on the back of my shoulder blade, but it's stopped bleeding now. Below the fresh cut, there's a deepening bruise, a mixture of purple and blue. I prod it with my fingers, and it stings from the pressure, creating a dull ache beneath my skin deep under the surface. I'd grab myself some ice from the kitchen, but I'd have to pass the living room, and the last thing I want to do is draw attention to myself. It's after eleven. I should be asleep by now. I have school in the morning.

I get to my feet and stash the remaining painkillers back in the cabinet above the sink, at the very back of the second shelf from the top, because it's the highest I can reach. I already know I'll need them tomorrow. When I click the cabinet door shut again, my empty reflection stares back at me in the mirror, and that's when I notice the tiny cut in my lower lip. I edge forward, pinching my lip between my thumb and forefinger as I examine it up close in the mirror. I can't remember when I got it, but it's not fresh, so I know I didn't get it tonight.

I shake my head and step back. It doesn't matter when I got it, because as soon as it heals, there'll be another to replace it. The same way there'll be more blood, the same way there'll be more bruises.

My reflection is still there, my eyes lifeless and sunken into my face, my shoulders slumped low, and my lips set in a permanent frown. I press a hand to my forehead and push my hair back to reveal a deep cut that runs parallel to my hairline. It's taking forever to heal, and I'm starting to worry that it's going to turn into a scar. Quickly, I smooth my damp hair back down over it, then turn away from the mirror.

I grab my shirt and pull it on. There's a row of fading brown bruises along my lower back that I need to cover, so going shirtless is never an option anymore. There's always something new to hide. I slip into a pair of shorts, then toss my towel into the drained tub and glance at myself one last time in the mirror before I leave the bathroom. Nothing is on display, so I'm good to go.

Carefully, I push open the door a few inches, and as silently as I can, I step out into the hall. There are no lights on, and it's dark. I can hear the sound of the TV from the living room and the sound of my parents laughing in unison at whatever show they're watching. I keep my steps light as I edge along the hall toward the stairs, but I notice the living room door is open a crack as I grow nearer, and instead of disappearing upstairs like I should be doing, I creep over and peer around the doorframe.

Mom and Dad are on the couch, their bodies entwined. He has her held close against him, his arms wrapped securely around her, his chin resting on top of her head. Although she's laughing, she still seems tired. She only got back from the office just as I was locking the bathroom door and climbing into the tub an hour ago.

I back away from the living room and spin around, running up the stairs as fast as I can, two steps at a time. Against the carpet, my footsteps are almost silent. The door to my room is wide open, the light is still on, but I stop for a second to peer into the room on my right, my brothers' room.

I squint into the dull room as my eyes slowly adjust. In the bed on the left, my youngest brother, Chase, is asleep. He's on his stomach, his face pressed into his pillow with one leg dangling over the side of the mattress. Over in the bed to the right, Jamie is snoring softly. There's a bruised lump on his forehead from earlier in the day, when another kid on his fourth-grade baseball team hurled the ball at his face by accident.

I wish my bruises were only accidents too.

Stepping out of the room, I pull the door closed, but not completely. Chase is still scared of the dark and he likes it to be left open, so I leave a safe crack of a couple inches and then turn for my own room.

It's exactly as I left it. My math homework is spread across my floor, nothing more than worthless scraps of paper that aren't good enough to hand back in next week. One of the sheets is torn into three uneven pieces. It's the one that contains the single equation I messed up on. But one simple error is apparently one error too many, even if it is only seventh grade algebra. I'll need to fix it tomorrow, and then pray my damned hardest that everything is finally up to his standard.

I gather up the papers and stuff them into my backpack, then I turn off the light and climb into bed. Only it hurts, so I wince and breathe out, moving onto my right side. I pull my comforter up to my chest, and I lie there in the dark for what feels like forever, staring aimlessly at my wall. It always takes me a long time to fall asleep.

I raise my left hand and hold it up in the air. I flex my fingers, then roll my wrist in a circular motion three times. I'm supposed to do this a bunch of times during the day, but I keep forgetting. After having my wrist in a cast for the past four weeks, it's super stiff. It could take another few weeks before the fracture fully heals.

There are sudden footsteps against the stairs, and I drop my hand back down immediately, squeezing my eyes shut and pretending to be asleep. I do this a lot, so I'm pretty good at it. I even open my mouth a little, deepening my breath.

My door opens, and there's a moment of silence where he hovers for a couple seconds before he takes a step inside. And I know it's him. It's always him.

He enters, closing the door behind him with a soft click. There's no sound other than his breathing for a while, and then I begin to sense him slowly moving around my room. I don't know what he's doing, and no matter how badly I want to roll over and open my eyes to check, I don't want to take the risk, so I stay as still as possible.

I hear some fumbling, and I think he could be searching through my backpack, because there's the shuffling of paper, and after what happened earlier tonight, it seems likely that it's my math homework he's after. Silence again. More shuffling. A long sigh that sounds almost like a groan.

And then he speaks, letting his voice break the silence. His words are low and hushed as he murmurs, "I'm sorry, Tyler." I don't know if he thinks I'm asleep or awake, but I do know that he says he's sorry a lot. I also know that he doesn't mean it. If he did, he wouldn't have to say it again tomorrow, and then the day after that. I'm scared he's always going to have something to apologize for.

I continue to keep still, because the quicker I can convince him I'm asleep, the quicker he'll leave. And I think he's buying it, because he hasn't said anything else. I don't think he's moved either, and I don't know where in my room he is. A few minutes pass where nothing happens, where I focus on my breathing, where I pray that he'll leave. And then there are more footsteps that are hard to hear against the carpet, and then the opening of the door, and then one final pause. He sighs again, but he sounds annoyed, and I can't tell if he's annoyed at me or if he's annoyed at himself. I think it's me.

It usually is.

My door is pulled shut, and he's gone.

I exhale in relief and open my eyes. At least I know it's over for tonight. I can get some sleep now—only I won't, because I haven't had a full night's sleep in months. I'll wake in a few hours, where I'll stare at my ceiling for a while before I fall back asleep, and then repeat.

Yet although I can never sleep well, this is always the best part of every day. That time where I know that for the next seven hours I'm safe. I like that feeling, but I also hate knowing that tomorrow I'll have to do this all over again.

Tomorrow, I need to go to school and keep on acting normal in front of everyone.

Tomorrow, I need to try my best to keep tonight's fresh injuries hidden from Mom.

Tomorrow, new bruises will develop and new cuts will appear.

And they will all be caused by Dad.

2

SOMEONE'S BEEN FUCKING AROUND with my beer. It doesn't taste the same as it did ten minutes ago. I close one eye and tilt the rim of the bottle toward me, peering inside, trying to figure out if someone has been pouring other drinks into it while I haven't been looking. I'm getting a strong scent of rum. I glance over to the kitchen. Jake is there, his back to me, bent over the countertop as he mixes together a bunch of different drinks as though he's a fully trained bartender. I fucking hate that guy.

"What's wrong?"

I drop my glare down to Tiffani. She's been sprawled across me for the past five minutes, her long bare legs folded over my knee and her head resting against my bicep. She's been running her nails slowly around my chest in a circular motion, but I haven't realized she's stopped until right now. Her face is tilted up to look at me, and her bright blue eyes are studying me through a thick set of eyelashes that didn't exist yesterday. "Jake thinks he's hilarious slipping rum into my beer," I tell her, then I press my lips together as I set my bottle down on the small table beside the couch. "Come here," I murmur, pulling my arm out from beneath her and sliding it around her shoulders instead, pulling her closer against me. She presses her head to my chest, and I know for a fact she's going to get at least five layers of her makeup on my shirt, but I don't care because now I'm running my eyes up and down her legs. I move my free hand to her knee, then slide it across the smooth skin on her thighs. Her tiny black dress is too short and too tight, but that's nothing to complain about. "What time are we heading out?"

"I was thinking eleven," she says, but I know she's distracted because she reaches for my hand and places hers on top. Slowly, she moves my hand higher up her thigh, under her dress. I can feel the lace of her underwear beneath my fingers, and when I look down at her, she's smirking as she leans up toward me, her lips brushing my ear as she murmurs, "Are you staying here tonight?" I used to love that thing she does with her voice, where she lowers it to a breathy whisper that would have driven me insane a year or two ago, but it just doesn't do it for me anymore. She's only trying to keep me interested with the promise of sex.

But whatever, right now it's working. I sit up a little and pull her entirely onto my lap, my hand still gripping her hip beneath her dress and my other moving her blond hair to one side so that I can press my lips to her neck. She tilts her head back fully as she runs her fingers through my hair, her eyes closed. I take her skin beneath my teeth, leaving my all-too-familiar mark on her body. Tiffani claims she hates hickeys, but she never attempts to stop me, so I beg to differ.

Suddenly, she pulls away, springing off me and getting to her feet, straightening up fast. Over the sound of the music that Jake's controlling from the speakers in the kitchen, I haven't heard the front door open. Tiffani has, and now she's setting her drink on the coffee table and pulling at her dress, willing it to cover more of her thighs.

7

Right now, it hardly covers her ass. "Mom," she splutters, taking a few barefooted steps across the hardwood flooring. "I thought you said you were working late."

"It's eight thirty," Jill states. There's a black folder held to her chest as she moves further into the kitchen, her heels clicking against the floor. "This *is* late." She purses her lips in disapproval as she looks around. First at the alcohol lining the countertop, then at Jake, who is leaning over to quickly lower the volume of the music, and then at Tiffani. "You didn't tell me you were having friends over."

Tiffani is still pulling at her dress, because if there's one thing I know for sure about her mom, it's that she won't be impressed right now. "Because I thought we'd be gone before you got back," she admits, shrugging. She has her arms folded across her chest now, but it's obvious she's only attempting to hide how exposed her body is in that dress.

"And where exactly are you planning on heading?" Jill asks in that hard tone she seems to always have. In the past three years that I've been dating Tiffani, I don't think I've ever seen her mom crack a smile. She's kind of a bitch. They both are.

"There's a party," Tiffani says, pouting. "I thought we could all just hang out here until it was time to show up, because c'mon, Mom, we never turn up early to house parties. That's just embarrassing."

"Fine," Jill says, but the stern tone to her voice makes it clear that she's not happy we're here. "Keep the music down. I have a pounding headache." She rubs her temples as though to prove this, then flicks her hair over her shoulder and spins around, back toward the door. As she leaves, she throws me a disgusted glance as her eyes narrow, and I raise my hand and wave back at her. I grin only because I know it'll piss her off.

The thing is, Tiffani's mom doesn't like me. She never has from the very first moment I met her, back when Tiffani and I were nothing more than friends. Even then, she didn't want her daughter around a kid like me. Bad influence, she thought, and in some ways, I was. Over the years, her dislike for me has grown into seething contempt, which she doesn't even attempt to hide. But I don't even care all that much about Tiffani, let alone her mom, and I know this relationship isn't going anywhere, so I'm not worried about winning over her parents. The second Jill is gone, Tiffani relaxes back into her dress and says, "She's such a pain sometimes." Rolling her eyes, she tells Jake to turn the music back up as she joins him by the speakers. He's careful not to play it as loud as before.

Pushing myself up from the couch, I get to my feet and head toward them both as they hover around the kitchen countertop, debating over which songs to add to the playlist and which drink to have next. I push my way in between the two of them and throw my arm around Tiffani's shoulders, and as she leans in closer against me, Jake watches us out of the corner of his eye. Jake Maxwell can get any damn girl he wants, but he can't get Tiffani. I think it'll forever infuriate him knowing that three years ago, she chose to get together with me rather than with him. Sometimes I like the satisfaction of knowing I'm with a girl so many other guys would kill to have by their side. Other times, I *wish* Tiffani had chosen Jake over me. That way, it would be him she puts through hell and back and not me.

I reach over and pluck a new bottle of beer from the pack, and as soon as it's in my hand, Jake is lifting his head and asking, "What's wrong with the beer you already have?" The asshole smirks at me as he raises an eyebrow, and again I think how this whole "*let's pretend to be friends for the sake of everyone else*" thing is nothing but bullshit. I just want to knock the guy out.

9

I sharpen my glare, fixing him with a threatening hard look. More often than not, I don't need words to warn someone not to fuck with me, but with Jake, he's used to it by now, so instead of backing off, he only snickers and passes me the bottle opener. Seriously, I think he just pisses me off because he's hoping I'll snap eventually. It's like he lives to test my patience.

"What the hell are Dean and Megs doing upstairs?" he asks as casual as ever, glancing down at the watch on his wrist. When he looks back up, he motions to the drink he was working on five minutes ago. "I've created an exotic signature cocktail, and I need Dean to be the guinea pig who drinks it first."

I lean over and steal a glance into the cup, and the only exotic thing about it is that it's a deep green. "I'll go get them," I say. Releasing my hold on Tiffani, I pop the top off my beer and take a swig as I head for the stairs. My steps are slow, my beer held loosely by the tips of my fingers, my other hand in my hair. It pisses me off that I'm not drunk yet. We've still got a few hours to fill before we head over to the party, so I've got time to change that. I can't do parties sober. I never have.

The door to Tiffani's room is open a few inches, and I can see Meghan having a breakdown as she paces across the carpet, both her hands pressed to her face while she lets out a long groan. Dean only watches her and scratches at the back of his neck.

"You guys are taking your time up here, ain't you?" I say, pushing open the door wider and stepping into Tiffani's room. They both look at me, although Meghan looks more exasperated than anything else, and she seems to scream under her breath through gritted teeth as she throws herself down onto Tiffani's bed. That's when I notice that her dress is open and her back exposed. I lift an eyebrow at Dean. "Have you guys been hooking up?"

"Funny," Dean says, sighing. He shakes his head and nods back to Meghan. "The zipper is stuck."

Meghan dramatically sits up and sniffs, telling me, "I'm going to have to borrow something of Tiffani's," as though it's the worst thing in the world. I know she'll kill me if I roll my eyes right now, but it's hard not to when she's up here having a breakdown over a damn dress. After being with Tiffani for three years, I'm somewhat used to outfit dilemmas.

"Come here," I say. Setting my beer down on Tiffani's dresser, I move over to the bed and reach for Meghan's hands, pulling her up to her feet. I step behind her and run my eyes over her pale skin, down to the zipper that's jammed just above her waist. It's caught in the blue material, and with a firm tug downward, it comes undone. With ease, I smoothly zip it up fully to the top, and Meghan breathes a sigh of relief while spinning back around, claiming that I'm a lifesaver.

My gaze moves to Dean as Meghan skips across the bedroom to fetch her shoes. He's making a face while he takes a sip of his beer, his eyes rolling to the back of his head, and it's evident by his expression that he's waiting for me to taunt him. It's hard not to.

"C'mon, man," I start. "You seriously struggled with that?" My lips curve into a grin and as I step toward him, I thump his bicep twice as though there's nothing there. Dean's a nice guy, though he could do with some toughening up, because sometimes he can be *too* nice.

"I thought I'd leave it to the expert. You know, given the number of dresses you've unzipped in your lifetime," he fires back. It's an exaggeration, but we share a laugh anyway, and he hands me my beer. We clink bottles and take a swig.

As I swallow, I wipe my mouth with the back of my hand and glance back over at Meghan. She's perched on the corner of Tiffani's bed, sliding her heels onto her feet. "Where's Rachael anyway?" I ask. In the past few hours that we've all been here, I haven't even noticed that Rachael is missing until right now. She's usually here too, and she would usually be drunk by now, and Dean would usually be helping her stay upright, and Jake would usually be continuing to pass her shots. Rachael thinks I'm a dick, so I don't particularly care that she's not here tonight.

"Her mom needed her to go do something," Meghan tells me, "so she's just gonna meet us at the party. Does anyone remember the name of the girl whose party it is anyway? Was it Lucy?"

I don't remember either, so I look at Dean. He knows everyone and anyone, whether they graduated three years ago or if they're a freshman. I don't know how he can even be bothered to remember their names. "Yeah. Lucy," he says. "A junior, I think."

"No idea," I mutter. Whoever the hell she is, it's no surprise we're invited to this party she's throwing. We get invited to a lot of parties by people we don't know.

Someone clears their throat from the door. All three of us look over, and Tiffani is there, leaning back against the doorframe. Her smile is tight and closed as she curls a strand of her hair around her index finger, her gaze on Dean and Meghan but not on me. "Jake has made you guys some drinks," she says slowly, and then, with a firmer edge to her voice, she adds, "You should head down and try them." Her smile grows wider, revealing her teeth.

"In other words: Get out of your room?" Dean jokes, but he's right. That's exactly what she's asking, and in reply to his words, Tiffani only bats those crazy eyelashes of hers. "C'mon, Megs," he says. "Better leave these kids to it."

He takes Meghan by the hand and pulls her up from the bed,

steadying her as she totters slightly on her heels. As he leads her out of the room, he throws me a knowing look over his shoulder, and I find myself smirking. Tiffani isn't the best when it comes to keeping her intentions subtle. They're usually completely obvious, like right now, as she watches Dean and Meghan head downstairs before she shuts her bedroom door and turns back around. Now we're alone.

"You couldn't wait until later?" I tease, pressing my beer to my lips and finishing it in one gulp. I abandon the bottle on her dresser and roll the sleeves of my flannel shirt up to just below my elbows as I close the distance between us. It's all so familiar, so part of the routine, that my hands are already gripping her hips of their own accord, my mouth on the edge of her jaw. I almost choke on the overbearing taste of her perfume.

For some reason, she isn't reciprocating, and after a few seconds, her hand is against my chest and she's pushing me a step back. I stare at her, my lips parted and my eyebrows raised, dumbfounded. Tiffani *never* shuts me down. Her expression is suddenly a lot more twisted than it was a minute ago. "You left your phone downstairs," she says sharply, holding it up.

Even though I know it's my phone, I still pat the back pocket of my jeans, and sure enough, it's empty. I shrug and raise my hand to take it from her, but she quickly moves her arm away. She shakes her head very slowly but very firmly, and I sigh and scratch my temple. I know she's pissed about something, and I know I'm going to have to suffer for the rest of the night unless I can find a way to make her happy again. "I read your messages with Declan," she states after a moment. And I think: *That's it?*

"So?" I don't get what her problem is. Sure, I'm expecting him to hook me up with some joints later tonight, but that's nothing new.

Tiffani is used to that, so it shouldn't come as a surprise to her, and especially with Declan Portwood. Everyone knows him. Those on the good stuff are his best friends. Those who aren't tend to hate him.

Tiffani steps closer, her head tilted back a little to glare up at me. "I read *all* of your messages with Declan," she rephrases. And this time, it only takes a split second for me to realize what it is exactly that she's talking about. I freeze in front of her, racking my brain for something to say that can possibly justify the messages she's read, but I come up empty-handed, and I'm left standing in front of her like a fucking deer caught in the headlights.

"You're not serious, are you?" she asks, her voice much softer now. Her narrow shoulders sink a little. "You can't be. You already do enough stupid shit that I put up with, but I swear to God, Tyler, I'm not going to put up with this. You're taking it too far. I don't want to be that girl whose boyfriend ends up in jail. Do you even know how that will look?"

I press my lips together, still unsure how to handle the sudden confrontation. Over the years, I've learned that it's better not to argue back with Tiffani and to admit to being wrong as quickly as I can in order to shut her up. I've also learned that she doesn't ever *really* give a shit about what I do; she only gives a shit about how it affects her.

"I haven't done anything yet," I mutter. I still don't think it's even that big of a deal. "We were only talking."

"But *why*?" she presses, throwing a hand up in frustration at my apparent lack of good decision-making. "Why would you even consider doing it in the first place? It's not like you need the money, so what could possess you to do something so fucking stupid?"

I can do nothing but shrug, because I don't actually know the answer myself. "What is there to lose?"

Tiffani looks at me as though I'm seriously deranged. "Uh. *Everything?*" she says. "If you think dealing drugs is a good choice in life, then you're an even bigger idiot than I already think you are."

I close my eyes and exhale, trying to keep my cool. She's blowing this way out of proportion, but I'm more inclined to defend myself tonight for once rather than apologize. "It's just pot."

"Yeah, and that's exactly what you said when you first started smoking it, and look at where we are now." She reaches for my hand and slams my phone against my palm. "You're gonna start selling pot to freshmen, then you're gonna end up selling coke to losers just like yourself." She shakes her head again, this time in aggravation, then she holds her hand up and turns her face to the side. "Don't talk to me tonight. You're disgusting, and if I see Declan, he's gonna get slapped."

I grind my teeth together but still manage to keep my mouth shut. Saying anything more will make this worse; I know that. I'm pissed off, but I have to remain calm before I seriously flip out on her. The alcohol in my system isn't helping either. It only makes it harder, but I focus all of my concentration on steadying my breath as Tiffani turns her back on me and heads for the door.

And this whole conversation should be over now—at least for a while—where I take a few hours to calm down before I start kissing her ass again, but she does the most remarkable thing. She stops, turns around, and opens that pouty little mouth of hers one more time.

"You know, Tyler," she says, her lips forming a smug, cruel smile, "sometimes I think you *want* to end up in jail just like your dad."

The tiny, tiny amount of self-control that I've been clinging to snaps. *She did not just say that.* My fists clench and I need a way to release the fury that erupts in my chest and the rage that spreads through me like a wildfire. I snatch the closest thing to me: My empty bottle of beer on the dresser. I don't even realize I've hurled it across the room until it smashes against the far wall, shattering into pieces that cascade to the floor. I'm breathing too heavily and my eyes are wide and wild, and when I force myself to look back at Tiffani, her mouth is agape with shock.

"I'm leaving," I growl through gritted teeth. I shove my phone back into my pocket and grab my car keys from the other one, pushing past her.

"Good!" Tiffani yells back, pointing to the shards of glass on her carpet. "You're a complete douche bag."

I could say so much more and so much worse about her, but I know I need to get out of here before my temper flares up even more than it already has. I wish I was better at keeping my anger under control, but I just can't. I was raised this way. As soon as I throw open Tiffani's bedroom door, I can already hear the music from the kitchen. I can hear Meghan laughing too, but I'm in no mood to join them tonight. I storm down the stairs, desperate to get the hell out of this house and as far away from Tiffani as I can. I keep my eyes locked on the front door, and even though Dean calls my name, I don't glance up. I keep walking, straight past all of them and over the threshold, slamming the door behind me.

My car is parked against the sidewalk directly outside the house, and although I've had several beers, my desperation to get away from here overpowers my will to stay on the right side of the law. Right now, I couldn't care less.

I unlock my car and slide in behind the wheel, pulling the door shut at the same time as I aggressively tug my seatbelt on. The engine roars to life and I slam my foot down on the gas, accelerating so harshly that my tires screech against the road. There's a stop sign just ahead, but I don't slow down. I never do.

3

THE BRUISE ON THE back of my shoulder seems to have worsened during the night. It's grown bigger in size and doubled in pain, and even now, sitting at the kitchen table forcing cereal down my throat, I'm trying not to think about how badly it hurts.

It's almost seven thirty. I'll be leaving for school in ten minutes, but I don't want to go. I have track and field today, and the last thing I want is for anyone in the locker room to see the mess my back is in. The very thought of it makes me feel sick, so I know I'll have to skip it even though I can't afford to get into any more trouble this week.

"Are you still asleep?" Mom teases, her voice alone enough to snap my attention back to reality. I blink and look up at her, my hand holding my spoon in midair, slightly dazed. Mom's setting more plates down on the table, but she's smiling gently at me, her eyebrow raised. She's already wearing her suit for work, heels and all. The jacket is hung over the door.

"Uh-huh," I lie. I rub at my eyes with my free hand then return to my cereal, scooping up spoonful after spoonful, sitting at the table alone in silence. I prefer it like this in the mornings, just Mom and me, but it never lasts long. Jamie and Chase will be down soon once Mom yells at them to hurry up. So will Dad, once he's finished shaving and once he's found his tie from somewhere in the laundry room.

"Good schedule for today?" Mom asks. She always puts in too much effort in the morning with me because she thinks I'm an introvert until noon, but really, I'm only quiet because I'm thinking of reasons to keep breathing.

I shake my head. "Science, math, gym."

"Hmm," Mom says, and she stops moving around the kitchen and stands still opposite me at the other end of the table. "Speaking of gym class, I got a letter from your teacher yesterday." My eyes fly up to meet her sudden stern gaze, and she looks at me like she's expecting an explanation, but I don't know what to tell her. I sit still, fumbling with my hands in my lap as she turns around to retrieve a sheet of folded paper from the drawer. She opens it up and clears her throat. "*I'm growing concerned over the increasing number of times Tyler has been absent from my class this past month. I've overlooked the issue too many times already, and if this behavior continues, I'll be sending a formal report to Principal Castillo,*" she reads, then studies me intensely over the top of the paper. "What's the deal? I thought you liked gym class."

"I do," I say quickly, but I know I'm about to lie to her, so I have to look away. "It's really weird, but I always feel sick before gym class. Like, really, *really* sick. That's why I keep skipping. I keep going outside to get some air."

Mom doesn't seem to believe me, but it's the only excuse I can think of that makes sense. It's not like I can tell her the truth; that I keep skipping class because I don't want to change in the locker rooms, that there's too many bruises to hide, that taking part in anything physical hurts too much.

"Maybe I should take you to see Dr. Coleman if you're feeling so sick all the time," she says, pressing a hand to her hip with concern evident across her features.

"No," I protest immediately, shooting upright in my chair. My pulse quickens and my throat feels dry, so I have to swallow hard a couple times before I can speak again. "I won't skip class again. I swear." I'm pleading with her now, but the conversation is cut short by the sudden sound of Jamie and Chase thundering down the stairs.

My brothers come flying into the kitchen a few seconds later, pushing each other out of the way as they fight to be the first through the door. Jamie shoves Chase into the wall before he scrambles into the seat next to me, looking pleased with himself. Chase isn't so happy.

"Mooom!" he whines, rubbing his shoulder. He makes a face and sends a glare in Jamie's direction, right before he marches over to Mom, sulking.

"I wish the two of you would settle down a little," she murmurs, but as always, she pulls Chase into her arms and squeezes him, ruffling his hair. "Oh, Chase," she says, "your shirt's on backward."

As she laughs and starts tugging his shirt off, Jamie turns to me, eyes wide and alert as though it's the middle of the afternoon. His constant energy drives me insane. "I knew he was wearing it backward," he confesses, "but I didn't tell him."

"Why?"

"It's funny when he looks dumb," he says. Sitting up on his knees, he leans across me and grabs the box of cereal, sticking his hand inside.

"Jay," Mom snaps in disapproval. "Bowl." She wags her finger at him as she helps Chase up into the chair opposite us, then she pushes a bowl across the table. I don't think she likes mornings. She always gets a little stressed out with all of us, especially Jamie. All she can do is sigh when he spills half the cereal across the table as he's pouring it.

"Oops," he says. He flicks some toward Chase.

"Now," Mom says as she pops some bread into the toaster. When she turns back around to examine all of us, she leans back against the countertop and folds her arms across her chest. "Is any homework due today done?"

We all nod. I always nod. My homework is always done as early as possible. Dad makes sure of that.

"Backpacks packed?" she continues. "Got everything you need for today?"

Again, we all nod. I don't think I like mornings either. I hate this routine. It's always the same questions and it's always the same answers. The entire time, I feel nauseous as I wait for Dad to join us.

Jamie's eating his cereal with his mouth open, purposely crunching it loudly in my ear. Mom's turned her attention to the TV mounted on the wall, messing around with the remote as she tries to get the news on, and when she does, she lowers the volume and watches the screen out of the corner of her eye as she spreads some jam on Chase's toast. He grins when she sets the plate down in front of him, and they all seem to be satisfied, just like they always are.

I feel so far away from them. And I know truly that I'm right here beside them, but sometimes it feels like I'm not really. Everything is just so numb, so empty. I've grown so used to tuning everything out that I can't remember how to tune back in. I feel lost halfway between being here and being elsewhere. The truth is, I don't really know where I am. I'm just *somewhere*. I'm torn back from my trance when I hear Dad coming down the hall. His footsteps are heavy as he whistles the same tune he only whistles on his good days. I think I'm the only one who ever notices. Mom doesn't even know that he has bad days.

I take a deep breath and squeeze my eyes shut, composing myself.

When I open them again a few moments later, he's stepping through the door with a smile on his face. I hate it when he's happy in the mornings. Does he remember what happened last night? If he does, there's no guilt, and that makes me feel like I could throw up.

"The things I would do for coffee right now," Dad murmurs. He runs his hand through his hair and down the back of his neck as he walks straight past the table, straight toward Mom. I watch him closely, just like I always do.

"Right here," Mom says. She slips a steaming cup of black coffee into his hand, and he gently tightens his fingers around hers as they exchange a smile. She does this every morning; she always has his coffee ready. It's all part of that routine we seem to have gotten so comfortable with.

"Thank you," Dad tells her, then presses the cup to his lips and takes a large mouthful. He swallows and passes her his blue tie. He tilts his chin up and watches her with warm affection as she fastens the top buttons on his shirt, slips the tie around his neck, and ties it with the utmost care. "Thank you," he says again, then leans forward and kisses her cheek.

"Dad," Chase says, calling for his attention. "Jamie pushed me."

"You call that being pushed?" Jamie fires back across the table, shooting upright onto his knees again as he holds up his fist. "I can show you what being pushed is like.'

So could I, I think.

Dad turns around, furrowing his eyebrows in disapproval as he glances back and forth between them both. He pulls out the chair next to Chase and sits down, leaning back. "When will the two of you quit fighting? C'mon now, Jay, you're ten in January. Double digits. Did you know that you can't keep picking on your brother once you're into double digits?"

Jamie sinks in his chair. "Really?"

"Really," Dad says. He widens his eyes and nods, right before he cracks into laughter and glances sideways at Chase, nudging him with his elbow. He takes another swig of his coffee, and that's when he looks at me for the first time this morning. His eyes find mine over the rim of the cup, and the warmth in his expression disappears as he sets the cup back down on the table. "Someone's quieter than usual this morning," he says.

"Most likely because of this," I hear Mom comment, and the color drains from my face the second I look over and see her reaching for that letter again. *Please don't show it to him. Please, please, please.* "He's skipped gym class five times recently," she tells him, and my stomach clenches with nausea as she leans over his shoulder and hands him the piece of paper. "I need to write back and let Mr. Asher know it won't happen again. Right, Tyler? You promise?"

I feel so sick, I can't even speak. I just nod as fast as I can, over and over again. Dad's reading the letter with his mouth nothing more than a bold line, and I hate the way the expression in his eyes keeps on hardening with each word he reads. The second he is finished, he locks his glare on me. "Why the hell are you skipping class? You're ruining your attendance."

"Someone's in trouble," Jamie snickers from beside me, and he's right—I am.

Today is no longer one of Dad's good days. Today is now a bad day, and I'll feel the force of another one of his bad days later.

I can't get any words out and Dad's expecting an explanation. For a moment, I feel like I can't breathe. If we were alone, I wouldn't even answer him, but I know I have to say *something*, so I stick to my earlier excuse. "I felt sick," I finally mumble.

Dad raises one eyebrow in suspicion. "Five times in a row?" I should have thought of something better. He isn't believing this. Why would he? I'm lying and he knows it. All I can do is shrug and drop my eyes to my lap, staring at the small cut on my palm that I hadn't noticed until now.

"No more skipping class," Mom reminds me, this time with a sterner tone to her voice than before. I nod without looking up, and all I know is that it's a relief to hear her increase the volume of the TV. It's a relief to hear Chase ask for more toast. It's a relief to know the conversation is over.

For what feels like five minutes, I can't bring myself to lift my gaze. I can't look at anyone, especially Dad. My stomach still hurts. I know he's mad at me, and I know that he isn't going to let this go. I hate Mr. Asher for sending that letter.

"Right," Dad says loudly. I force myself to look at him as he finishes off his coffee, wipes his mouth with the pad of his thumb, then gets to his feet. He runs his eyes over the gold Rolex on his wrist. "I better get you to school." Even though he doesn't bother to look at me, I know who he's talking to. Dad always drives me to school on his way to work. Mom always drives Jamie and Chase on the way to hers.

"Go and get yourself ready," Mom tells me over her shoulder from the sink. I don't think she's even sat down yet. She never does in the mornings. "And don't forget to brush your teeth."

I'm desperate to leave the kitchen. I'm scared of Dad's glaring eyes and my shoulder stings and I'd rather go anywhere but school right now. I kind of hope I *do* hurl so that I can stay home, but I know that won't happen, so I slide off my chair and head straight for the door. I'm just about to take the first step upstairs when Dad sticks his head out into the hall.

"Tyler," he says, and I freeze. I don't turn around, but I do look back at him as he slips on his jacket and straightens his tie. He doesn't look so angry anymore, but he isn't smiling either. His entire face is just blank, and I receive nothing but a single, firm nod. "I'll wait for you in the car."

And as I turn back around and run upstairs, I'm really wishing that he wouldn't.

4

FUCK, I THINK. *THE BARBECUE.*

I can see the commotion in the backyard the second I pull up outside my house, braking so hard that I end up skidding a little. There aren't any cars parked out front, but that's because Mom only invites our neighbors. She does this every year, and every single year without fail, half our neighborhood comes strolling down the street with their crates of beer. I don't know why Mom continues to insist that I be here each year. I can't think of anything more uncool than this, especially considering I hate half our neighbors. Mrs. Harding from a couple doors down? She once called the cops on me for walking across her lawn. Mr. Fazio from across the street? He decided to let my mom know about that time I threw a party while she was out of town. Mrs. Baxter at the very northern end of Deidre Avenue? She does nothing but complain about the amount of noise my car makes every time I drive past her house.

So yeah. I usually pass on this annual tradition.

Killing my engine and pulling the keys out of the ignition, I kick open my door and step out. I can hear the music from the yard now and the disgusting scent in the air makes me feel almost nauseous for a moment. I hate barbecues, not because of the social nature of them, but because of the gross smell of burning meat. I haven't eaten meat in years, and I have to shove my hand into my hair as I take a second to compose myself. I'm already pissed off and coming home to this definitely isn't helping.

Narrowing my eyes, I head for the backyard. I may be furious, but I have an act to keep up, so I slam my fist against the gate to throw it open. The mixture of voices immediately hushes until only the music is left, and I spot Mrs. Harding in the corner, glaring at me in disgust.

"Sorry I'm late," I announce. My eyes search the crowd in front of me as I try to spot Mom, but I'm glad when I can't find her. I don't want to see her face right now because I know I'm embarrassing her, but with this many people around, I can't afford not to. So I may not spot Mom, but I do spot my asshole of a stepdad over behind the barbecue. Dave's already fixing me with a threatening look that warns me not to say anything else, which gives me every reason to continue. "Did I miss anything besides the slaughtering of animals?" I flip him off at the same time, and there are some murmurs of disapproval that I choose to ignore. I could cause a bigger scene than I already am; I could kick over the stack of beer that's on my right, but I decide not to, only because I'm still trying to figure out the argument I just had with Tiffani. "I hope you guys enjoyed the cow you just ate." I have to laugh, because it's the only thing I can bring myself to do right now. If I don't, I think I will seriously throw a punch at someone, anyone.

I turn away before my temper flares up again, and I hear Dave say, "More beer?" There's some awkward laughter from the guests as I head inside through the patio doors. I slide them shut again as harshly as I can, and I blow out a breath of air, relieved to be inside at last. The AC is on and the kitchen is refreshingly cool as I stride into the hall, ready to bolt my way upstairs to my room so that I can chill out and calm myself down.

But just as I'm turning onto the stairs, Mom's voice calls my name, and I know I have to talk to her despite how angry I am right now. I hang my head low for a second before I turn around, gathering my thoughts and my excuses. I hope she can't smell the beer on me. She would flip if she knew I've been driving like this.

"What the *hell* are you thinking?" she snarls under her breath.

She's gritting her teeth when I turn back around to look at her, and at first, all I can do is shrug. I'm not great at answering questions I don't know the answers to.

"Where have you been?" she asks, demanding more answers. She's mortified, I can tell, and I feel slightly guilty as she glances over her shoulder to ensure no one is here, then grabs my elbow and pulls me into the living room. "I told you to be here tonight and you think you can just stroll in here *now* acting the way you just did?" She closes her eyes in exasperation and massages her temples, like I'm a headache she's trying to soothe away.

I'm still super aware that I've been drinking, so I take a couple steps back from her, increasing the distance between us. I don't want to add any more fuel to the fire. "I'm not even late," I mutter, because, technically, she told me to be here and I am.

"You're two hours late!" she yells at me, her eyes flashing open again. She usually lets me off the hook a lot quicker than she is now, and I really wish she wouldn't choose right now to argue with me.

I laugh again, but only to stop myself from losing it. "You really think I'm gonna come home to watch a damn barbecue?"

Mom exhales as her gaze softens. "What is your problem this time?"

27

she asks, pacing back and forth in front of me as though she's trying to figure out the underlying reason for my behavior tonight. Admittedly, I'm not usually as agitated as this. "Forget about the barbecue. You were acting like a little kid before you even got out of the car. What's wrong?"

I've never been able to look Mom in the eye when I lie, so I clench my jaw and turn my face away from her, looking at the window. "Nothing."

"It's clearly not nothing," she snaps back, and the softness to her expression is gone. I hate it when she gets like this. She gets mad at me a lot, but usually more in the frustrated, helpless sort of sense. This time, I really have pissed her off. "You just humiliated me again in front of half the neighborhood!"

"Whatever," I say.

Mom goes silent for a second, and when I look back over at her, she's shaking her head at the floor and murmuring, "I shouldn't have let you leave. I should have just made you stay, but no, of course I didn't, because there I was trying to cut you some slack, and you throw it back in my face as usual."

"I would have left anyway," I argue, because this is true. Even if I didn't already have plans tonight, there's no way I would have stuck around here, and Mom knows that. I don't know why she even tries anymore. I wish she'd just give up on me. "What are you gonna do? Ground me again?" I take a challenging step toward her, failing to hold back my laughter again. I've been grounded for the past two years, I believe. It's nothing but an empty threat that Mom never follows through with.

"You're impossible." She looks away then, staring straight past me and over my shoulder as her expression shifts. Her frustration with me seems to dissolve, and she furrows her eyebrows instead as she gently pushes past me and heads for the door.

I sigh and push my hand back through my hair, tilting my head back so that I can stare at the ceiling. If I have another argument tonight, I might just combust.

Mom says something and I quickly spin around to find her lingering just outside the door, only it's not me she's focused on. I don't know who she's talking to, so I move across the living room and peer around the door.

There's a girl awkwardly spread across the stairs, eyes wide with alarm as though she's absolutely terrified. I don't know who the hell she is, because I don't think I've ever seen her around before. I'm sure I haven't. I narrow my eyes at her, studying her more intensely. She doesn't look that much younger than me, so I seriously can't figure out why I've never seen her around school before, and given the fact she's a brunette, I'm sure I would recognize her. Her anxious gaze doesn't leave mine, which makes me begin to wonder why she's so nervous in the first place, but I don't wonder for long because I become distracted by how plump her lips are as she presses them together and swallows. This girl definitely isn't from here. I know for sure that I would recognize her if she was. How couldn't I?

The muscle in my jaw tightens when I realize what I'm thinking. Tiffani would kill me if she heard my thoughts right now.

"Who the hell is this chick?" I finally demand, tearing my eyes away and looking expectantly at Mom instead.

She takes a minute to think about her answer, and even she seems a little nervous too. "Tyler," she says quietly as she places her hand on my arm, "this is Eden. Dave's daughter."

At first, I don't quite process her words. "Dave's kid?"

The girl straightens up, standing up, and she opens those plump, wet lips of hers and says nothing but, "Hi."

My eyes are drawn back to hers at the sound of her voice. It's low and husky, even a little raspy, and it is so different and so new to me that I freeze on the spot, paralyzed by a single syllable. Even on her feet, she's still several inches shorter than me, so I stare down at her, trying to make sense of the information that's pushing down on me. This girl... This brunette girl with the full lips and the husky voice... is my stepsister?

No. Fucking. Way.

When Mom said Dave's kid was going to be living with us over the summer, I didn't even pay that much attention, and now I'm really wishing that I had. I didn't realize she'd be around my age. How old is she anyway? I want to ask, but I can't even part my lips, let alone form words. I feel like someone has knocked the air out of me. I swallow hard and look at Mom again. "Dave's kid?" I repeat, but it's almost a whisper. I'm in complete and utter disbelief.

Mom sighs. "Yes, Tyler," she says, almost like she's exasperated. "I already told you she was coming. Don't act stupid."

Although I'm looking primarily at Mom, I'm also looking at the girl as surreptitiously as I possibly can out of the corner of my eye, because I seriously can't look away. The makeup around her eyes is smudged a little. "Which room?"

Mom's expression flashes with confusion. "What?"

My throat is starting to feel dry. "Which room is she staying in?" I urge.

And then Mom says it, the answer I was dreading: "The one next to yours."

I groan, finally becoming unrooted from the spot. We have two spare guest rooms upstairs, and of course Mom has to give her the room next door to mine. I don't want to be anywhere near this girl, not because

I have a girlfriend, but because this girl is my stepsister. God. I never thought I'd ever have to stay away from a girl because of *that* reason.

My anger is surfacing again, and I don't even realize I've been glaring at her until I feel the strain in my forehead from narrowing my eyes for too long. I couldn't stick around at Tiffani's place, but now I can't stick around here either. Everything that has happened in the past hour is seriously starting to get to me.

Nudging my way past Mom, I storm upstairs, and I have no choice but to brush past this girl who is going to be in my way for the entire summer. I knock against her shoulder, and I can't bring myself to apologize, because all I can think about is getting the hell away from her. I march into my room, slamming the door behind me and pacing around in a circle for a good minute or so until I collect my thoughts. They're all over the place, and I have to play some music as loud as I can through my speakers in order to distract myself. Once my breathing has calmed, I pause and glance around. Mom has made my bed and picked up my clothes from the floor again. They're folded and left in a neat pile on top of my dresser. I should put them away, but I've discovered that if I leave them there long enough, then Mom'll give in and put them away herself. I've also discovered that the only reason Mom doesn't mind tidying up my room every morning is because she likes to raid the place in search of anything she doesn't approve of.

I press my lips together and get down onto my knees, ducking to check underneath my bed. Sure enough, like always, she's stolen the pack of Bud that I put there last night. I get up and move to my bathroom to check inside the cabinet, and again, it's no surprise that she's swiped the packet of Marlboros too. I don't even smoke cigarettes that often, but I still like to have them on me, just in case.

Walking back into my room, I sit down on the corner of my bed and press my hands to my temples, staring at the floor while I decide what I want to do. I'm in the strangest mood, and all I want right now is a hell of a lot more beer and a joint. They're the only things that I can always rely on to distract me when there are things I don't want to deal with. I want to go to that party tonight, despite the fact that I'd rather avoid Tiffani. Sticking around here isn't an option anymore, so I take out my phone and text some of the guys for the address. Kaleb is the first to reply, and I tell him I'll be there in twenty. I get to my feet and spray on some cologne, then turn off my music as I grab my car keys from my pocket. I feel entirely sober after all of the arguing, but I'm still livid, and it doesn't help that the second I push open my door, that damn girl is there again.

She looks up at me with those same anxious eyes as before, only this time I'm noticing that they're hazel, and an intense hazel at that. I can't decide whether or not they're more golden than they are brown. "Hi," she says again. "Are you okay?"

That voice. I blink a couple times and try to keep my expression as blank as I possibly can to hide the fact that that voice of hers is seriously doing something to me. "Bye," I say, stepping past her. I don't want to be around this girl. I've already decided that, so I follow through by making my way downstairs and out of the front door without looking over my shoulder, despite how badly I want to.

As soon as I step outside into the front yard, I can hear the music from the back again. Laughter too. Luckily, no one is around out front to notice me leave. I doubt Mom would put up a fight anyway. She never does.

Unlocking my car, I slide back in and pull the door shut. I start up the engine, but I don't drive off immediately. I sit there for a minute, my elbow resting against the window as I run the tips of my fingers along my jaw while I think.

Sighing, I get my phone out again and pull up my messages with Tiffani. It's better to warn her.

I'll see you at the party.

I type out the text, and then I hit send at the exact same time as I hit the accelerator.

5

FIVE YEARS EARLIER

FORCING MYSELF ACROSS THE lawn and over to Dad's silver Mercedes is always the hardest part of every day. My legs feel stiff as I drag my feet, keeping my eyes on the grass as I tighten my grip around the strap of my backpack. I know he's watching me, waiting, and I know he's going to have a lot to say during the ten-minute ride to school. I wish Mom hadn't shown him that letter.

I'm still staring at the ground as I reach for the handle and open up the door, avoiding Dad's harsh glare. I slide into the passenger seat and pull my backpack around onto my lap, then click on my seatbelt. I focus my eyes on my sneakers. All I can hear is the soft purring of the engine until Dad releases a heavy sigh and starts to drive.

He increases the volume of the radio and groans when he hears that there's already a forty-minute delay on the freeway. I know how much he hates the drive to downtown LA each morning, and it really doesn't help that I've already ruined his good mood for the day. Now he's more aggravated than usual at this time. He shuts the radio off entirely.

"So," he says, "what the hell are you playing at? Skipping class because you felt sick? Bullshit."

I look at him out of the corner of my eye. He's shaking his head at the road ahead of us, and I can feel his anger in the air around us, thickening it. "I…I just didn't want to go," I tell him. I'm lying again, but at the same time, I'm thinking, *Isn't it obvious?* "It's track and field. I hate running."

"Bullshit," he says again. "Are you trying to rebel? Is that it? Are you trying to get in trouble just to test me?"

"No. No," I stutter. I pick at a fraying edge on my backpack as I try to think of something to say, anything. "I'm not trying to do anything. It's just…well, it's the locker rooms." I bite down on my lip and hold my breath as I shut my eyes. Being honest with him is the only way I'm going to get out of this car alive.

"What about the locker rooms?"

I squeeze my eyes shut tighter. I just hope he isn't looking at me right now. I hope he's still looking at the road. "Um. I don't…I don't want anyone…I don't want anyone to ask questions." My mouth is dry as each word sticks in my throat.

"Ask questions about what?"

My eyes flash open and I angle my face to fully stare across at him. "Dad…" I murmur. "You know what."

"No," he says more firmly, "I don't. There's nothing to ask questions about."

He's in denial. He has to be. That, or he's crazy. "Okay," I mumble, dropping the subject. I keep picking at the frayed edge on my backpack until it starts to get worse, splitting open completely. Dad hasn't looked at me since he started driving. I hope it's because he feels guilty and not because he couldn't care less

"Now tell me," he says, "you have math today, don't you?" Before I can nod, he brakes to a halt at a stop sign. The intersection is clear to go, but he wrenches up the parking brake and shifts in his seat, angling himself toward me. He snatches my backpack from my grip and pulls it onto his lap. Unzipping it, he rummages inside and pulls out my math homework that's due next week, including the page that's torn into three. I don't know what he's looking for, but whatever it is, he spends a few moments searching the pages for it.

"The second you get home from school today, I want you to sit down and fix this question," he orders calmly, holding up one of the torn pieces for me to see that same equation from last night again, the only one I got wrong. "And you'll need to write all of this out again." He shakes his head at the ruined pieces of paper in his hands as though it was me who destroyed them, then he crumples them into his enclosed fist. His strained knuckles are pale from pressure, and I watch in my usual unsurprised way. My balled-up math homework is tossed into the cup holder in the center console, and my backpack is thrown back at me.

"I could have kept the other pages," I point out as I zip my bag up again. "They weren't torn."

"That's too bad," Dad says as his eyes drift to the road ahead while he puts the car back into drive. "You can go ahead and do each question all over again. Consider it extra practice. You need it."

That homework had thirty questions. It took me over an hour to complete last night, and the thought of doing it all over again because of one mistake is enough for me to grind my teeth together until my jaw hurts. Dad does things like this all the time, and although it no longer surprises me, it still aggravates me. But I can't let him know that, so I try to relax my features as I focus my gaze on a spot on the dashboard as Dad switches the radio back on. *He just wants the best for me*, I remind myself.

It's always a relief each morning when we pull up outside Dean's house. It's when Dad starts smiling again and it's when his cold tone disappears, and I know that for the final five-minute drive to school, he definitely won't lose his cool. He can't. Not while we have company.

The front door of the Carter house swings open as if on cue, and Dean's dad appears on the front step, holding his hand up to wave. Dean rushes to his side several moments later, struggling to put his backpack on. His dad, Hugh, helps him with the strap and then they both make their way across their lawn toward us.

We've been picking Dean up for school every morning for as long as I can remember. The Carters are practically family, and Dad does the morning run to school, while Hugh does the pickup. Dean opens up the car door and climbs into the backseat at the same time as Dad rolls down his window to talk to Hugh.

I crane my neck and turn around slightly in my seat, looking back at Dean as he tugs on his seatbelt. When he clicks it in place, he glances up at me and curls his hand into a fist, holding it up to me. I bump my fist against his and give him a smile, tuning out Dad and Hugh's conversation.

"Did you do that science project?" Dean asks, sinking back against the leather of the backseat. "I got my mom to do half of mine."

"Yeah. I handed it in last week," I tell him.

Hugh clears his throat and ducks down a little at the window, looking past Dad at both me and Dean. "Right, you two," he says, "I'll be there waiting at three." When he smiles, it's genuine, and he throws us a thumbs-up before stepping away from the car. I like Hugh. Sometimes I wish *he* was my dad and not the guy sitting next to me.

Dad rolls the window back up and drives off. The radio is on again, but the volume is low enough to allow him to maintain his friendly persona, where he fills the remainder of the drive to school with questions about our classes for the day and football and if Dean's excited for his birthday next week. I don't know what's worse: Dad when he's mad or Dad when he's nice. It's always so confusing to me.

By the time Dad cuts the engine just around the corner from the school entrance, I've already got my seatbelt off and my hand on the door, ready to escape his constant expression of disapproval for a few hours. Dean hates school. I like it because it's the only place I can really get away from Dad for a while.

"I hope you both have a great day," he tells us with that tight smile of his. He leans over into the backseat, holds his palm out, and lets Dean low five him. Then, as both Dean and I push open the car doors and jump out onto the sidewalk, he quickly adjusts the cuff of his shirt.

"Tyler," he says right before I shut the door behind me. I glance over my shoulder to find him leaning over to look at me, his expression neutral. He stares at me for a long moment until his features begin to shift again. His eyebrows pull together as the corners of his lips pull into a small, sad smile. For the first time all week, I see the tiniest hint of guilt in his green eyes. "Work hard," he murmurs, swallowing. "I love you."

No, I think as I turn away from him and slam the door shut. *You don't.*

6

PRESENT DAY

IT'S NEARING TEN BY the time I'm driving across the city. I've already stopped by the liquor store and now have two six-packs taking up my passenger seat. Not to mention the fresh pack of Marlboros. The cashier demanded twenty bucks in exchange for him turning a blind eye to the fact that I'm four years off of twenty-one, but lucky for him, I'm a loyal customer. And most likely his favorite considering the hefty tips I give.

The party is being thrown by some girl named Lucy who I can't quite put a face to, and although I'm turning up earlier than I usually do, Kaleb also says that mostly everyone is already there. I can't remember the last time I showed up at a party on my own. At the very least, I always have Tiffani by my side. But tonight I'll have to deal with being that fucking moron who only has beer by his side rather than his friends.

It's almost dark out as I crawl along Stanford Street on the very outskirts of the city until I arrive at the address Kaleb has given me. There are already several cars parked outside and a couple guys lingering on the porch, cups in their hands and lazy grins on their faces. I recognize them only vaguely from school. Their attention shifts to me as I pull up against the sidewalk across the street and kill my engine, and I notice them cocking their heads to the side as they check out my car. I pretend to ignore it, but their jealous attention is still satisfying; it always will be.

I remove my seatbelt, then roll my window down a couple inches to allow the faint pumping of music to enter my car, then I reach over and yank a bottle of beer from the pack. Not only have I never turned up at a party this early and alone before, I've also never turned up at a party sober. I've dried out from the booze from earlier, and now I'm left dreading the idea of walking through that front door sober. It's a whole lot easier to maintain my act in front of a crowd when I'm drunk. Cracking open the cap with my teeth, I take a single swig of my beer, swallow it back, then chug the remainder of it. Shoving the bottle into my glove compartment, I sigh and shift my gaze to my reflection in my rearview mirror. My eyes seem more intense, more of a vibrant green than usual, yet my expression seems too soft for my liking. I press my lips together, clenching my jaw while narrowing my eyes slightly until my entire expression is sharper, more hardened, and then I grab my keys, my cigarettes, and my beer.

I step out of the car and nudge the door shut behind me. I set the beer down on the hood, shove my keys into my back pocket, and retrieve my lighter instead. I pull a cigarette out of the pack, place it between my lips, then light it.

One of the guys from up on the porch takes a sip of his drink and then calls across the lawn, "Are you here for the party?"

I take a long drag as I study him, allowing the smoke to fill my lungs for several seconds before I exhale, blurring my vision with the plume of smoke that fills the air around me. "Nah. Here for the view,"

I deadpan. What a fucking moron. Placing the cigarette back between my lips, I grab my beer and head toward the house, cutting across the lawn and over to the porch. The music grows louder the nearer I get, but it's still not as loud as it should be, which makes it pretty obvious that the host is a first-timer. That and the fact that the house doesn't appear to be packed.

"I didn't know that you'd be coming," the guy says when I reach him and his friend on the porch. Very quickly, he looks me up and down, and when I move my cigarette from my lips again to exhale, he holds his breath. They both look too young to be here, and I begin to wonder that they might not even be juniors, but maybe sophomores. Yikes.

"Is this your first party?" I ask, my words muffled against my cigarette. I raise an eyebrow while stepping past them. The last thing I want to do is stop and end up in a conversation with some dumb-ass sophomores. I want to get inside and see who's here. I want to crack open another beer. I want to hunt down Declan Portwood.

"Yeah," the guy says.

He exchanges a confused glance with his friend, and I don't even attempt to hold back my laugh when I reply, "I can tell."

I push open the front door a crack and immediately the music floods my ears, laced with laughter and the sound of a drink being smashed. Before I head inside, I turn around and press my back against the front door, smirking as I push it open backward. "Words of advice?" I offer, as I flick the butt of my cigarette to the ground and step on it. "Stop standing out here on the porch and get your asses inside."

Spinning back around, I'm greeted with a party where personal space seems to actually exist for once. There's no one that I immediately recognize, besides the familiar faces I've seen at parties before, but I know that Kaleb is already here, so I weave my way across the living room in search of him. I don't smile at anyone as I pass them, despite the fact that I keep receiving small nods of acknowledgment, and I edge my way through a small group of girls blocking my path into the kitchen.

"Tyler!" Kaleb calls at the exact same second that I spot him perched up on the countertop. The center island is covered in all sorts of booze, which makes it the most popular spot in the house, and I have to squeeze my way around everyone in order to reach Kaleb. "You're finally here, man," he says, resting his hand on my shoulder once I step in front him. I can smell not only the beer on him, but the weed too, and his bloodshot gaze scans the kitchen as though he's missing something. "Where's Tiffani? Dean? Everyone else?"

"They'll be here soon," I say. I nudge his hand off me and slide my beer onto the countertop, pulling a bottle free from the pack and cracking it open. "What about Declan? Is he around tonight?"

Kaleb props his elbow on the coffee machine and just shrugs, but at the same time he gives me a knowing grin. He's high as fuck. "Later. What are you game for tonight?" He leans forward again and raises an eyebrow at me, then taps the front pocket of his jeans twice with his index finger. "You don't have to wait until Declan gets here," he murmurs, his voice hushed as the music around us thumps continuously. "I can hook you up."

I study him intently as I swig at my beer. Sometimes I wonder how Kaleb even ends up at these parties. Both he and Declan are college freshmen, but Kaleb has the face of a fourteen year old, so I can understand that perhaps he fits in better at high school parties than he does at the college ones. As for Declan, he seems to be friends with everyone. He once told me that having good connections is the first rule in business.

Shaking my head, I take a step back. "I'm alright for now. Let me know when Declan shows up."

"At least take a shot first," Kaleb says, grabbing a bottle of vodka from his side that's almost half empty. The cap is already off, and he slides off the countertop and accusingly points the bottle at me. "Why aren't you drunk?"

"Maybe because I only had my first drink five minutes ago," I fire back at him, then snatch the bottle out of his hand. He has a point. I can't be seen at a party sober. That's not me, so I tilt the bottle against my lips and drink for as long as I can possibly bear the burn of the vodka at the back of my throat, then I pass the bottle back. "I'm gonna go and see who's all here."

"Alright," Kaleb says as he pushes himself back up onto the countertop. He takes a swig too, then lets the bottle hang in his fingertips. "If you change your mind, you know where to find me."

I decide to turn around and walk away from him before I really do change my mind. I could seriously do with a hit right now, but I figure I'll crave it even more as soon as Tiffani turns up. That's when I'll really need it the most, so for now I'll wait. I can hold off for another hour, but I need to keep myself distracted, so I head off on a tour of the house to see who exactly is here. So far, Kaleb is the only person I know, give or take a few people I've spoken to only briefly before.

In the kitchen, people are pouring drinks. In the living room, people are spilling them. Outside in the backyard, there's a game of beer pong kicking off among half a dozen guys who are too drunk to stand, let alone aim, so I don't even bother to join in. Instead, I come back inside to toss my empty bottle of beer into the trash and to open a new one, and I notice that Kaleb has already disappeared from his reserved spot up on the countertop. So much for knowing where to find him. The guy couldn't even last fifteen minutes waiting there.

With a fresh beer in hand, I head off again, this time upstairs. The house isn't huge, and neither is the guest list. I'm so bored that I've resorted to counting how many people are actually here, and so far, I've counted twenty-seven. No one appears to even be upstairs except the girl throwing up in the bathroom.

"Are you alright?" I ask her, sticking my head around the doorframe. She doesn't lift her head from the bowl, only raises her hand and gives me a thumbs-up, so I close the door and leave her alone.

"Tyler? I thought that was you," a voice says from behind me. When I spin around, there's a girl quickly making her way up the stairs toward me, a drunken smile on her face. I know her, but it takes me a minute to remember her name.

"Hey, Naomi," I say. I can't bring myself to smile at her, probably because I'm still stuck in this weird mood, so I sip at my beer instead. I don't know what to say to her. She sits in front of me in English lit, and the only time I ever speak to her is when I need her to translate Shakespeare for me.

"What are you doing up here?" she asks, stopping a mere foot away from me. She leans out to press her hand against the wall, steadying herself to prevent her from swaying. She drunkenly giggles while adjusting her skirt, then pouts up at me. "Shouldn't you be downstairs? You know, where the alcohol is?"

I shake my head and take the final swig of my beer, leaning down to abandon it on the floor. I can't remember if it's my third or my fourth, but either way, I'm still nowhere near drunk, and I'm starting to get frustrated. Naomi's way ahead of me, but I do notice that her hands are empty. "Good point," I say. "How about a drink?"

"Shouldn't you be hanging out with Tiffani?"

"She's not here yet." I glance at the watch on my wrist. It's just after ten thirty, so she should be here in around half an hour. I'm dreading the idea of having to face her, which means that I only have thirty minutes to consume as much alcohol as I can in order to blur out the argument that'll most likely break out between us.

"Oh," Naomi says, but she's smiling as she nods. "A drink sounds nice."

"What do you like?"

"Hmm." She tilts her head to one side and pretends to deeply consider her answer, right before she grins and leans back against the wall entirely. "Surprise me."

"Alright. Stay right here."

Brushing past her, I make my way back downstairs as the music engulfs me all over again. Someone has definitely increased the volume, because it's now at the point where people have to yell in order to hear one another, and I shove a guy out of my way so that I can get into the kitchen. I may not be drunk, but I'm not exactly sober either. I'm starting to feel slightly more relaxed, a little more at ease here without Tiffani on one side of me and Dean on the other like I'm so accustomed to.

Kaleb is back up on the countertop again, exploding into laughter with some guy he's talking to, but when he spots me, he winks and mouths, "*Pot?*" I shake my head no.

Half my beer has been stolen by the time I find the packs, and there's only four bottles left. It's to be expected at house parties, so I steal a random bottle of Bud from someone else and crack it open, then find a cup and scour the center island. I spot a box of Red Bull, so I grab a can and then mix it into the cup with what I'm pretty certain is more than a double measure of vodka. I shrug, crush the can in my hand, then toss it onto the countertop.

"Tyler," Kaleb says, just as I'm turning to head back upstairs. I glance over my shoulder, and he motions for me to come over with his index finger, so I deeply inhale and then make my way back over to him. "You know the rules," he says, his words a little slurred. "Every time you come into the kitchen, you gotta take a shot."

I raise an eyebrow at him. This rule has never existed until right now, but who am I to argue with him? Only idiots turn down free shots. "C'mon then." With both my hands full, I step closer to him and tilt my head back, parting my lips.

Kaleb grabs the bottle and raises it to my mouth. The vodka hits my throat as he tips the bottle up even higher, but he doesn't stop, only grins in satisfaction as I continue to swallow and swallow and swallow until my stomach physically burns. I can't keep going, so I clamp my lips shut, only for Kaleb to spill the vodka down my neck and onto my shirt.

"That's how you do it," he comments, taking a shot himself with a nod of appreciation. I don't know how much I just drank, but I'm glad he's enjoying how queasy I suddenly am. I focus on my breathing for a moment or two until I'm convinced I won't throw up on the floor.

"You're an asshole," I mutter once I've recovered. I set Naomi's cup down so that I can pull my shirt up to dry my neck, then I run a hand through my hair and pick the drink back up. I'm not sure if the house has been this hot the entire time, but heat seems to hit me out of nowhere, and I need to get away from this pounding noise and the bodies pressing all around me. Quickly, I manage to snatch the almost-empty bottle of vodka out of Kaleb's grip, balancing both it and my bottle of beer between my fingers. He narrows his eyes at me, but all I can do is wink back at him. "You know the rules," I mimic, backing away. "Every time you leave the kitchen, the bottle goes with you."

Kaleb rolls his eyes and says, "Touché." It's not like there's much left anyway. A couple shots worth, max, and he's already both drunk and high, so he doesn't need it. At least not as much as I do.

Someone touches my shoulder and says *hey* as I make my way back through the living room, but I don't bother to turn around because I have three drinks in my hands and my focus is on the cup I've thrown together for Naomi. It's filled to the brim and when someone else accidentally knocks against me, I spill a little on the carpet, so I quickly keep moving before anyone notices. Given how drunk half the people around me already are, I'm surprised no one's thrown up on the carpet yet.

It's a relief to get back upstairs again. The hallway lights are still off and everything is so still up here with no one around, not even Naomi. I peer around the bathroom door, but even the girl from earlier is gone, so I take a step back out into the hall and call Naomi's name, though it sounds more like a question. She's probably not even here anymore.

"In here!" she replies almost immediately, and I don't know why, but I feel myself exhale in relief at the thought of her still being up here. Who else am I supposed to talk to when there's no one else here I know besides Kaleb, who's too fucked up to do anything but smirk?

I follow the sound of Naomi's drunken voice into the room across the hall, and I carefully knee the door open, balancing the drinks as I take a few steps into the bedroom. I can't remember the name of the girl whose party this is, but I doubt this is her room, judging by the NFL posters on the walls. Naomi is leaning against the dresser, her hand on her hip as she studies the poster of Philip Rivers in front of her.

"Her brother likes the Chargers?" she says, glancing over her shoulder at me with a look of exaggerated disgust. Her knowledge takes me by surprise.

"Looks like it," I say. I could have an entire conversation with her about football, about how much I hate the Chargers, that the 49ers are better, but instead I add, "Here," and move across the room toward her, closing the distance between us and offering her the drink I've mixed up for her.

"You know," she says, leaning back fully against the dresser and tracing the rim of the cup as she stares down at the drink, "you're not as big of an asshole as everyone says you are." Her eyes flash up to meet mine the second she tips the cup to her lips, and I watch her as she drinks while I try to figure out if her backhanded remark was actually a compliment. I think, maybe, it was.

I'm unsure how to reply, so I swig awkwardly at my beer and then ask, "Is it too strong?"

But apparently it's not, because she holds up a finger and tilts the cup back even further, finishing it off in one. She sucks in a large breath of air once she's done and slams the empty cup down against the dresser, crushing it beneath her hand. "Did you say it was too strong?"

I blink down at her. Who knew Naomi from English lit was such a drinker? Because I certainly didn't, not until now, and although she's wasted and unable to handle it all, I'm still impressed by the way she shotgunned that drink, given the amount of vodka I put in there. "Wow," is all I can say, and I pass her the vodka bottle, and she finishes that too.

"Can Tiffani drink like I do?" she asks, stepping closer to look up at me with a challenging smirk on her lips, and it pisses me off that she's brought up Tiffani's name. I'd only just stopped thinking about her, and I can feel that anger returning as Naomi presses her hand to my chest and moves the empty vodka bottle back to her mouth. Her mascara is smeared beneath her eyes, but that doesn't stop me from seeing the devious expression that dominates her features. She parts her lips and then encloses them around the bottle neck, her eyes never leaving mine as she slowly runs her tongue around the glass. Then, her voice nothing more than a hushed slur, she presses even closer against me and whispers, "Can she?"

She's so close I can almost taste the alcohol on her, and her body is warm, almost too warm, and there's a lump in my throat that feels as though it might just stick straight through my skin. I swallow hard, but I'm rooted to the spot, paralyzed by her body against mine. "I think this is my…my cue to leave," I murmur, but before I can take a single step back, her hands are on my jaw and her lips are against mine.

It's so abrupt that I stumble back from the force, but then I regain my balance and grasp her waist and pull her closer, my beer against her hip, my mouth fast in sync against hers, fueled by the alcohol in our bloodstreams. I weave my hand into her hair, but it's a tangled mess that I only end up pulling, yet I continue to hold her against me as her hands run down my chest, grabbing fistfuls of my shirt. She tastes like the vodka she's just consumed, and I'm not thinking straight, too distracted by someone's body against mine that I can't bring myself to put a stop to it. I don't want to. I like distractions.

Naomi bites down on my lower lip in what I think is an attempt at being seductive, but she bites too hard and for too long, and I swear that for a second I think she may have torn my lip open. There's no time to wonder if blood has been shed, because her hands are under my shirt now, running across my chest, all over my skin, until suddenly her fingers are hooked over the waistband of my jeans.

I tense up, and I firmly reach for her wrists and move her hands away before she can go any further. I tear my lips from hers but keep my eyes closed as I absorb the reality of what we're doing, and then, my breathing heavy, I slowly open them again to look at her. "Naomi…" I murmur, shaking my head. "I can't."

The irritation is clear on Naomi's face as she harshly pulls her wrists free from my grasp. "Why?"

"You know why," I say quietly, sighing and running a hand back through my hair as I turn away from her, moving over to the bed where I sit down and set my beer on the bedside table.

I've done this before, but only this. Never anything more. I couldn't do that. I can be an idiot sometimes, but not *that* much of an idiot. Tiffani may put me through hell and back, we may only be putting on a show for the most part, we may not actually be in love with each other, but I'd never dare fuck her over.

Naomi drifts over and drops to her knees on the carpet in front of me, purposely blinking up at me from beneath her eyelashes. Her devious expression is no longer a turn-on. In fact, it turns me off as she purses her lips together and says, "Tiffani's never going to know. I'm not going to tell her and neither are you, so what's the big deal?"

"Naomi," I repeat, but more firmly this time, more annoyed. When she places her hand on my knee, I promptly push it off again. "No."

"Fine," she huffs. Pushing herself up from the ground and back onto her feet, she sways in front of me, adjusting her hair. Then, she grins and tells me, "The dare was only to make out with you anyway," before turning and walking straight out the door.

I stare after her as the muscle in my jaw tightens. *What the fuck?* Groaning, I throw both hands into my hair and collapse backward onto the bed. I stare at the ceiling for a while, focusing on maintaining a steady breathing rate, wondering what time it is. The music pulsing through the house from downstairs is hard to ignore, and I know that I can't disappear for long, because I should be in the kitchen, calling the shots but also pouring them, because *that's* what I do at parties. I don't hide upstairs, that's for sure.

Sitting back up again I sigh and pull myself together. I have to mentally remind myself to glare at every sophomore guy I pass from now on, and to smile only briefly at the girls, and to laugh whenever someone cracks a joke even if it isn't even remotely funny. I have to remind myself to be convincing, to put on a good act.

Before I leave the bedroom, I fix my shirt and try to tame my hair with my fingers so that it doesn't look so ruffled. That would raise suspicions. I almost gather up the empty cups and the bottle of vodka that's lying on the carpet, but cleaning up after himself is not the sort of thing Tyler Bruce would do, so I quickly finish my beer and then toss the empty bottle onto the floor.

As I'm heading for the door, I notice the flashing alarm clock on the dresser for the first time. It's eleven fifteen exactly, and I have no doubt in my mind that Dean will be here by now, and Meghan, and Jake. But also Tiffani, who I dread seeing the most, especially now.

7

DAD'S CAR HAS DISAPPEARED down the street within a second of me closing the door, but I like that he never sticks around. The quicker he is gone, the sooner I can breathe a sigh of relief. My shoulders sink as my body relaxes from its tensed state, and I fall into step next to Dean as we make our way across campus. We still have ten minutes until first period, so everyone is sort of milling around, leaning against lockers, waiting for the bell to ring. I only have a couple friends, but I still smile at the other kids in my classes whenever I pass any of them, and they sometimes wave back. I'm pretty good at the whole smiling thing. I find myself doing it even when I don't want to.

"There's Jake!" Dean says, pointing off toward the main office. He seems to speed up, so I keep up with him while I search for Jake, and when I spot him, he's already walking toward us.

"I've been here since seven thirty because my mom had to start her shift earlier," he complains as he comes to a halt in front of us, but there's something different about him today. I tilt my head to one side as I study him, but his hair is still the usual shaggy blond that covers his eyes, and he's wearing the same old blue hoodie that he always wears.

But when he adds, "I had to speak to that weird kid from gym class," I hear the lisp to his words and I see the shine of metal on his teeth.

"Did you get your braces?" I ask.

"Oh yeah," Jake says, as though he's totally forgotten all about them, despite only having them for less than twenty-four hours. He grins wide to show them off. "What do you think?"

"Why did you choose green?" Dean questions.

"Because I like green, idiot," Jake answers, and then thumps him on the shoulder.

We've only known Jake for a little over a year, since we first started middle school, but we may as well have known him forever. It feels that way, at least, and I like that there's three of us now instead of two. We all love football, we hate math, and we play too much *Madden NFL* on PlayStation 2.

"They, like, totally *pried* my mouth open!" Jake tells us as we begin to walk, headed inside toward our classes, though I'm not listening too closely. I feel far away again, that disconnected feeling surrounding me. "But my dentist is rough as hell, so my dad started yelling at him, telling him to stop tearing my mouth apart. Now I have to eat nothing but soup all day."

I glance over at Jake. He always talks a lot, always rambles on about pointless stuff, but this time, he has grabbed my attention. "Your dad wouldn't let you get hurt?" I quietly blurt out without thinking. I am always curious about everyone else's parents. If it was me, Dad would have rolled his eyes and told me to man up.

"Uh, no. Would yours?" Jake shoots back, then dramatically presses his hand to his face. "My jaw was in agony! I could barely *breathe*! I shouldn't even be at school today. I'm in *pain*."

I tune back out and tilt my head down, my eyes on the ground as we navigate the school hallways. It's loud. People are yelling, people are laughing, people are nudging me, pressing against that deepening bruise on the back of my shoulder.

Jake doesn't know pain. Jake doesn't know how hard it is not to physically flinch whenever someone touches you. Jake doesn't know what real agony feels like. I am jealous of him and Dean, of every other person laughing around me, who get to go home at night and not feel as though their heart is going to beat straight out of their chest whenever their dad comes anywhere near them.

"Aren't you at science?" Dean asks, and I glance up from the ground to realize that we are passing my class. I can't remember the past five minutes. That seems to happen a lot. "Crap. Yeah." I grind to a halt and turn for the door of my class, that bruise on my shoulder still throbbing. "Catch you guys at lunch."

Science is okay. It's the easiest class to fade into the background in, mostly because every twenty seconds someone has their hand in the air, asking Miss Fitzgerald for further explanation on points she's already covered at least five times already. So I sit at my seat by the window with my elbow propped up on the table and my chin resting on my palm, my stare boring through the dusty glass and over to the sports field. It's empty, but the sun is shining on the patchy grass and after a while, I stop looking. My eyes are open but I'm not really there, not really seeing. I zone out entirely as Miss Fitzgerald's voice drifts off into silence until silence is the only thing that surrounds me, but I like it this way. I like the quiet and the still, because it makes me feel alone. It makes me feel safe.

I think about Dean's dad, Hugh, again. He'll be waiting for us outside school in his truck a few hours from now. A smile on his face and his hand up in the air, waving just in case we haven't spotted him as he gets out of the truck to greet us. Dean doesn't like it when he does that. He thinks it's embarrassing, but I love seeing Hugh waiting for us. He always pats me on the back the same way he does Dean, and as crazy as it makes me feel, I like to pretend, even just for a second, that Dean and I are brothers and Hugh is my dad. That would be pretty sweet. Hugh wouldn't get angry if I messed up my homework, I'm sure of it. He wouldn't raise his voice or his fists. I would know that he loved me.

I love Dad, but not always. I hate him a lot of the time, actually. Maybe I could run away. I could sneak out of school right now, grab a bus to Union Station, and hop on a train to wherever the hell I could get to for five bucks. Which is absolutely nowhere.

"Tyler." Miss Fitzgerald's voices echoes from my right, and I snap out of my daze, pulling my attention back to her. She is towering over my desk, hand on her hip, her face set in a disapproving frown. "Would you like to share with the rest of the class what exactly it is that you find so interesting outside?"

"Uhh." Everyone's eyes are on me, and they are all collectively smirking with glee at my misfortune of getting caught. I rack my brain for an answer, but what can I tell her? I glance around the expectant gazes of my classmates, and I know what they're waiting for. They're waiting for me to break under the pressure, but I refuse to. I never do. Not here, not at school. I refuse to be weak here.

Slumping further down into my chair, I shrug and lazily glance back up at Miss Fitzgerald. "I can't help it that the grass is more exciting than your class," I finally tell her, my voice flat. *I don't care*, I think, and the hushed wave of laughter that makes its way around the room fills me with satisfaction. *Distract them so that they can't figure out what you're really thinking.*

Miss Fitzgerald purses her lips. I can see it in her eyes, that flicker of disappointment that I am all-too familiar with. Most of my teachers have given me that exact same look recently. A year ago, I was quiet. Kept my head down. Scribbled down notes as fast as I could. Tried my best. But lately? I don't see the point. Dad is never happy, no matter how hard I work. It's just so much easier *not* to care.

"Then perhaps you'll enjoy waiting outside," Miss Fitzgerald says. Her lips twitch now, and she gives a pointed nod toward the door, folding her arms across her chest.

On the outside, I roll my eyes and smirk, but inside I feel guilty. I like Miss Fitzgerald, so I can't look at her as I get up out of my seat and weave my way around the desks. The faces surrounding me are lit with amusement, and to keep everyone even more entertained than they already are, I even close the door a little too harshly on my way out.

The hallway is silent, and it reeks too. There's only fifteen minutes to go until class wraps up, so I pace back and forth for five of them, praying that Dad won't find out that I've just been kicked out of class. A couple months ago, Mr. Tiller sent me out of his math class for talking back too. At the time, I thought I was funny. I thought I was cool. But what I didn't know was that later that afternoon, Mr. Tiller called Dad. He was waiting for me when I got home, his anger brimming.

It was a bad night.

I have a scale now, one that I've invented.

There are the awesome nights, the way every night should be, the ones where Dad grins at me across the living room and slips me extra cans of soda when Mom isn't looking. The nights that I actually laugh with him. It's the kind of night that's rare, the kind that makes me wonder if maybe things are changing for the better.

But then there are the good nights, where nothing really happens at all. A good night is when Dad keeps to himself, usually huddled over paperwork at the kitchen table, a pen between his teeth and his foot tapping a relentless beat.

There are the bad nights too. They're the nights that happen too often. A bad night begins the moment I mess up, the exact second I do anything that isn't good enough for Dad. I can handle a bad night now. I am numb to them. Usually, I close my eyes so that I don't have to look at him. I stare into the darkness instead, wondering if Mom is okay working late by herself down at her office; wondering if Jamie has beat the next level on his game yet; wondering if Chase is laughing at his cartoons. Before, I would wonder when Dad was going to stop. Now I just don't bother.

And then there's the highest point of my scale: the really, really bad nights. The kind of night where I don't even recognize Dad. He doesn't usually scare me, but on the really, really bad nights, the crazed, wild look in his green eyes is always enough to send a stab of fear straight through me. There's no stopping him on those nights. The last time one of those nights went down is still fresh in my mind. It was only a month ago. It was the night Dad broke my wrist for the second time. I can't even remember why he was so furious with me, because I blacked out for most of it. Mom thinks I fell down the stairs. If only. It would break her heart if she knew the truth.

I glance down at my hands. Lift my left one, roll my wrist a couple times. It still hurts sometimes, but it's improving. I sigh and lean back against the wall, sliding down to the ground, closing my eyes. I'm so tired. Tired of overthinking. Tired of inventing distraction techniques.

I draw my knees up to my chest and force all of my thoughts out of my head, focusing instead on the sound of footsteps in the distance. They grow closer, louder, nearing me. Until they stop.

"You got kicked out of class?" a voice asks.

I open my eyes and look up. Rachael Lawson is staring down at me with curiosity from behind her big round glasses, her blond hair wrapped up in a high ponytail, loose strands framing her face. We share some classes. We hang out sometimes. We're friends, I guess.

"Yep," I say. Back to being Tyler the cool kid. Not Tyler the overthinker, not Tyler the kid who gets thrown around. That guy isn't cool. I don't like being him. "I talked back to Miss Fitzgerald. She isn't impressed."

"You're crazy." Rachael shakes her head at me, then laughs as she walks away.

"You bet I am!" I call after her. Yeah, right. Crazy for acting like someone I'm not, more like. I can't remember when I first started doing it, but it's starting to feel comfortable. I'm starting to like this Tyler better, but yet, as soon as Rachael is out of sight, I am back to being myself.

Sitting on the floor, my back against the wall, the bruise on my shoulder aching, my mind in overdrive.

8

PRESENT DAY

AS I MAKE MY way back down the stairs and as the music becomes louder and louder, I find myself off-balance. My legs aren't working the way I want them to, so I take each step one at a time, grabbing pathetically at the wall to stabilize myself. I know I look high, but I'm not yet. I just can't see in the dark, so it takes me two minutes of drunken navigation and staring intensely at the floor before I finally get back to the living room.

The house appears fuller now, though maybe I'm imagining it. The vodka I've consumed too fast is taking control of me. I feel lighter in a way, more at ease, but I know that I need to avoid Naomi, and I know that I need to find Kaleb. If I find Declan, then that's even better.

Glancing up, I make a beeline through the crowd straight to the kitchen, but I immediately bump into someone before I get very far. I stand on their feet, only to be tutted at and shoved back again. I hold my hands up in surrender, trying to seem apologetic even though I don't care, and then I focus my gaze to realize that actually, it's Rachael.

"God, Tyler," she mutters, glaring at me in disdain and tucking a strand of her curled blond hair behind her ear. "Wasted before midnight. No surprise there."

"Nice to see you too," I fire back, my voice flat. I'm supposed to like Rachael. She's supposed to like me. We call ourselves friends, but we're not, really. I've known her since middle school, but she's hated me ever since freshman year. *Apparently* she doesn't want to put up with my bullshit like everyone else does. Her words, not mine. I'm cool with her disdain though.

Rachael takes a sip of her drink via a straw so as not to smudge her red lipstick. She continues to glare at me through her heavily lined eyes. "So," she says, leaning in closer to me, "what was up with you earlier?"

I raise an eyebrow and step back from her again. I don't know what the hell she's taking about. She wasn't even at Tiffani's place earlier. "Huh?"

"At the barbecue," Rachael clarifies, cocking her head to one side. The music is so loud I can hardly even hear her. Most of the time I don't want to anyway. "When you stormed in like that?"

Huh. So that's what she's talking about. The barbecue. I'm surprised that she even went. It's not exactly her scene. "You were there?"

"Yeah. Your mom invited me over to meet Eden."

I squint at her. There's that name again, that girl. I try to picture her again in my head, but right now, I can't quite remember what she looks like all that well. I do, however, remember those lips and that voice. There's no chance in hell I'm forgetting that. I wish I could form a clearer picture, but my thoughts are blurring. "Eden?"

"Your stepsister?" Rachael says, rolling her eyes at me. Almost in pity, she purses her lips and looks me up and down. Then shakes her head like she feels sorry for me. I hate when people do that. "She thinks you're a jackass, by the way, so she has pretty good judgment. But whatever, enjoy your night, Tyler. Looks like you're already enjoying it a little too much." She seems so far away from me, disconnected, but I know it's just the alcohol that's putting her out of focus.

"Rachael." I reach for her arm as she turns to walk away. "Is Tiffani here?"

"Kitchen," Rachael says, then shrugs my hand off her before she disappears.

I stand in the middle of the living room for a few more seconds. Or maybe a minute. I can't concentrate on anything but Tiffani. I need to find her, and I need to resolve the argument we had earlier. We never fight for long. Neither of us have the confidence for that. We're not cut out for being on our own. She needs me by her side almost as much as I need her by mine, and we usually get back to putting on a show less than twenty-four hours after whatever fight we've had. At least that's usually how it goes.

I rub at my temple and take a deep breath. I'm good at this. I'm good at acting. Now I gotta be sweet and charming, apologetic and convincing, even when I'm not.

I weave my way across the living room through the distant faces of everyone around me, and then I hover by the edge of the kitchen, searching for her blue eyes. They meet mine from across the room, and she comes into focus, her mouth a dazzling smile as she laughs at whatever joke Dean has just made. Her gaze sharpens, and she presses her lips together, glancing away from me again. She is pouring herself a glass from the bottle of wine she's brought over, slowly and with a certain degree of deliberation to her movements, her chin held high.

I start toward her, nudging Meghan gently to one side as I squeeze past her, and as I approach, Tiffani raises the glass of wine to her lips and takes a sip, watching me closely over the rim, trying not to screw up her face as she forces it down. She hates wine. "Tiff…" I say, reaching for her free wrist.

"Tyler!" she exclaims. Immediately, she plasters a wide grin across her face. It's so forced and so fake that it's enough to make me feel sick. *Does anyone else see it? Does anyone else see that this is all just bullshit? All just a fucking act?* She throws her arm around the back of my neck and pulls me toward her, pressing her lips to mine.

Her mouth tastes like mint and the cheap wine she's drinking. She intertwines her fingers through my hair at the nape of my neck, pulling too hard, and she bites my lower lip in an effort to convey her anger at me. I kiss her back though, because we have an audience. Even grasp her waist like I know she wants me to.

Finally, she tears away first and fixes me with a forced smile, but I can still see the aggravation in her eyes. My hands still on her waist, I bury my face into the crook of her neck and against her warm skin, I mumble, "We need to talk."

Her blue eyes meet mine again and she gives me a tiny fraction of a nod, then slips her hand into mine. Around us, I can see Kaleb watching me intensely with an impressed, teasing smirk, and it's clear that even Dean is fighting the urge to roll his eyes as Tiffani flicks her hair over her shoulder and begins to pull me toward the door. I follow in silence, my hand still in hers, mostly because I'm just glad to have some support to keep me balanced. My head feels too heavy.

"We'll be back in a minute," Tiffani says over her shoulder, as though every single person in this damn kitchen actually gives a shit about what we're up to, and then she pulls open the door, allowing the fresh air to hit me smack in the face.

Shit, I think. *I really am drunk.* I grab Tiffani's shoulder with one hand and press the other to my forehead, wondering if I've felt this dizzy the entire night. I really can't tell, but what I do know is that the backyard is spinning around me, and Tiffani has pushed my hand off her body. I grab fistfuls of the air instead until I finally settle against the wall of the house, breathing deeply while I try to meet Tiffani's gaze again.

Now that we are no longer putting on a show, her smile is gone. Her arms are folded across her chest, her eyes are narrowing. I shouldn't be surprised that she's still pissed at me from earlier, but I'm thinking that maybe now isn't the right time to attempt to fix this. Not when I'm like this, but what choice do I have? I'm still mad at her for bringing up my dad earlier, but she's like a crutch to me. She's a part of the picture-perfect life I'm trying to pull off, and I don't want to lose that. Besides, the sex is on tap, and it's worth apologizing for that alone.

"I'm sorry for storming out earlier," I start. I'm not sorry at all, really, but I know that it's what she wants to hear. She wants me to beg for her forgiveness. That'll satisfy her ego. So, although I am wasted and she is blurry, I fake the apologetic frown on my face and the guilt in my eyes.

"*And* for smashing your beer all over my wall," Tiffani remarks. She exhales and looks away, staring across the backyard through the darkness. She is tense, her patience thin, so I fight harder.

"Yeah, that too." I step forward, unstable, and gently reach for her wrist. I try to force her gaze back to mine, but she is refusing to give in. "Babe, I'm sorry. You know what I'm like. I overreact. You were right to call me out." I want to tell her not to ever mention my dad again, but I know that will only start another fight, and honestly, I don't even want to think about it. Tiffani can be cruel that way. She already knows that she's not allowed to talk about him, but at the same time, she knows it's my weakness.

Her eyes finally flicker back to meet mine, and they immediately soften as she sighs. "You know, Tyler, you may be an idiot, but I do actually *like* you. At least enough to feel as though I would have to let someone know if you got involved with drugs more than you already are," she says with an air of innocence, and it's a subtle reminder that she'll ruin my life if she has to. As long as she's in control of my every move, ensuring that everything I say and do coordinate with exactly what she wants, then there are no problems between us. She glances down at my hand on her wrist and then pulls away from me, shaking her head in disapproval. "Because what good are you going to be to me if you end up in jail or dead? I mean, look at yourself. You're wasted. Are you high too?"

"No," I say bluntly. For once, I'm not lying. I try once more to reach for Tiffani's wrist, and this time, she doesn't pull away. I step closer to her and move my free hand to her chin, tilting her head up to look at me. She likes it when I do that. "I just drank too much again."

She's quiet for a minute as she studies my eyes, most likely measuring the size of my pupils, and then she frowns again. "You aren't seriously considering helping Declan Portwood out, are you?"

Here we go again. Questions that I don't want to answer. I step back from her and shove my hands into the front pockets of my jeans, shrugging. My head is hung low. "I don't know."

"Why, Tyler? It's not like you need the money." She grits her teeth and flicks her hair over her shoulder. I watch her closely as she exhales deeply, and for once, I do actually think she might just care about me a *little*. "Do you really want to be behind bars for dealing while the rest of us are in college, partying, and getting our degrees? If you do this…you're absolutely crazy. Tell Declan to find someone else to deal his shit."

I don't have the energy to argue over this again, so I do what I do best: I give in and let her win. It's not worth the grief. Besides, I am craving another drink. "You're right," I tell her. "I'm not going to do it. It was stupid to even consider it."

Tiffani's face lights up. "You swear, Tyler?"

"I swear, now come here." Teasingly, I place my hands on her shoulders and squeeze her, pulling her toward me. I wrap my arms around her tiny body and hold her against my chest, my chin resting on the top of her head. I fixate my eyes on a spot in the distance, trying to keep myself stable so that I don't topple over and bring her down with me. "Now *this* is better than arguing, isn't it?"

"Mm-hmm," she agrees against my shirt, then her body locks up beneath my grip as she pushes me back a step. "But you're smudging my makeup."

I roll my eyes, almost fall over from the dizziness, then kiss her.

9

HUGH'S TRUCK IS PARKED across the street. I spot it from a mile away, but only because I am desperately searching for it. Dean is by my side, and we're making our way out of school and across our campus. Today hasn't been *so* bad, and having Dean's dad pick us up makes it better. I may have gotten kicked out of science, but I participated during gym class and survived it, so I consider it an alright day. I just hope it stays that way. "*Why* does he have to get out of the truck?" Dean moans from beside me as Hugh pushes open his door and steps out. Of course, he is smiling, pleased to see us, and when he raises his hand in the air, Dean groans. "Oh, crap. Kill me before anyone sees."

I don't know why Dean hates it so much. My dad would never get out of the car to greet me. He barely even smiles when I climb in. That's why I find Hugh so cool. I give him a thumbs-up back, and Dean fires me a sideways glance of betrayal, but I don't care. He doesn't realize how lucky he is. "Hey, boys!" Hugh says as we approach. There's a smudge of grease on his chin, and I figure he must have just gotten off work. He has his own garage, and he wants Dean to work with him when he's older. Dad wants me to work for him too one day. That's why he pushes me so hard, but I don't even know if it's what I want.

"*Dad*, please stop embarrassing me," Dean says and throws open the passenger door of the truck and climbs inside. I follow suit, pulling myself up into the backseat and clicking on my seatbelt.

"Embarrassing you?!" Hugh repeats in mock disbelief as he joins us inside. He widens his eyes at Dean and then leans over to ruffle his hair. "Never."

"Stop!" Dean pushes his hand away and then sulks against the window. I know he's embarrassed only because I'm here, but I wish he knew how jealous I was. Last week, Dad grabbed my hair and dragged me across the kitchen. So, if your dad waving to you and ruffling your hair is embarrassing, then I would happily be embarrassed every single day.

"Oh, lighten up, Deano," Hugh says with a laugh. He starts the engine and it growls to life, and as he pulls on his seatbelt, he glances over his shoulder at me. "Hey, Tyler. How about you come back to our place and throw a football around for a couple hours? How does that sound?" He smiles at me, and it's not the fake kind of smile that Dad gives me.

"Really?" I ask. Playing ball with Dean *does* sound good, but in the back of my mind I know I have homework that needs to be done. Although, none of it is due tomorrow…

"Absolutely," Hugh says, and he begins to drive. "I'll let your parents know."

We head back to the Carters' house and during the entire ride, all I can do is pray that Dad will be working late today. I hope he doesn't mind that I'm going over there. I have all night to do my homework, so he should be fine with it.

We stop for a break only when Dean's mom brings us some juice, and we lie on the lawn, out of breath and staring up at the sky. I glance sideways at Dean. "What if we were brothers?" I ask.

He looks back at me, furrowing his eyebrows. Then he smiles. "I thought we already were."

"Okay. Can I ask you something then?" I sit up and cross my legs, anxiously pulling at the grass. I've been trying to find the opportunity to talk to him about this for a while, and now I finally have the chance. We are alone. We're friends. Brothers, even. I can talk to him about this.

Dean sits up too, angling his body to face me. "What?"

"Does your dad ever get mad at you?"

"Uh, *yeah*," he says, almost matter-of-factly, and then rolls his eyes. "I spilled his coffee all over his shirt on Sunday right before church. He was sooo annoyed."

"No," I say, shaking my head. I glance away. He doesn't get it. "Like, really mad."

I'm just trying to figure out whether it's normal or not. I don't think it is. I don't think your dad is supposed to get that mad. I don't think he's supposed to be that strict. Maybe it's just the way my dad is. Maybe there's something wrong with me, something that makes him so angry, something that makes him flip. Everyone else makes him happy, so why don't I?

Before Dean can answer, we are distracted by the sound of a car approaching, and when I glance over my shoulder, my chest tightens when I realize it's *him*.

Dad's Mercedes pulls smoothly to a stop by the sidewalk, and my heart is pounding as I stare, frozen with fear. The engine dies and the door swings open. Dad steps out, his tie loosened after his day at work, and he rests one hand on the top of the car door, the other on his hip. I can see the Rolex that Mom got him last Christmas shining in the sun.

"Tyler," Dad says, and the firm hardness to his voice immediately tells me that he isn't happy. The coldness in his green eyes as they meet mine only reinforces this. "You're supposed to be at home. Studying. You know that."

I scramble to my feet, and my voice catches in my throat as I try to blurt, "We're just playing…playing football. Hugh said I could come over."

As if on cue, Hugh steps outside onto the porch with a beaming grin. He must have been keeping his eye on Dean and me from the window. He holds up his hand, giving Dad a small two-finger wave of acknowledgment. "Hey, Peter!"

"You were supposed to take Tyler straight home," Dad states. He isn't smiling back. No, his mouth is a bold line and his gaze is sharp.

The grin on Hugh's face slowly fades while his eyebrows furrow with confusion. He scratches at his head. "Ella said it was fine so long as I had him home before six?"

"No," Dad says, shaking his head. They are calling across the lawn to one another, and although Dad and Hugh are good friends, Dad isn't hiding the fact that he's pissed off at him. "He should have been at home studying, *not* messing around playing football." Dad's attention shifts to me again, and he gives me a strict nod. "Tyler, grab your stuff."

"Oh, c'mon, Peter!" Hugh says with a laugh, attempting to lighten the mood. "They're just kids. It's only seventh grade, not college. I'll make sure he's home by six, alright?"

Dad fixes Hugh with a threatening glare but doesn't reply. Instead, he looks back at me again and in a harsher tone he says, "Tyler. I *said* grab your stuff."

"You're going home?" Dean asks, looking up at me from the grass.

"Sorry," I say with a shrug, my voice quiet. Dad is angry, so I don't have a choice. I already know exactly what I'm in for when we get home. It would be a stupid move on my part to attempt to argue over staying here, so I run across the yard to the porch where my bag is. I sling it over my shoulder as Hugh watches me.

"Sorry, buddy," he says with a small smile, and then pats my head. I think he knows Dad can be pretty strict, but I wish he knew how bad it really was. I wish he would say something so that I won't have to. I don't want to be the one to get my dad in trouble.

Please don't let me go, I'm thinking. *I want to stay here with you.*

I can't say it out loud. I just stare up at him instead, praying that he can read my expression, that he can see how terrified I am to get into Dad's car, that he can help me. But of course he doesn't notice. Why would he?

With no option left, I force myself to walk toward the car, but my legs feel stiff, like my body is trying to override my decision, telling me not to go. I fight against it and keep on pushing. I can't look at Dad as I approach, even though I can feel his intense eyes watching me the entire time, and I stare down at my sneakers as I climb into the passenger seat and pull on my seatbelt.

I don't want to go home. I don't want to be alone with Dad. I don't want to get hurt again.

Dad joins me in the car, slamming his door shut behind him. He turns on the engine, his dark eyes set on the road ahead, then he casts me a quick sideways glance. It's the exact same warning look he always gives me right before he makes another one of his mistakes. Already, I can hear his apology in my head.

10

I AM STANDING ON my own lawn, staring at my front door, wondering how the fuck I got here.

It's the middle of the night. I'm wasted. I can't even see, let alone stand. Did I walk home? If I did, then I am impressed with my ability to navigate a two-mile walk while drunk. I glance around me, and thankfully, my car is nowhere to be seen. At least I didn't drive. Did someone give me a ride? Who? I can't remember the past couple hours. I was supposed to stay at Tiffani's place tonight. Where is she?

"Tiffani?" I call out, but no one replies. No one is here. My street is empty, houses are dark.

I look down. I'm still holding a damn beer. It's almost done, so I press it to my lips, wobble a little, then finish it off. I crush the empty can in my hand and toss it away. I should get some sleep, or else I'll suffer for this even more than already necessary.

I reach into my pocket for my keys, but the only keys I pull out are for my car. I fumble in my other pockets, pat myself down, pull out an abundance of lighters and gum and my phone, then realize that I didn't even have my damn house keys with me in the first place.

"Fuck," I say. Then again, louder. "Fuck!"

I turn back, tilting my head while I study the house, groaning. There is no life inside; everyone is asleep. Mom would flip if I woke them all up to let my sorry drunk ass in. I could call Jamie to wake him up and then get him to open the door. Or I could break a window around back.

"No," I tell myself, shaking my head. "No." I'm not waking anyone up, and I'm not breaking any windows either. That's stupid. I'll sleep out here on the lawn tonight. There's a breeze, but it's not cold. I slump down onto the grass, running my hand through the dry blades. Comfy. "What the hell is going on? When did it pass midnight?" I laugh out loud then, because honestly, I know I'm pathetic. I'm sitting on my lawn talking to myself, goddamn.

Suddenly I hear something that sounds like a *hey*, but I can't tell if I'm imagining it or not. I've never had hallucinations from alcohol before, and I really doubt we have a neighborhood ghost, so I tell myself I've imagined it. Until I hear something again, and this time it's louder and as clear as day, a female voice whispering, "Up here!"

I glance around, searching for the voice, until finally my gaze lands on someone peering down at me from the guest room window upstairs. They are so far away and blurry at first, so I narrow my eyes at them for a few seconds as they come into focus. And it's her, that girl again, that damn girl with the husky voice. My... No, I'm not saying it. It's too weird. Has she been watching me this entire time? "What the hell do you want?"

"Are you okay?" she asks, frowning down at me with those full, plump lips of hers, concerned.

No, I'm not okay, I think. *I'm drunk and I'm stuck outside.*

It hits me then that actually this girl has just become my savior. This girl is going to be the one to let me sleep with my head on a pillow rather than a beer can. "Open the door," I tell her, then quickly push myself up from the lawn and head toward the front door. I feel as though I could throw up, but that's stupid. I can handle the alcohol. At least I think I can, but I am desperate to get inside, and this girl certainly isn't rushing to help me. I stand by the door for a few minutes, focusing on my breathing so that I don't hurl, until finally I hear the lock turning. The door swings open and there she is. She's pulled on a pair of jeans and a T-shirt, her hair piled into a heap on top of her head, her eyes tired. I can't remember her name. Emma? Ellie? I know it, I do. It's on the tip of my tongue. It's_.it's Eden. That's it. *Eden.*

"You took your damn time, huh?" Oh God, I really am going to throw up any second. I clamp my mouth shut and push my way into the house.

Eden wrinkles her nose at me with disgust, then locks the front door behind us again. "Are you drunk?" she asks, although I'm pretty sure she doesn't even need to ask. Isn't it obvious?

"No," I answer, just to tease her. "Is it morning yet?"

"It's 3:00 a.m.," she states blankly, her eyebrows furrowed.

Huh. That's still early. I laugh, but then I feel it again, that sickness rising in the pit of my stomach. I quickly turn for the stairs, fumbling for a grip as I try to climb them, but I fall several times and almost break my damn leg. "When did these get here? They weren't here before." I pat the stairs, and I know I'm talking shit, but it's funny to me. Everything is funny right now.

Eden stares up at me from the bottom of the stairs, chewing her lip as though she doesn't know what to do "Do you want water or something?"

I need water, desperately, but I can't. This girl doesn't know me, and she never will, so I'm going to stick with being the Tyler Bruce I am so used to being. "Get me another beer," I joke over my shoulder, and then I force my way back up the remaining stairs. It's such a relief to push open the door to my room, to see my bed still unmade from this morning, to see my bathroom.

I leave Eden behind, close my door, and then dive straight for the toilet, only barely reaching it in time before I promptly throw up.

"Unbelievable," Mom is mumbling under her breath. She's been walking around my room for at least five minutes, furiously picking up clothes from my floor and emptying my trash. I think she's doing it on purpose just to torture me, because it's not even 9:00 a.m. yet. "*Unbelievable*," she says again. She moves to my window and yanks open my blinds, allowing the morning sunlight to flood my room and set my eyes on fire.

I groan and bury my head further under my pillow. "Mom, *please!*" My head is pounding, I'm sweating buckets, and I still feel so damn queasy. I can't deal with Mom right now. I need more sleep, more water. My throat is so dry, I think I might choke.

"Do you think I'm oblivious, Tyler?" Mom stands by my bed, glaring down at me with her arms folded across her chest. "You thought I wouldn't know that you were drinking last night? You *stink* of alcohol. Look at you! You're a mess." She shakes her head in disgust at me. "Get up. You don't get to spend the day in bed. Kids who are capable of drinking are also capable of mowing the back lawn."

"*Mom*," I try again, my voice pleading. My body is aching, and I think I would rather die than suffer this hangover. "Please just leave me alone."

"You know," Mom says quietly, her forehead creasing with concern as her shoulders relax, "there *are* better ways than this to deal with things, Tyler." I know exactly what she's talking about and I know where this conversation is heading, but right now, I just can't deal with her attempts at promoting more healthy methods of dealing with the past. "You don't have to be reckless. Bottling everything up isn't good for you. Maybe you should talk—"

Right then, my phone rings and cuts Mom off. It vibrates wildly on my bedside table, and Mom raises an eyebrow as she snatches it before I do. "It's Tiffani," she tells me, then rolls her eyes at the inconvenient interruption and tosses me the phone. I expect her to leave at this point, but she doesn't budge. She just stares at me, watching in disapproval. She's never really liked Tiffani all that much, and I wonder if it's because she knows me well enough to realize that I'm not even in love with the girl I've been with for three years. Mom's not stupid. I bet she knows the relationship doesn't mean anything.

I roll over so that my back is to her, then I press my phone to my ear. "What?" I mutter. Is Tiffani insane? Why the hell is she calling me at this time of day? Did she even get home last night?

"Wakey wakey, baby," she says, her voice way too cheerful this early in the morning, and I almost throw up again in my mouth right there and then. Isn't she hungover too? I can't remember if she was even drunk last night. I can't remember anything. "I'm picking you up in half an hour. I need to go shopping, and you're coming with me. I'm thinking the promenade, and then we can go pick up your car too."

"Are you kidding me?" I groan again and press my hand to my forehead. My skin is blazing with heat and my hair is damp. A cold shower would be amazing right now. "I'm dying, Tiff."

"Well, that's what you get for being an idiot," she says with a bitter laugh, then quickly adds, "See you in thirty!" before she hangs up on me. We are back to normal again.

Aggravated, I throw my phone onto the floor and grind my teeth together. If I didn't have to suck up to her after our argument last night, then I for sure would *not* be going anywhere today.

"What now?" Mom asks. I wish she would stop heaving those sighs. It's all she ever does, and I fucking hate it. It makes me feel like all I do is drive her insane.

"Looks like I'm headed downtown," I mutter, throwing my sheets off me and sitting up.

"You're not going anywhere. You're grounded," Mom reminds me as firmly as she can, but the threat is empty and she knows it. She can't handle me. She doesn't know how to. I hate disappointing her, but I don't know what else to do either. This is just the way I am these days.

"I'm going to the promenade," I state slowly, and that's enough for her to finally give up. She releases another one of her signature sighs, shakes her head at me, and then leaves me alone at last, shutting my door behind her. I like that she has never expected me to be perfect, but I wish that I could be. She deserves that and so much more.

My legs feel weak as I make my way over to my bathroom, and when I see my reflection in the mirror, I realize that I really am a mess. I look like I've been through hell and back, and my entire body feels damaged. I fumble around in the cabinet, take my antidepressants, pop a couple painkillers, then I force myself under the cold shower until I physically can't take it for a second longer. I'm hoping it helps wake me up, and it certainly does, but it doesn't make me feel any better.

It's a mission in itself just trying to get dressed. I have to stop every couple seconds to take a deep breath, and by the time Tiffani is laying on her car horn outside, I'm only *just* ready. I grab my wallet and my keys, and then I stuff them into my pockets. That's when I remember something from last night. I remember *not* having my keys, and I remember that girl opening the door for me.

Eden.

Eden let me in last night and saved me the humiliation of having Mom find me asleep on the lawn this morning.

I freeze in the hall, stopping right outside the door to the guest room. Or Eden's room now, I guess. It's closed, and I don't know if she's awake or not yet, but for a very, very split second, I lift my hand and contemplate knocking. I know I should thank her, but then I remember that look of disgust she had on her face last night, and I quickly drop my hand and keep on walking. Tiffani is waiting, and I doubt Eden wants to see me. So far, I don't think she's impressed, but no one ever is. I prefer it that way. When people don't like you, they stay away from you.

Stealthily, I creep my way downstairs, glancing around over my shoulder to figure out where Mom and Dave are, but I can't see them. The front door is in sight, so I make a clean break for it, throwing it open and quickening my pace across the lawn toward the neon red car that is waiting.

And as soon as I have opened the door and sat inside, Tiffani is running her eyes over me. "You look like shit," she informs me, which is easy for her to say. Honestly, there is no way in hell she drank enough last night if she was actually able to get up early this morning to do her hair and makeup. She looks good, but I don't have the energy to tell her. "You want me to walk around with you by my side looking like that?"

"Yeah, well, I feel like shit too," I mutter. I yank my seatbelt over me and click it into place, slumping down against the passenger seat.

I close my eyes and focus on my breathing. "My head is pounding, so please don't talk to me."

"So *boring*," Tiffani says, and I can just sense the dramatic eye roll as she begins to drive.

For once though, she *does* actually shut up. She remains silent on the drive downtown, though she keeps the radio on, and I'm sure I'm not just imagining the volume gradually increasing. It makes my headache even worse, and I have to roll the window down to let some fresh air into the car. I decide then, as I'm feeling like I've been hit by a bus twice, that I'm never getting as drunk as I did last night ever again. It's not worth the blackout, it's not worth this suffering. Next time, I'll stop once I've had enough. Though that's easier said than done.

"I know what'll cure you," Tiffani says, her voice teasing as we're parking. I open one eye and look at her. "My mom's going out tonight," she continues, killing the engine and removing her seatbelt. She angles her body toward me, and I don't miss the way she seductively bites down on her lower lip. "And I was thinking that me and you..."

I sit up. That's one way to get my attention. "Me and you could what?" I urge, raising an eyebrow. I already know the answer. I just like hearing her say it. I love the way she blushes when she does.

"Maybe," she murmurs, leaning in closer, "me and you could continue this?" She bats her eyelashes at me and presses her hand against my chest as her glossy lips find mine. It's the same old routine. She tries to maintain dominance, but I'm stronger than her, and within a matter of seconds my hands are tangled in her hair, and I'm pulling at her lower lip with my teeth. She doesn't offer too much, because she pushes away from me after less than a minute. "Hmm? What do you say?"

"Do you really need to ask?"

Tiffani's not all bad. She's hot, and she distracts me from all the other shit that goes on in my head, and I know that I'm using her, but she's using me too. We'll most likely break up next summer after graduation once we've successfully dominated our high school for four years, then she'll move on to college and find some other guy to partner up with to enhance her college experience. We know where we stand with one another, and we know exactly what this relationship is, so we're on the same page.

And I'm cool with that. I don't want to spend my life with her. In fact, I don't think I want to spend my life with anyone. It's not exactly something I've imagined, because I try not to think about the future too much. I don't even know if I'll still be here a few years from now, and honestly, it all seems way too hard to figure out. I'm not good enough for college. Not good enough to be anyone's husband or father. Not good enough for anything, really. That's why I take every day one day at a time, and I try to cope as best I can in the present.

Still feeling nauseous, I follow Tiffani toward the Third Street Promenade, Santa Monica's second pride and joy after our pier and beach. It's Saturday and the sun is out early for once, so the promenade is heaving with crowds dodging the freaky street performers and dipping in and out of clothing stores and food joints. Tiffani and I are soon doing the same.

We are hand in hand as she pulls me along behind her down the center of the promenade, her hips swinging in an effort to turn heads, but no one gives a shit. She does this a lot, and I let her, because it's kind of amusing. I'm exhausted, but getting out of the house for some fresh air is definitely helping me feel a little better.

"What about these jeans?" Tiffani asks. We are in American Apparel and she waves a pair of jeans in front of my face for what feels like the fifteenth time already. I don't know how they can be any different from all the other pairs.

"I…honestly…don't know." I don't care either. I'm leaning back against a rack of discounted tops, scanning the people in the store, because I am bored out of my fucking mind, when I spot some fitting rooms over in the far corner. There's a sign stuck to the door stating that these fitting rooms are closed, but it's not exactly clothes I intend to take with me.

I glance back at Tiffani, who is posing in front of a mirror as she holds the pair of jeans against her body, tilting her head from side to side. I step toward her, reaching for her waist. "Why wait until tonight?" I mumble against the back of her ear as I press my body firmly against hers and brush my lips over the soft skin of her neck. "Why can't we continue…right now?"

"Tyler!" Tiffani twirls around and whips me with the pair of jeans she's holding, her lips parted and her cheeks red. I know she's down though. I can see the mischief behind the dramatic, horrified expression she has.

"Come on." I snatch the jeans from her and toss them onto the nearest table, then reach for her hand and swiftly pull her toward those closed fitting rooms. I need to stay on her good side, and there is nothing she loves more than feeling wanted. Even when it's for all the wrong reasons.

I glance around us, scouring the store in search of staff, but the coast is clear. No one is around, so I go ahead and push open the door to the fitting rooms, pulling Tiffani with me.

"God, this is a bad idea," she mumbles, squeezing my hand. "*Such* a bad idea…"

I spin around to face her and press my mouth against hers, mostly just to shut her up before she freaks and backs out. I kiss her hard, both of us fighting for that dominance again, and I push her back into a cubicle, pulling the curtain closed behind us. She hooks her arms around the back of my neck, holding me close while I wrap a hand into her hair. We're never all that gentle with one another, and if I get the chance to pull her hair, then I'm doing it.

"Stooop," Tiffani whispers with a laugh as she pulls away from me. Her blue eyes are glossy and bright, and I know she is enjoying this.

"Babe." I grab a fistful of her blouse and pull her against me again, and then I kiss the corner of her mouth as I begin to undo the buttons. I trail my lips down to her jaw, and then her neck, where I close my eyes and get to work.

"What is that you're wearing?" she asks, her voice breathy. She tilts her head to one side and pulls on my hair with both hands. "Is that Montblanc? It smells like it."

I wish she would stop talking. "No, it's Bentley," I say. "Come here." My mouth finds hers again, and I push her back against the wall of the cubicle. Right now, I definitely do not feel hungover. I am kissing my super-hot girlfriend in a damn American Apparel fitting room, and I'm enjoying it. I would be fucking crazy not to.

My hand is under her blouse, my lips are planting kisses all over her chest, we are stumbling. She is grabbing my shirt, one hand still slung over the back of my neck. I can feel her breathing deeply into my hair as she rests her chin on the top of my head.

"What are you doing?"

"What?" I mumble, refusing to tear my lips away from her body.

"Whatever it is that you're doing right now," she says. Her breathing is still heavy. "It feels nice."

I don't even know *what* I'm doing. I'm just kissing her, just touching her. My hands are all over her body, in her hair and under her shirt and on her hip. "Of course it does." I pull away for a second, grabbing my

T-shirt and pulling it off. I reach for the belt of my jeans, but Tiffani is quick to grab my wrist.

"Tyler!" she gasps. She's shaking her head at me, but her eyes flash in amusement. "We're not doing that here."

I am just about to narrow my eyes at her, just about to ask her why the hell not, when I hear a voice call out, "Eden, are you still in here?"

Instantly, we both freeze. We aren't the only ones in here anymore.

"Shhh," Tiffani hisses sharply, and the alarm is written all over her face. Then, she raises her voice and asks, "Who's here?"

There is a silence. And then, "Tiffani?"

"Rachael?"

Thank God. I would much rather be caught by Rachael than some store employee, and both Tiffani and I exchange a glance of relief. She slides the curtain open and steps out, but I don't join her.

"Um, I didn't know anyone was in here," Tiffani says, and I can hear the embarrassment in her voice. Though at the same time, she's probably ecstatic that we've been walked in on. It's just the type of gossip she loves. *Did you hear Tiffani and Tyler were caught hooking up in American Apparel this weekend?* It reminds everyone that yes, we're still together, and yes, we must just be *so* in love with one another that we can't keep our hands to ourselves.

"What are you doing?" Rachael questions, and then louder she adds, "Tyler, are you in there too?"

I grit my teeth, rub my temple, and then finally say, "Yeah, I'm here." I step out of the fitting room, pulling my T-shirt back on. My hair is a mess, so I run my hand through it in an attempt to tame it. I'm not exactly happy to be interrupted. "Ever heard of privacy?"

Rachael is staring at me with that disapproving, disgusted look of hers that she always, always gives me. "Ever heard of not hooking up in the middle of American Apparel? That's gross." Awkwardly, Tiffani begins closing the buttons of her blouse.

Rachael isn't alone. Next to her, Eden is staring at me with a pile of clothes in her hands. She keeps her head down slightly, but I can see that she's curiously watching us.

"What the hell are you guys even doing here?" I ask, staring straight back at Eden again, wondering what she thinks of me *now*. Was she in here the entire time? She saw me turn up late for the barbecue yesterday, then she saw me wasted on the damn lawn, and now, she may not have seen anything, but I'm pretty sure she knows I was just getting it on with my girlfriend in a damn fitting room. She probably thinks I'm an asshole. Good.

"Trying on clothes," Rachael answers with the roll of her eyes, "which is a normal thing to do in fitting rooms."

Tiffani isn't too happy about being disturbed either, because she fires Rachael a threatening look and then seems to notice Eden for the very first time. I don't know if they've met yet. She cocks her head to the side and asks, "And you are?"

She is back to being the Tiffani she *wants* to be. We are both good actors, and Tiffani is quick to establish her imagined authority whenever she meets someone new. That's why she's looking Eden up and down in an effort to intimidate her, and I feel a little bad when I see just how uncomfortable Eden looks. "Eden," she says with apprehension. God, her voice sounds so good when she says her name like that, all nervous and quiet, bringing out that husky tone again. She glances at me and adds, "His stepsister."

"You have a stepsister?" Tiffani angles her body to look at me, her gaze sharp. I don't think I ever mentioned it to her. I didn't find it necessary. It's not like Eden lives down here, and honestly, I totally forgot she was even coming for the summer. But Tiffani likes to keep tabs on every single part of my life, so this information is a big deal to her.

All I can do is shrug. "Apparently."

Tiffani stares at me, blinking. She is annoyed now, I can tell. "Why were you in here?" she demands, turning her glare back to Eden. "Were you spying on us?"

"Chill, babe." I reach for her arm and give her a look. After Eden helped me out last night, I owe her one. The least I can do is stop Tiffani from grilling her just to fuel her own ego. "It's not even a big deal. Stop tripping out."

She shrugs my grip off and then crosses her arms over her chest. She will be pissed at me for stopping her, but whatever. "I'm just saying," she mumbles.

"Yeah, well, don't." I steal another glance at Eden. She is still watching us closely. "She doesn't care. Let's just go. I need to go to Levi's." I don't, actually. I just want to get the hell out of these fitting rooms. I throw my arm around Tiffani's shoulders and pull her in close, but she doesn't even budge.

"I'll see you on Tuesday," she tells Rachael. "You're still coming to the beach, right?"

"Yeah," Rachael agrees, and then she looks at Eden, and it's pretty clear what she's about to say next. It makes me wonder when the hell Rachael and Eden even became friends. That damn barbecue…"Eden can come too, right?"

Tiffani sighs slowly, pursing her lips. She is quiet for a while, making it all the more painful for Eden as it becomes more and more evident that Tiffani doesn't want her there. Our circle of friends was established in middle school, and Tiffani hates having anyone else around us. She knows she can control not only me, but our friends too, and she doesn't like that certainty being threatened. "I guess."

I've had enough at that point. Enough of Tiffani's ego, enough of Rachael's glances. That's why I pull Tiffani away again, and this time, she is happy to leave with me. We can continue this later. Tonight. That's if she doesn't stay pissed off. As we head out of the fitting rooms and back into the bustling store, I try to steal one more glance over my shoulder, but the door has already closed behind us. *Damn*, I think. I wanted to see Eden's expression again, because I haven't had enough of *her* yet.

11

FIVE YEARS EARLIER

THROUGH THE SILENCE, DAD taps his index finger against the top of the steering wheel. His jaw is clenched, his eyes are set on the road ahead. He hasn't turned on the radio. That's how I can tell that he's not just annoyed but *seriously* angry with me. And I know why. It's because I was supposed to be redoing my math homework that he tore up last night. I shouldn't have gone to Dean's after school. I should have just asked Hugh to take me straight home. I should have known better.

"I was…I was going to do it tonight," I quietly volunteer. I'm playing with my hands in my lap, interlocking my fingers over and over again. I can't look at Dad. Not when he's mad at me.

"You *know* I wanted you to work on that homework right after school," he says through gritted teeth. I see his hand tighten around the gearshift lever. He once told me only real men drive stick shift. "We know exactly what happens when you leave everything until too late in the evening. You start whining that you're too tired, that you can't concentrate as much."

"I'll do it right after dinner!" I tell him, glancing up, my eyes wide. Maybe there's still time to salvage this. It's not like I *wasn't* going to redo that homework. I just wanted to throw a football around first, like how Dean gets to.

"Tyler, just be quiet right now," Dad says. His voice is low but firm. As always. His eyes are locked on the road and with his free hand, he rubs his temple. "Please."

I drop my eyes back down to my backpack on the floor by my feet. I give it a small kick, frustrated. Like Hugh said, it's only seventh grade. I wish Dad didn't take it all so seriously, like my whole future would blow up if I failed one test. I'm not even in high school yet! No one else studies as hard as I do, but that's still not good enough for Dad.

I do as he says and keep quiet for the rest of the ride home. It's not too far, only five minutes, so I stare at my hands and trace the lines on my palms. Without the radio playing to distract us, the tension is more noticeable, the silence unbearable. It's just after four, and Dad always works from home in the afternoons, which is a routine I've grown to hate. It means that for a couple hours every day, I'm alone in the house with Dad. Mom is usually down at her office until at least five thirty most nights. She's an attorney who always has case after case to work through. That's why her car isn't in the driveway when we pull up.

The silence continues even as Dad is pulling his keys from the ignition and stepping out of the car. I slip my backpack on and scramble after him across the lawn, but dread is weighing me down. I thought I knew what I was in for, but now I'm not so sure. It's still early. I can still have that homework finished by dinner.

"Dad, I'll go and do it right no—" I splutter as we're walking through the front door, but my words are cut short when Dad abruptly slams the door shut behind us.

"Get upstairs," he demands, setting his green eyes on me. Grabbing me by my backpack, he drags me down the hall and then upstairs. His strides are too wide, so I have to fight to keep up or risk being knocked off my feet. Dad shoves open my bedroom door and hauls me inside behind him, then throws me down onto the chair in front of my desk. "One hour, Tyler. ONE," he states very clearly, his voice raised. He yanks my backpack straight off me, almost twisting one of my arms as he does, and then he begins rummaging around inside it. He throws a handful of chewed pens at me. "Disgusting," he says, still searching through my bag. Finally, he pulls out my math homework and slams it down on the desk, dumping my bag on the floor. He grabs my shoulder, one hand resting on the desk, and he crouches a little so that we are at eye level. His gaze is intense, his vibrant eyes piercing straight through me. "Every single one of these questions better not only be done but be *correct* too. Got it? Your mom wouldn't want to know that you're slacking, so c'mon. Impress her."

I nod, already reaching for paper, a pen in my hand. Dad's grip on my shoulder becomes even tighter, his fingers pressing into my skin. "Got it," I mumble. An hour to complete this entire worksheet again? I run my eyes over the thirty different equations. There's no way.

Dad finally lets go of my shoulder and turns away, kicking my bag to one side. "*El trabajo duro siempre vale la pena*, Tyler," he mumbles under his breath. Whenever Dad speaks Spanish, the hint of an accent is clear. Grandma *is* from Mexico, after all. "*No lo olvides.* Okay?"

I don't know what he's saying. I should, because he's been teaching me since the moment I could talk, and I'm pretty close to fluent now, but my mind goes blank as I try to process his words. I try to translate them in my head, but today, I'm just not getting it. My heart is pounding in my chest. What did he ask?

Dad doesn't like my silence, and he is obviously waiting for a reply, because he glances back over his shoulder, sees my blank, wide-eyed expression of confusion, then slowly swivels around to face me again. "You don't even know what I just said, do you?" He shakes his head as though I've betrayed him, and he places his hands on his hips, narrowing his gaze at me. "Do you?"

"*No. Lo siento,*" I apologize. Saying sorry is all I can do. I've messed up twice now today. There's nothing more I can do. "*Lo siento,*" I say again, quieter. I don't even know why I still attempt to appeal to Dad's better, sympathetic nature these days. I discovered a long time ago that he doesn't have one.

"God, do we have to go over basic fucking Spanish again tonight too?" he yells, his hands in the air. He's swearing now. That's a bad sign. "I was trying to tell you that hard work always pays off. Do you understand *that*?"

I nod fast and turn my eyes back down to my homework in front of me, but it's a blur. My hands are trembling. Dad doesn't like it when I don't answer him, but I can't bring myself to open my mouth right now. My chest is tightening, restricting my breathing. I can't breathe. I can't.

Dad's hands are grabbing my shoulders, dragging me up out of the chair, slamming me against the wall. He shakes me. Says something. I can't hear him. I'm tuning out, focusing on a tiny scuff on my wall at the opposite side of my room, forcing my mind to be anywhere but here. The numbness sets in, my head is fuzzy. Dad is yelling. I still can't breathe. One second I'm here by my desk, the next I'm over by the door. Then back again. I'm on the ground. Dad's hold is too tight. I close my eyes.

12

I'M LYING ON MY bed, staring at the ceiling, my head propped up by three pillows. My TV is on, but I'm not watching it. I have my earphones in, listening to music. Depressing shit. Shit that gets me overthinking. Shit like You Me At Six and All Time Low that I would never tell anyone I listen to. I'm supposed to be heading over to Tiffani's in an hour, but ever since I got home earlier, I've managed to think myself into one of my bad moods. It's frustrating because it usually only happens when I've forgotten to take my pills, which is often, but I definitely took them this morning.

I do this a lot. The overthinking. Most days, I am fine. Most days, I can bear it all. It's easy when all I have to do is act. But then there are the days when I'm *not* fine, when it all spills over for a little while before I force myself to get back in check and continue being *the* Tyler Bruce.

But I'm okay just being me right now. I am alone in my room with no one to perform for. I can lay here for as long as I want with my hood up and my earphones in, questioning my life and wondering what the fucking point is. And no matter how many nights I spend trying to figure these things out, I am still no closer to finding the answers.

I just wish I knew where I was headed. I'm too scared to think about my future, because I am terrified I don't have one. I keep on messing things up for myself, because the only thing I can focus on is surviving another day without having an absolute breakdown, and the only way I know how to survive is by distracting myself from all of my fucked up issues.

I tug on the drawstrings of my hoodie and roll over onto my side, staring at my wall. I stare into space sometimes, mostly out of habit. I became real good at zoning out when I was younger, but right now, I am finding it difficult to put my mind elsewhere. It is in overdrive.

I wish I *was* the Tyler I pretend to be. That guy doesn't care. That guy is cool. That guy has the hot girlfriend, the nice car, the biggest group of friends. That guy is happy. But what people don't know is that the hot girlfriend doesn't care about him. The nice car left him with an empty trust fund. The big group of friends is all fake.

And all that is left is me, the pathetic Tyler. The Tyler who doesn't know who he really is, the Tyler who hates disappointing his mom, the Tyler who cares *too* much, the Tyler whose dad ruined his life.

Sometimes, I wonder if there are even words strong enough in the dictionary to describe the hate I have for him. It tears me up inside every day, starting in my chest and spreading through my body, until the anger becomes too much. I lash out at Mom. At my brothers. At Tiffani. At my friends. At teachers. At strangers. I can't control it. I am an angry, impossible person, and for that alone, I will forever hate him.

Dad is in prison. He has been for almost five years now, and I hope he despises it. I hope he is going insane without anyone who loves him enough to visit. I hope he regrets every single fucking time he laid his hands on me. He lost everything, but so did I. Does he have nights like these too? Where he can't stop going over old ground, turning everything over in his mind? Where he asks himself where he went wrong—and never finds the answer?

I bet he thinks my life is better now that he's no longer in it. But I wonder if he knows that my life is even worse than it was before. That although he got locked away, his abuse never stopped. It's always there, ingrained in my mind. It has fucked me up, and I so badly wish he knew that dealing with the psychological damage that he inflicted is a million times harder than putting a Band-Aid on a cut or waiting for a bruise to heal or a fracture to mend.

I'm worried it will never go away. I'm scared I'm never going to be okay, that I'll always just be this person whose life is in pieces.

Over the sound of my music, I hear Mom's voice calling up the stairs. I sit up and pull one earphone out to listen to her, but she's only calling to let me know that they're about to leave. They're all heading out for a meal together, but I'm not going. She knows my mood is low, so I'm grateful she isn't forcing me to join, which is why I know I should at least have the decency to get up and say goodbye.

I force myself out of bed and head for my door, pulling it open, my hood still up and my music still playing. I step outside my room, and the very first person I lay eyes on is Eden. It's the first time I've seen her since the awkward interaction at American Apparel this morning, and I narrow my eyes at her. She's wearing a pair of sweatpants. Definitely not appropriate attire for a family meal. "Aren't you going?" I ask.

"Aren't you?" she throws back, her tone sharp. I take it that no, she isn't going. Which means I'm going to be stuck here with her. Fuck.

Immediately, I pull my earphone out and push my hood down. I am such a pro at this whole Tyler Bruce act, I can switch into character without even thinking about it. And right now, I need to be him. Not me. "Grounded," I tell her, only because it sounds way cooler than telling her I'm feeling depressed as hell. I press my fingers to my temple, feeling the heat on my face. "What's your excuse?"

"Sick," she says, though it's far from convincing. She spins around and continues downstairs, but I follow her, watching the way her hair swings around her shoulders. I don't know if she just has an attitude or if she doesn't even realize she's doing it. "And that's weird: being grounded didn't stop you from going to American Apparel," she adds, glancing over her shoulder at me from beneath her eyelashes. Thankfully, she keeps her voice low.

Who even is this girl? Does she have any idea who she's dealing with? "Shut the hell up."

Down in the hall, the rest of this weird, thrown together, poor excuse of a family is waiting by the front door. Mom and Dave are dressed nice, and Jamie and Chase are discreetly elbowing one another in the ribs.

"We won't be too late," Mom tells us, and her soft gaze locks on mine. I can see the worry in her eyes, but I'll be fine. I always am. These low moods never last for more than a few hours. "Don't even think about leaving," she adds for good measure, just to reinforce the fact that I *am* still grounded. Though I don't care.

"Mom, I wouldn't dare," I reassure her, crossing my arms over my chest and leaning my shoulder against the wall. Gotta play it cool in front of Eden. First impressions are everything, and right now, she is still forming hers.

"Can we go now?" Chase whines. "I'm hungry."

"Yes, yes, let's go," Dave says. Even for a stepdad, he's pretty shitty. He doesn't so much as acknowledge my existence as he opens the front door to let Jamie and Chase run to the car. He only frowns at his daughter and says, "I hope you feel better, Eden."

Eden gives him a tight smile. She's lying, but he doesn't see it. "Bye," she tells him, and I almost laugh at her bluntness. It's the first time I've seen the two of them interact, but there doesn't seem to be much warmth there.

"Behave yourselves," Mom adds quickly, though she must know that the warning isn't actually going to prevent anything, and then they all finally head out the door, leaving Eden and me in the new silence that has formed in the hall.

I'm staring at her, running my eyes over her body as I try to analyze her. At first, she seemed quiet, almost reserved. But she just spoke back to me *and* she's lying to her dad? Nice. Not so quiet after all.

She angles her head to look at me, and she scrunches her nose when she realizes I'm already staring at her. "Um."

"*Um*," I mimic, raising the pitch of my voice. This girl is new and I have yet to figure out her personality, so I need to test it while also letting her know who exactly Tyler Bruce is. Or at least who he *wishes* he was.

"Um," she says again. It's clear by the look she's giving me that she's not my biggest fan, but that's okay. I don't want her to be.

I glance at the clock on the wall behind her. It's six, and Tiffani wants me over at her place by seven, but I think I may just head over there early to save me from having to stick around here with Eden. It's already awkward enough. "I'm gonna grab a shower," I tell her. She is standing between me and the stairs so, putting on my act as best I can, I add, "That's if you'd get out of my way."

Slowly, she moves to the side, her eyes still narrowed at me in what appears to be disgust. Whatever. I brush past her, my shoulder hitting hers, and I march back upstairs and into my room. At least I am no longer stuck in my cycle of analyzing my life too much. There is only one thing on my mind now and that's Tiffani. She's good at distracting me. Real good. It's partly why I'm with her in the first place.

I dither around my room for a while, flicking through TV channels and pulling out a fresh pair of jeans and a shirt, and then I jump into the shower. I imagine the water rinsing away all of the shitty thoughts that have been running through my head for the past couple hours, and I feel much better by the time I'm done. I step out feeling ready to perform, ready to be *that* Tyler Bruce.

I am just pulling on my shirt when I hear footsteps on the stairs. I pause to listen, waiting to see if Eden is only heading to her room or if she's coming to talk to me, and I'm kind of hoping it's the latter so that I can try to push her buttons. But I quickly realize that it's not Eden at all.

"Jesus Christ," Tiffani says as she barges into my room. Her cheeks are flushed red and she looks mortified. She pushes my door closed behind her, then throws her hands up at me. "I thought you had a girl over!"

I blink at her, confused. I didn't know she was coming over. Last I knew, I was supposed to be going to *hers*. "What?"

"That damn stepsister of yours who came into existence out of nowhere just gave me a damn heart attack!" she explains, shaking her head fast. Her hair is tied up into a high ponytail, and it swings rapidly around her shoulders. "Honestly, I was ready to march up here and kill you."

"Tiffani," I say firmly, and she stops talking. I step toward her, place my hands on her shoulders, and just look at her. "Calm down. It's only Eden."

She is breathing heavily, but she nods. Her blue eyes pierce mine, and she cocks her head to one side. "You're right. You wouldn't do that to me, would you? Because I don't know what I would do if you ever did."

I think about Naomi last night, but then I remind myself that I was drunk. It doesn't count. I was drunk when I kissed Ally Jones a couple months ago too. And I'm pretty sure I kissed Morgan Young once, but I can't remember exactly. It only ever happens when I am way too drunk, but still, I don't want to find out what Tiffani *would* do if she knew. She once got me suspended from school for cheating by claiming she wrote my English lit essay all because I forgot her birthday and didn't make a huge deal of it like she expected me to. And the only reason Mom knows I often smoke weed is because Tiffani told her. Again, all because I forgot her fucking birthday.

I give Tiffani the smallest hint of a smile. She can't ever find out. "And throw away *you*? Never." God, I hate myself so fucking much. I wish I could just tell Tiffani that I don't care, that she's hot but I don't even like her very much, that I'm only using her as a distraction. But no, I'm too much of a pathetic loser who has to maintain this bullshit relationship to convince everyone that my life is good, that I'm fine, that I've got everything figured out. I started high school with every intention of ensuring no one ever saw me as pathetic and someone to be messed with, and hooking up with the coolest girl back in my freshman year was a surefire way to guarantee that. Without Tiffani, I'd have to find my own status all over again.

I sling my arm around Tiffani's shoulders and pull her close against my chest, guiding her back over to the door, but she quickly pushes me away from her. "I've been waiting for you to come over," she tells me, her tone changing. It becomes sharper, back to its usual. "What the hell have you been doing this entire time?"

I follow her down the stairs, and I'm thinking, *Here we go again.* Demanding Tiffani is back. "Chill out," I say, rolling my eyes behind her. "I was gonna head over in an hour, like you said."

"You could have at least answered my calls. You know I need you to always answer them so I know where you are."

"I couldn't hear them over my music." That's a lie. I saw her calling, but I just wasn't in the right mind frame to answer. She was the last person I wanted to talk to. It's not like she would understand, because she doesn't know the truth. No one does.

We stop in the hall, and she turns around to face me, most likely to start another unnecessary argument, but before she can say anything more, I spot Eden. She is on the couch in the living room, her eyes glued to us, watching. It's all she ever seems to do.

"Now what the hell is your problem?" I ask her.

Eden continues to stare at me, her expression blank. She looks unfazed. "Geez."

"Shut up, Tyler," Tiffani says, and I sense her shaking her head from beside me. As if she's on Eden's side.

"Whatever." I turn back to Tiffani, and although she is grinding my gears, I still expect our plans to follow through. "Let's just get outta here."

"Actually…" she says slowly, and she pushes out her lower lip, something she always does when she knows she's about to piss me off. That's why I know that whatever she says next, I'm not going to be happy with.

I sigh. "What now?"

Tiffani turns away and walks into the living room, stepping in front of the TV, much to Eden's irritation. She's wondering what the hell is going on too. It's obvious from her expression. She's not very good at hiding her true thoughts, it seems, but maybe she doesn't realize how readable her expression can be. "New plan," Tiffani says, and I step curiously into the living room, listening. She is glancing between both Eden and me, and I don't like it. "Austin's throwing a last-minute party and we're going. You too, Eden. It's Eden, right? You don't really look the partying type, but Rachael says I have to invite you along. So come."

"Back up a second," I blurt. What the hell? Another party? I barely survived the one last night. The absolute last thing I want to do right now is go to another, where I will have to laugh at jokes that aren't funny. Where I will have to nod to music I don't like. Where I will be the one to have to drink the most because everyone thinks I can handle it when I definitely can't. I just want to relax, to be with Tiffani, to let her distract me. I head over to her, placing my hand on her hip and moving my lips to ear. "I thought we were going to your place. You know…"

"Reschedule that," she murmurs. She moves around me and claps her hands together, moving her attention to Eden, the goddamn stranger who she only met a few hours ago. "Okay, so you're coming, Eden. And you too, Tyler. You're coming and you're not getting wasted for once."

So I'm not even allowed to get drunk in order to survive the party? "The fuck?" I hate that she always makes decisions for me.

She already has her car keys in her hand, ready to leave. So much for early notice. "Rachael and Megs are already at my place getting ready, so come on, let's go!"

"Wait," Eden says, and when I flash my eyes at her, she is getting to her feet. She doesn't look too enthusiastic about the idea of a party, but she isn't objecting to it either. If anything, she only looks apprehensive. Like Tiffani, I wouldn't have taken her for the partying type of girl, but I guess she's only going to continue surprising me. "I need to get an outfit. Give me five minutes to find something."

Tiffani laughs out loud, a laugh of pity, but Eden probably can't even tell the difference as Tiffani reaches for her arm and yanks her forward. "You can borrow something of mine. Now come on! We're leaving for the party in two hours." She lets go of her and makes for the front door, car keys jingling in her hand, her chin held high. I follow her, but only because it seems like I don't really have a choice right now.

"I thought you were grounded," I hear Eden murmur as I'm leaving.

I stop, turning back around once more to study her. Who even *is* this girl, really? I figure she must be from Portland, but only because I know Dave is from there. I know she's only here for the summer. And I know she doesn't know who *I* am yet, because she keeps testing me whether she realizes it or not. She keeps watching me, keeps talking back, keeps questioning everything. I know she lies to her dad. And I know her eyes are hazel, because I can see them now, staring back at me without breaking contact. I smirk at her, impressed. Most people can't do that. Most people look away after a few seconds. "And I thought you were sick."

She doesn't say anything more after that, even when we're in Tiffani's car en route back to her place. I'm riding shotgun, and I push my seat as far back as it will go, just to see if Eden will tell me to fuck off or not. She doesn't, but I wish she would, just so I can hear the way it sounds in her voice. She remains quiet in the backseat instead, staring out of the window, looking slightly more anxious now.

Tiffani, on the other hand, won't shut up. She is filling me in on the latest petty drama that I honestly could care less about, so I nod and murmur, "Really?" every once in a while just so she believes I'm listening. I'm not though, because all I can think about is how much I am dreading this party. They suck. The only reason I bear them is because they distract me. They help me forget, just for a while, so I'm focused on something else other than how fucking messed up my life is.

When we pull up outside Tiffani's place, Rachael's and Meghan's cars are already in the driveway, and I know they're already inside getting ready. I can picture it all already: I will be subjected to hours of giggling. I will be grilled about my opinion on their outfits. I will be the one to bring them drinks. "Your mom's still out, right?" I ask once we're inside and lingering in the hall, listening to the music that's already pounding from upstairs. Eden looks way out of her comfort zone as she hangs back behind us, and I quickly glance around. Tiffani's mom wouldn't approve of me being here again, and she's always such a buzz kill.

"Yeah. There's beer in the kitchen. Kick back down here while we get ready, but take it easy," Tiffani tells me, and the thunderous look she gives me is all the warning I need. I embarrassed her last night, I know I did. She reaches for Eden's hand and begins pulling her toward the huge marble staircase that I have stumbled down drunk so many times before, and halfway up, she calls back, "We won't be long!"

Eden looks terrified as she is dragged away into the hell that is being under Tiffani's control. Honestly, I feel sorry for the damn girl. She's been here for—what?—a day? I don't know what the parties in Portland are like, but I doubt they are anything like ours. She doesn't know what she's getting herself into, and I can already tell that she's going to regret it tomorrow. I run my hand back through my hair and make my way into the kitchen. There's a stack of alcohol already there, waiting to be brought to the party, and I grab the first beer I find. I pop the cap and take a swig, but I can't even enjoy it. I drank enough last night to last me the entire summer.

I force it down nonetheless as I lie sprawled on the couch in Tiffani's living room, flipping between sports channels on the giant TV in the dark for what feels like forever. I keep the box of Bud Lights next to me, so that I can easily grab another. And another. And another. Take it easy? I wish I could, but Tyler Bruce doesn't take things *easy*.

"We shouldn't be too much longer," I hear a voice say after a while, and it startles me a little because the beer is making me drowsy. I prop myself up and crane my neck. Rachael is hovering at the door, a drink in her hand. "You know, you were really, really wasted last night."

"Yeah. Thanks for the reminder." I roll my eyes at her, then purposely take a long sip of the beer in my hand just to remind her that I don't give a shit.

"I'm just saying," she mumbles, taking a step into the living room. She glances at the TV for a moment, and then back at me, her eyebrows pinching with concern. "You don't have to drink that much, you know."

"Says you, Lightweight Lawson," I retort, turning away from her. I get bored of Rachael so easily. All she ever does is shake her head at me and comment on everything I do. What is up with everyone in my damn life trying to control me?

"That's different," she says. She takes several more steps into the room, standing directly in front of me so that I have no option but to look back up at her, even though I'm not interested in what she has to say. "I get drunk *because* I'm a lightweight. You get drunk because you *want* to."

I sigh and keep my expression blank. "Are you done with your lecture?"

"Not really." Taking a swig of her own drink, she sits down on the arm of the couch next to me and crosses one leg over the other. "I'm just letting you and that ego of yours"—she taps her index finger against my forehead—"know that you won't be any less cool if you have a limit. It's okay to turn down a drink." She drops her gaze to the empty bottles of beer on the floor around us, and she frowns. "I think you've had a lot already."

"Whatever, Rachael." I nudge her away, pushing her off the couch, and she doesn't put up much of a fight. I hope she's happy now that she's done her good deed for the day. She doesn't say anything more, only sips at her drink as she turns and walks away. I listen to the sound of her footsteps on the stairs until they disappear, and then I drink from my own beer again.

I wait around for another half hour, texting Dean and Jake to see if they're at the party yet or not, before I finally crack and lose my patience. I have been waiting two entire damn hours for the girls to get ready, and it's becoming a joke. I finish off the beer in my hand, my seventh, then get to my feet. A wave of dizziness hits me, but I force my way through it and head for the stairs. If the girls aren't ready, then screw it. I'll go without them.

I push open the door to Tiffani's room, and it smells of burned hair and perfume. The music is loud and pumping, and it feels stuffy in here. But, thankfully, the girls are all dressed and have their hair and makeup done. "Alright, can we head over there now?" I ask, stepping into the room and leaning against the doorframe. Out of the corner of my eye, I notice Eden as she emerges from the bathroom.

She looks different. She looks like…them. Like Tiffani, like Rachael, like Meghan. Like a girl who is trying way too hard to impress. She's wearing one of Tiffani's tiny black dresses, and the only reason I know it belongs to Tiffani is because I remember tearing it off her a month ago. It's tight and it's short. I try not to look, even though I want to. But that would be weird. *Stepsister*, I think. It's still an alien concept to me.

"Dean and Jake are already there," I add quickly, trying to focus on something else.

"Do I look good?" Tiffani asks, not exactly answering my question. She twirls around in a circle, showing herself off, but she looks exactly the same as she always does. Way too overdressed in too few clothes, on the brink of suffocation, and slightly tacky.

"Baby, you look fine," I tell her. Again, it's what she wants to hear. I finish off the beer in my hand and set it on her dresser, then move closer to her. I'm aware that Eden is watching, so I grab Tiffani's waist.

"Real hot." And then I kiss her, right there and then, because if there's anything Tiffani loves more than herself, it's having me kiss her while we have an audience. But I'm not doing it for her. No, I'm doing it to show Eden more of me. More of Tyler Bruce.

I want her to believe that I'm an asshole. A jerk. A moron.

13

FRIDAY NIGHT BASEBALL GAMES have become almost a tradition in our family. We like the Dodgers, and Dad has been taking me to games ever since I was young. And then Jamie came too when he was old enough, and then Chase, and now Mom wraps up early at the office on Fridays, so she comes along too. Every time the Dodgers play a home game on a Friday night, us Graysons are there.

That's why we're here now, at Dodger Stadium among the buzz of noise. Because it's Friday night, and the Dodgers are playing at home against the Diamondbacks. Empty seats around the stadium are slowly filling up as the stragglers roll in, the commentator's voice echoes out over the field, the evening sun is low. The game has just started.

I'm sitting forward on the edge of my seat, my hands interlocked between my knees. The Diamondbacks are batting, so my focus slips and I glance sideways at Jamie. He's on the edge of his seat too, his eyes wide as he stares down at the field, invested in the game. I lean forward, looking beyond him to Chase. We're up in the top deck, and he's too short to see over the people in the row in front, so he's on his feet, watching the game on the big screen instead. He's wearing a Dodgers cap that's too big for his head, so it keeps falling down over his eyes. I sigh and look past him too, over to Mom and Dad. They're talking among themselves, and Mom is leaning in close against him, her head resting on his shoulder. She's wearing a cap too. Dad's arm is around her, and they both laugh, their smiles genuine, their eyes locked on one another. I like it when they're happy. I like that they *make* each other happy.

"Oh, Chase!" Mom laughs. She sits up and nudges Dad's arm off her. Placing her hands on Chase's shoulders, she gently pulls him closer to her and swipes his cap, then she places it on his head backward instead. "I think your dad should buy you a smaller size on our way out."

"That's right, buddy," Dad says, leaning forward to look at Chase past Mom. He grins wide, and he and Chase bump fists in agreement. His gaze flickers up to meet mine, and his smile widens as he glances between Jamie and me. "Are you guys hungry?"

Jamie tears his attention away from the field and looks at Dad, confused. "But it's still the first inning," he states. We usually wait until the third before we get hot dogs—another of our traditions.

"By the time I get to the front of the line, it *will* be the third inning!" Mom says, getting to her feet. She grabs her purse from the floor. "Hot dogs coming right up!" She squeezes around Dad, but before she leaves, he reaches up for the bill of her cap and pulls her down toward him, kissing her. Then, she shuffles off along the row.

"Tyler," Dad says. He fixes his gaze on me and nods after her. "Help your mom."

Quickly, I stand up and push my way past Jamie and Chase, then practically climb over Dad's long legs. He watches me closely, his mouth still showing a hint of a smile. He's relaxed tonight. He usually is on a Friday. I awkwardly sidestep my way down our row and then race to catch up with Mom further back inside the stadium. There's food and merchandise stalls every few hundred yards, and the lines are long and weaving. "Oh, Tyler," Mom says as I approach her at the back of one of the food stall lines. She looks down at me, unaware that I've been following. "You're missing the game!"

"It's okay," I say with a small shrug. "Dad asked me to help. The Diamondbacks are batting anyway." I don't even want to think about the look Dad would have given me if I'd said no to him, if I'd whined and told him I wanted to stay and watch the game. He's been in a good mood today and he's been smiling a lot, but I don't want to test him. Dad never stays in a good mood for too long, at least not with me.

"Hmm," Mom says teasingly, pursing her lips as she pretends to think. She smiles wide at me, her blue eyes sparkling. Why don't I look like her? "Who raised you to be such a good kid?"

"You did," I answer. I smile back up at her, but it's sort of fake. Dad raised me too, and I'm not *allowed* to be anything less than good. I *am* a good kid, but only because I'm too scared not to be. That's why I always try to remember my manners, always work hard in school, always do my best to stay out of trouble. Sometimes, even that isn't enough.

Mom laughs and runs her hand through my hair, playfully ruffling it before she rests her arm over my shoulders. We move forward in line. "Ketchup, no mustard, right?"

I nod and she turns her attention to the food stall as we slowly progress toward it. She doesn't notice that I'm staring at her, watching her calm features and wondering if she would ever believe me. I want her to know the truth. I want her to know that I'm scared, that I don't know what Dad will do next to hurt me, but I don't know how to tell her. She loves him. Would she still love him if she knew? Dad would never forgive me if I ruined all of that. And Mom... I want her to know so that she can help me, so that maybe she could ask Dad to stop. But I also don't want to see her sad. I like it when she smiles. I like it when she's happy. I like it when they both are.

That's why I've never told her. That's why I never will. I can't. I'm terrified to, because I don't know what will happen if I do. Would Mom still love *me*?

"Hold this for your dad," Mom says, and she slides a cold cup of beer into my hand. I blink fast, realizing that we're suddenly at the front of the line and Mom has already ordered our food. Did I zone out again? I need to stop doing that. "Keep it down low."

I glance down at the beer. Dad likes to have a few at every game since it's the weekend and all, and this is his second. It's freezing cold in my hand, so I shift it to my other, then try to disguise it behind my leg.

"C'mon, let's get back," Mom says as she grabs the tray of hot dogs. She spins around and nods at me to go ahead as she follows. "Quickly."

I begin to carefully weave my way around the thick crowd of people, but there are bodies darting back and forth in different directions, and the beer is too cold in my hand, and my steps are growing faster, and I'm glancing between the beer and my route back to our seats, and I trip. Just like that, straight over my own feet. I fall to the ground with a hard smack, landing on my hands and knees on the concrete, and Dad's beer spills all over the ground in front of me. It happens so fast that I don't even register any of it until my knees sting with the pain of fresh scrapes.

"Tyler!" Mom gasps, and she rushes to my side, crouching down next to me. "Are you okay? Oh, you're bleeding! I've got Band-Aids in my purse." Balancing the tray of hot dogs against her hip, she reaches for my elbow and gently pulls me to my feet.

People are staring at me. My heart is pounding too fast. Numbly,

I glance down and see that I've broken the skin on both my knees. There's a little blood, not much, and it stings, but it's nothing I can't handle. I look up ahead at the empty cup that's on its side on the ground. There's a stream of Dad's beer running along the concrete. He's not going to be happy. My hands tremble, and the panic spreads through my chest until my entire body is shaking. I can't help it. I'm a quivering mess as I stare at that empty cup. "Dad's…Dad's beer…" I mumble. He was happy tonight. He was smiling. I've ruined that again. I always do.

"Hey. Hey!" Mom says, stepping in front of me and crouching down again, looking at me with concern from beneath her eyelashes. "It's okay, Tyler. I'll just get him another later!" She's trying to reassure me, but it isn't enough to stop me from trembling.

Mom throws the empty cup into a nearby trash can and then places her hand on my shoulder, guiding me back to our seats. I feel sick, like I'm going to throw up right here and now in front of everyone. I don't want to go back to our seats. I don't want Dad to narrow his eyes at me and clench his jaw like he does whenever he's mad at me.

We shuffle back along our row as my knees continue to sting. I brush past Dad as quickly as I can, keeping my head down and refusing to look at him, and then I almost run past Jamie and Chase until I collapse into the safety of my own seat at the opposite end from Dad.

"Where's my beer?" I hear him ask as Mom sits down next to him with the tray of hot dogs. I peek at him out of the corner of my eye, and he's furrowing his eyebrows at her.

"Oh," Mom breathes, rolling her eyes, "Tyler had a little fall. I'll grab you another later. Here, hold this." She pushes the tray onto Dad's lap and opens up her purse, searching for Band-Aids.

Slowly, Dad's gaze moves to me. His eyes meet mine and I freeze under their power, rooted to my seat, unable to breathe. He presses his lips together. His jaw twitches. "When did you get so clumsy?" he asks.

I can't answer him. I'm not clumsy. I'm just too caught up in the mental battle I am constantly fighting with myself. Mom sits back and leans over Jamie and Chase, passing me a couple of Band-Aids. She gives me a sympathetic smile, one that's reassuring, and I focus on that warmth rather than the negative vibes I can sense radiating from Dad.

Tearing the plastic off the Band-Aids, I lean forward and quickly place them over the cuts on my knees. Band-Aids have become a necessity over the past couple years, but they can only fix so much.

14

I AM CRAMMED INTO the backseat of Meghan's shitty, beat-up Corolla as she slowly drives us across town toward Austin's house. It's getting dark now and Rachael is controlling the music from up front, while I'm stuck in the back with Tiffani and Eden on either side of me. I have a box of beer in my lap, and it's tempting to crack another one open just to help me survive this journey. I lock my eyes on the parking brake and fold my arms across my chest, keeping to myself.

Tiffani and Rachael are doing what they do best: gossiping and wondering who will be at the party. They refer to a couple people as losers, but I'm not listening. I never, ever do. I don't have the energy for it.

Instead, I am thinking about Eden. She's on my right and I can sense her looking at me, so I glance over, and our eyes meet for a fraction of a second before we both look away again. *Yeah, she was definitely staring.* It's weird, I guess. I figure she's not used to this either. This whole step-sibling thing. I'm trying to figure her out the same way she seems to be trying to figure *me* out, but I'm not really getting anywhere. I peek at her again, and because she is staring out of the window now instead, I take the opportunity to fully study her. Her dark hair is straight and lays flat against her back, though thick strands keep falling over her shoulders and framing her face. She's wearing a lot of makeup. Eyelids painted dark, like smoke. Thick lashes that seem to grow longer every time she blinks. Red lips. I have only seen her a handful of times so far, but I've seen enough to know that this isn't her.

She senses me watching her, because she turns her eyes back to me, but I've already glanced away again. She catches me more than once during the rest of the drive, mostly because I can't help it. It gets pretty awkward after a while, so I eventually stop looking. I focus on staring straight ahead at nothing in particular again for the rest of the trip, never saying a word, even when Tiffani presses her body against mine and starts touching my thigh.

It's a relief when we finally pull up outside Austin's place. I don't even know the guy that well, but of course, he knows us. It's still super, super early, barely eight thirty, but already the place is bouncing. There are several cars parked out on the street, and there are people standing on the lawn talking to one another. As soon as Meghan cuts her engine, I grab my beer and follow Tiffani out of the car, stretching my legs. I can hear the music already, and I fight the urge to groan. I don't want to go through all of this again. The excessive drinking, the loud music…

"Hey, Tyler!" someone calls out, and when I glance up, I spot Austin rushing across the lawn to greet us. He's a short guy, but his grin is big enough to make up for it. He waves his beer at me and, knowing I have to put on a show for the next however many hours, I give him a fist bump. "Glad you could make it," he tells me.

"Yeah." I bet he is. I bet he's glad Tiffani's here too. We are a permanent fixture at parties, and if we turn up, then it pretty much verifies that the host isn't a loser. I nod to my beer, desperate to open another. "Kitchen?"

He points to the house and smiles wider. "Yeah. Dump it and come join us."

I begin to walk, heading across the lawn toward the front door, but I do throw a final glance back over my shoulder at the girls. Tiffani is saying something to Austin, and Meghan is trying to ram her car keys into her purse, and Rachael is staring at the bottle of vodka in her hand. Eden, however, is wearing her usual unreadable expression, but her eyes are wary as she takes everything in. She's going to regret coming. I just know she will.

Shaking my head, I continue into the house, murmuring *heys* to everyone who nods at me. A few hours ago, I was in my room, thinking. And now I'm here, at another party, buzzed off beer, acting. I hate this. I hate that this is what I have to do to forget.

I navigate my way through the house, keeping my head down as I enter the kitchen. There is alcohol covering every countertop, and the floor is already sticky with spilled drinks, and I accidentally step on a shot glass, crushing it. I kick the broken pieces out of the way in aggravation.

"I've been wondering when you were gonna show up," someone says, and Kaleb steps in front of me. His eyes are bloodshot, his smile is lazy. He's high, but that's not surprising. I can't remember the last time I saw him sober. "Austin's letting us do our thing as long as we stay out of the way, so we're in the fucking backyard shed." He begins howling with uncontrollable laughter as he reaches up to open the first cupboard he finds, and he steals a packet of cookies. I watch in silence as he stuffs one into his mouth, closes his eyes, and sinks into euphoria. "Oh my God. *Amazing*," he mumbles. He opens his eyes again and tries to focus on me. "So, are you joining? It's good shit tonight, I swear. Look at me! I'm *baked*." Right now, I really *could* do with some relaxation. Just a couple hits to put my mind at ease, to numb it. I grab a bottle of beer, pop the cap on the edge of the countertop, and then nod.

"Count me in."

Kaleb smirks with delight, only because he knows he's about to make some money off me, and then he turns around, cookies in hand, and heads back through the house. I step behind him, swigging my beer, when someone grabs my shoulder just as I'm about to follow Kaleb outside into the backyard. I pause; it's Jake.

"You finally made it," he says. "Where are the girls?"

"Just coming," I answer bluntly. I don't want to talk to Jake. I don't even like the guy, and I just want to smoke a joint. I begin to walk away, but he grabs my shoulder again and pulls me back.

"Where are *you* going?" he questions, raising an eyebrow. He glances at Kaleb as he continues across the backyard, and then back at me. I think he already knows the answer.

"Where the fuck do you think I'm going, Jake?" I snap, shrugging his hand off my shoulder. God, I wish my friends would leave me alone sometimes. I've already been lectured by Rachael tonight, and I don't need Jake questioning me too. It's not like they don't know I smoke.

"Alright, asshole," he mutters, then finally walks away.

I head outside and stride across the yard after Kaleb toward the shed in the corner. Talk about a drug den. I can smell the weed in the air and hear the laughter before Kaleb has even opened the door. And when he does, I'm not surprised to spot Clayton and Mason inside. I've smoked with them before. I share some classes at school with them too.

"It's about time you made an appearance," Mason says. He's stretched out on a lawn chair in the corner, his feet resting on the lawnmower, and he has an almost burnt-out joint in his hand. He looks scruffy, but whatever. He's high as shit. They all are.

"I know." I grab my wallet from my pocket, pull out fifteen dollars, and offer it to Kaleb. Usually, I prefer to buy from Declan directly, but he's been laying low lately, so I will have to steal a gram off Kaleb instead. "Hook me up?"

"Maaan," Clayton murmurs. He's leaning against the wall, his eyes closed, exhaling a plume of smoke into the air around us. There's not a lot of room in here, so it's extremely cramped. "Blissful."

Kaleb takes my money, fumbles around in his pockets for a minute, then presents me with two prepared joints. "Already rolled two for you," he says proudly. "I knew you'd be game tonight."

I take them both from him and study them in my hand. Then I think, *Fuck it.* "Light me up," I order, and Kaleb pulls out a lighter and sets one of the joints alight for me. He watches closely as I press it to my lips, eagerly waiting for my approval, and I inhale, taking that first hit.

The smoke fills my lungs, the burning familiarity satisfying my desire. I haven't smoked in a week, so it feels real nice. I hold the smoke in my lungs for several long seconds, and then I exhale, feeling the difference already. It'll take me a lot more hits and another five minutes or so before the buzz truly hits me, but I can feel it, that weight on my shoulders losing its pressure.

"Hey, where the fuck did you get those cookies?" Mason asks, shooting upright in his lawn chair. He points his joint at Kaleb, and Clayton opens his eyes.

"Stole 'em from the kitchen. Munchies are kicking in," Kaleb explains, and all three of them burst into laughter. I'm not high yet, so I don't laugh, though I do crack a smile.

I lean back against the wall and close my eyes, taking another drag of the joint, focusing on my breathing. *Just relax.*

"Declan came through for us tonight, by the way," Kaleb murmurs, nudging me with his elbow. When I open my eyes, he nods down to the small table next to Clayton. In perfect, neat lines, there is coke. I stare at it for a minute. "I told you it's good shit."

"Man…" I shake my head slowly. Tempting, but no. I'm not that desperate. I have done it before. I do it often, I guess. But only on the nights where I can't take things any longer, and ever since I took a bad trip once, I've been more cautious. I hold up a hand in surrender. "Count me out for tonight."

"Booo," Mason drawls, rolling his eyes. "We were waiting for you!"

"More bumps for us then," Clayton jokes, and again, the laughter continues. The three of them are so stoned, and I wish my own buzz would hurry up and kick in. That's why I take another hit, holding the smoke in my lungs for as long as I possibly can before it burns too much, then I tilt my head back and release it into the air.

I am just about to close my eyes again, to relax into the warm sensation, when the door of the shed swings open. We are so fogged out in here that it takes me a minute to see who is here to join us.

Shit.

It's Eden. Her hand is over her mouth and she coughs, stepping back, retreating from the door. "Is that weed?"

"No, it's cotton candy," Mason jokes, and Clayton and Kaleb immediately howl with laughter as though it's the most hilarious reply they have ever heard in their entire lives.

I don't join in again, not because I'm not high yet, but because there is panic running through me. I need Eden to know who Tyler Bruce is, but I don't want her to know about *this*. Not when she lives in the same damn house as me. Not when she can tell my mom. Quickly, I try to hide my burning joint behind me, hoping she doesn't notice that I'm involved. "Are you serious?" she asks, staring at me wide-eyed.

Clearly, I am too late. She's already seen it, and I know that there is absolutely no way I can deny it.

"Dude, get this chick outta here," Clayton mutters, waving his joint at her. I don't look at him though, because my attention is all on Eden. Her eyes are fixed only on me as they dilate with complete and utter disgust. "Unless she wants to come in here and keep us company."

"Bro," I murmur, turning to fire Clayton a look. I swallow hard. *Play it cool. Be Tyler Bruce. You don't care.* "You really want that kid in here?"

Clayton and Kaleb chuckle while Mason starts coughing to death in the corner. Of course, this is amusing to them, but to me, it's far from it. I am frozen in place, wondering how the hell I am supposed to get myself out of this situation.

"Who the hell is she?" Clayton finally asks, and I'm definitely not going to answer him. I can only imagine the number of jokes they would crack if they knew she was my stepsister. "Has no one taught her the rules?" He turns to Eden, and I don't like the way he grins at her. "No interrupting, babe. Get the fuck out of here unless you're here to ball with us." He steps toward her and holds out his half-smoked joint, offering it to her as if she would actually take it.

Automatically, I step in between the two of them, facing Clayton, Eden behind me. "What the hell are you doing?" I quickly put out my own joint and shove it into my pocket, saving it for later, and then I narrow my eyes. "C'mon, Clayton, where's your common sense?"

"Offering her a hit *is* common sense," he says. He moves his joint back to his lips and takes another hit though I don't think he needs it. "It's called good manners. It would be rude not to. Am I right, new girl?" He looks at Eden again over my shoulder.

"Dude, take the damn hint," I growl under my breath. He is pissing me off now, mostly because I don't like the way he is talking to her. "She doesn't want it. Look at her." I cast a glance over my shoulder at Eden again, and my chest tightens when I see the way she is looking at me. Most people look at me the same way, with that horrified, disgusted look on their faces. But seeing that same expression in Eden's eyes is different, like I am seeing it for the very first time, and I can't figure out why, for a second, I actually feel disappointed in myself. Those hits I just took must be kicking in. I am feeling lighter, feeling fuzzy.

"Alright, alright. Just get her outta here then. Why do we have some random kid in here anyway?" Clayton asks.

"I'm wondering the same thing," I mumble, then turn around to face Eden directly. She is shaking her head at me, and that feeling of disappointment rises in my chest again. I need to get her out of here, away from these morons, away from me. I step toward her, but I hit my hand against the table next to us. It catches Eden's attention.

There is a silence for what feels like forever. Or maybe I'm just imagining it. *Shit*. This is the *worst* time for my high to be kicking in. I need to maintain a clear head in order to bullshit my way out of this, because I know Eden isn't stupid. I know she is staring at the coke on the table, and I doubt she thinks it's sugar.

"Oh my God." Her face pales with disbelief, and I can see questions flashing across her face one by one. She parts those lips of hers, her mouth open. "Oh my God?"

"Dude, seriously, I'm not kidding," Clayton orders, his voice sharp now. "Get her out of here before she calls us out to the cops or something."

"Yeah, yeah, she's leaving." Desperate to get Eden away, I grasp her elbow and guide her away from the shed and across the yard until we're a safe distance away. It feels like it takes me twenty minutes to walk her across the lawn, but in reality, it's more like twenty seconds.

"You're unbelievable," she hisses at me. She shakes my grip off her arm and then stares me straight in the eye. "Coke? Really, Tyler?"

I think it's the first time I've heard her say my name, and I figure it's the weed, but it sounds like absolute heaven in that husky tone of hers. I want her to say it over and over again for the rest of my life. Yep, I'm stoned.

My gaze meets hers, and I am silent for a while. I'm not sure how to explain myself without telling her that my life is a mess. I cover my face with my hands and groan out loud. "This isn't the place for you," I tell her. I shove my hands back down into my pockets, and I can feel those two joints waiting for me. Right now, I need them more than ever. "You should—you should go back inside."

Eden only continues to stare at me with her mouth agape, shaking her head. She looks furious, but I don't know why. She doesn't even know me. She shouldn't care, but it's clear that she does, and I have this awful feeling that she's going to tell my mom about this when she gets home. Mom already knows that I smoke, though she doesn't know just how often, and she certainly doesn't like it. The coke, however, she has no idea about. I'm not sure how much longer it'll stay that way.

I turn around and head back toward the shed—another twenty-minute walk to my buzzed mind—and the guys are waiting for me with curious expressions. There's no way I'm telling them who Eden is, so instead I stick to being Tyler Bruce, and I roll my eyes and say, "Got rid of that loser."

More laughter erupts and the shed feels as though it is shaking. I laugh too this time, but not for long, because we are interrupted when I hear Dean's voice call out, "Dude, come on. That's low. Chill out."

I flash my eyes over at him. He's standing a few feet away from us, shaking his head in disapproval. He looks sober as hell, but that's not surprising. Dean's like that. He's a nice guy, always keeps himself in check, always looks out for people. That's why he has so many friends. Real ones.

"Shut the fuck up, Dean," I mutter, and he just sighs in reply and sprints across the lawn toward Eden. I stare after him, my eyebrows furrowing as I watch the two of them talk. Have they even met yet? They talk for what I feel like is an hour, but they're too far away to hear what they're saying.

"C'mon, get lighting up," Kaleb urges, tossing me his lighter.

I swiftly catch it and then reach back into my pocket to pull out my joint from earlier. I place it between my lips and relight it, and just as I'm about to take another hit, I see her again. Eden, watching me over her shoulder as she lingers by the door to the house. I wish she didn't care. I wish she'd just shrugged, rolled her eyes, and left. I don't know her well enough yet to predict what she will do with this information. In fact, I don't know her at all, so now I'm worried that she is the type of girl who will tell. And then I'll be kicked out of the house. And then I'll need to find a way to survive.

I look away from her, dropping my eyes to the ground, and Clayton says something as he shoves a new beer into my hand, but his words don't register. I can still feel Eden's gaze on me, so I move further into the shed, away from the door, out of her sight so I can no longer see that disgusted look on her face.

The guys are laughing again, but I don't know why. I am focused on something else now. I know I swore to Tiffani that I wouldn't do it, but I don't care about her enough to feel bad about breaking any promises. Tyler Bruce does whatever the hell he wants.

I glance sideways at Kaleb, then elbow him in the ribs to get his attention. "Tell Declan I'm in," I murmur into his ear. "I'll sell his shit for him."

When I wake up the next morning, my head is a little foggy. It takes me a long minute of squinting at the sunlight streaming in through the window to realize that I'm not even in my own room; I'm in Tiffani's. Quietly, I groan and roll over, and I almost jump straight out of my skin at the sight of Tiffani already awake, dressed, and sitting cross-legged on the bed next to me. Her blue eyes are boring into mine.

"Mom wants to kill you," she states. I could think of better ways to be told *good morning*.

I raise an eyebrow, still half asleep. "Huh?"

"You cleared out half our refrigerator last night," Tiffani explains, pursing her lips. I don't know what time it is, but she already has her hair and makeup done. "And we woke her up when we got back here, so now she's pissed, and I need to take you home ASAP." She swings her legs off the bed and gets up, then begins scooping my clothes up from the floor, throwing them at me at full force. My jeans almost knock me out.

"And take Eden's shit home too," she huffs and begins tossing even more clothes at me as she drifts around her room. She throws me a phone too. "Oh, and thanks for fucking embarrassing me last night. I just *love* having a drugged-up boyfriend."

I force myself to sit up, rubbing my eyes. I feel so groggy, but I know it's just from my comedown. I wonder what happened last night. I remember smoking all night and laughing a lot. I remember drinking too many beers. But I don't remember coming home with Tiffani. I don't remember what happened to Eden. "Where did she go last night?" I ask, squinting at Tiffani again. My eyes are a little sensitive, and my throat is dry. I'm so thirsty. "Eden?"

"She left after, like, half an hour," Tiffani says casually, disinterested.

"How uncool is that? Dean took her home; now it's my turn to take *you* home, so get your ass in gear."

"What time is it?"

"Only eight."

"Eight?" I repeat, glaring at her now. We probably only got here a few hours ago. "Fucking *eight?*"

"Do you want my mom to kill you?" she asks, spinning around to give me a stern look. Her hands are on her hips, her brow arched high. "Do you want *me* to kill you? Because the longer I have to look at you, the more I want to. So let's go." Groaning, I slip on my shirt from last night and haul my ass out of bed. I could do with a few more hours of sleep, and I dread going home now. Mom hates it when I don't come home without telling her first, so she'll be pissed about that for starters, plus the fact that I snuck out last night too… She definitely isn't going to be happy. And if Eden told her what she saw last night, then I may not even have a home to return to.

I pull on my jeans and before I've even had the chance to finish stepping into my shoes, Tiffani is latching onto my arm and tugging me desperately toward the door. I barely manage to grab Eden's clothes in time, but I do, and I allow Tiffani to drag me downstairs without resisting her rough hold. Her house is silent, so I figure her mom must still be asleep, which explains why she wants me out of here so fast.

The morning sunlight burns my eyes as we step outside, and by the time I am slumped in Tiffani's passenger seat, I am already falling back to sleep. It's nice though, because it means that she doesn't even attempt to talk to me. I've had enough of her for one weekend, so now I could happily go a couple days without her, though I know that's unlikely to ever happen. I seize the opportunity I have to take a ten-minute snooze before I'm forced to face up to Mom.

"Alright, get out," Tiffani says a short while later, and when I peel my eyes open, I realize we are parked outside my house. *Here we go*, I think. It's time to explain myself to Mom. I sit up and pull down the sun visor to check my reflection in the mirror. My eyes look fine, though they're dry. I blink a couple times and then close the visor again, opening the car door. I swing one leg out and pause. "I'm sorry, you know," I say, glancing back over at Tiffani. I don't really know *what* I'm even apologizing for, probably for getting high all night, but I do know that I don't want Tiffani to be mad at me. I've grown too comfortable having her around, and even though I know she would never break up with me, I still hate the thought of her giving me the cold shoulder. It's like she knows this and does it on purpose just to punish me for stepping out of line.

"Go, Tyler," she mutters, staring ahead at the road, her hands gripping the steering wheel. How high was I last night? What stupid shit came out of my mouth?

Whatever it is that I've done to irritate her this time, I'm too hungover to stay and figure it out right now. I just want to climb into bed, pull my sheets up over my head, and sleep for the next twelve hours. That's why I don't say anything more as I step out of the car. Tiffani doesn't wait around. As soon as I've shut the door, her foot is on the gas and she's off, flying down the street.

With Eden's clothes still in my hands, I stare at my house for a moment. And then I sigh. I'm used to Mom's yelling, and even though I hate letting her down, I've learned to tune it out. It will last for five minutes, max, and then she'll give up. At least that's how it usually goes.

I walk up to the front door, my steps slow and almost reluctant, and I try the handle. It's unlocked. I squeeze my eyes shut, take a deep breath, then push the door open. There is silence at first as I creep into the hall, clicking the door closed behind me again as quietly as I possibly can, and I look at the stairs, on a clean getaway to my room, but then I hear it, the worst sound in the world: "Tyler?"

I freeze on the spot and surrender to my fate. I wait in the hall, and a few seconds later, Mom walks in from the kitchen.

"*Finally*," she breathes, pressing her hand over her heart as though she's been worried sick. I don't know why. It's not like I've never done this before. Her expression quickly hardens, and she throws her hands up in frustration. "Where the hell have you been, Tyler?"

I glance down at the floor and shrug. "Out," I answer. Usually, Mom can see straight through me anyway, so there's not much point wasting my breath.

"Where?" she presses.

"What does it matter? I'm home now."

Her blue eyes are full of both anger *and* concern, which is what I hate the most. I want her to think I'm okay, even though she knows I'm far from it. I wish I could be okay just for her just so she doesn't have to go through this. "Have you been out drinking all night?"

"No," I say, running a hand back through my hair. It's a mess. "I slept at Tiffani's place."

"And before that?"

"Mom, I'm tired," I mumble, hoping she'll feel sorry for me, but it's a weak attempt.

"Tyler." She goes quiet as she runs her eyes over me, and the expression in them changes. Not anger, not concern, just that same old look of disappointment that she gives me too often. "You've been smoking, haven't you?"

"What? No," I lie, instinctively stepping back from her.

"You think I can't smell it?"

I glance down at myself. I'm wearing last night's clothes. I haven't showered. *Of course* I stink of weed. I'm a fucking idiot. "Alright, I was at a party. Some guys there were smoking. Not me," I blurt out quickly, and because I don't know what else to say, I brush past her and attempt to make my escape up the stairs.

"You're lying to me," I hear her state, her voice quivering. "God, Tyler. Why? I can't deal with this!"

I stop and turn back. She has her hands pressed to her face now, and I want to hug her, to tell her that I'm sorry, that I *need* to do all of these things to cope, that I love her and wish it was all different. But then Dave decides to get involved. He steps into the hall as though he's been listening the entire time and says, "Did he finally show up?" in the most patronizing of tones.

I narrow my eyes at him. I've never liked Dave since the moment Mom first introduced him to us years ago, and it's not just because I don't like father figures. It's because Dave's an asshole who has never once taken the time to get to know me better. He knows my history, but yet he still comes along with all his condescending remarks and eye rolls that just make me want to hit him square in the face. "Yep, here I am," I reply, flashing him a grin.

"And what exactly is it that makes you think it's okay to stay out all night?" he questions, moving closer to Mom. He puts his hand on her shoulder and squeezes her for support. "You're grounded. You weren't even supposed to leave the house last night."

I make a face at him. It makes me want to laugh whenever he attempts to act strict with me. He may be my stepdad, but I still don't believe that gives him the right to act like my parent. "Dave, please do me a favor. Give up." I roll my eyes, and I spin around and storm up the stairs.

"Tyler!" Mom calls after me. "Get back here."

I ignore her, instead muttering under my breath about how much of an asshole Dave is. I have my eye on my bedroom door when I realize I'm still holding Eden's clothes. I also realize that, unbelievably, Mom didn't just yell at me for the coke. Which means she doesn't know. Which means Eden didn't tell her. At least not yet.

I come to a halt outside of Eden's room for a second, and then I push the door open without even knocking, and I walk straight in. Not only do I need to give her her stuff back, I also need to talk to her.

She's awake, luckily, and is just pulling a hoodie on over her head when I enter. It doesn't take long for her gaze to sharpen into a glare. "Did you know there's this thing that exists called—oh, I don't know—privacy?"

I close the door behind me and tilt my head to one side, studying her. She's obviously still mad at me from last night. "Here's your stuff," I mumble, feeling awkward as I dump her clothes down on the end of her bed. Then, I fumble around in my pockets for her phone, stepping forward and offering it to her. "And your, uh, phone." I can't meet her eyes, but I like to think it's because I'm tired and *not* because I feel ashamed.

"Thanks," she says bluntly.

The tension is almost unbearable as she stares at me, inscrutable but most likely judging me for every single action I took and every single word I spoke last night. I feel so scrutinized by her that I turn to leave her room, but then I remember that there's something I'm forgetting.

"Look," I say, turning back around. "About last night—"

"I already know that you're a jerk and you do drugs and that you're pathetic as hell," she cuts in quickly. Even in that low voice of hers, the words cut straight through me. "You don't have to explain it to me."

125

At least she knows who Tyler Bruce is. He's a jerk, yeah. He gets high, yeah. He's pathetic? No, wait. That's not Tyler Bruce. That's me, and suddenly I feel exposed, almost like she can see straight through me. But I don't know how that's possible. "Just—just don't say anything." God, I even *sound* pathetic.

Eden crosses her arms over her chest, and her gaze softens a little. She looks at me for a while, almost with amusement, and then says, "Are you asking me not to snitch?"

"Don't tell my mom or your dad or anything. Just forget about it," I beg, and I really do feel like a fucking loser. Here I am, begging some girl I barely know not to ruin my life even more than it already has been.

"I can't believe you're involved in that stuff," she says quietly, dropping her eyes to her phone and then throwing it onto her bed. Her gaze meets mine, but I can't remember what color her eyes are. She's too far away to be able to tell. "Why do you even do that? It really doesn't make you look cool if that's what you're trying to do."

I do a lot of things to look cool, to look like I have everything figured out, but getting stoned isn't one of them. If only she knew I did it to numb myself from all of the bullshit I have to deal with, to forget about everything Dad did. "Not even close."

"Then what?" she asks, frustrated. I still don't know why she cares so much.

"I don't know," I answer. As if I'm going to tell her the truth. I don't intend to ever tell *anyone* the truth, and if I did, it certainly wouldn't be Eden. She's a stranger. "I'm not here for a lecture, okay? I just came to give you your stuff back and to tell you to keep your mouth shut." I run my fingers through my hair and look at the door. I need to get out of here. I need sleep.

And then, just as I'm about to leave, I hear Eden almost silently ask, "Why do you hate me so much?"

My eyes flick back to hers. Is that what she thinks? That I hate her? Nothing I have said or done to her is anything personal. It's just me being Tyler Bruce. Maybe I come across as hateful, and that's because I am, but not toward her. "Who said I hated you?"

"Um. You kind of insult me every chance you get," she tells me, furrowing her eyebrows as though she doesn't know why she even needs to explain it, like it should be obvious. "I get that it's weird having a stepsister all of a sudden, but it's weird for me too. We got off on the wrong foot, I think."

"No." Laughing, I shake my head. Incredible. She thinks I act this way because I'm not used to having a stepsister? She's so wrong. I act the way I do because I have no other choice, because it's a defense mechanism to save myself from becoming vulnerable and exposed. That's something she'll never, ever understand. "You don't get it at all." I don't want to talk anymore, so I finally spin around and head for the door.

"What don't I get?" Eden asks, raising her voice. It's firm, demanding. She wants an answer.

I don't even turn around. I just say, "Everything."

15

FIVE YEARS EARLIER

"HOW'S THAT HOMEWORK GOING?" Dad asks me late Sunday afternoon.

I glance up from my desk, my legs numb with pins and needles from sitting cross-legged on my chair for so long, and my hand is beginning to cramp. Dad is at my door, leaning back against the frame with his hands stuffed into his pockets. He's wearing a pair of faded jeans and flannel shirt, and he hasn't shaved. He never does on Sundays. That's why I love the weekend, because Dad is always much more relaxed and easygoing without the stress of work looming over him. It's like the weekend rolls around and suddenly the pressure to be perfect, both him and I, disappears for a short while.

"Um," I mumble, swallowing as I look down again and run my eyes over the work in front of me. I've spent the afternoon working on an assignment for my history class, but even when I wrapped it all up, I was too scared to take a break. "I finished it an hour ago. I've just been going over the notes I took in class."

"Good job," Dad says. His mouth transforms into a smile and he gives me a nod of approval, then he quickly straightens up, removes his hands from his pockets, and rubs them together. "Alright, put down that pen. You're done for the day. Come on, there's something I want to show you outside."

I stare blankly at him, mostly wondering if I've heard him right. Did he just say I was done for the day? No more studying? I've only done a couple hours. It doesn't seem like enough.

"C'mon!" Dad says, clapping his hands together, urging me to hurry up.

I don't dare challenge him, so I throw my pen down onto my desk and scramble off my chair, feeling lightheaded as I stand up too fast. Despite the numbness in my limbs, I make my way toward him, and he throws his arm over the back of my shoulders, pulling me in closer against him as he guides me downstairs.

"What's outside?" I ask quietly. Maybe I shouldn't question it, but I'm curious. And besides, Dad is in a good mood, so I don't think he'll mind me asking questions.

"You'll see!" he answers, and when I steal a glance up at him out of the corner of my eye, he's beaming down at me with a wide grin. It's definitely not a first, but it's still a rare occasion.

We head outside through the front door. The sun is shining from clear blue skies, and our neighborhood is busy with other kids riding down the street on their bikes, and Mr. Perez from next door is out mowing his lawn. It's a typical California day. On our own driveway, however, Jamie is fighting to snatch a basketball out of Chase's arms as he hugs it tight to his body. I didn't even know we *owned* a basketball. I squint at the two of them through the sunlight, then at the basketball hoop mounted above the garage door that definitely wasn't there yesterday.

"What...what's that?" I splutter.

"A basket," Dad says from beside me, stating the obvious. He moves his arm from over my shoulders and walks across the lawn toward the driveway, but then he pauses when he realizes I haven't followed. He looks back at me as I stand in surprise on the porch, and he rolls his eyes, his grin widening even though that should be impossible. "To shoot at, Tyler. C'mon."

Still confused, I walk over to join him on the driveway, and I linger by his side, chewing my lower lip. "I thought…no sports?"

"No *football*," he clarifies. "I don't want you getting hurt. This is much better." He dives forward and playfully plucks the basketball straight out of Chase's arms and out of Jamie's grasp, then dribbles it to the back corner of the driveway with a smug smile on his face.

"Hey! I was just about to get that, Dad!" Jamie whines, throwing his hands into the air in defeat as he glares at Dad.

"No, you weren't!" Chase protests. "I was about to score!"

He places his hands on Jamie's chest and shoves him back a step, and they begin to argue back and forth.

I stand on the edge of the driveway, blinking fast as I watch them, and when I glance at Dad, his features are soft, and his gaze is gentle. He smiles again and then hurls the basketball through the air straight to me. I catch it, barely, getting knocked back a couple steps from the force. I hold the weight of the ball in my hands for a minute, staring aimlessly down at it. Dad's really letting me play ball on the driveway instead of studying?

"You're not supposed to hesitate, Tyler!" Dad calls across to me with a small laugh. He nods up to the basket above the garage door. "Give it a shot."

I look up at the basket, and I don't even bother to aim, I just throw the ball up into the air and watch as it bounces off the garage door with a clattering echo. It bounces onto the ground, and both Jamie and Chase race to fetch it.

"Ain't nothing some practice can't fix," Dad comments as he approaches me. Why won't he stop smiling today? He runs his hand back through my hair, then spins around and joins Chase in blocking Jamie as he attempts to dribble his way down the driveway. "Chase, you're with me," he says once Jamie shoots the ball straight over their heads and into the basket. He looks at me, smirking. "Tyler, Jay…good luck."

I relax then. Dad is happy. It's a good day. He's playing ball with us on a hot Sunday afternoon, and I forget just how much fun Dad can be sometimes. I grab Jamie's elbow and pull him over to the side so that we can discuss our game plan, and Dad keeps wiggling his eyebrows at me from across the driveway, and I even smile back at him. *Game on.*

We play for a couple hours. Jamie and I run around, out of breath, dribbling the ball back and forth and attempting to utilize teamwork by occasionally passing the ball to one another. Even Mom comes outside with juice for all of us and eventually gives in and joins us after some begging. She's on mine and Jamie's team, but she won't stop kissing our opposition, so she's utterly useless.

We're winning though, but only because I think Dad is letting us. He has Chase on his shoulders as he dribbles the ball with one hand down the driveway, then he aims and shoots the ball straight into the basket. Chase is too tired out to take part, but he does throw his hands up into the air with a cheer, then reaches down and high fives Dad. Mom plants a kiss on both of their cheeks.

It's a good day. One of the best in a while. We're all laughing. My brothers are competitively trash-talking one another. Mom's smile is wide and pure, full of love and pride. Dad is just like the man I used to adore, the same man I know he still is deep down. We're all happy.

This is the family I'm trying so hard to protect.

16

PRESENT DAY

I GLANCE BETWEEN THE two cards on the table in front of me and my phone in my hand.

It's been soooo hot today down at the beach! Just got home. BTW we're thinking of all heading out tonight. Maybe Venice or the Hollywood sign. Can you take Eden with you and meet us wherever we decide to go? It's just easier that way.

Tiffani has texted.

I lift my head and glance off into the distance, over beyond the bustling pier. For June, the weather is good. The morning smog burned off quickly, leaving behind clear blue skies and burning sunshine all day. For a Tuesday, the crowds are pretty hectic too.

I've been at the beach all afternoon too, but on the south end, the opposite side of the pier. As far as Tiffani is concerned, I've been at home all day, and luckily, we haven't bumped into each other.

Maaaan, sounds good. Mom's still grilling me about Saturday, but I'll try make a getaway later.

I text back, and I cringe as I send the message. Lying to Tiffani isn't anything new, but I still feel shitty every time I do. It's also risky. She hates it if I don't even pick up a damn phone call, so she would flip if she knew I was lying to her.

I set my phone back down and focus on the game as cards are dealt and as cash is placed down, even though I don't really have a damn clue what I'm doing. I've been down here at the beach for a couple hours now, sitting around this old rickety table playing blackjack with a couple guys I've never met before. They're older, at least midtwenties, and they've been eyeballing me with distrust the entire time. Kaleb's here too, though he's not playing because every half hour or so he disappears on a drop-off.

The elusive Declan Portwood is also here. He's been laying low for the past couple weeks, so it's good to finally see him around again. Declan wears a very taut expression almost constantly, his gaze always serious, but he's well dressed and clean-shaven. The gold watch on his wrist shines when the sun catches it. To those who don't know him, he's just some rich college student. The rest of us know that he makes big bucks from the shit ton of weed he grows in his attic.

I guess that's why he invited me here today. To get me in on the circle, to do exactly what Kaleb and these other guys do. So far, it seems pretty straightforward. He'll sell me his shit, and I do the distributing and keep the profit. I don't have much to lose. I wouldn't be here if I did.

"I had an idea," Declan announces. He finishes dealing the cards and then leans back in his chair, kicking up sand. "How about a little party?

You know, a party among ourselves. No strangers, just the people we're cool with."

Warren sits up and rests his elbows on the table, leaning forward with an eyebrow raised. He has huge shoulders and tribal tattoos snake their way around his impressive biceps. "When?"

"This weekend," Declan says. He pushes his sunglasses down over his eyes and lowers his voice. "I'll have some real good stuff ready, and I wanna move it quick. It's risky, but there'll be good money in it. Your rent is due, isn't it, Liam?" Liam nods, falling victim to Declan's smooth convincing.

Liam is a walking stereotype. There are bags under his eyes and his stubble is unruly, and the fact that he has two fucking phones laid out on the table in front of him is an absolute giveaway. He also twitches every once in a while, and I honestly can't tell if he's high or if he's sober. "Count me in," he says.

"Sorry, guys, gotta get back out there," Kaleb says as he rises to his feet for what feels like the fifth time. "What's up with everyone needing a hookup today? It's fucking Tuesday," he mumbles, and without another word, he turns around and walks off, keys to his truck in hand.

"Hear that, Tyler?" Declan says, angling his jaw toward me. I can't see his eyes behind his dark shades, but the corner of his mouth does quirk into a smirk. He rubs his thumb against his index and middle finger. "Dirty, dirty money."

Warren fires me a look, cocking his head to one side. He looks me straight up and down, then he asks, "What's a rich white boy like you doing here anyway? You obviously don't need the extra cash." He scoffs and throws a pointed glance over his shoulder toward my car, parked not even a hundred feet away from us in one of the south parking lots. Then, he narrows his eyes at Declan. "Portwood, how do you even know this kid? 'Cause he looks like a cop's son or some shit to me. I bet he's voice recording us right this second."

"Relax," Declan orders with a minute shake of his head. "He's cool. Been fucking with me since, like, what? Freshman year? Isn't that right, Tyler? I can trust you, can't I?" He edges in closer to me and lifts his sunglasses, his dark eyes studying me. He's still smirking.

I reach for my cards and toss a fifty-dollar bill onto the table. I don't even care if I win or lose this game, I just don't want these guys thinking I can't keep up with them. I'm younger, sure, but I'm probably slicker. "If you couldn't trust me, you wouldn't have asked me to come out here," I state.

Declan's smirk grows and he sits back again, lowering his shades back over his eyes. He gives me a small nod and then focuses his attention back on his own cards.

"That ain't explaining why he's here," Warren speaks up, but I wish he would stop questioning me. Why is *he* here? I bet it's for the money, and not because his life is a fucking mess like mine.

"Man, what does it matter?" Liam asks, rolling his eyes. Still can't tell if he's stoned or not. "Let's just get this round played."

But Warren won't stop pursuing an answer, and I honestly don't know why he gives a damn. "You know, us guys only get involved in this shit when we don't have any other choice. So, Tyler with the flashy sports car, what left you with no options? Did Daddy stop paying for all your shit?"

I throw my cards down and shoot to my feet, pressing my palms down flat on the table. My jaw is tight as I lean toward Warren, narrowing my eyes at him as fiercely as I can so that he gets the memo not to say anything more. "*Daddy's* locked up, asshole."

Usually, I would never square up to anyone twice my size and nearly a decade older than me, but there are some things that I can't stay rational about. Like whenever Dad is brought up. No one knows the truth about why he's really in prison, which means no one knows how agonizing it is when I'm reminded of him. I snap way too easily.

Warren doesn't so much as bat an eyelid at me, nor flinch an inch. "Well, that makes sense then," he says slowly, looking up at me, laughing. "You're following in his footsteps, bro."

There it is—the snap. My chest tightens and I grind my teeth so hard my jaw aches as I launch myself at him, swinging my fist straight into the corner of his mouth. I don't even register what I'm doing. I have learned by now that when I snap, I am uncontrollable. The adrenaline floods through me as Warren jolts back in his chair, and then he scrambles to his feet, hoists up his pants, and raises his fists.

"Oh, cut it the fuck out," Declan groans. He sighs and stands up, stepping in between Warren and me. Liam watches silently, and I decide then that, yes, he's high.

My glare is fixated on Warren as I breathe heavily, my heart pounding in my chest, and his nostrils are flaring angrily. He wipes a spit of blood from his mouth and shakes his head, dropping his fists.

At the same time, I hear a voice yell, "What the hell are you doing?" and when I glance up, my heart almost stops when I see Dave marching across the sand toward us. Two thoughts run through my mind at once: One, what the hell is Dave doing here at the beach? And two, my stepdad cannot come over here right now, not when I'm standing next to fucking Declan, who deals a lot more than just a hand of crap cards.

"Declan, I'll hit you up, okay?" I splutter quickly, and before Dave can get any closer, I break into a sprint and head over to him instead. At this point, I'm willing to let him yell at me, just so that we can get away from here.

"What the hell was that, Tyler?" Dave asks, his voice raised. He throws his hands up in frustration and stares at me in disbelief. I never fail to surprise him. It's like whenever he thinks I can't get any worse, I go ahead and prove him wrong. "You're grounded, which means you're supposed to be at *home*. Not here! Are you gambling?" He takes a step around me to look back at Declan and the others, but I step closer to him, blocking his view. He doesn't need to know who Declan is. Ever.

"We're just messing around. It's only a game," I explain, lying through my teeth.

"A game where you throw punches? Huh?" He gets all up in my face, his eyes wild. I've figured by now that either Dave has a tough love sort of approach to parenting, or he just hates me. "Did you just blow a bunch of money? Is that why you're pissed?"

"Yeah, I lost," I lie, stepping back from him. Lying is much easier than admitting I threw a punch because I can't bear the thought of my dad, though I'm sure if I told Dave this, he'd understand. At least I'd like to think so. He knows how badly my dad hurt me when I was a kid.

Dave pinches the bridge of his nose and inhales deeply. "Get in your car and follow me home. Right now," he orders.

"Dave, c'mon—"

"No," he cuts in. "I said right *now*. You're going home to your mom." He grabs my shoulder and firmly guides me across the beach, back up to the parking lot where both our cars are parked. I don't put up a fight and I don't glance back over my shoulder either, because I know Warren is probably laughing his ass off at me being escorted home by my fucking stepdad. Now I really do feel like a kid, so I keep my head low. Once we reach our cars, I shrug Dave's hand off my shoulder and pull open my door, sliding inside. But Dave slams his hand down on the roof of the vehicle before I can close it again.

"Straight home, Tyler," he says firmly, fixing me with a look. "I know you've got a lot to deal with, but you can't keep doing stuff like this."

I roll my eyes at him as I pull my door shut. He really thinks I'm going to take off as though I'm scared of him? I really don't have the energy, and honestly, I don't even care that much. I was planning on heading home soon anyway.

It's only a fifteen-minute drive back to the house, but it feels like forever, mostly because I am stuck behind Dave, and every time we are stopped at a set of lights, I can see him glaring at me in his rearview mirror. I pretend not to notice, and I play my music too loud with my window down all the way back to Deidre Avenue.

Dave says nothing more to me and I say nothing more to him as we both park and head for the front door. I even let him march off ahead first into the house while I stroll nonchalantly after him, and honestly, it's almost amusing just how heated Dave can get when it comes to dealing with me. I really grind his gears, but I have ever since Mom first introduced us a few years ago. It's like he moved down here to LA, hoping for this new, perfect life, and he almost has it. We've got the big house in the nice neighborhood. He drives a nice car. He's pretty high up at the company he works for, I think. He's got Mom, who's amazing, and he's got Jamie and Chase, who I guess are pretty cool. But then he's also got me, and I'm not exactly perfect, so I can't really blame him for getting frustrated at me. Who cares? I'm over it.

"Ella!" he yells as soon as we walk inside the house. I scrunch up my face in disgust when I realize Mom's cooking steak, because the scent wafting down the hall is enough to make me feel nauseous. "You'll be glad to know I found Tyler!"

I follow Dave to the kitchen, and Mom spins around to look at us both as soon as we enter. Her hair is clipped back and she stares mostly at me, frowning as her shoulders sink.

"Do you want to know what I just witnessed?" Dave asks, his voice raised. He sounds like an asshole right now, like he enjoys throwing me under the bus to Mom. He's wasting his breath though. "So here I am, heading down to Apian Way to drop off some paperwork on my way home, and guess who I happen to spot at the beach?" As though it isn't already obvious who he's talking about, he gives me a pointed glance.

Mom looks at me and I can see her physically fighting back a sigh. "I told you not to leave," she mumbles.

Dave ignores her and goes on with his story. "So I think, *Hey, he's grounded*, and I head over there to ask him what he's playing at, and he's sitting around some table with these guys who looked ten years older than him, and I stood there and watched him toss ten-, twenty-, fifty-dollar bills onto this table," Dave tells her, and it's only then that I actually wonder how long he had been watching me.

"Tyler," Mom says, and I look at her. There's that look of disappointment on her face again that I hate so much. It's even worse when she doesn't say anything. Her silence always speaks louder than words.

"This is bullshit," I mutter, shaking my head.

"Shut the hell up," Dave orders, and I'm surprised he says this in front of Mom. He and I both know it makes her uncomfortable when he says shit like that to me. He loosens his tie, then rolls up the sleeves of his shirt, and presses his hands to his hips. "So I'm standing right there watching him gamble and throw away cash, and guess what happened when he lost the bet?" He hesitates for a second, probably for dramatic effect to make it all sound even worse. "He started swinging."

"That asshole was cheating," I lie. Only about the cheating part though. Warren *is* an asshole, and I feel aggravated just thinking about his words again. I lean back against the countertop to stabilize myself, and I add, "I wasn't gonna let him get away with it."

Dave gets up in my face again, and if Mom wasn't here, I definitely would be hitting him too. "Do you want to get arrested for assault? Spend your life in juvenile hall? Is that what you want?"

"Tyler, you have to stop all of this," Mom says quietly, and the soft pleading in her voice makes me feel like hell. She finally releases that sigh she's been holding, and it just sounds...sad. "I don't want you to get into trouble."

I don't want to get into trouble either, I want to tell her, but I can't find the words. How do I tell her I'm only doing all of this because I don't know anything different? Because trouble is all my life has ever revolved around? Because I'm just trying my best to get by?

"This isn't Las Vegas," Dave huffs, drawing back my attention. He is even closer to me now and I can see the anger in his eyes, but I'll never understand it. I'm not his son. I'm nothing to him. "What the hell were you playing at?"

I stare evenly back into his eyes, my expression stoic. "Live a little."

"I'm done with you," Dave says, and he finally retreats from me, hands thrown up as though he's giving up. He shoots Mom a look as he shakes his head, then he disappears outside into the backyard.

Amazing. I wonder how long it will be before he tries his hand at parenting me again. Probably not long at all. I have to laugh at him though; after that last attempt, it would be rude not to. I see Mom opening her mouth to say something, but I can't bear to hear it. I also can't bear the smell of those damn steaks that are cooking behind her. They smell burned by now, and I don't even think she's realized.

I turn around, unable to look at her, and walk out of the kitchen. I have no idea what time I'm supposed to be heading out to meet Tiffani and the rest of the crew tonight, but I refuse to stick around here, so I decide to leave early. I have my eye on the front door, my hand already reaching into my pocket for my car keys, when lo and behold, I spot her again. There Eden is, standing in the corner of the hall with her back pressed against the wall. She stares at me, frozen, and even though I'm wondering what the hell she's doing, I've remembered something. "I've gotta give you a ride, right?"

Eden hesitates for a while, looking uncomfortable *yet* again. Am I really that intimidating? "I think so," she finally mumbles. She still doesn't look all that sharp, but her uncertainty is sort of cute.

"I'm leaving right now," I tell her, "so either come or stay here." I'm not waiting around any longer, and certainly not while Eden makes up her mind, so I turn back around again and continue toward the front door.

"Tyler! Please don't leave again!" I hear Mom's voice bounce from the kitchen, but even though I can hear how hurt she is, I can't bring myself to stay.

I keep on walking, my head down, out the front door and across the lawn. At first, I assume Eden isn't coming, but then I hear the front door open again behind me, and a husky voice calls out, "Wait up!"

And, honestly, I'm glad to hear it.

17

BY THIRD PERIOD ON Wednesday, I've run out of energy to even listen during history class. I didn't get much sleep last night. Dad was mad again, and I still don't know what about. I can barely stay awake, and my eyelids keep drooping every five minutes until I shake myself in an effort to become more alert, but it's no use.

To stop myself from constantly drifting into another world, I turn my worksheet over and begin to trace one big circle, around and around and around... My eyes close again, and I flinch, blinking fast. I sit up, hoping that maybe if I don't slouch so much, that'll help. But it doesn't. I glance to my left, looking across the class at Dean's desk. He's already staring back at me with a smirk.

"*Wake up,*" he mouths. Is it that obvious?

I bury my face into my hands, rubbing hard at my eyes until I see stars, and just as my sight is coming back to me, I see Mrs. Palmer putting down the phone at her desk. Her eyes flicker and she looks straight at me, swiveling around in her chair to face me more directly.

"Tyler," she says gently with a small smile, "Mr. Hayes would like to see you in his office."

Mr. Hayes wants to see me in his office? Why does the school counselor want to see me? Jake said he was called to his office last week to talk about his grades because they suck, but my grades are fine. *I'm* fine.

I was falling asleep a second ago, but now I'm wide awake. I swallow hard and set my pen down getting to my feet. Half the class is working on the worksheets, the other half is watching me closely. As I weave through the desks, I glance back over my shoulder at Dean. He raises his eyebrows at me, curious as to why I've been called to Mr. Hayes' office, and honestly, I have no idea, so I just give him a small shrug and turn back around. I keep my head down as I walk out of class. I've only ever been in Mr. Hayes' office once before, and that was last year when everyone was called up one by one to talk about what our plans for the future are, as though we're supposed to know the answer to that in middle school. I told him I wasn't sure, but that I'd probably end up working for Dad. That's what I'm expected to do, at least.

When I reach Mr. Hayes' office, I take a deep breath and zip up my hoodie to cover the Band-Aid on my neck. Then, I knock on the door and I wait.

A few seconds later, the door swings open and Mr. Hayes smiles down at me. "Ah, Tyler. Thanks for coming," he says. He steps back from the door and motions for me to come inside, which I do. He closes the door behind me again. "Sit down, please."

I stuff my hands into the pockets of my hoodie and sit down on the edge of the seat in front of his big old desk. I can't relax. My foot is tapping against the floor as Mr. Hayes sinks down into his chair across from me. He's young, Mr. Hayes. Younger than Dad, with thick stubble, a crooked nose, and dark eyes that are studying me closely.

"You've just come from history, right?" he asks gently as his way of initiating a conversation, interlocking his hands together on the table in front of him. His smile never falters.

"Right," I agree. *Why am I here?* I ball my hands into fists inside my pockets, feeling even more anxious than I did a minute ago.

"Relax, Tyler," Mr. Hayes says with a small laugh, reading my expression. He can sense how nervous I am. "You're not in trouble. I've only called you down here to talk. I just want to check in and see how you're doing."

"Check in and see how I'm doing?" I repeat, confused. Why does he need to check up on me? It's not like it's some mandatory thing. Have I done something wrong?

Mr. Hayes' smile tightens into what I think is a frown, and he leans back in his chair, his gaze never leaving mine. "Several of your teachers have said you've been acting up lately," he finally tells me. "And skipping gym class?" He arches a brow. *Uh oh.* My hands are sweating now, so I pull them out of my pockets and twiddle my thumbs instead.

"I haven't…I haven't been acting up," I lie, my words sticking in my throat.

"Hmm." Mr. Hayes cranes his neck and looks at the screen of his computer for a few moments. "Not listening. Talking back to your teachers. Not finishing work during class." He looks at me again and cocks his head to one side. "Any reason for the change in attitude? Your grades are still perfect, so what's going on, Tyler?"

"I don't know," I say bluntly. I lock my eyes on a random spot on his desk, refusing to meet his gaze. I know exactly what's going on. The cut on my neck stings again.

"Who are your friends?" Mr. Hayes questions.

"Dean Carter and Jake Maxwell," I mumble. Why does it matter who my friends are? I still can't look at him, but that doesn't mean I can't still feel his eyes boring into me.

"Alright, so you're not hanging around with the wrong people," Mr. Hayes muses to himself. He goes quiet for a second, as though he's considering other possibilities, and then he asks, "Are there any people in this school you dislike? Any people you should let me know about?"

I look up at him, gritting my teeth. Why is he questioning me like this? Why does he care? "I'm not being bullied, Mr. Hayes," I state clearly and slowly. I'm fine. *I am fine.* "Can I go back to class now? Like you said, my grades are perfect. I can't be missing out on class." I begin to stand, prepared to walk straight out of this office.

"Tyler," Mr. Hayes says firmly. He folds his arms across his chest and narrows his eyes up at me, but not in anger. Concern. "You're giving me attitude, and yet you say you're not acting up." He stands up too and leans back against the window, his hands in the pockets of his pants, his eyes still analyzing me. I'm afraid if I stick around any longer, he'll figure me out. "Is everything okay at home?" he asks.

My heart skips a beat in my chest. "What's that supposed to mean?" I mutter, glaring across the desk at him. I'm angry now. Does he know? No, he can't possibly know. No one does.

"Well," he says, "maybe your parents have been fighting? Anything going on that may be affecting you?"

"No, they love each other," I spit. I'm clenching my jaw so tight I think it may shatter. They both love me too. Dad loses control too easily, but it's because he's stressed. He wants the best from me. He wants me to succeed. He doesn't mean to hurt me; he just can't help it. I want it to stop, I do, but I also don't want anyone to take him away from us. From my brothers. From Mom. "I'm going back to class, Mr. Hayes." This time, I really do turn to leave. I storm toward the door and reach for the handle.

"Tyler," Mr. Hayes says one last time. I hesitate at the door, but I don't turn around. I stare at the door handle instead, breathing heavily, listening. "If you figure out why you're acting like this, then please come and talk to me. I'm here to help you, remember," he says gently, his voice quiet. "Okay?"

I squeeze my eyes shut as I pull open the door, refusing to answer him and stepping out into the hallway. Aggressively, I slam the door shut behind me, because he's a liar. He can't help me. No one can.

18

I PULL OPEN MY car door and then turn around. Eden comes rushing across the lawn toward me, like she's terrified I'll leave without her, and I study her as she approaches. Her hair is wavy, her lips are glossy, and there are weird black ticks next to her eyes. The past couple days, we've only been awkwardly passing each other around the house, but neither of us have been willing to speak first. On Sunday, she was calling me pathetic. She's right, though I don't want her to be. That's why, although I'm annoyed, I know I have to put on my game face. I have to switch back to being the cocky asshole that everyone knows as Tyler Bruce.

"What?" Eden asks. I realize that I'm staring too hard.

"Well?" I ask. I nod to my car because it's the first thing I think of. This is the first time I'm giving her a ride, but I'm pretty sure she'll have noticed it by now. It usually grabs attention pretty quickly, though Eden's expression is indifferent. "Do you even know what car this is?"

She walks around the car, looking over the bodywork, and then finally says, "An Audi?" once she spots the badge. She looks entirely disinterested and almost perplexed as to why I'm asking about it.

"An Audi R8," I correct, expecting more of a reaction.

"Okay. Do you want me to applaud you or something?" Eden deadpans, staring back at me with her arms folded across her chest. I guess it makes sense. She's from Portland, where I'm pretty sure everyone is a hippy that rides a bike, so I'm not even surprised that she doesn't know a nice car when she sees one.

"Girls are clueless," I say with a laugh. "You'd probably pass out if you saw the figures on this thing."

Mom almost passed out too when I first told her I wanted it a year ago. At first, she said there was absolutely no chance that she was letting me blow half my trust fund on a damn sports car, but she caved within a few days. She thought a nice car would make me happier, and it did for a while, especially because our trust funds are mostly made up of the money from Dad's shitty company, and it felt nice spending all his hard-earned cash on something so meaningless. Now I couldn't care too much about the car, and what most people don't know is that it's, like, four years old with a whack gear shift lever and brake pads that need replacing almost constantly. But at least it makes me look like I've got my life figured out.

"Get over yourself," Eden tells me, and then climbs into my passenger seat. I blink a few times. Who actually is this girl, honestly? I need to step up my game, because so far I really haven't done a good job of intimidating her.

I sigh and join her inside the car, and as I get the engine growling to life, I toss her my phone. "Call Tiffani," I order.

"You mean your girlfriend who you like to either be all over or completely ignore?"

Damn, so she really has been watching me. I haven't just been imagining it. For someone who apparently doesn't like me, she sure does seem interested in what I'm into, which is sort of amusing to me, but also slightly terrifying. I don't like it when people focus on my life too much. They'll see the cracks if they look too hard.

"You're an ass," she mutters under her breath, turning away. I didn't realize I've smiled in reply to her question. She tries way too hard to stare out the window, as though she's letting me know that she doesn't want to speak to me anymore. She's still holding my phone.

"Call her," I say again as I step on the gas a little too hard, sending us flying down the street a little too rapidly. "I have no idea where we're going."

Eden dramatically sighs, as though I'm asking her to give me a kidney, and she sits up and looks at my screen. "Pass code?"

"4355," I tell her without hesitation. Besides some raunchy pictures from Tiffani and some pretty incriminating evidence in my messages with Declan Portwood, my phone is pretty clean. I do watch my screen out of the corner of my eye as Eden unlocks it just to make sure she doesn't do any snooping.

"Is that your favorite number or does it stand for a word or—"

"It spells out hell," I cut in sharply. Hell, because my life is hell, because I feel like hell, because I'm going to hell. I *did* create that pass code on one of my low nights. I hope she doesn't ask why, because I don't have the energy to explain. "Call her."

Eden frowns and scrolls through my list of contacts, past Declan and Kaleb, past Mom and Dave, past all of the hundreds of names in between, and all the way down to Tiffani. She calls her and presses my phone to her ear.

"It's Eden. Tyler's driving," Eden explains once Tiffani picks up. "Where are we all going tonight? Has it been decided yet?"

I watch her again as she listens, biting down on her lower lip. She nods as Tiffani speaks, and I don't know if she realizes just how focused she looks. "Yeah," she says, and then listens some more. I'm so distracted by watching her that I almost drive straight into the curb, and Eden fires me a sideways look when I swerve back. She lowers my phone, puts it on speaker, and then holds it up by my shoulder.

"Yeah?" I ask. *Of course* Tiffani was going to ask to talk to me. I steal a glance down at the screen, and then I have to slam hard on the brakes at a stop sign. I'm usually not such a distracted driver, but I also usually don't have strangers riding with me, so I guess I could say it's actually Eden's fault.

"I haven't spoken to you all day!" Tiffani says through my phone, and her voice is high-pitched and overly sweet, a total act. It's only because she knows Eden can hear us, and I really do have to roll my eyes at how pathetic we *both* are. Why do we try so hard to convince everyone that we are this perfect, happy, dream couple when we are the exact opposite? We are toxic, trapped by each other, hating one another but also being unable to let go because of how dependent we've both become. "Did your mom let you out of the house?" she asks. Stuck at the stop sign, I pull up my parking brake and look at Eden. I'm pretty sure she was eavesdropping on the conversation with Mom and Dave in the kitchen, which means she knows exactly where I was this afternoon. And with Tiffani on speaker, I can't afford for Eden to be blurting out the truth. I sharpen my gaze at her and shake my head slowly, letting her know not to dare say a word.

"No, I was stuck inside all day," I finally tell Tiffani. Again. For like the fifth time today. I swear she never pays attention to a word I say, but that's a good thing, because everything I tell her is usually a lie anyway.

"That sucks," she says. And then her voice hits that high octave again as she adds, "I can't wait to see you! We won't be too long. Just wait for us by the Sunset Ranch."

Okay, so we're heading to the Hollywood sign then. That's okay with me. I like it up there. It gets you away from everything for a while. "Sure."

"Love you," Tiffani says to finish the call, but again, it's all just so fucking fake. She doesn't love me. She just wants everyone to think she does.

That's why I only say "Yeah" and hang up. I refuse to say it back.

As I toss my phone down into the center console, I run a hand through my hair and lean back in my seat, getting comfortable. It's not exactly a short drive over to the Hollywood sign.

"You're unbelievable," Eden says in disbelief. "Stuck inside all day?"

I don't even look at her. I try to just stay focused on the road as I cross the intersection. "That's what I'm going with."

"You're really going to lie to her like that?" she questions, and I think, *Here we go again.* What is with Eden interrogating me as though she's my mom? I glance at her to see if she's actually mad at me or not, and she *does* look disgusted. "You were at the beach gambling and fighting and you're going to act like you were inside all day? I feel so bad for her."

I laugh out loud, hard. She feels bad for Tiffani? Incredible. It's funny the way things can appear to the people on the outside looking in. Behind closed doors, everything is so different. "Yeah, you're definitely Dave's daughter," I say. It must be a Munro thing to hate me as soon as they meet me, to question everything I do, to be repulsed by me. "You gotta learn to mind your own business, kid."

"Stop calling me kid," Eden orders, and she's serious. It's settled: I *definitely* don't intimidate her. "You're only a year older than me, and you've got fewer brain cells."

"Alright, kid," I say again, smiling to let her know I'm not doing it out of malice. I'm only messing with her. "Your dad's an asshole."

"At least that's one thing we can agree on." We both go quiet, and the only sound is my car engine rumbling and Eden sighing as she stares wistfully out of the window. "I don't even know what his problem is," she says after a while. "I get that you must be super annoying to live with, but it's like he looks for reasons to yell at you."

I drum my fingers against my steering wheel. "Tell me about it."

"My mom's better off without him," she comments, but then her eyes go wide as she glances at me, panicking over her words. "Not that it's unfortunate for your mom or anything like that," she babbles too fast. "What about you? Where's your dad?"

I slam on the brakes so hard that the car jerks to a complete stop in the road and our bodies fly forward against our seat belts. My eyes flash over to look at her in disbelief. "What the fuck?"

Eden stares at me, her eyes even wider and her face paling. For the very first time, I think she is actually scared of me. I don't mean to yell at her, but fuck, man. What is she thinking asking me something like that? "Sorry—I—" she splutters, but her voice is nothing more than a small squeak.

I clench my teeth hard to stop myself from losing it with her. I've already lost it once today and I really don't want to lose it again, but it's so damn hard. The anger is building as Dad's face creeps its way into my head, and the only way I can think of to release it is to step on the gas and floor it. The engine roars and the tires screech; it's a satisfying feeling. "Don't talk," I spit, forcing the words out as calmly as I can through gritted teeth. Eden is *so* lucky I'm keeping my temper in check. She hasn't seen me angry yet, and believe me, she doesn't want to.

"I didn't mean to offend you—"

"Shut the hell up," I demand harshly. Does she know? Does she fucking *know*? Did Dave tell her? No... He wouldn't have. Dave is a jerk and I find him insufferable most of the time, but I do trust him enough not to share a secret that is only mine to tell. Mom has him well warned on that one, so no, Eden can't possibly know. She was only asking a question, a question that is pretty normal to anyone else, but an agonizing question to me.

She doesn't know, I tell myself over and over again. *She didn't ask to be cruel. She was only making conversation.*

I can't bring myself to speak for the rest of the journey; instead, I spend the entire time with my gaze fixated on the road while I keep on telling myself to just calm down. It was only an innocent question. I wish I didn't snap over the mere mention of Dad, but I always do and I hate it. Now Eden can add anger issues to her never-ending list of my flaws.

Thankfully, she doesn't attempt to make conversation again either, and honestly, I appreciate the silence while I get my head together. She stares out of the window the entire time, and I can only assume she's thinking about how much of an asshole I am, because there's nothing exciting about the freeway to distract her. It's rush hour and it's LA: We end up stuck on the I-10 in crawling bumper-to-bumper traffic. It's way more unbearable than it usually is, but that's only because I'm stuck in this confined space with Eden, feeling the tension. I play music in an attempt to cover it up, but it's still impossible to ignore. The only time I *do* actually speak again is an hour later when I let her know that we're almost there.

I drive up the winding streets off North Beachwood Drive toward the Sunset Ranch, the Hollywood sign towering high in front of us, and I feel the final dregs of my anger subside when Eden leans forward to peer up through the windshield at it, fighting back a smile. I feel like shit for yelling at her now. A few minutes later, we finally reach the Sunset Ranch, and when I pull into the tiny parking area by the side of the road, I'm relieved to see that everyone else is already here. I see Dean and Jake grabbing bottles of water from the trunks of their cars, and then there are the girls—Tiffani, Rachael, and Meghan, flailing around and applying lip gloss. We're an alright group, I guess. We've been friends for a long time, and even though both Rachael and Jake hate me, we all tolerate one another.

I park, cut my engine, and glance at Eden. I'm considering apologizing to her for snapping at her the way I did an hour ago, but she already has her back to me as she gets out of my car. A sigh escapes my lips and I follow suit, stepping out the car just as Meghan comes over and asks, "You took the freeway, didn't you?"

Tiffani follows after her, her grin widening when my eyes meet hers, and she immediately throws her skinny arms around my neck and hugs me tight. Even though she is clinging to me, I still manage to quickly tell Meghan, "Yeah, did you guys go through Beverly Hills?" Tiffani's body is pressing against mine and she moves her hands to my face, cupping my jaw and guiding my lips to hers. I know it's all just a show, but I kiss her anyway, only for a second. I free myself from her grasp, stepping away and placing at least a foot of distance between us, and then I notice Eden's eyes on me. She's most likely thinking about that phone call with Tiffani earlier, the one where I lied and didn't say *love you* back. And now here I am, kissing Tiffani like a damn hypocrite. I drop my eyes to the ground, kicking at the dirt.

"Easiest way to speed and not get caught," Jake says, and I can't even remember what I asked. "We didn't want to keep you waiting for an hour."

"It's incredible," Eden says quietly, her voice breathy and forever husky. I look up at her, and everyone else looks at her too. Her head is tilted back, her eyes squinting up through the evening sunlight to the sign. "Thanks for showing it to me." God. We all laugh, and I really can't fight it. She thinks this is it? She thinks we drove all the way here just to look up at the damn sign from the bottom? And she actually would have been grateful for that? Man, her innocence is cute.

"We haven't shown you it yet," Rachael tells her, and I can see the color rising in Eden's cheeks. "We're taking you all the way up."

"Up?" Eden says. She furrows her eyebrows as she glances back up at the sign. Sure, it's pretty high up there on top of Mount Lee, but it's really not a bad hike.

"Yeah, up," Dean confirms. "We better get moving if you want to see it before the sun goes down. And it's hot. So here." He passes out a bottle of water to her, and then bottles to Jake and Meghan.

"Who remembers the route?" Rachael asks. She comes to Tiffani and me, shoving a warm bottle of water into my hand.

"It's not that damn hard, Rach. Sharp left and then right," I remind her. I drop my hand to Tiffani's waist, guiding her toward the Hollyridge Trail that starts just ahead. It's been at least a year since all of us came up together, but the trails are simple and straightforward, so the route is impossible to forget.

Tiffani and I lead the way, but that's nothing new. For as long as I can remember, we've always been the leaders of the group. Maybe because we both like to be intimidating. Maybe because we're both good actors. Maybe because we care the most about what others think of us. I'm not too sure.

"Sooo," Tiffani says, running her fingers down my arm and interlocking our hands. "Bet you're happy to get out of the house, huh?"

"Sure am," I murmur. If only she knew what I was *really* up to today.

I honestly think she would kill me if she found out, especially since I've already promised her I *wasn't* going to get involved with Declan Portwood. Yet that's exactly what I'm doing. "How was the beach? Topped up that tan?"

"I don't know," she says, and as nonchalant as ever, she continues, "You'll be able to tell me when I take my clothes off later."

Well, damn. It didn't take Tiffani long tonight to start with all her teasing. It only reminds me yet again that we are so, so wrong for each other. We have nothing to talk about besides sex, parties, and social status. After all these years, it just feels so repetitive and so boring. I glance sideways at her and she gives me the best innocent smile she can pull off, but it still comes across as a smirk. I don't know what to say at this point apart from, "Alright. Sounds good." She doesn't look all that pleased with my weak reply.

As we keep on walking, heading up and up, I glance over my shoulder. Everyone has already fallen behind us, and the five of them are trailing by a short distance. I notice Eden at the back, talking with Rachael, listening closely. Dean's laughing with Jake and Meghan about something, and honestly, I wish I wasn't stuck up ahead at the front of the pack with only Tiffani as my companion.

We talk about the most mundane shit ever during the entire hike, and if I wasn't walking up a damn mountain, I definitely would have fallen asleep by now. The conversation never used to be so lacking a few years ago when we first started dating, but over time, we have just gotten *so* used to each other. And when you are so used to someone you don't even like all that much, you seriously lose the will to even try anymore. I put my hand on her shoulder occasionally to keep her happy, and she touches my bicep every so often. It's all just so meaningless, but I never really expected there to be anything more, anyway. I knew from the beginning that there were never going to be any true feelings between Tiffani and me, but sometimes I wish there had been.

I check over my shoulder again, and I don't know why, but I clench my fist when I realize that Eden isn't with Rachael anymore. No, she's with fucking Jake. The two of them are way behind the rest of us, and seeing the two of them alone together makes me uncomfortable. I narrow my eyes at Jake, wondering what kind of crap he's up to. Eden's gaze catches mine and she notices me watching, and she just confidently glares straight back. Is she still mad at me for snapping at her in the car? Does she think she's the one I'm glaring at?

"Oooh, I've never been so glad to see this damn fence in my life! Finally!" Tiffani says. She grabs my hand and yanks me along with her as she breaks into a jog around the bend toward the sign, and she calls over her shoulder, "Eden, come see this!"

We round the corner, and there it is, the Hollywood sign sitting before us, the huge letters facing out over the city of LA. When the skies are clear, like tonight, you can see the skyscrapers of downtown LA off in the distance. We've made it up here in just under an hour, and because the sun is now beginning to set, we're basked in a warm, orange glow. But I've seen it a bunch of times before, so it's not as cool as I once thought it was.

Everyone catches up to us, rushing around the bend, but Eden is the only one I keep my gaze trained on. Her expression lights up, her eyes widening, and she presses her hands to the chain link fence as she peers through it. She's silent for a long while, taking in the view. I bet they don't have shit like this in Portland, that's for sure.

"Worth the hike?" Dean asks her, and all she does is nod, still staring.

"It's so beautiful," she murmurs.

Meghan says something, but I don't hear her. I've stopped listening because now I'm looking at the sign too. We've all jumped the fence a couple times before to touch those letters, and even though it's illegal, we've never been caught. We usually get the hell out of there pretty fast, and if Eden has hiked all the way up here, then she deserves the full experience. Plus, I want to put her through her paces and figure out if she's the type for an adrenaline rush or not. She doesn't look like she would be, but I'm not going to assume anything, because so far, she's done nothing but surprise me.

I reach up and grab the top of the fence, looking back at everyone. "What are you guys waiting for?" I ask them with a smirk, and, being the leader of the pack and all, I haul myself up and swing my body over the fence. I land on the other side pretty smoothly, like a damn acrobat. I'm impressed with myself. "C'mon."

I set my eyes on Eden, looking back at her through the chain links. I can see the fear in her gaze as she glances around, first at the tower of security cameras, and then at the trespassing signs, and then finally at me. I smile at her, challenging her to do it. I *dare* her.

"We have, like, ten minutes before they send out the helicopter," Tiffani states, and she's the first of the group to actually begin climbing over. "Eden, touch the sign and then we'll get out of here."

Eden frowns and then shakes her head at us. "Really, it's okay. I don't need to touch the—"

"Just touch the fucking sign," I cut in, growing frustrated. I really wanted her to surprise me. She's doing exactly what I expected her to do, and that's no fun at all. It's more interesting when she proves my assumptions wrong.

"We won't get caught," Rachael reassures her, and as she climbs over with Dean and Meghan, she adds, "We do this all the time." Which is a fucking lie. We've only jumped this fence, like, twice.

"Don't worry," Jake says, and my chest tightens when he grasps Eden's hand and places it on the fence, encouraging her. What *is* he up to? Because that's weird. "If we get caught, we'll all go down together. But we gotta be quick."

Eden finally gives in, and she grabs at the fence and pulls herself up and over. I give her a nod of approval, but she doesn't even notice, so I turn around and begin edging my way toward the giant letters as everyone follows. It *is* steep, so we do have to be careful, watching our footing the entire time. "I love this place," Dean says once we reach the letters. He touches the "O" and then sighs. "I wonder how many people around the world would kill for the opportunity to do this. We're lucky."

My gaze sharpens as I fire him a look. Dean does this a lot. Everything is always so deep with him. "Dude, stop getting all sentimental, it's just letters on a mountain," I tell him. It's really not a big deal, and I don't know why it has become one. "This city is stupid as hell and so is this sign."

"You're so negative," Tiffani says, shaking her head. She walks over, stepping directly in front of me and hooking her fingers around the belt loops of my jeans. Probably so I can't get away. She looks up at me from beneath her thick, fake eyelashes. "What's with the shitty mood?"

I refuse to look at her, and instead I stare off into the distance. "I'm not in a shitty mood."

"You are," she says. "You always are. It's seriously annoying. Can you smile sometimes? So, you know, you don't look like a permanent asshole? We're supposed to be happy."

My gaze drops down to meet hers and I clench my jaw, ready to tell her to fuck off and leave me alone, to stop trying to tell me what to do, when I vaguely hear, "How about that date then?" from somewhere to my left.

My eyes flicker over and I see it: Jake and Eden standing way too close together with both their hands side by side on the "H" of the sign. Did I hear that right? Did he seriously just ask her for a date? Goddamn, he only just met the fucking girl!

"What the hell, man?" I yell over to him, and I push my way past Tiffani, marching straight over there. He's up to something, I just *know* it. Eden isn't even his type.

"What?" Jake says, turning around to face me. Clearly, my interruption has pissed him off because he stares at me as though he's fed up, with his lips pressed together and his eyes rolling.

"What the hell did you just say to her?" I demand, my voice ragged. I close the distance between us, our chests only inches apart, and because I'm slightly taller, I glare down at him. Who the hell does he think he is, asking my damn *stepsister* on a date?

"Bro, get outta my face," Jake mutters, stepping back. He turns away and throws up his hands as though he isn't looking for a fight, making me look like the bad guy for squaring up.

And that's when I realize: Is he doing this to piss me off? To get a reaction? Is he seriously still hung up over losing out on Tiffani?

"No," I argue. I follow Jake, stepping back in front of him again, refusing to back down. He doesn't get to use Eden to piss me off. That's just being a jerk. I jab his chest with my index finger and my eyes never leave his. "You two are not happening. I'll kick your ass if you even think about it," I threaten, and I hope he knows I'm being serious. I *will* floor the guy.

"Tyler, baby, chill," Tiffani pleads in that fake, sweet voice of hers. She pushes her body in between Jake and me, pressing both her hands to my chest and attempting to shove me away, to remove me from the situation. I still haven't broken eye contact with Jake. "Don't be an asshole. Stop trying to start a fight."

Dean tries to help too, and since Tiffani has a hold on me, he steps in front of Jake to block him. "C'mon, guys. Quit it."

I'm just about to search for Eden to check her expression, to see if she's thankful that I intervened or if she's pissed at me again, when I hear the faint sound of a helicopter. All of us are completely silent, and I know everyone else has heard it too. Within a matter of seconds, the blades cutting through the air become louder and louder. I tilt my head back and look up, right as the LAPD helicopter emerges from the other side of Mount Lee.

19

I HEAR THEIR VOICES from the kitchen before I'm even downstairs. It's late and I should be in bed by now, but I can't sleep yet. I've only just finished up in the bathroom, cleaning up the cut on my shoulder and popping some more painkillers. What I really want is some ice.

Every single light in the house is off except for the glow that shines through the open crack of the kitchen door. Silently, I edge down the stairs one step at a time. I just checked on Jamie and Chase, and they're both asleep and snoring, so I keep quiet, not only so my parents don't discover me creeping around, but so that I don't wake my brothers.

I drift down the hall toward the kitchen door and when I reach it, I lean back against the wall and squint through the open crack. I'm holding my breath, because I'm scared they'll hear me if I breathe.

"Can't you just replace him internally?" Mom is asking, frowning at Dad as he paces back and forth across the kitchen. She looks tired and she's wearing sweatpants, her hair tied back and her makeup already washed off. "Give one of your other guys a promotion?"

"Replace Evan Kroger?" Dad says, abruptly coming to a halt. He stares back across the kitchen at her, his eyes wild. He's still wearing his shirt and tie, though it's loosened around his neck. He reaches up to undo the top buttons of his shirt too. "None of my other guys are *capable*, Ella. How the fuck can Evan just walk out like that? No damn warning!" He shakes his head in aggravation. "Now the Seattle office doesn't have a project manager two days before we break ground on our biggest project of the year. We're *fucked*."

Through the dark, I roll up the sleeve of my T-shirt and glance down at my arm. Just below my shoulder, a new set of bruises is developing. I wasn't sure what I did wrong tonight, but now I know why he was so mad. Something has gone badly wrong at work.

"Stop cursing," Mom says. I drop my sleeve and peer through the crack in the door again. She is looking at Dad with sympathy now. She's always there for him. "You'll figure it out, Peter. You always do."

"I'm sorry," Dad murmurs with a sigh. "But goddamn it!" The muscle in his jaw twitches as he spins around, slamming his fist down against the countertop. I haven't seen him this furious in a while. He leans back against the counter, his head hung low, rubbing his temples and exhaling deeply.

Mom walks over to him and wraps her arms around his back, burying her face into his chest as though to offer him some comfort and reassurance. "You're just stressed. Relax," she whispers, tilting her chin up and pressing her lips to the corner of his jaw. She kisses his mouth too.

Yeah, I figured he was stressed two hours ago when he came home late from work and stormed into my room. He didn't like that I was watching TV, even though I'd done all of my homework.

"I should probably catch a flight up there tomorrow to figure out how much of a mess Evan has left me with," Dad says with a groan. He rests his arms over Mom's shoulders and pulls her in closer against him, looking down at her with an apologetic smile. "Will you manage with the kids on your own? If not, I can ask my parents to watch them after school in the afternoons until you get out of the office. Is that okay? I don't have to go if you don't want me to. I can manage it over phone calls."

"I don't have any court appearances until Monday, so I'll just work on my cases here. I'll take care of everything," Mom reassures him. "Go to Seattle, Peter."

Dad sighs a sigh of relief and presses his forehead down against Mom's, cupping her jaw in his hands and weaving his fingers into her hair. The smile he gives her is full of warmth and gratitude. "You're my lifesaver," he murmurs, and just as he is about to kiss her, his eyes dart over her shoulder and his gaze lands on me. He abruptly leans back from Mom but doesn't let go of her. "Tyler," he says, raising his voice. His tone is hard, his features harder. "You should be asleep. Go back upstairs and get to bed."

Mom cranes her neck to look back at me, and despite the smile she gives me, I think even she's annoyed at the interruption. I can hear the strain in her voice when she asks, "What's up, Tyler?"

They've spotted me now. I can't turn and run at this point, so I push open the kitchen door further and take a single step into the room. Dad is glaring at me, so I focus only on Mom. "I'm…I'm thirsty," I lie. My throat is dry, sure, but not because I need a drink. "Can I get some water? With ice, please."

"Sure," Mom says, and she pulls away from Dad's embrace and walks over to the sink.

The kitchen falls into a tense silence as Mom fetches a glass and turns on the faucet. Dad is still leaning back against the countertop, gripping the edge of it with both hands, and his eyes are fixed on me. With

Mom's back turned, I can see him looking me up and down, searching for his mistakes. Uncomfortable under his scrutiny, I reach for the sleeve of my T-shirt again and try to pull it down lower. I drop my eyes to the floor, listening to the sound of the faucet running, and then the crushing of ice from the ice machine that's built into our refrigerator.

"Here you go," Mom says, walking back over to me. She slides the glass into my hand and raises an eyebrow at me with a small nod. "Now goodnight, Tyler. You've got school in the morning." She kisses my forehead and I turn around, water in hand, and leave the kitchen. I can't look at Dad again before I walk out, and I even pull the door closed again behind me, leaving that same small crack.

I take a few steps down the hall and then come to a halt. Before it can melt, I stick my hand into the glass of water and grab some of the ice. It's freezing cold and it numbs my fingertips, but I'm desperate. I glance back over my shoulder one last time before I head upstairs. Mom is against Dad again, her arms around his neck, his mouth against hers, his hands on her hips. They stumble. I close my eyes and turn away, and as I make my way back upstairs to my room, I pull back my sleeve and press the ice against the fresh bruises on my arm that Dad's fingers have left behind.

20

"SHIT!" I YELL OUT, and I slam my hand down hard against the giant "H" in aggravation. It stings my palm, but I'm too panicked to care. I pull on the ends of my hair, completely frustrated. "How the hell do they always get out here so fast?"

"Don't trip!" Tiffani calls out. Right now, it is everyone for themselves, and she slips her hand into mine and begins pulling me with her as she takes off. And, despite how steep Mount Lee actually is, it is much quicker to just run through all of the shrubs and dirt rather than heading back to the trails. It's dangerous, but right now, our safety is the least of my worries.

I can't afford to get caught. I've been arrested and cited for trespassing before. With all of the shit I'm about to get myself involved in with Declan Portwood, I need to keep myself off the cops' radar as best I can. They don't need to be aware of me.

"Oh my God, my mom will *kill* me if I get a citation!" Tiffani panics, her breathing all over the place. We are still hand in hand as I lead the way down, testing out the ground first as quickly as I can while she follows. There are random dips, random holes. It's so easy to roll an ankle up here, and as much as Tiffani annoys me, I don't want her to get hurt.

We are in a race against time to get back down to the base of the mountain before the cops have a cruiser there waiting for us. That's why we don't wait for the others. I can hear them all a few hundred feet behind us. I can hear Rachael and Meghan shrieking every few seconds, and I can hear them all calling out to one another, but I don't turn around.

I'm totally relieved when Tiffani and I finally reach the bottom again without any injuries and without any cruisers in sight. It still doesn't mean we're in the clear though. Out of breath, we force ourselves to keep running back to the small parking lot where we left the cars, and I begin fumbling in my pockets for my keys. I can still hear that damn helicopter above us.

"Let's just get out of here," I murmur, unlocking my car. I hop inside and Tiffani slides into my passenger seat. The others will understand why we've left without them. I know I should probably wait for Eden to take her home, but I can't risk it. I'm sure the others will give her a ride.

"Yeah," Tiffani agrees, then places her hand on my thigh. "Let's go back to my place."

We do go back to Tiffani's place, but only to drop her off. She slams my door and calls me an asshole again as she leaves, furious at the rejection, then storms into her house, all the while swinging her hips and flicking her hair as though to show me what I'm missing. But I'm seriously not in the mood. Today has been weird.

By the time I do get back home, it's almost dark, and Mom and Dave are watching TV together in the living room. I stand in the hall in silence for a few minutes, deliberating whether or not I'm going to even speak to them, and I decide that, after everything that has happened today, I should at least have the decency to let them know I'm home. It's not like I *want* to infuriate them. I just sort of…do. So if I get the chance to actually be tolerable, then I'll take it.

I knock on the glass panels of the living room door and gently push it open. Both Mom and Dave glance over at me, almost like they're surprised I'm actually home before midnight for once, and then mute the TV.

"I'm home," I say quietly. I even throw in a smile. I know Mom was disappointed earlier, so I want to make it up to her.

"Where were you?" she asks. She keeps her voice equally as soft, as though we've made an unspoken agreement to forget about what happened earlier.

"With Tiffani," I say. It's not a lie. More like an omission of the truth. As if I'm going to tell them we almost just got arrested for trespassing our way to the Hollywood sign.

"Where's Eden?" Dave joins in, and although his voice is still pretty abrupt, it's not as gruff as it usually is. He also looks slightly concerned.

"She's with Rachael," I guess. Again, *definitely* not telling him that his daughter just ran from the cops. I'm pretty sure she'll be home any second anyway. I notice the empty food containers on the coffee table and I raise an eyebrow. "You ordered Chinese food?"

"Your mom burned the steaks," Dave says, and he wiggles his eyebrows at Mom, who blushes in embarrassment. Usually, she's a pretty amazing cook.

"Great!" I drawl sarcastically. "So that cow died for nothing!"

Mom's face falls. "Tyler…"

"I'm kidding!" I say, holding up my hands as I let out a laugh. God, I can't even make one of my vegetarian jokes without them thinking I'm about to burst into a fit of rage. It's kind of sad, actually. Have I really gotten to the point where people just expect me to be aggressive all the time?

"Tyler!" I hear Jamie say as he comes bounding down the stairs. He slides across the hall floor in his socks and bumps straight into me. He grins wide and looks up at me with his blue eyes that are identical to Mom's. "You're home. Good. I need you to come play *Madden* with me because Chase honestly *sucks*."

"He'll be trying his best, Jay," Mom says.

"No, he's not," Jamie argues, groaning. "Even *you* could play better than him, Mom! Now c'mon, Tyler." He grabs my arm and begins yanking me toward the stairs, but before I disappear out of sight completely, I flash Mom a smirk, rolling my eyes as Jamie continues to tug at me. She smiles, probably just glad to see me relatively at ease for once. I follow Jamie upstairs and into his room at the end of the hall. Chase is sitting cross-legged on the floor in his pajamas, waiting patiently, and *Madden NFL* is paused on the TV. "Move over," Jamie orders, nudging him with his knee. "Tyler's taking your place."

"What? Why?" Chase asks, widening his eyes. All of the lights are off, so the glare from the TV screen is the only light source in the room, and it reflects in his blue eyes. Both of my brothers got Mom's blond hair and blue eyes. For some reason, I was the only one to inherit Dad's Hispanic genes in my looks, so I always look a little out of place in this family now that Dad's gone.

"Because you suck," Jamie says.

"I don't!" Chase huffs, but he throws the PlayStation controller down anyway and reluctantly shuffles over to make room for me.

It's funny. The three of us are all so different. I'm the fucked up one, the angry one. Jamie is the smart one, the perfectionist. Chase is the innocent one, the people-pleaser. They're only fourteen and eleven, but I already know they're going to be way better men than I'll ever be.

I sit down next to Chase on the floor, leaning back against Jamie's bed and stretching out my legs in front of me. I grab the controller. "Sorry, buddy, but the pro has arrived," I tease. And, to make it more dramatic, I crack all of my fingers and then my neck. "Ready, Jay?"

"Ready," he says from on top of the bed. He takes the game off pause and it kicks into action, picking up midgame play, and I stare at the screen while I try to figure out which team I'm playing for. Yeah, Chase really is trailing behind. He's scored nothing. *Nothing.*

I haven't played in years. When I was their age, I used to play *Madden* with Dean and Jake. All. The. Damn. Time. Not anymore. Now I spend my free time ruining my life. That's why I suck at the beginning of the game too until I get into the groove of it, and Jamie insults me the entire time while Chase fidgets next to me, glued to the screen. We do laugh a lot though, and I wish I did this more often. Man, I love the pair of them, but I've usually got so much going on in my life that I don't ever make the time to actually hang out with them. But they're happy and carefree, and I could really use some of that positive energy that they radiate.

"Boom!" Jamie says, tossing his controller to the floor and raising his arms into the air as he makes the final touchdown and the game ends. There was absolutely no way to salvage the damage that Chase had already done, so of course he was going to win. "You see that, Tyler? Huh? Now who's the pro?"

"Not you," Chase mumbles, folding his arms across his chest. He's sulking, but I'm cracking up. It's a damn game!

"What did you say?" Jamie growls playfully, and he launches himself off the bed at Chase, wrestling him. They roll around on the floor next to me for a minute or so, pushing each other around and laughing, both trying to get on top of the other. I watch them in amusement, laughing along with them and rolling my eyes.

If there is one thing that I am absolutely thankful for, it's that Dad never, ever laid a hand on either of them. I would have taken triple the amount of abuse if it meant they would never get hurt the way I did. I don't think I would have been able to bear that. They were so young. I look at Chase now, out of breath as he gives up in defeat and pushes Jamie off him. He's so young, so childish and pure. There is no way anyone could ever hurt him. He's only eleven.

But I was eleven once…and the cuts and the bruises didn't stop until I was twelve.

I was young too. I didn't deserve it. I was just a kid. I was just like them.

How could Dad have looked at me, like I am looking at Jamie and Chase now, and even consider the thought of hurting me?

Chase doesn't know about Dad. The truth would hurt him, and he doesn't need to know that our father is a monster. Mom couldn't protect me and she couldn't protect Jamie, but she wants to protect Chase. He is so much better off believing that Dad is in prison for grand theft auto. That's what most people think anyway. But Jamie knows the truth. Jamie discovered it. Jamie stopped me from nearly being killed five years ago. We never talk about it though. I think it scares him.

"Can you guys promise me something?" I say, reaching for the remote and turning off the TV. The room goes silent. I stand up and turn on the lights, and then I sit down on Jamie's bed and look down at them on the floor. I'm not laughing anymore. My expression is serious.

"What?" they both say in unison, staring back up at me with curious, wide eyes.

"Don't do anything stupid when you're my age. Okay?" I say. Unlike me, they actually have a shot at a decent life. A shot at a college, a good job, healthy relationships…a shot at being happy. I really don't want them to mess that up. They have the head start that I didn't. "I don't want to see either of you getting into trouble."

They stare at me blankly, and then Jamie gives me a goofy grin and asks, "So what stupid stuff is it that *you* do?"

I laugh and lean forward, ruffling his shaggy hair. "You think I'm gonna tell you?"

"I'm hoping you will, and then I can blackmail you into buying me *Madden 12* in August," he says, and his grin widens.

"How about," I say, reaching into my back pocket for my wallet, "I just give you some cash toward it right now? Don't tell Mom." I'm feeling generous because they've put me in a good mood, so I grab thirty bucks and hand it to Jamie as his eyes light up in disbelief.

"Hey!" Chase says. "What about me?"

Damn. I pass him twenty, and luckily, he doesn't notice that I've fleeced him. Fifty bucks is a small price to pay to see the pair of them grinning as though they've won the damn lottery. I shove my wallet back into my jeans and stand up, tell them goodnight, and then leave the room.

I'm crossing back over to my own room when, as I'm passing the stairs, I notice Eden running up them at full throttle. She *just* got home? She was only a few minutes behind Tiffani and me when we left the Sunset Ranch. She should have been home ages ago.

"Eden?" I stare down at her, wondering where she's been, because she clearly didn't come straight home. "Where the hell did you go?"

She freezes on the stairs for a split second and fires back, "Where the hell did *you* go?" She walks up the last few stairs and stops in front of me. She's much smaller than I am, but she holds a mean stare down. "You just ditched the rest of us. Nice teamwork."

Shit, so she *is* mad at me. But for what? For the way I snapped at her in the car? For the way I squared up to Jake? I've done a lot of things that could have potentially pissed her off today, and I groan at the thought of them. "I don't work well with cops, alright? I can't get caught again."

"Again," Eden repeats, scoffing. Yet *another* con of mine to add to her list: *gets arrested*. "When did you get home?"

"Twenty minutes ago," I say. "Mom finally stopped grilling me about the whole beach thing earlier."

"Cool," she says with absolutely zero emotion. As though I've disappeared into thin air, she strolls straight past me and walks into her room. I wasn't done talking to her, so I aimlessly follow. She runs her eyes over me and deeply inhales. "What do you want?"

I don't know. To figure out why she's mad at me, I guess. "Nothing," I say, and then look at the floor. God, what the hell is wrong with me? I should get out of her room. She obviously doesn't want to talk to me. Feeling embarrassed, I quickly turn around and walk next door to my own room.

"What was your problem with Jake?" I hear Eden ask, and when I look over my shoulder, she has followed me this time. Her arms are folded across her chest and her stance is confident as she stares at me, an eyebrow raised as she awaits an answer. "I asked you a question," she says.

"I'm not answering it," I say. Is my room even tidy? I glance around. No, of course it's fucking not. I didn't make my bed this morning.

There's beer on my bedside table. There are pairs of my boxers by my bathroom door. I need to distract her from noticing, so I grit my teeth and turn around to face her. "Wait, I will. That guy is the second biggest asshole I've ever met. Don't waste your time. He'll screw you over."

"Who's the first? Yourself?" she quips, and I wish she wasn't being sarcastic, because the first is Dad. My own blood.

"Close enough," is all I say.

"Okay, well, Jake's actually really nice. Unlike some people around here." She steps back and I can see her gaze shifting around the room, checking everything out. "And you don't really get a say in whether I want to hang out with him or not."

"You're kidding, right?" She is, isn't she? She has to be. Jake is a stranger. She doesn't know him like the rest of us do. She doesn't know that he's a player and he's proud of it. She doesn't know that he's combative, argumentative. "Alright," I say. "Don't say I didn't warn you."

"Why do you even care?" she asks.

"I don't," I say, my voice defensive. Or do I? If I don't care, then why am I getting pissed off at the thought of Jake messing with her?

"You clearly do."

I walk away from her, shoving my hands into my pockets as I think of how I'm going to change the subject. I have a pile of old DVDs by my TV, and I sound like a damn idiot when I blurt out, "What's your, um, favorite movie?"

Eden stares at me. She's probably thinking I'm an idiot too for changing the subject to movies, out of everything I could have possibly chosen. "*Lady and the Tramp*," she eventually confesses.

"The Disney movie?" I almost laugh. There she is, surprising me again. If she were Tiffani or Rachael or Meghan, I would be teasing her to hell and back right now. But I think it's sort of cute that she wasn't too shy to give me an embarrassing answer. So I ask, "Why?"

"Because it's the greatest love story of all time," she explains. "Romeo and Juliet have got nothing on Lady and Tramp. They were so different, yet they made it work. Lacy was totally normal and Tramp was totally reckless, yet they fell in love." She smiles as she talks, not really looking at me, and I've never seen anyone look so happy over a damn Disney movie. "And plus, the spaghetti scene is totally iconic," she adds.

"Totally," I agree, laughing. I've never seen the movie, but I think I know how it goes. "And I'm pretty sure Lady wasn't normal. She was boring and didn't know how to have fun. Tramp's my kinda guy."

"What, because he roams the streets the same way you do when you're stumbling home drunk on the weekends?" She tilts her head to one side, those hazel eyes of hers sparkling as she gives me a teasing smile. I laugh again, and she glances around my room once more. "You play football?" she asks.

"Huh?" I look over my shoulder to see what she's talking about. Dean's varsity football jacket is hanging over the edge of the top shelf in my closet. It's been there for like a year, and it brings back bad memories. I took a bad trip once. Last summer. I don't remember much, but I remember waking up with Dean's jacket on. Apparently, I'd been shivering too hard and they wanted to keep me warm. I'm much more careful now. "No," I say. "That's Dean's. I'm not really the football type."

"Dean plays football?" she says slowly, as though she's surprised. "And you don't?"

"Yeah. So does Jake." I walk over to my closet, subtly kicking my boxers to the side as I pass. "I used to play when I was younger, but I stopped back in middle school."

"Why?"

"According to some people, football is a waste of time." My throat tightens. I used to love football. I couldn't wait for high school so that I could try out for the team, but Dad never let it become a priority. "*Why waste your time on sports?*" I recall. "*Throwing footballs around isn't going to get you into Ivy League schools. Stay inside and study instead so that you can actually be successful.*"

Eden is watching me closely. "Who told you that?"

"Just someone." Someone she is never, ever going to know about. "So that's why I wasn't allowed to play."

"Allowed?" She raises an eyebrow.

Crap. I really need to censor what I say sometimes. "I mean, that's why I stopped," I say, reaching up to push Dean's jacket further back onto the shelf. I run my eyes over my clothes and decide that I need a fresh shirt after all the shit that's happened today. I feel gross, so with my back to Eden, I quickly pull off the shirt I'm currently wearing and then swap it out for a new one. "I really have to give Dean his jacket back. He's been bugging me about it for ages," I say over my shoulder.

A few moments of silence pass, and then I hear Eden quietly ask, "What does your tattoo mean?" I spin around to look at her, confused, and she adds, "I'm going to ignore the fact that you clearly got it illegally."

"My tattoo?" I only have one. It's on the back of my left shoulder, and she's right: I *did* get it illegally last year in the basement of some guy Declan knows. "Uh, it says *Guerrero*," I answer, feeling a little awkward. I scratch the back of my head, and before she can ask, I say, "It's Spanish for *fighter*." I still don't know why I chose that. I guess at the time, it was sort of a *fuck you* to Dad. He used to always tell me to fight hard for success. So I decided, in that basement that stank of weed and stale beer, that I was going to do exactly as he asked of me. I was going to fight for my own version of success, which is to not let what he did ruin my life. Though I haven't exactly done a great job of that so far.

Eden is still staring straight at me, and she's genuinely curious, which is sort of nice, I guess. Tiffani once told me the tattoo is stupid, but she doesn't know the meaning of it. "Why Spanish?"

"I'm fluent," I admit. "Both my parents are. My dad taught me when I was a kid." I don't speak it much anymore. It only reminds me of him.

"I don't know any Spanish," Eden says. She bites her lip and then gives me a playful smile. "I speak French. Like the Canadians," she jokes. "*Bonjour.*"

What the fuck? Did that husky voice just become foreign? I didn't know French could sound so good. "*Me frustras,*" I reply in Spanish, running my hand back through my hair. She looks confused, but it's entertaining. "*Buenas noches.* That means 'Goodnight.'" I don't translate the first part for her. I don't tell her she frustrates me.

She seriously does though. She questions me constantly, but she also pays attention to me. One minute she's all shy and embarrassed, and the next she's confident and challenging. She listens, but she also doesn't put up with my bullshit. That's sort of cool to me.

"Oh," she says. The corner of her plump lips curves into a small, sweet smile and as she turns around and walks out of my room, I'm so glad to hear that mesmerizing voice of hers murmur, "*Bonsoir.*" Maybe it means goodnight in French? Whatever it is, it sounds amazing on her tongue.

My gaze remains glued to her until she disappears back into her own room. I'm smiling as I stand rooted to the spot, staring out into the empty hall. Something doesn't quite feel right. I don't know what it is, and I stand in silence for a few minutes, racking my brain and trying to figure out why I'm feeling so off. It's not until I catch a glimpse of my reflection in the mirror that it hits me.

My smile isn't the same as it usually is. It's not a smirk, it's not challenging, it's not cocky. My eyes aren't as narrowed or as fierce. My heart sinks in my chest when I realize that for the past few minutes, I wasn't acting. For the first time in a long time, I forgot to be Tyler Bruce.

I was just me, and that is the biggest mistake I could ever possibly make.

21

I LOVE IT WHEN Dad is out of town, because when he's out of town, he isn't here, and when he isn't here, he can't hurt me. He's been in Seattle for the past two days, and I don't think he's coming home until tomorrow night. I wish he would stay away longer, but I'm hoping that by the time he gets back tomorrow, he won't be so stressed. I'm hoping he'll come home happy and play basketball with us out on the driveway again like he did a couple weeks ago. That would be real nice. It's Friday afternoon, and I've been allowed to skip last period only because I have an appointment with Dr. Coleman. We're sitting in his waiting room now, Mom and me, and I'm staring at the clock on the wall in front of me, watching it tick on. It's been a while now since I got the cast on my wrist removed, and now Dr. Coleman wants to follow up and check how the fracture is healing. I've been constantly forgetting to do the exercises he asked me to, so in a last-ditch effort to make a difference, I quickly hold up my left arm and begin rotating my wrist in a full circle. It still hurts sometimes. "Isn't it too late to start doing that?" Mom asks teasingly as she glances at me out of the corner of her eye. She's been on her phone for the past five minutes, rapidly typing, probably because she's been working from home the past couple days and needs to stay in touch with the office. She's even taken the afternoon off to take me here, and she's promised we'll stop for ice cream down at the promenade afterward.

"It might still help," I tell her with a shrug, but then quickly give up and drop my wrist back down onto my lap. I look at the clock again.

"Tyler?" I hear a voice say, and when I look over, Dr. Coleman is smiling straight at me from the door of the waiting room. He's sort of old, with deep wrinkles and graying hair and a pudgy stomach, but he's always super nice. It's not enough to put me at ease though. "Come on in!"

Mom tosses her phone into her purse and gets to her feet. I try not to wince as she places her hand on my shoulder and guides me over to Dr. Coleman as he leads us down the hallway to his office. Dr. Coleman is a childhood friend of Grampa's, and he's been our family doctor since forever. Mom asks him how he's doing, but I don't listen for the answer, because now I'm nervous. I get anxious every time I have to see him. Despite the high temperatures outside today, I'm wearing several layers of clothes, including a hoodie. I don't want him to notice the bruises, and I make it difficult.

"So, how's that wrist doing?" Dr. Coleman asks once we've all sat down and are comfortable inside his office. He flashes me a warm smile and interlocks his hands in his lap as he watches me through the thick lenses of his glasses, waiting for a reply.

"It still feels sort of stiff sometimes," I admit, glancing down at my hands. I just want to get this over and done with as quickly as possible.

"Normally, it'd be fully healed by now given how small the fracture was, but it's taking longer due to how weak the bone is after breaking it the first time," he explains with a frown, then edges forward in his seat and reaches out his hand. "Let's take a look."

I roll the sleeve of my hoodie back up to my elbow and hold out my wrist to him. I've done this all over before, earlier this year when Dad fractured my wrist in the exact same place when he grabbed me too hard, so I know the routine. Dr. Coleman bends my hand in different angles. Rolls it. Prods my skin deeply with his thumb.

"Just stiffness?" he asks once he sits back again, angling himself toward his computer.

"Yeah," I say. Quickly, I pull my sleeve back down.

Dr. Coleman begins typing and over his shoulder he says, "It's feeling pretty good to me. Give it a couple more weeks, and if it's still feeling tight, come and see me again." He stops typing and swivels back around in his chair to face me, moving his glasses an inch down the bridge of his nose. "I still don't understand how you were unfortunate enough to break that wrist *twice* in the same year. Some odds those are, Tyler. When you turn eighteen, make sure you try out the lottery!" He laughs and gives me a wink.

"He can be so clumsy," Mom says. Even without looking at her, I can sense she's rolling her eyes. "We can't keep him on his feet half the time!"

"Must run in the family. Old Pete was always tripping out on the field when we were young!" he says. We get to our feet, and he exchanges a smile and shakes hands with Mom. I'm pretty sure Grampa must have been genuinely clumsy, whereas I'm not. "Make sure he does those exercises."

"Of course," Mom says, placing her hand back on my shoulder again when I stand up.

I feel sick now. Even Dr. Coleman doesn't know what's really going on. But I guess I make it difficult for anyone to figure out. Half of me desperately wishes someone would, but the other half of me knows better.

"Tyler," Dr. Coleman says as we're heading for the door. Mom and I pause to look back at him, and he shakes his head with a small laugh. "No more running down the stairs too fast, okay? I don't want to see you breaking that wrist for a third time!"

If only I could promise him that.

22

PRESENT DAY

AS THE WEEK PROGRESSES I make every best attempt I can at emphasizing who Tyler Bruce is whenever Eden is around. I fucked up big time on Tuesday night, and I need to salvage that. She can't figure out that I'm not *actually* as bad as everyone thinks I am. So, I've put my skills to the test and have been delivering the ultimate performance all week. I've been ignoring her mostly, only glaring at her, but I sometimes mutter cocky remarks or demand that she gets out of my way. And, so far, it's working.

Even now, I can hear her. Our rooms are right next door to one another and for the past five minutes, I've been subjected to hearing her talk on the phone. It's not clear enough to make out *exactly* what she's saying, but it's clear enough to hear her voice. That's why, as I'm lying across my bed flicking through text messages, I don't have my TV on or any music playing. I already have background noise to listen to.

You better get over here pretty soon if you wanna have a shot at making any $$$

Declan has texted. His party is tonight. I'm supposed to be going, but I haven't found the energy to get ready yet. It's still early though.

It's the perfect night for this party to be taking place. Once a month, Tiffani stays at her dad's place, which means that one weekend each month I have to survive without her. But for once, I'm glad she's at her dad's tonight. If she was here and knew I was heading out to a party thrown by Declan Portwood, there'd be no way in hell I'd ever get anywhere near it.

But I guess I'm sort of nervous about it. Declan says it's the perfect opportunity to get me started, to meet the right kind of people, but I'm starting to have doubts. I haven't thought this through too much, and now I'm getting wrapped up in it way too fast. I'm not sure if I really want to go down this path.

I hear Eden's voice again. All husky and low. I wonder what *she's* doing tonight. Probably nothing. Maybe she'd like a party. There are two benefits to inviting her: One, she gets to see me as Tyler Bruce, and that should distract her from the fact I was actually *nice* to her the other night. And two, I won't have to go to this party alone.

I roll out of bed and glance at myself in my mirror. I narrow my eyes, testing out their intensity, and I tighten my jaw a little. Even tame my hair. Then, I clear my throat and walk out into the hall. I pause outside of her bedroom door for a second, listening in closely, and I hear her tell someone not to miss her too much.

I push open the door without much consideration over whether or not she's still on the phone and I take a single step into the room. "Who were you talking to?"

Luckily, the call seems to be over. Eden's cross-legged on her bed and her gaze flicks up to meet mine. I can literally *see* the irritation in her eyes. "Did I say you could come in?"

"Who were you talking to?" I ask again. I'm trying to sound like as much of an asshole as possible, *but* I may also be slightly curious. "You got a boyfriend back in Portland or some shit?"

Eden stares blankly at me, barely impressed by my interruption. "Were you eavesdropping?"

"My room is right next door. The walls are thin as hell."

"Okay, well, I was talking to my mom," she finally tells me as she stands up. Good. Does that mean there's no boyfriend, then? I don't want to ask, so I just stay silent. Eden looks at the clock. "Shouldn't you be out doing something?"

"That's actually what I gotta talk to you about." Thank God she asked, because I wasn't sure how to bring it up. I close the door—I don't want anyone overhearing—and walk over to her. I keep a safe distance of at least three feet between us and she is watching me closely with those curious, big eyes of hers. "You're not doing anything tonight, right?"

"No," she says. "Everyone's busy."

"Alright, you're coming with me," I tell her. Tyler Bruce doesn't ask. Tyler Bruce demands. She's not getting a choice. "Party down on 11th Street. Don't mention it to your dad." Without giving her the chance to reply, I quickly turn my back on her.

"Tyler," she says as I'm leaving. I reluctantly pause, slowly spinning back around. She's folded her arms across her chest now and has an eyebrow raised. "Who says I want to go to a party with you? Sorry, but you're sort of the last person I want to hang out with."

So it seems she still hates me. Success. "Get ready," I order.

"No."

"Yes," I say, my voice hard. Why does she do this? Why can't she just be like everyone else and actually *do* what I tell her? Why does she

185

have to fight so hard against me? Time to be a jerk. "What else are you gonna do? Sit here all night in your room like a damn loser with no social life?"

Her expression falters and she doesn't look so tough anymore. She glances up at the ceiling and then back down, almost like she's considering it, and then she quietly asks, "What will I wear?"

That's more like it. Thank God I don't have to go to this party alone. "Anything," I say. My voice loses its firmness. "It's not the same kinda party as Austin's. This one's more…chill. You could turn up in a pair of sweats and you wouldn't be out of place." Everyone will be too stoned to care, but I don't even dare mention this. She'll figure that out when we get there.

She definitely picks up on it though, because she looks perplexed. "Chill?"

"Yeah. Are you up for pre-drinks while you're getting ready?" I offer. Did she even drink at Austin's party last weekend? I'm not sure. I wish I'd paid attention. "My stash is running a little low, because Mom's constantly searching my room, so all I've got is beer and some Jack and a little vodka. You know what, I'll surprise you." I smile at her, relieved she's given in, and also relieved she's not telling me no.

I drift back to my own room and immediately drop to my knees, searching under my bed for all of the shit I stash under there. I grab a bottle of beer and then mix up some Coke and some vodka for Eden. I don't make it too strong. I don't wanna kill the girl. My hair is still a mess, so I try once more to tame it a little before I head back through to her room with the drinks.

"I'll probably be ready in twenty minutes," she tells me. She's by her closet, searching through it on the hunt for an outfit.

"No problem. Here," I say. I pass her the drink and she takes it from me, but our fingertips brush, and I don't know why, but it feels weird to me. I don't think she notices though, so I play it cool.

"Vodka and Coke?" she asks. Probably double-checking that I'm not poisoning her with weed killer.

"Yeah. Always a safe bet," I confirm. I crack off the cap of my beer on the edge of her dresser, and then suddenly I realize it may not be what she wanted. "You like it, right? If you want beer, I can get you some—"

"This is fine," she interrupts. Her lips may even be forming a smile. "I like it."

"Okay, good." Shit, what's wrong with me? Why does she make me so awkward? I look up at the ceiling and chug my beer while I try to gather my thoughts, and then when I glance back down, I can't look at her for some reason. "Just, uh, come get me when you're ready."

"Are you guys drinking?" a voice asks.

Both our eyes flash over to Jamie. He has appeared at Eden's bedroom door, staring at us suspiciously. I can see his gaze resting on the drinks that we're holding, so I quickly move my beer behind my back, but I don't know what the point is. He's already seen it, and now I'm about to be blackmailed by my little brother. I know him so damn well.

"No," I lie anyway. My voice has softened. I can never pull off my Tyler Bruce tone whenever I'm with my brothers. "You know we're not twenty-one. Why would we be drinking?"

"I can see it right there," Jamie says. He nods to Eden's drink, but I can already see it in his eyes that there's a plan forming in his mind. "Does Mom know?"

I strain my neck and exhale. "It's only a little. Can you give us some space?"

"Twenty bucks," he demands. He holds out his palm flat to me, expecting cash, and he smiles at me with that devilish but charming grin that he's mastered over the years. He waits patiently.

"I gave you thirty the other day," I remind him. There's no point in arguing though, because I know he will only twist my arm until I give in anyway. I put my beer down on the dresser and then pull out my wallet. "Because you wanted that video game, remember? Don't think I forgot, because I haven't."

"Hmm." Jamie goes quiet, tapping his lips with his index finger. "I'll take ten then."

"Fine, ten," I agree with a laugh. I hate that he can play me so well. I really need to stop doing so much dumb shit that lets him blackmail me so easily. I pass him ten bucks, then push him away. "Now get outta here."

He shoves the bill into his pocket, and as he turns around and runs back down the hall, he snickers, "I would have taken five."

All I can do is laugh while I fetch my beer again and take another swig of it. "Kid treats me like an ATM," I say with a sigh. Then, as I leave too, I tell Eden, "Get ready."

I still haven't texted Declan back, but whatever. I head to my room, finish the beer I'm drinking, then hop into the shower to fix my mess of hair. I take my meds that I forgot to take this morning, and I pull on some jeans and a plain T-shirt. I manage to drink another two beers in the time that it takes Eden to get ready—which is definitely more than twenty minutes—and I begin lining the empty bottles up on my window ledge.

"Okay, I'm ready and my drink is finished, so we can go now," Eden says as she *finally* enters my room. It's much tidier than it was the other night. I've even made my bed.

"It's about damn time," I tell her. Her hair is up and she's wearing some makeup, and thankfully, she's dressed casual. Just jeans and a hoodie, and unlike most people, she actually pulls it off and makes it look cute. I knock over the bottles of beer and then grab my car keys. Declan is gonna kill me if I don't turn up soon, so we need to get going. I'm not drunk, and it's not far.

"What are you doing?' Eden says, her expression horrified. She shakes her head at me. "You've just drank all those beers."

"Jesus," I say. There she goes, doing that thing again, practically scolding me. None of my friends would have even batted an eyelid, except maybe Dean. "Fine, I'll get us a ride. Happy?"

"Yes," she says.

Rolling my eyes, I throw my car keys onto my bed and then pull out my phone. I call Declan, because if there's anyone who'll be able to hook us up with a ride, it's him. He answers on the second ring.

"Where the hell are you?" he snaps at me. "I've got a house full of people looking for hookups and only Kaleb and Liam are here. I need you and Warren to get over here ASAP."

"Yeah, yeah, I'm just coming, Declan," I reassure him. He sounds desperate but also slightly mad at me. He clearly doesn't want to get his hands dirty, and I wonder again about what I'm getting myself into. "Who's driving tonight?"

"Kaleb is," he says, his voice returning to its usual smooth, calm tone. "Or I can ask around, but everyone is pretty...well, not sober." He stifles a chuckle.

"Give me Kaleb," I say I'm surprised he's staying sober tonight. "Can you ask him to get over to my place as fast as he can? Couple doors down, actually." Declan agrees to send Kaleb our way, and I say, "Thanks, man. See you in twenty," before I hang up the call.

"Kaleb?" Eden asks.

"Kaleb's alright," I say. "He's in college, but he still looks like a high school sophomore. He knows how to have a good time though." I laugh, because honestly, I'm realizing that maybe this is a bad idea. I shouldn't be taking Eden to this party, but it's too late now. I don't mention that Kaleb's a dealer, or that he makes a good profit from me.

Keeping my footsteps light, I make my way out into the hall and then downstairs. Eden follows behind me in silence, neither of us saying a word. I figure she's smart enough to know that I shouldn't be sneaking out, so I'm glad she just goes along with it as we discreetly slip out the patio doors into the backyard.

"Shouldn't I have told my dad I was going out?" Eden asks.

She looks panicked for a moment, and she looks back over her shoulder at the house as we're sneaking around it. "I mean, I get that you need to sneak out, but I'm not on lockdown. He's going to kill me when he realizes I've left without telling him."

"Don't get worked up about it," I advise her. "Just drink a lot and in a couple of hours you won't care." Which is probably the worst advice *ever*. Tyler Bruce is an idiot.

We walk down the street, away from our own house—too risky to get picked up there—and then hang around on the sidewalk almost six doors down. It's dark and there's a breeze in the air, but it's still warm outside, and I lean against a tree, watching Eden closely. The more I think about it, the more I realize this is *seriously* a bad idea. I'm testing my luck here. She didn't tell Mom about the drugs last weekend, but I doubt she'll let me off the hook a second time.

"Is it a big party?" she asks, meeting my eyes. She looks anxious now, most likely because I haven't given her much detail on what to expect.

"Not too big," I say, then shrug. I'm feeling nervous now too. She's going to flip out when we get to this party. Honestly, what was I thinking? Sure, I didn't want to head over there alone, but *shit*. Why did I ask Eden, of all people? I can't bring myself to speak to her as we wait, so I kick at the ground and stare at the sky instead.

I'm glad when Kaleb rolls up in his beat-up Chevy, engine spluttering and all. He rolls down his window and leans over his passenger seat to look at us. "Get in, bro!" he says, and I flash him a dubious look. I'm not sure if I trust Declan or not when it comes to Kaleb being sober.

I climb into the passenger seat while Eden clambers into the backseat, and thank God the truck doesn't reek of weed. Only tobacco.

"Who's this?" Kaleb asks, eyeing Eden in his rearview mirror, scrutinizing her. He's not a huge fan of strangers. He clearly doesn't recognize her from last weekend, probably because he was so high at the time. He doesn't know she walked in on us. "My, um…" I begin to say, but then my words get stuck in my throat. The word feels too weird to say, too foreign. She doesn't feel like that word to me. I swallow hard and turn up the music, then finally choke out, "My stepsister."

"Didn't know you had one," he says, then narrows his eyes at Eden even more, staring at her for a moment longer. Then, he finally begins to drive. "So how've you been, dude? Feels like I haven't spoken to you in weeks!"

"I saw you on Tuesday," I tell him, nodding along to the beat of the rap. Eden remains silent in the backseat, and I can't turn around to check on her without it being completely noticeable, so I just stare out of the windshield instead.

"Shit, you're right!" Kaleb says, and then howls with laughter as he smacks his palm to his forehead.

"How's the party anyway?" I ask him. "Thanks for giving us a ride."

"It's alright. Pretty mellow. It's good." He shrugs and takes a sip from a can of Sprite that's in his cup holder. "Good luck for when Warren sees you though."

"He crossed the line," I mutter. Am I supposed to be worried? I don't give a shit about Warren. He shouldn't have said what he did. I'll hit the guy again if he tries anything with me.

"Yeah, a damn thin line," Kaleb snorts.

We roll up to Declan's place across town ten minutes later and of course, it looks pretty dead. The party *does* have to stay under the radar. The cops would have a damn field day if they busted us. That's why no one is hanging around out front. There's no music to be heard. There's only, like, four cars parked outside too, and that's including us. The three of us jump out of the truck and Eden is asking, "Are you sure this is the right house?"

"Yeah." I begin to head for the door. I really don't know what she's going to make of this. "Remember it's a smaller party. Twenty people, max."

I push open the front door and the music descends over us, drilling into my ears. I don't know who the fuck is playing this weird techno shit, but it's awful and someone else needs to take over as DJ. I glance sideways at Eden and she's wrinkling her nose in disgust—the smell of weed in the air is impossible to ignore, and she's not an idiot. She knows what it is. I can hear laughter and voices, and only a couple people are in the hall. I've been to one of Declan's parties before, and I know he keeps all of the alcohol in the spare room down the hall, so that's exactly where I head. Eden follows me, sticking to me like glue while Kaleb dashes off without another word.

As soon as we walk into the room, the very first person I lay eyes on is Declan himself. Although he expected me to be here earlier and sounded pissed on the phone, he greets me with a cunning smile. "Tyler, you made it," he says, moving over to us. He gives Eden a pointed glance. "Who's this?"

"My stepsister," I blurt out without hesitation this time. She really shouldn't be meeting him, but I introduce them anyway. "Eden, this is Declan. She's hanging with me for the night if that's alright with you."

"Woah." Declan's eyes go wide as he shoves a beer can into my hand. He's sober, most likely so that he can keep an eye on everything going on around him to ensure there's no trouble. "Dude, when the hell did ya get a stepsister?"

"Last week, bro," I say as casually as I can. Before he can ask me anything more on this new piece of information, I quickly turn to Eden and flash her a smile. I'm hoping she hasn't realized what kind of party she's at yet. "What do you want?"

"Anything," she says. She scans the table that is overflowing with everything from beer to vodka to rum to fucking absinthe. Who the hell brought *that*? "Actually," she says, "I'll just take another Coke and vodka."

Easy. I fetch a cup and mix up the drink for her, pouring the Coke in first so that she can't tell how much vodka I'm adding in. I make this one much stronger than the one back at the house. She'll need it if she's to survive the night. "I'll show her around," I tell Declan as I pass Eden the drink and guide her back out into the hall, my hand on her shoulder. Quickly, I leave her there and turn back to Declan, grabbing his shirt and pulling him over to the corner. "Can I at least get a bump first before I start helping you out or not?" I hiss into his ear, keeping my voice low. Sure, I smoked last weekend, but I kind of need something stronger tonight. It's been a while.

Declan gives me a nod. "Meet me outside when you've got a second."

I sigh, already imagining the sweet, sweet relief, and I walk back over to Eden, who, of course, has been staring at me the entire time. There's no way she could have heard though, so it's cool. I guide her toward the living room, ignoring the couple of people who say my name, and then I point my can of beer toward the group of people who are hanging out on the couches. "Alright, you see these people?" They're all stoned as fuck, headbanging to the music or staring at the TV screen. I don't really recognize anyone. A lot of the people here are in college.

"Yeah?" Eden's eyebrows pinch together as she looks up at me, expecting more of an explanation. "They look bored."

"They're far from bored," I mumble with a laugh that I just can't fight. God, she still isn't realizing where she is. Out of the corner of my eye, I notice a cat trembling under the hall table with wide, cautious eyes. "Hey, check out this guy," I tell Eden, pointing my beer at it too. It looks terrified, and it's probably gone deaf from all this shit music. "Aw, man." I place my beer on the table and then crouch down to the floor, gently scooping the animal up into my arms. It fidgets a little, and I ruffle its fur as I stand back up. "Why not date this little guy? It's probably got bigger balls than Jake."

"Put it down," Eden orders. She doesn't look impressed. She better not tell me she hates animals, because that…that would be unforgivable.

The cat settles down and begins crawling over my chest, up my arms, and over my shoulders. "What can I say?" My lips form a smug smile as I scratch behind its ears, and I smolder my eyes at Eden from over the top of its head. "I'm a pussy magnet."

Eden scrunches her face up at me in mock disgust and rolls her eyes as she turns away. I burst into laughter and set the cat back down on the ground, and as it catapults off down the hall, she remarks, "Look, even that cat has had enough of your bullshit."

There's Eden again. I grab my beer and take a sip, noticing the clock on the wall. I shouldn't be in here laughing with Eden. I should be outside with Declan. "Go talk to some people," I say, and there's a demanding edge to my voice. I'm not smiling anymore. "I'm heading out back for a while."

The smirk playing at Eden's lips immediately disappears. "Are you kidding me?"

"Huh?" I sip at my beer again as I look straight into her eyes, wondering why she's staring at me with such outrage and disbelief all of a sudden. What the hell did I do?

"Don't act stupid," she growls at me under her breath. It's the first time I've ever heard her sound so aggressive, so threatening, and she steps right up against me and moves her mouth to my ear. She nearly spills her drink down my shirt. "I didn't come with you to this bullshit party so that you could just leave me by myself while you stand around in the backyard smoking joints and making pretty little coke lines to snort," she hisses.

"It's none of your business," I snap back at her. How dare she talk to me like that? No one has ever been so upfront and straightforward with me in such a confrontational tone before. Especially a damn stranger. I step back from her, creating distance. "Go make some friends and leave me to do whatever the hell I want."

I'm not listening to this shit, so I turn around and storm down the hall toward the door to the backyard. Now I need that hit even more. I can feel Eden rushing after me, and she throws her body in between the door and me, physically blocking it. Is she serious? She's really doing this right now? *Eden, please don't do this*, I'm mentally begging her. She didn't like it when she saw me angry the other day, so she definitely does not want to see me furious. She is going to make me uncontrollable if she doesn't quit this.

"You're not going out there," she states, her breathing heavy, her eyes frantically searching my expression. "It's so stupid."

I slam my can of beer into the wall behind her and it splits open, crushing beneath my hand as the beer spills to the floor. My eyes are fierce as I lock them on hers. She has no right to challenge me. She doesn't even *know* me. "Get out of my fucking way," I hiss slowly, spitting my words.

"No!"

I grasp her wrist, pulling her toward me, eradicating the few inches that separated us. She needs to stop. I am glaring down at her with the most threatening of looks that I can possibly pull off, but she only stares straight back at me. "Eden," I whisper, fighting hard to keep my voice calm. "Don't." *Please, Eden. Please don't do this. Please don't anger me.*

"No." She yanks her wrist free, and despite the flash of fear in her hazel eyes, she asks, "Why do you do it?" Her voice is laced with frustration, and I can hear the desperation behind each word.

"Because I need to, okay?" I yell at her. It's the only answer I can give, and I quickly glance around us to make sure there's no one listening. With the music so loud, our yelling is almost unnoticeable.

"You don't *need* to," she says, lowering her voice. Her eyes soften with disappointment. "You *want* to."

She's never, ever going to fucking get it. No one is ever going to understand me. She thinks I *want* to throw my life away like this? She thinks I *enjoy* having to resort to this shit? I don't have a choice! It's the only way I can keep my mind in check, to feel some damn peace in my life for *once*. I take a deep breath and exhale, running a hand through my hair. "You don't get it," I whisper. I feel so weak all of a sudden that I can't even speak. I feel so deflated, like all of my energy has just evaporated. For the first time, I think Eden may have just defeated me.

Numbly, I nudge her out of the way, staring into space as I swing open the door to the backyard. I slam it shut after me, leaving Eden behind inside, and I throw my head back to the sky, my eyes squeezed shut, and I let out this weird, crazed sort of guttural groan.

When I tilt my head back down and open my eyes, I realize I'm not alone. Declan's shoving a wad of cash into his pocket as he furrows his eyebrows at me. Liam's slouched back in a deck chair, his feet up on the patio table with a joint between his lips, his bloodshot eyes fixated on me.

"What the fuck?" Kaleb says, cracking up with laughter.

"Hey, man," I hear someone say from my left, and as I turn around, I catch sight of Warren approaching. In the space of a single second, I see him smirk, right before he slams his fist into the corner of my jaw.

23

FIVE YEARS EARLIER

MOM LETS US STAY up late. It's Saturday and Dad isn't home yet, so she's letting us stay up and wait for him. Jamie and Chase are in my room, the lights off, our eyes sore from the glare of my TV. We're playing *Madden NFL* on the PlayStation 2 that we got for Christmas last year to share, though I like to think that it's mostly mine, because Chase barely remembers that it exists and Jamie sucks at every game he tries to play. I haven't lost once tonight, and we've been playing for over an hour.

"Is it true that there's a PlayStation 3 coming out?" Jamie asks midgame. I think he's giving up at this point, because I can sense him looking at me rather than at the screen.

"Yeah. In November," I tell him with a shrug. On the screen, my team scores a touchdown. My sixth already within this game alone. We're sprawled out on our stomachs on my bedroom floor, suffering carpet burn on our elbows, and Chase is lying on my bed half asleep.

"Really?" Chase says, growing alert. He sits up, excitement capturing his expression. "Will Santa bring us one?"

Jamie snorts from beside me, rolling his blue eyes, and in the darkness I whack his arm and fire him a threatening glance. "I don't know, Chase," I say, pausing the game and pushing myself up from the floor. "Add it to your list and you'll find out."

At that exact moment, Mom's voice echoes up the stairs as she cheerfully calls out, "Boys! Your dad's home!"

Jamie throws the console controller halfway across my room and springs to his feet while Chase leaps off my bed. The two of them run straight out of my room, wide grins on their faces, and I listen to the sound of their footsteps on the stairs as they race to greet Dad. For a very, very split second, I consider joining them. But then I remember that I don't *want* Dad here, and I definitely don't want to rush downstairs to give him a hug.

I get up, close my bedroom door, then return to my position on the floor and sit down cross-legged in front of the TV again. I end the current game and begin a new single-player one, increasing the volume and focusing my attention solely on the screen. My three days of guaranteed safety are over, and I know Dad hates it when I play video games too much, so I'm taking advantage of the freedom while I can.

Ten minutes pass, and I haven't heard any of the commotion downstairs. I don't want to hear it. I don't want to hear his *voice*. But then my door opens and the sound of it sends a shiver down my spine.

"You know, Tyler, it's considered rude not to come and see your dad after he's been gone for three days," he states, and I don't even pause the game as I glance up from the floor. Dad is standing in the doorway, his hand resting on my door handle, and he is narrowing his eyes down at me. Suddenly, he pushes my door open fully and flicks on the light. "And why the hell are you playing this?" he demands, storming into the room.

My eyes hurt from the sudden brightness, and I squint at Dad as he strides toward me, snatching the controller straight out of my hand. "Mom said we could," I tell him, but there's no point. He doesn't listen to me anyway.

"Have you been playing this the entire time I've been gone?" he questions, shaking the controller in front of me, his free hand already balled into a fist. "You have, haven't you?"

"No, only tonight," I splutter, flinching at the abruptness of his voice. How is it possible that I can make him so angry so quickly? What's wrong with me? I scramble up onto my feet and hold my hands up in surrender. "I swear, Dad. All my homework is done… I've already studied this morning!" Dad throws the controller straight back at me, and it hurls against my shoulder and swipes the edge of my jaw despite my efforts to dodge it. Furious so suddenly, he turns to the TV and reaches around the back of it, yanking out wires. My heart is beating so fast it hurts as the fear begins to rise through me. Dad is so unpredictable when he's angry, so I find myself defensively taking several steps back.

He grabs the PlayStation 2 and tucks it under his arm, wires dangling to the floor, and he fixes me with one of those disapproving glares that I hate so much. It makes me feel guilty, and I really don't know why. I haven't done anything wrong. Or have I? I was only having some fun.

"You don't get to play this anymore," Dad tells me through gritted teeth. There are several feet between us, but I wish there were more. "Now get to bed, Tyler. Right now." He turns around and heads back to the door with the console still in hand, and I don't know where he's taking it or why he's so mad. He glances over his shoulder before he leaves and when he sees that I haven't moved an inch, he almost throws the console at me too. "Don't fucking test me," he growls, nodding over to my bed. "I've had the worst couple of days, and this is the *last* thing I need."

He doesn't need to tell me a third time. I learned the hard way what happens if it comes to that. My eyes feel damp as I quickly turn around and crawl into my bed, pulling my comforter over me. I lie on my back, trembling slightly, and I watch him over the edge of my comforter as he turns back to the door, switching off the light again. "Dad," I whisper. I really don't know what I've done wrong, so I can't help it. I'm crying. "I'm sorry."

I'm sorry that I make him so mad. I'm sorry that I can never be good enough. I'm sorry that I can't make him happy the way Mom does, the way Jamie does, the way Chase does. I'm sorry for letting him down.

Dad pauses in the hall, but he doesn't turn around. His shoulders rise and fall in sync with his breathing, and slowly, he shakes his head. Right before he pulls my door shut behind him, I hear him murmur, "It's not enough."

I squeeze my eyes shut in the dark silence of my room, my lips quivering as I cry even harder.

His apologies are never enough either.

24

I'M SLOUCHED ACROSS THE couch in the living room, staring at a random spot in the ceiling, trying to fight the dizziness I'm feeling. My head feels heavy, my chest feels tight, but I always get this way during a comedown. Chase is sitting cross-legged on the floor as he stares at the TV, glued to his Sunday morning kids' shows, and the volume is low enough to serve as distant background noise. I take a deep breath, close my eyes, hold it, then release. God, I feel sick.

Last night was a mess. I remember Warren flooring me in a single punch—and my jaw still aches enough to prove it—and everything else after that is a blur. I do know I was stoned on more than just weed. That's why I feel like shit this morning. I also remember Dave still being awake when I came home in the middle of the night, not because he was worried about me, but because he was worried about Eden. She hadn't come home.

She *still* isn't home.

I'm getting sort of concerned too, I guess. I'm to blame because I was the fucking idiot who brought her to that party in the first place. And then I stormed outside and left her. In hindsight, that was a bad move.

Eden wouldn't have known anyone. Did she try to walk home? Get lost en route? Is she lying in a ditch somewhere? Shit. If I had her number, I would call her, though I doubt she would answer. Dave's already called like a million times to no avail. and he's been pacing the house all morning. He says he's waiting until noon before he takes action, whatever the hell that means. He'd kill me if he knew it's my fault she's not here.

I press my hands over my face, my eyes still squeezed tightly shut. I haven't had enough sleep. I'm exhausted.

"Tyler," I hear Mom say as she enters the living room, her voice quiet, soft. I drop my hands and open my eyes, glancing up at her. She seems wary as she sits down on the arm of the couch across from me. As she folds her arms across her chest, she gives me a smile, but it's not a happy one. "Just checking in. Has it been a bad week?"

Mom always does this. At least once a week, she'll check up on me in this serious sort of manner, like she's my own personal therapist. She likes to check up on my mental state, and usually I understate everything in order to protect her. If I told her the complete truth, then most weeks she'd have a complete breakdown. How do I tell my mom that I wouldn't care if I died tomorrow? How do I tell her that I hate myself, that my life is all over the place, that I'm not really sure how to make any of it better? I can't. So I just shrug and divert my gaze back to the ceiling. "It's been worse," I say. I would rather lie and keep her happy than tell her the truth and break her heart.

She exhales and keeps quiet for a moment. I can feel her blue eyes studying me. "Are you sure? It's seemed like you've had a pretty bad week to me, Tyler. You've been acting out more than usual. What's going on?" She reaches over and angles my chin toward her, forcing me to meet her eyes again. She looks desperate. Afraid, even, like she doesn't want to hear the answer. "Talk to me."

"I don't know, Mom," I tell her. I do know though, and she does too. I'm like this because of Dad. I wish I was strong enough to move on, to not let it affect me as much as it has, but I think I'm forever going to be this way. I'm always going to be angry, I'm always going to be insecure, I'm always going to be fucked up. I know deep down that I should try harder, I should quit all of these distractions, I should get help. But I just don't know where to begin. The only peace of mind I have is knowing that I'm already at rock bottom and things can't possibly get any worse. Only better, I guess. One day.

Mom glances over at Chase. He's so invested in the TV that he doesn't even notice us talking. Her gaze meets mine again, and she frowns as the corners of her eyes begin to crinkle. "Please don't push me away, Tyler," she begs in a mere whisper. "I'm always going to be on your side. I understand why you act the way you do, but I hate it. There's other ways to deal with this than to rebel against everything. You were such a happy kid…" She stops herself and closes her eyes, pressing a hand to her mouth as she chokes up.

"Yeah, until you-know-who made me his personal punching bag," I mutter as I sit up. Chase is in the room, so I have to watch my words. He can't ever find out. Mom shakes her head, her eyes still closed, my reminder tearing her apart. But it's the truth, and that's what she wants. "Do you expect me to be happy, Mom?" I gently ask her, my tone solemn. "After everything?"

"No," she whispers, opening her eyes to look at me. They are full of so much remorse, so much guilt. "But I just desperately wish you could be."

My chest tightens. I hate that I can't give her that, that I'm letting her down. I lower my head and drop my eyes to the floor. "I'm sorry."

"Don't you dare say sorry, Tyler," she abruptly cuts in, dropping straight down onto her knees so that she can look up at me. She places her hand on my knee, and her eyes are doing that thing again where they flood with an agonizing pain that only we can understand. "You have *nothing* to be sorry for."

"You always say sorry too," I whisper, my voice weak. Mom does that to me. I love that she cares so much, that she's so protective, but I feel the exact same way about her. I hate it when she says sorry for what Dad did, because it was his mistake, not hers. I hate it whenever I see the flash of guilt in her eyes, because I wish she didn't blame herself. She thinks she's a bad mom for not noticing the abuse I was suffering for years, but I fought hard back then to make sure she *didn't* suspect anything.

"That's because *I* do have something to be sorry for," she murmurs, then hangs her head low as she blinks at the floor. "I should have been there for you, Tyler. I should have…I should have noticed. You're my *son.*" Her eyes brim with tears and her lower lip quivers as she whispers, "How didn't I see it? How didn't I see it in your eyes that you were hurting?" But she's not talking to me. No, she's questioning herself, and I wish she wouldn't.

I grasp her hand on my knee. "Stop. Please," I say, hunching forward and looking down at her on the floor in front of me. It breaks me when she gets like this, and my heart is beating a little too fast. It's hypocritical of me to expect her to move on when I can't even move on myself.

"Let me do something," Mom begs, interlocking our hands. She squeezes tightly as though she's afraid to ever let go. "Let me get you help. I'll find you the best therapist in Los Angeles. Please, Tyler, just give it a shot."

"I can't," I say, shaking my head fast. We have this discussion a lot, but my answer always remain the same. "I'm not ready to talk about it yet." I can almost sense Mom's heart sinking in her chest. She has been fighting for me to seek therapy for years now, and I know it *would* be for the best, but I just can't bring myself to open up to anyone yet. I squeeze Mom's hand back. "But I will one day," I add, and her gaze lights up through the tears. "I promise I will. Just not yet."

"Okay, Tyler," she breathes. "I love you, okay?" I nod, and she clasps my face in her hands and kisses the top of my head before reluctantly leaving the room.

I blow out a long breath of air and release the pressure in my chest as I sit back. My gaze rests on the window, staring out onto the street, and that's when I notice Jake's car parked outside. I get to my feet and walk over to the window, peering through the blinds more carefully, and… No. No way.

Eden gets out of the car. She closes the door, turns toward the house, and pulls her hood up. She's still wearing last night's clothes. Has she been with Jake the entire time? What the hell? That asshole.

"Hey! Eden's back!" Chase says, finally looking up from the TV.

"Yeah, I can see that," I mumble, grinding my teeth together. Now she's in trouble with not only Dave, but me too. I *told* her to stay away from Jake. Is she naive? She has to be. That, or she's an idiot, which I've already decided she isn't. As she heads across the lawn, I quickly stride out of the living room, down the hall, and swing open the front door to meet her. She's already standing on the other side of the threshold, mouth a small "o" with surprise, and I reach for her arm and pull her quickly inside.

"Um," Eden says, her voice groggy, like she's half asleep. As I shut the front door again, she takes a step back from me.

"You're kidding," I say as I turn back to face her. Her hair that was up last night is now a tangled, lopsided heap with loose strands sticking out from all over the place. There's still the smudge of mascara under her eyes. Where did she even sleep? *Has* she slept? Or has she been up all night making out with Jake Maxwell in the back of his car? Fuck. I hope not. "Right? You've got to be kidding."

Eden exhales and tugs on the drawstrings of her hoodie, staring at me in silence. "I could say the same to you," she finally says, but it's not the reply I was looking for. I was hoping for some reassurance that she *isn't* under Jake's spell. She shoves her hands into the front pocket of her hoodie and tilts her head to one side. "You took me to a party with all your pothead friends and crackhead losers. Are you insane?"

"Shhh. Keep your voice down," I order, holding up a finger to her. I glance down the hall to the kitchen where our parents are.

"Sorry," Eden says, though she doesn't even bother lowering her voice. She presses her lips together, her gaze challenging. Her stance is defensive and her tone is bitter. I took her to that party and then got into a heated argument with her. Yet again, she saw a flash of my absolute worst side, the side of me that I just can't control. "I forgot your mom has no idea about how pathetic her son is."

I wish she'd stop saying that word. *Pathetic*. I know I am, but hearing her say it is a harsh reminder. It's like she can tell it gets to me, like she knows it hurts to hear. That's why she keeps saying it. Not because it's a fact, but because it's the one thing she can use against me. My own damn weakness. It's almost cruel of her, so I don't feel guilty when I yell out, "Dave! Eden's home." I even throw in a smile for good measure.

Eden parts her lips, her eyes widening. "Seriously?"

"Face the consequences," I say, taunting her. Face the consequences for sneaking around all night with Jake fucking Maxwell.

"Your consequences," she snaps back. She is growing more and more aggravated each second. It's like I make her blood boil. "You forced me to go to that party."

"Yet I remember you agreeing to it."

"I'm surprised that you even remember anything," she mutters. And then, to get back at me, she decides to become condescending. "Was it a sober night for you? I doubt it." She pushes her hood fully down and takes a deep breath as we hear movement from the kitchen.

"Good luck," I tease sarcastically and I laugh, leaning back against the wall and crossing my arms over my chest. This should be good. Entertainment at its finest.

"Where the hell have you been?" Dave explodes as soon as he steps foot in the hall. He comes marching down toward us, but for once, his glare isn't directed at me. No, not this time. It's Eden's turn. "Do you even know the time? It's almost noon. Where have you been all night?" he interrogates, all of his worry releasing itself as anger. His eyes are nearly bulging out of his damn head. "The least you could have done was answer your phone. I've been worried sick, Eden."

"I'm sorry, I—" Eden begins, but then her words seem to get stuck in her throat. What is she supposed to say? What explanation can she offer him? That I dragged her to a party and then abandoned her, only for Mr. Player of the Year to swoop in and rescue her, and that she's been with some guy who's pretty much still a stranger the entire night? As if she's telling her dad that. He'd kill me first, and then Jake, and then her. Fear is flashing across her face as her eyes dart all over the hall, and I realize just how vulnerable she looks. She's usually pretty confident, saying whatever's on her mind, but right now, she looks small and terrified. It's not as entertaining as I'd hoped.

"She was at Meghan's place," I cut in quickly. I'm not throwing her under the bus. Not after what I did to her last night. My eyes meet hers and I fix her with a firm look, one that tells her to keep quiet while I fix this for her, and then switch my attention to Dave. "I already told you that," I lie.

Dave stares at me for a few seconds, perplexed. His eyebrows draw together. "No you didn't."

"I'm, like, pretty sure I told you last night when I got back, because she asked me to let you know," I say, feigning innocence. I even pull it off in my eyes, which is hard for me because I'm *never* innocent. "Remember?"

"No."

"Man, I must have forgotten." I shrug as though I'm deeply sorry, and then look back at Eden once more. "Sorry, Eden. My bad."

Dave is silent as he glances between Eden and me, confused. He's not buying this, but at least I tried. Eden looks stunned that I have. I *do* feel guilty about last night so saving her from getting into trouble over it is seriously the least I could do. She just stares at me, her expression twisting with disbelief.

"Next time, don't leave in the first place without telling me," Dave finally mumbles. Amazing. He actually let me get away with my shitty act of innocence, though he still doesn't sound too pleased about it all. "By the way," he says just as he's about to turn around to leave, "we're going out for a late lunch. All of us. That means you too, Tyler. Dress nicely." He gives me a stern look. I take it I'm not getting a choice in the matter.

"You get off the hook so easily," I comment once Dave heads back into the kitchen. Sure, I helped Eden out with a bullshit cover story, but she *did* still stay out all night without letting her dad know. When I do that, he puts me through hell and back.

"Why did you do that?" Eden asks. She's staring at me, much calmer now than a few minutes ago, and her eyes are bright with curiosity.

"Do what?"

"Lie for me," she clarifies with a small shrug. "I don't get it."

"I owed you one," I say, and then, just to be clear, I quickly add, "For taking you to that party last night. I didn't think it through. Sorry." I'm not one for apologies, so although I'm being blunt and straight to the point, it's the best I can give her. I also mean it.

"Why did you even invite me along in the first place? Did you honestly think I'd want to be around that stuff?" she questions, and her annoyance has returned. It's always such a subtle change in her tone of voice, but I notice it every time. It's when her voice deepens a little more, bringing out its huskiness. I like it when she's *not* annoyed, or angry, or in disbelief. I like it when she just...talks. But we don't often do that.

"I'm sorry," I say again. I *know* it was a bad decision on my part, and I *am* sorry for it, so I hope she knows I'm not just apologizing for the sake of it. I'm mad enough at myself already, because maybe she wouldn't have ended up with Jake if I hadn't taken her out with me. Which reminds me..."So you were with Jake, huh?"

"What does it matter to you if I was?" she shoots back, which confirms it: she *has* been with Jake the entire time. He's got a lot to answer for the next time I see him. "You have your opinion of him, and I have mine. I don't want to talk about it again because it's got nothing to do with you."

She's right; it *doesn't* have anything to do with me, but if she just took a damn second to consider why it gets to me, then she'd realize that maybe I just don't want to see her get hurt. And not just because she's my stepsister who I'm *expected* to look out for, but because I genuinely don't like the thought of Jake messing with her head. She seems too switched on, too wise, to fall for his bullshit. I'd hate to see that. She wouldn't deserve it.

"I need to take a shower," I say, changing the subject. There's no way I'm admitting it out loud that I actually *care*. Because Tyler Bruce doesn't. "We'll talk about this later. After this bullshit meal that we've gotta sit through."

"We'll talk about it later?" Eden echoes. It sounds like she doesn't want to, but if it's the last thing I do, I'm *not* letting Jake play her.

"Yeah." I head for the stairs so that I can make a start on getting ready for this first broken family outing. It's not something I'm particularly looking forward to, but I don't have the energy to put up a fight. As I make my way upstairs, I glance back at Eden one last time. She's staring after me, watching me leave. "And remember what your dad said," I say. "Wear something nice."

I don't know what it is about this girl, but I'm so damn changeable around her. I've never slipped up as much as I have around anyone as much as I have with her. I messed up again last night too. When we were fighting... She wasn't fighting with Tyler Bruce. She was fighting with me. *My* weaknesses. *My* honesty. *My* fear. And even now, in this split second, I'm just being myself.

And the way I can tell? I'm smiling at her.

25

FIVE YEARS EARLIER

I'M NOT HUNGRY ENOUGH to eat. I'm too distracted, so I just numbly move forkfuls of food around on my tray, my eyes set on a random spot on the table and my mind in a complete trance. It's lunch and the cafeteria is wild. It always is. The buzz of chattering, the random shrieks, the echoing laughter. I hate it. I wish everyone would just sit down and shut up.

"Hey," I hear Jake say sharply, right as he throws an eraser across the table at me. I blink and force myself to tune back into my surroundings again, slowly lifting my head to look at Jake. He grins across the table, the fluorescent lights shining against his braces. "Are you in?"

"On what?" I ask. I glance sideways at Dean for backup, but he just rolls his eyes at me and continues chewing a mouthful of food. I think they're used to me zoning out a lot, though it's something I wish I could stop.

"We're gonna try out for the varsity team in high school. All three of us. Deal?" Jake says, and then holds out his fist and bumps it with Dean's. He holds his fist out to me too, and when I only stare blankly back at him, his smile fades and he sighs. "Football, you idiot. Are you in or are you not? Everyone knows that if you want to be cool in high school, you *gotta* be on that varsity team."

"You do know that high school is still two years away, right?" I ask him, furrowing my eyebrows. "And I don't think it actually works like that in real life."

"Sure it does!" Jake says, retracting his fist. Before he can say anything more, our conversation is cut short when Rachael Lawson appears out of nowhere and slides onto the bench alongside him.

"What are you guys talking about?" she asks, resting her elbows on the table. She glances around at the three of us from behind the smudged lenses of her glasses. Sometimes, she and her friend Meghan join us for lunch.

"Rach, why are you so obsessed with me?" Jake teases, smirking at her as he nods down at her arm brushing against his. Jake is such a joker. I wish I was like him sometimes.

"With those braces? Keep dreaming," Rachael fires back, then dramatically shifts a few inches away from him. "Mr. Hayes has asked Meghan and me to show the new girl around, so be nice. Here they come."

"There's a new girl?" Dean says with curiosity, but there's no time to get an answer.

Meghan Nguyen walks over, her dark hair swinging around her shoulders, and behind her, a girl I've never seen around before is following. I didn't know we were getting a new girl either. Meghan sits down on our side of the table next to Dean, and the new girl joins Rachael opposite us.

"Are you gonna introduce yourself?" Jake says, leaning forward to look at her over Rachael.

The new girl gives him a small, confident smile as she tucks her mousy blond hair behind her ears. Her eyes are seriously bright blue, like ice, and she studies all of us one by one, her gaze shifting around the table. "I'm Tiffani. Just moved here. And you guys are?"

"Someone ain't shy," Jake snickers under his breath, covering his mouth with his hand, but we all hear him anyway. Then, he flashes Tiffani a smirk. "You can call me Jake, and I hate to break it to you, but Rachael and Meghan are both already *in looove* with me, so hands off."

"Shut up, you freak," Meghan hisses across the table while Rachael digs her elbow into Jake's ribs. The three of them do break into laughter though. Jake teases them all the time, and it's only ever playful.

"Aren't you nervous?" Dean asks quietly amid the bickering. He cocks his head to one side as he looks at Tiffani suspiciously. No new girl is *ever* that comfortable so quickly. Usually, they don't even speak until at least their second week. "I'm Dean, by the way."

"Why would I be?" Tiffani asks, blinking at him, her over-glossed lips still curved into what seems to be an innocent, gentle smile, but it really isn't. I've learned to read expressions more carefully than other people. Her bright blue eyes flicker over to meet mine, and she pouts at me. "What's up with you, quiet boy? Do you have a name?"

"Tyler," I mumble, dropping my eyes back down to my tray of untouched food. I hate strangers. The more people who know me, the more people who have the potential to figure out that there's something wrong.

"Can I just call you Ty?"

I look up at her, my expression blank. "No."

"Whatever," she says, rolling her eyes and turning her attention away from me as though I'm not worth it. She pulls out her class schedule and looks it over, biting down on her lower lip. "Does anyone have science with Miss Fitzgerald next?"

"Tyler does, I think," Meghan says, and when I glare at her, she only gives me a small shrug.

"The quiet one," Tiffani murmurs. Her eyes lock back on mine again exactly as the bell rings, and the noise in the cafeteria amplifies even more as everyone gets to their feet, including us. "You can walk me to class, Ty," she says, throwing one strap of her bag over her shoulder and flicking her hair. As I walk around the table, she hooks her arm around mine. "Let's go." Over her shoulder she calls, "Catch you guys around!"

I sigh but I don't bother fighting against her. She's new, probably trying too hard to make an impression, and is just latching onto the first group of people she can find. I do, however, mutter, "It's Tyler."

26

"THIS IS NICE, HAVING all of us together," Mom muses. She glances around the table at all of us, a warm smile lighting up her face. It's the first time we've been together as a family of six, rather than a family of five. "We should do this every Sunday."

"Agreed," Dave says. They exchange a glance, and I swear he reaches for her hand under the table.

"Disagree," I add, just for the sake of making things awkward. My smile is beyond sarcastic and I tilt my head down, fold my arms, and stare at my silverware. I don't want to be here, especially with Mom and Dave both emphasizing this whole "family" thing. We're *not* a family. Dave's not my dad. Eden's a stranger.

"How long do we have to sit here for?" I ask soon after we've ordered our food. I'm not participating in the casual conversation that Mom and Dave have got going on, but neither are my brothers or Eden. She keeps quiet next to me, and every time I surreptitiously steal a glance at her, she's twiddling her thumbs in her lap. I stare across the table at Mom and Dave as I loosen my tie. It's hot in here. "I've got better things to do," I state, even though I don't.

Dave fixes me with a threatening look, almost as though he's *daring* me to ruin this momentous occasion, and his hand tightens around the glass of his drink.

"Stop being so moody," Mom says, almost jokingly to begin with, but then her expression quickly grows taut and she sits up a little, meeting my eyes. She looks concerned, the exact same way she did earlier this morning. "Did you take your meds today?"

"Mom," I say with a strain to my voice. Did she seriously just ask me that? Right now? In front of everyone? I steal a quick glance at Eden to see if she's heard, and of course she has. *Now* what is she going to think of me? "I'm gonna go get some air," I mumble, exhaling.

I push myself up from the table and turn away, my pace quickening as I weave my way between tables, my eyes set on the door. It's Sunday afternoon, so of course the place is packed. I tear off my tie as I push my way through a group of people, desperate to get outside. And as soon as I do, I inhale the longest breath of air I possibly can, holding it in my lungs. Then, I release it and lean back against the wall. It's clear blue skies today, and the sun beats down on me as I glance down at my tie in my hand. It reminds me of Dad.

The older I get, the more I see him in my reflection every time I look in the mirror. I'm starting to look more and more like he did when he was in his twenties and I hate it. Every time I see myself in a shirt and tie, it just brings back memories of when Dad would get home from work, pissed off about something, only to then take out his anger on me. Dad was rarely ever happy when he was wearing a shirt and tie.

There's no way I'm sticking around here. I want to go home and tear off this damn shirt and grab a beer, then relax. Mom was right. It *has* been a bad week, and that's why I'm pleased when I shove my hand into my pocket and realize I have Mom's car keys. She hates parallel parking, and so I parked for her when we got here. Nice. I have a getaway vehicle.

Pulling the keys out of my pocket, I head across the parking lot toward the Range Rover. Dave's Lexus is parked next to it, because as we discovered when leaving the house, as a family of six we no longer all fit in one car. I don't feel so guilty about heading off in Mom's now, because at least they still all have a ride home.

I climb into the driver's seat and sling my tie back over my shoulder. I don't start the engine though, because I end up staring through the windshield at the shrubs lining the parking lot.

No, I didn't take my meds today. Did I take them yesterday? I don't even know, but what does it matter? I've been on them for years and I *still* feel like hell, so it's not like they work. I'm constantly feeling like this, always so low and so bummed out, so I'm over it by now.

There's a small knock at the passenger window. I snap out of my thoughts and look over. It's Eden, standing on the other side of the door, staring back at me through the glass. Her dark hair falls over her shoulders in loose waves, and she plays with the ends. Maybe she's nervous, I don't know. But I like that she's come out here. For as much as I figure she hates me, she sure can't stay away. Maybe she actually gives a shit, unlike most of the people in my life. That's the only reason I roll down the window.

"What?"

She anxiously steps back, retreating away slightly and putting more distance between us. Probably because I'm in a crappy mood, which means I can be unpredictable. "Are you coming back inside?" she asks.

"Screw that bullshit," I tell her. "I'm not heading back in there." I turn back to face the shrubs, clenching my jaw. As if I'm going back inside. Not with Mom and Dave trying to turn us into some sort of happy family, and *especially* not after Mom mentioned my meds. It's embarrassing, and it only reminds me that I've got something wrong with me that pills are supposed to fix.

"You're kind of melodramatic, don't you think?" Eden says, and I can hear it in her voice that she's holding back a sigh. "It wasn't that big of a deal. She only asked you a question."

"Are you stupid? For real—are you?" I flash my eyes back over to her. Only a question? It's a big fucking deal to me. "You don't understand shit, goddamn Eden Munro." Sometimes I wish people knew the truth, so that maybe they *would* understand. But at the same exact time, the truth is the very last thing I would ever want people to know. People would never look at me the same.

"There you go again, overreacting about every little thing. I'm trying to understand what the hell is wrong with you, but you treat me like shit every time I talk to you, so forget it," Eden mutters, rolling her eyes. "Now I'm going back inside, because I'm not a self-centered douche bag who throws tantrums when things don't go my way." Without waiting for my reply, she turns around and struts off across the parking lot, her hair swinging. I watch her in the side mirror, and I realize I don't want her to leave.

God, why does she do this? Why do I *like* it when she tells me the truth so brutally? Sighing, I lean across the passenger seat and out of the open window. I softly call out, "Eden!" and pray that she hears me. And she does because she looks back at me over her shoulder. "Come here," I gently order. "Come get in the car and I'll be honest with you, and then we'll go back inside."

It's like it's an offer she can't resist, because her eyes light up for a fraction of a second, and then she turns around and walks back over.

I start the engine just before she pulls open the passenger door and climbs inside. "Okay, what?"

Man, I've got to stop focusing on her damn lips. I grip the steering wheel a little harder as I stare at her, taking in her gaze. I like that I can see the green of my own eyes in hers. A perfect hazel. I don't want her to go back inside. I want to be selfish, to keep her here with me, so that I can watch her lips move as she tells me everything I can't bear to hear.

"Alright, you want honesty?" I ask her. As subtly as I can, I move my free hand to the gearshift. We're sitting in park. But not for much longer. "Okay. I'm being totally honest right now when I tell you that we're getting the hell out of here." I slam the gearshift into drive and step on the accelerator, and Mom's Rover spirals out across the parking lot, wheels spinning until it gains some traction. We're going home, and so I pull straight out of the lot and into the flow of traffic.

"Are you serious?" Eden screams at me, desperately pulling on her seatbelt as though she's terrified I'll drive us straight into the damn Pacific Ocean.

"Not serious," I say. "Just honest."

"Take me back," she orders, pressing her hand to the dashboard. She's facing me now, those hazel eyes piercing straight through me. Clearly, she isn't finding our spontaneous getaway as much of a relief as I am.

"You really want to go back there?" I ask her, my eyes flicking to meet hers. I accidentally swerve a little to one side, but I quickly correct and keep my eyes trained on Eden. "Look me straight in the eye and tell me that you want to go back to that place and eat that gross food and sit with your dad for an hour. Tell me that you honestly want to do that."

"No. I don't," she reluctantly answers, her full, wet lips moving slowly. God, I almost crash the fucking car. "But I know I have to, so go back before they kill us both. Are you even allowed to drive this?"

"Are you even allowed to look like that?" I mutter, mostly under my breath, because it's seriously beginning to frustrate me, but I say it too loud and she hears me.

She grits her teeth and snarls, "Okay, there's no need to insult me."

"It wasn't an insult, Jesus Christ." I slam on the brakes as we hit a set of lights, and I look over at her, throwing my hand into my hair. She's driving me crazy. "We aren't going back. We're going to the house so that I can get a beer and tell you that Jake's playing you, okay?"

"Thank you, Tyler," she drawls after a moment, her words dripping with sarcasm. "Thank you for getting me into even more trouble."

"Last night was on you," I remind her. She has her elbow propped up on the doorframe now, her fingertips massaging her temple. "Sure, I took you out, but it was you who chose not to come home, so don't try and call me out for that one."

"Fine," she says. "But new problem: your mom is going to flip when she sees that her car is gone. How'd you ever get the keys?"

"Chill out, they'll all fit in your dad's car." The lights flash to green, and I slam my foot straight down to the floor, letting the engine growl. "And I still had them from when I was parking. Now stop distracting me, I'm trying to drive."

"Try harder."

Eden doesn't say anything else after that. She's too pissed at me to speak, because she keeps her arms firmly folded across her chest and her body angled toward the door, her mouth a scowl as she watches the passing scenery.

I focus on the road as best I can, but I do keep glancing sideways at her every few minutes to gauge how she's feeling, and when we're nearing home, I decide to give Mom a call. She'll be wondering why Eden and I are taking so long to return.

"Tyler?" Mom's voice echoes across the line. She answers pretty fast, on the third ring. "Are you coming back inside?"

"Hey, so, we left," I bluntly state, my phone pressed to my ear, one hand on the wheel. Better to let her know. "I'm sorry but we couldn't care less about eating together as a *family*. We'll be at the house." And, before she can yell at me or beg me to come back, I quickly hang up and throw my phone into the center console.

Eden flashes me a look of disapproval, rolling her eyes and shaking her head, her jaw clenched. Then, she turns back to the window for the remainder of the drive, which isn't long. We pull up to the house five minutes later and I quickly park.

"Go to my room," I tell Eden as we're walking across the lawn. I search my pockets for my set of house keys, swinging them around my index finger. "I'm gonna grab a drink, and then we're gonna discuss that asshole you're so fixated on."

"I don't want to discuss anything with you," Eden says from behind me as I'm opening the front door. I look back at her, and she's standing several feet away, her eyes narrowed sharply. If she's trying to be threatening, it's not working. She just looks cute.

"Go upstairs and go to my room," I tell her again, turning toward the kitchen. A beer is all I want right now. "I'll be up in two minutes."

I hear the front door close behind me, and then footsteps on the stairs. "Just to clarify," Eden calls after me, "I'm going upstairs to my room, not yours."

"I'll be in your room, then, in two minutes," I yell back from the kitchen, rolling my eyes. I don't think we're ever going to be on the same page, but I can at least hope. I'll start with Jake, because I'm still not happy that she was with him last night. She might think I keep bringing it up just to be an asshole, but I'm seriously not. She needs to be warned, and as her stepbrother, I should be the one to look out for her. Shit, that sounds weird.

I grab a beer from the refrigerator and pop it open, then make my way upstairs to Eden's room. She's awkwardly lingering around by her bed when I walk in, giving me her usual attitude of crossed arms, pouted lips, and a glare to match.

"Okay, where to start," I say. I take a drink of my beer, considering the best way to get the message across to Eden, and then I remember that the truth bluntly delivered is her favorite thing. "Let me simplify it for you: Jake Maxwell is the biggest player of the year."

"Funny. I thought you were," she mutters.

Woah. What? Where the hell did she get that idea? I'm a lot of things, but a player isn't one of them. "No, there's a big difference between Jake and me," I state, shaking my head. "Girls want me; Jake wants girls. You know, I don't purposely go out of my way to find other girls. I just kind of bump into them at parties or whatever, maybe flirt a little, sometimes kiss them if I'm drunk and Tiffani isn't around. That's it," I admit. I take another drink, because now I need it. Eden is listening carefully, her eyes never leaving mine. "Jake, on the other hand, is a player. He leads chicks on for weeks and sometimes even months, sleeps with them, and then never talks to them again. Guy does this with like three girls at a time. I can guarantee you that the second you put out, he'll disappear. He always does. Pulls out either the 'Sorry, I'm not feeling it anymore' or the 'I can't talk to you anymore, because my mom's super strict and says I can't date until college' card."

"Why are you telling me this?" she asks, dropping her hands to her hips.

"Because I am," is the shitty middle school cop-out answer I give her. I'm telling her because I don't want her to get hurt. I'm telling her because maybe I'm selfish, because maybe I don't want her to spend time with Jake, because maybe I want her to focus on me instead. But I can't tell her that.

"That's not a valid reason."

I smile at her. "Neither was my reason for leaving the restaurant." Taking another swig of my beer, I turn around and walk out of the room.

It's later that night that I can't get to sleep. I'm tossing and turning, but all I can hear is Eden's voice. She's been talking to someone for a while on either loudspeaker or video chat, because I can very faintly hear another female voice replying. They've been talking about school, and boys, and college. And it's getting annoying.

I groan and get out of bed, then head out into the hall in the dark and crouch down to grab the internet router from beneath the hall table. I turn it off, throw the router back, and then walk back to my room. Instead of climbing back into bed though, I hover by the wall that separates mine and Eden's rooms. I can't hear her talking now, which leads me to believe it *was* a video chat. Thank God I've cut it off. I listen for a minute to make sure, and then when I'm certain the call has ended, I softly knock on the wall three times. I don't know why. I almost do it impulsively, like I'm *trying* to get her attention.

Several seconds pass while I wait, and then finally a knock returns from the other side of the wall. My face lights up, my features relaxing. Eden's no more than a few inches away from me, only a wall separating us. I knock back to her, four times, louder than the first.

"Can you stop?" Eden demands. Her voice is slightly muffled through the wall, but it doesn't stop me from hearing that threatening edge to her tone. And I fucking love it.

"I turned off the internet," I tell her. "Your conversation was giving me a headache. 'God, Amelia, isn't Chicago just so freakin' awesome? School is my favorite thing in the entire world! It's so great! I love psychology and homework and studying!'" I imitate, straining my voice to make it higher.

"I didn't even say that," Eden mutters, and then there's a thud against the wall as though she's punched it or something. She's probably pretending it's my face.

I stifle a laugh and press my back to the wall, sliding down to the floor. I stretch my legs out in front of me, tilting my head back to the wall and staring up at my ceiling through the darkness of my room. Just to tease her even more, I continuously drum my knuckles against the wall. "I could do this all night. I heard no one gets any sleep in college, so this is good practice for you. I'll turn you into an insomniac in no time."

"Has anyone ever told you how frustrating you are?" Eden asks as her tone begins to soften back into its perfectly deep huskiness.

"Hmm, I don't think anyone ever has," I joke. All I *do* is frustrate people, and Eden is no exception. In fact, I seem to frustrate her more than most. "How am I frustrating? Enlighten me, college girl." I'm only teasing her, and I hope she knows that. I'm not being a jerk. A jerk wouldn't be smiling right now.

"For starters, you disconnected the internet and now you won't stop knocking on my wall," she says.

"Technically, it's our wall." I knock against it again. I'm sort of wishing it wasn't there, that I could be looking at her right now. I want to read her expression.

"Either way, it's extremely annoying. Please stop," she says, but it doesn't hold much of a threat to it. Her words seem demanding, but her voice isn't.

"No can do." I begin tapping my knuckles against the wall again, over and over and over again. I like messing with her.

There's another thud, like she's hurled her fist straight into the plaster, and I burst into laughter. I'm getting to her, and I hate that it suddenly goes silent. She doesn't say anything else. She doesn't knock again. I figure she's given up, so I sigh and lay my head back against the wall again, listening for a while, hoping she'll come back. I was craving silence ten minutes ago, but not now. I close my eyes, still sitting on the floor with my back to the wall, and when I open them again, it's almost 2:00 a.m.

I quietly knock on the wall once, but there's still no reply. I try again when I wake at 4:00 a.m., but there's no reply then either.

I even knock one last time at 7:00 a.m., but when I fall back asleep, I'm left still wishing she'd come back.

27

FIVE YEARS EARLIER

"YOU KNOW, YOU DON'T have to be up here all night," Mom says as she enters my room on Sunday evening. She walks over to my desk and smiles down at me, gently rubbing my shoulder. She doesn't realize that she's rubbing a bruise. "Don't you want to watch the game downstairs? I think the 49ers are losing, but hey, who knows? They might turn it around. At least your dad is praying they will."

"It's okay," I mumble, keeping my head down, my hand never stopping. I'm writing out some notes from the work we covered in geography class over the past week. I have a test coming up soon, and failing it isn't an option. Besides, Dad has asked me to study tonight.

"You're always studying," Mom comments, and even though I'm refusing to look at her, I know that she's frowning. I can hear it in her voice. "Don't get me wrong, I'm definitely not complaining, but maybe you should live a little too."

"I *want* to study," I lie. I write even faster with more pressure, my pen leaving deep grooves in the paper. I wish she would stop rubbing my shoulder. It hurts.

"How did I get so lucky to get such a hard worker like you?" Mom muses with a sigh. I can sense her frown transforming into a smile now. I know her so well. "But seriously, enough for tonight. Either watch the game or help me with the laundry. Your choice." She leans over my shoulder and plucks the pen out of my hand. I was developing a cramp anyway, so I'm grateful.

I twist my neck to look at her for the first time now, and she's resting the laundry basket on her hip with an eyebrow raised as she smirks challengingly back at me. I force a smile onto my lips, even though I don't feel very happy. I feel drained, but I always do. "Okay, Mom. I'll watch the game."

"Good, now get going!" she says with a laugh, nudging me off my chair. Reluctantly, I get up as she drifts around my room, scooping up clothes from my floor, and I make my way downstairs.

I can hear the sound of the game echoing from the living room and with an overwhelming sense of dread, I force myself to man up and enter the room. As I push open the door, I keep my chin up and feign bravery. The 49ers game is playing on the TV, the volume up way too loud. Jamie is on the floor on his stomach, his chin resting on his hands, his eyes wide and fixated on the TV screen. He'll ruin his eyesight if he keeps sitting that close. On the couch, Chase is sitting cross-legged next to Dad, eating a bag of chips. Dad has a beer in his hand, and his eyes flash over to look at me as soon as I walk into the room.

Still, I keep my head held high and my gaze on the TV as I sit down on the opposite couch. I can't sit back and relax though. I'm rattling with nerves and my blood runs cold with fear.

"What are you doing down here?" Dad asks after a few minutes, keeping his voice relatively quiet amid the noise of the game. Slowly, he takes a swig of his beer and narrows his eyes at me over the rim of the bottle.

"Watching the game," I state. I try to keep my voice clear, strong. I look at him for only a split second and then I turn my attention back to the TV. *Don't back down.* For once, *once*, I just want to defend myself. I deserve to watch the game too.

I hear Dad release an aggravated sigh into the air, and then I watch him out of the corner of my eye as he gets up and walks over, sitting down next to me. His knee bumps against mine, and he angles his jaw toward me, hissing, "You're supposed to be studying."

"I already did," I tell him. I don't like him being so close. I can feel his breath on my face, and it's a mental battle with myself to stay rooted in position. If I move, I'm weak. If I back down, I'm weak. If I let him tell me what to do, I'm *weak*. "How come they get to watch the game and I don't?" I nod to both Jamie and Chase, who are still glued to the TV. We are keeping our voices low now, so they can't possibly hear us.

"Because they do," Dad says. He nudges me with his elbow. "Get back upstairs."

"No. I'm watching the game with you. Mom told me to," I bite back, and the adrenaline floods straight through me, sending a shiver surging down my spine. I've never spoken back to Dad before, not like this, not with determination. It's almost satisfying, but at the same time, it's terrifying.

Quickly, my courage changes to fear when Dad grinds his teeth together and grabs a fistful of my shirt with his free hand. Rising to his feet, he yanks me with him and shoves me hard toward the door. I glance back at Jamie and Chase, and they're so invested in the game that they haven't even noticed Dad throwing me across the room despite it happening right in front of them. Dad is glaring at me, daring me to stay here and challenge him further as he sits back down next to Chase. He takes another sip of his beer, and I finally give up and walk out of the room.

In complete and utter defeat, I storm back upstairs and into my room. Luckily, Mom isn't here anymore to ask why I've returned, so I shut my door behind me and slump down onto the floor, leaning back against my wall. Why can't he just let me watch the game? I've already done my work. Don't I deserve a break now?

I reach for the closest thing to me, my school backpack, and I throw it across my room. It hits the opposite wall with a soft thud, but it's not satisfying enough for me, so I even kick over my chair. But then I feel guilty, so I quickly pick it back up again.

"Tyler," Dad says, and I flinch at the sound of his voice and his sudden appearance at my door. I should have known I wouldn't get away with talking back to him like that, because he's followed me up here, his beer still in his hand. He walks into my room and slowly clicks my door shut behind him, and that's when it's confirmed: I've made it another bad night.

I stand frozen in the center of my room and already I'm trying to focus on something else, trying to numb my mind so that the next few minutes can be a complete blank to me. My stomach is twisting as Dad walks toward me, and just as I'm about to squeeze my eyes shut, he brushes straight past me and sits down on the chair at my desk instead. I peel open my eyes again and watch him carefully as he sets his near-empty bottle of beer down on my desk and exhales, hanging his head low.

"I'm sorry, Tyler," he says, but despite the softness to his voice and the guilt in his green eyes, I don't believe him. He always feels guilty, and I believe *that*, but I don't believe his apologies. He looks up at me from beneath his thick eyelashes. "Look, I wasn't going to tell you this yet, because I've been keeping it a surprise, but I've got us tickets for the game against the Chargers next month," he tells me quietly with the very small trace of a smile. It's apologetic. "We're heading up to San Francisco, just you and me, buddy. You know Hugh takes Dean up there to games all the time, right? We're joining them. How's that sound?" His smile widens a little, and the corners of his eyes begin to crinkle. This is Dad, really. This is him deep down. This is the dad I used to love so much.

"Really?" I ask, my eyes widening. Dad's never taken me to a football game before, but he knows I've always wanted to go. "We're going to a game?"

"I thought you'd like that," Dad says, and for once, he looks almost sheepish. He locks his gaze on his beer while he traces its rim with his thumb. He goes quiet for a few seconds as he runs his eyes over the notes that are still lying on the desk, then he frowns. "I *am* sorry, Tyler," he apologizes again, glancing back over to me. "You've worked hard enough tonight, so come on. Let's head back downstairs. We've got a game to watch." He smiles, wide and pure, just like he always used to.

28

MY NECK IS STIFF in the morning, so I roll it until it cracks as I'm walking downstairs. Not only did I sleep on the floor, I also slept upright. *Upright.* I'm suffering for it now, but I'm headed to the gym with Dean so I'm hoping to loosen up the stiffness with a workout. He's running late, so I make my way down into the kitchen to grab some water, ignoring Dave as I pass him in the hall, and then I see Eden slamming the dishwasher shut. "Morning," I say as I approach her.

She straightens up and turns around, wrinkling her nose at me, wearing her usual expression of repulsion. "Ugh."

"You're supposed to say good morning back," I say, purposely brushing my shoulder against hers and nudging her out of my way as I walk over to the refrigerator. I pull open the door and stick my head inside.

"You kept me up all night," Eden states.

I steal a glance back at her. I'm not sure what she's talking about. "Huh?"

"The knocking." She squints a little, her eyes locked on mine.

Oh, that. She heard it? Why didn't she knock back? "I wasn't knocking," I lie, letting out a laugh. "Didn't your dad tell you the house is haunted? Demons everywhere."

"Oh, shut up," she says, but I hear her almost laugh too. "Couldn't you get to sleep or something?"

"Not exactly," I say, grabbing a bottle of water and spinning back around. I push the door shut behind me and take a step forward, folding my arms and raising an eyebrow at her. "I was hoping you'd wake up and knock back."

"Sorry. I wasn't in the mood for communicating with you through the wall at 4:00 a.m.," she deadpans. I can see her gaze traveling all over my body, studying me.

"Ouch," I say, and I keep my eyes focused on her face until she glances up again. Then, more because I'm curious rather than just trying to be playful, I ask, "What about tonight?"

Her eyes slowly lower to my chest. "What?"

"Tonight," I repeat. My eyebrow arches even higher, my head tilted to one side. "Will you knock back?"

"No, Tyler," she says slowly, her eyes flashing back to mine, "I don't want to knock back and forth. It's just weird."

"Damn." I glance down at my watch to check the time, but just as I'm about to sigh at Dean *still* not being here, I hear him in the hall, greeting Mom.

He enters the kitchen a few seconds later, spinning his car keys around his index finger. "Ready?"

"Dude, you're twenty minutes late," I say, setting my eyes on him. Our gym always gets super packed after ten. And it's now after ten.

"My bad," Dean apologizes. "I had to stop for gas."

When I steal a glance at Eden, I realize I've been doing it again. Slipping up. But now that Dean's here, I can't afford to do that. That's why I glare at her and mutter to Dean, "You left me to hang with this fucking loser. Let's just bail already." I feel like such an asshole, but Tyler Bruce *is* an asshole. Tyler Bruce *is* a jerk. Neither Eden nor Dean is impressed though. They both stare at me in silence, Eden glaring while Dean gives me a more scolding shake of his head. "Chill, guys," I say quickly. "Just a little sibling rivalry, right, Eden?" The word slips off the end of my tongue, but it doesn't taste right. *Sibling.*

"We're not siblings," Eden says.

"And thank God for that," I shoot back. I'm glad she agrees, because honestly, I don't know if it's just me who's finding it impossible to think of her in that way. I can't look at her the same way I look at Jamie and Chase. It's different. She's just…she's just a girl to me. And a pretty cool one.

She exhales and walks away, slipping outside into the backyard through the patio doors until she's out of sight.

"Dude," Dean says. When I turn to look at him, he's shaking his head slowly at me as he leans back against the countertop. "Why did you talk to her like that?"

"I talk to everyone like that," I say, my tone defensive. I unscrew the cap of my water and take a sip, not quite meeting his eyes. I know I shouldn't have said what I just did, but Tyler Bruce is ruthless.

"Yeah, but…c'mon." Dean sighs. After Eden, he probably comes in as a close second on the list of people who seem to actually call me out on all my shit. There have been a lot of times when he's sat me down and asked if I was alright. I've always lied and said, yeah, of course I'm alright, I'm Tyler Bruce, the guy with the hot girlfriend and the nice car. "She's cool, you know."

"And how would *you* know?" I ask, my tone aggressive. I don't mean to be a jerk to Dean, but I can't help it. How does he know Eden's cool?

He doesn't even know her. Neither do I, really, but I've at least spent time with her.

"I took her home last weekend. After *you* were a dick to her at Austin's party," Dean says. He shoves his hands into the front pocket of his hoodie. "And we hung out on Saturday night at the La Breve Vita concert. Again, after *you* took her to Declan's place. I mean, seriously? Jake had to rescue her."

"Yeah, I already figured that," I mutter. I didn't know Eden had gone to some concert with Jake and Dean, but I do know she eventually ended up with Jake the entire night. "He brought her home in the morning."

Dean's eyes widen. "Woah. He did?" He looks away, blinking at the patio doors for a few seconds. "Damn, I knew she left with him after the show, but I…I didn't know she'd stayed the night." His voice goes quiet. "Seems like Jake's already got her in his clutches then. Whatever. Let's just go."

My heart is beating a little too fast, my gaze darting around, never quite focusing for too long on one spot. I keep shifting uncomfortably in my seat, anxiously running my hands around my steering wheel. I have over one hundred grams of weed in my glove compartment.

Why the fuck did some chick want to meet here, at the damn pier of all places? It's pretty packed for a Wednesday afternoon, and I'm parked in the main lot as people stream on by. I'm waiting for someone, but the longer I sit here, the more and more suspicious I feel I look. I've been helping Declan out the past couple days, but I've never felt as nervous as I have now. Probably because all of the other hookups I've done haven't been at the city's busiest fucking hotspot.

My phone buzzes on my lap and I flinch. I expect it to be Stacey, the girl I'm supposed to be meeting, but no, it's Tiffani. She's texted me a picture of her nails, freshly manicured and painted a glossy blue. Probably to match her eyes or some shit. I don't know.

Just got out of the salon. What do you think???

They're sharp and she tears half my skin off when she runs them down my back, so no, I don't like them. But I'd be asking for an argument if I told her that, so instead, I simply text back:

Looks nice. Good day with the girls?

It's much better to just stay on her good side.

Yeah, we've planned a party for Meghan's birthday. We're having it at Rachael's place on Saturday, so keep it free.

She replies. Just as I'm about to begin typing a message back to her, another text comes through and she adds:

Don't mention it to Declan Portwood or any of that crew. They're losers and we don't want that shit at Rachael's house.

I chew on my lower lip. If only she knew I was one of those losers, out here working for Declan right now as we speak. I promised her I wouldn't get involved, but I have, and so now I have to be extremely careful. If she finds out…I don't even want to consider how she'd react. I text back:

No problem

Even throw in a smiley face.

"Hey," someone says through my open passenger window. I glance over and there's a girl ducking her head into my car, her hair falling over her face. My heart beats even faster. "Tyler, right?" Her mouth curves into a small smile, and as discreetly as possible, she opens her closed fist and fifteen bucks falls onto my passenger seat. So, this is Stacey.

"Reach down," I murmur, but my voice is so dry. There are people milling around us. We're surrounded.

Stacey leans further into my car, and I can see her eyes searching the vehicle, and then after what feels like the most agonizing wait ever, she finally spots the gram of weed in a tiny plastic baggie in the storage compartment of the passenger door. She swoops her hand down and grabs it, then shoves it into the front pocket of her jeans. "Thanks," she says. "Catch you around." And just like that, she turns and walks off, casually blending into the crowd on the pier's boardwalk.

My shoulders sink with relief, and I let out a long breath of air. My heart is still rocketing back and forth against my ribcage, so I stay put for a while, breathing deeply until I feel it begin to settle. How does Kaleb do this every day? I've been doing it for three, and already I'm paranoid as fuck.

Suddenly, there's a knock on my window, right by my ear. I jump straight out of my damn skin and then quickly fire my eyes up, half expecting it to be Stacey returning for more, but it's even worse than a college stoner. It's a cop.

Hands on his hips, sunglasses over his eyes, name badge shining in the sunlight, he stares straight down at me through the glass. *He totally saw. He totally fucking caught me. He knows what's up.*

237

My heart rate is erratic again, thumping all over the place as my breath gets caught in my throat. My stomach twists as I roll down the window, and I just stare blankly up at the officer, praying he can't sense my fear.

"Nice car," he says with a couple nods of approval. "What year is it?"

What? I furrow my eyebrows, silent for a second while I figure out if he's kidding or not, and then I force myself to swallow hard and force an answer out. "Uh. '07." Is he seriously asking me about my car and not the quarter pound of weed that's in my glove compartment?

"Nice," he repeats, then takes a step back and cocks his head to one side as he checks out my rims. I sit in disbelief, my heart still pounding. Then, he steps closer again and places his hands on my door, leaning down to look at me. "You seem familiar," he says. He pushes his sunglasses up into his receding hairline, and it's enough for my heart to finally stop. I recognize him, and it doesn't take me more than a couple of seconds to piece it together once I read his badge. Officer Gonzalez. He's dealt with me before, back when I was younger. Years ago. More than once. He was there the night that Dad… The night that it all ended.

"Uh, I don't think so," I splutter quickly, glancing down at my steering wheel. I can't meet his eyes now. I don't want him to remember who I am. I don't want him to remember *how* he knows me.

"No, really," Officer Gonzalez insists. He leans even closer toward me, like he's trying to analyze my features. "Ella Grayson's son, right?"

I look up at him. He really still recognizes me? "It's not Grayson anymore," I mumble. There's no point in denying it. He's already figured it out. "But yeah, that's me. It's Tyler, by the way."

"That's it!" he says as his features ease with relief, but then he quickly straightens up and silently watches me for a few seconds. His expression grows solemn and wrinkles form on his forehead as he squints his eyes at me. Pity. That's what's in them. Fucking *pity*. "How are you doing anyway? Good?" he asks quietly.

"Yep, fine," I mutter stiffly, turning my eyes back to my steering wheel. Uncomfortable, I pick at the ripped knee of my jeans.

"I'm glad to hear that," he says, but I don't even look at him, let alone reply. I just continue to keep my eyes fixated on my steering wheel, my pulse racing. "Take care, Tyler," Gonzalez adds, and he pats his hand against my car door before he turns around and walks away.

I finally lift my head a little, watching him from beneath my eyelashes as he strolls over to the boardwalk, patrolling the pier. I always liked Officer Gonzalez. He was always nice, and he still is. I'm grateful that he didn't ask too many questions. I don't like questions, and I especially hate being asked if I'm okay, because I'm not.

29

FIVE YEARS EARLIER

DAD IS MAD AGAIN.

I don't know what I've done wrong, but what I do know is that it's always my fault. He doesn't get mad at Jamie. He doesn't get mad at Chase. He doesn't get mad at Mom. That means there's nothing wrong with Dad; there's something wrong with *me*. I was the kid he didn't plan for. The kid he changed his life for. The kid he puts too much pressure on himself for. He has become this monster because of me.

It's one of the worst nights. I'm already numb, already somewhere else, already praying it will end soon. Mom's out with her friends tonight. They get together for cocktails once a month. I can see her face through the darkness now, laughing. I like Mom's smile. It's bright and contagious. I wish she was here right now; I wish she could help me, but I also want her to keep that smile.

I think something happened at Dad's work again. I don't know what, exactly. But I was studying like he would have wanted me to do. I was finishing up my homework while he worked downstairs at the kitchen table, frantically flipping through papers and running his hands back through his hair. I should have had the homework done before I came downstairs for a drink. But I didn't. I only had one question left. It would have only taken me a minute.

He's yelling, he's cursing in both English and in Spanish. His green eyes are fierce and terrifying, so I close mine. I weigh nothing to him. I'm thrown across the kitchen, taking down one of the chairs with me, landing in a heap. I've landed on my wrist. A brief, sharp pain surges up my arm. But it's okay. It's not broken. The pain isn't bad enough for that.

I'm grabbed from the floor, my body is bruised, and I am aching. His knuckles are rock hard. I can feel them as they smash into the corner of my jaw. He yells something at me, but I don't register his words. I'm wincing in agony under his tightening hold on me. He shoves me away again. My forehead smacks against the corner of the kitchen table on my way down to the floor. I can feel the warm dampness of blood on my skin, trickling from the fresh cut. I reach up and touch it with my fingertips. I still can't open my eyes. I'm waiting for his firm hands to grab me again, for his harsh voice to scream at me.

But the only thing I hear is the sound of glass shattering. There's some more cursing. A groan. A deep breath. Then, footsteps that for once *don't* grow louder. They fade away into the hall, leaving behind the deafening slam of the kitchen door.

My breathing is out of sync, fast and ragged, and I slowly peel open my damp, wet eyes. The kitchen is a mess. Dad's business papers are scattered all over the floor, some torn. Three chairs are knocked over onto their sides. There are shards of glass lying just in front of me.

I retreat from the glass, crawling as far away as I can until I'm pressed against the corner of the room. I hug my knees to my chest, my wrist throbbing, my forehead stinging, my bruises deepening. I'm shaking uncontrollably, and as I bury my face into my knees, I break down in tears.

30

I'M RELIEVED WHEN SATURDAY rolls around. I've been a complete nervous wreck the entire week, and I'm refusing to help Declan out today. I need a break from it, to just take some time to clear my head and wonder what the fuck I'm actually doing. It's even better that Tiffani doesn't want to hang out today. Apparently, she's waiting for Rachael to call her over to her house at any moment to help set up for the party tonight. I'm not exactly in the mood for a party, but at least it's a small one. Or at least Rachael is hoping it is.

It's just after one and I'm sitting at the kitchen table on my own in a pair of sweatpants, slowly eating my way through the avocado, lettuce, and tomato sandwich I've thrown together myself. I'm not that hungry, so I've been trying to get through it for the past twenty minutes. I haven't even bothered to turn on the TV. I'm just staring blankly through the glass of the patio doors, my eyes fixed on nothing in particular outside in the backyard.

I already know it's going to be one of *those* days. I'm already feeling pretty low, but for no reason in particular. It'll pass though. Eventually. I'll mope around for a few hours, question my existence, and then I'll be laughing at that party tonight as though I'm the happiest guy in the room.

I release the sigh I've been holding and drop my eyes down to my plate, pushing it away from me. I don't really like being alone all that much, not when I feel like this.

"Not hungry?" Mom asks as she walks into the kitchen. She gives me a small, warm smile just like she always does, and I'm so glad she does, because I really need it right now.

"Not really," I mumble with a hopeless shrug. I prop my elbow up on the table and rest my chin on my palm, my gaze following Mom as she grabs my plate and carries it away.

"We're taking your brothers to the Dodgers game tonight," she casually muses over her shoulder. She tips the remainder of my food into the trash, then slides the plate into the dishwasher. As she turns around to face me again, she leans back against the countertop. Her smile has become a knowing one. "So wherever you end up sneaking out to tonight, look after yourself. Nothing stupid, Tyler." The way she arches her eyebrow at me is stern, and I know what she means. No drinking, no smoking, no staying out all night.

I frown back at her and shift my attention back to the yard. The sun is shining, its rays bouncing off the pool water, but I find it easy to focus on. I don't want to disappoint her tonight, though I know I will.

"Tyler," Mom says quietly, her tone different all of a sudden. Warily, she sits down next to me, her eyebrows pinching with worry. I don't like it when she looks at me like that. My heartbeat races that tiny bit faster as my eyes meet hers. "I found something last night," she murmurs, her voice breaking. She pulls something from her pocket and softly sets it down in front of me. Her blue eyes dilate with the heartache she is feeling, and she presses one hand to her chest, the other on my back. "We must have missed it."

I inhale deeply, exhale slowly. She gives me an encouraging nod, and then I glance down at the object she's placed in front of me. It's a photograph. A photo from forever ago. A photo of Dad and me. My chest tightens and I stare down at the memory in front of me as Mom soothingly rubs my back. She stays silent, giving me time to process it.

In the photograph, we're at the pier on the boardwalk. It's just getting dark, the sky a mixture of blue and pink streaks as the sun dips below the ocean behind us. I'm young, maybe six or seven, and I'm grabbing onto Dad's arm, huddled in close to him. Dad's young too, and as I look at him now, his smile beaming back at me and his green eyes full of warmth, I realize that we *are* similar. The older I get, the more I see it. Our eyes are identical. We have the same tanned skin. The same dark hair and thick eyebrows. The same damn jawline. We were both happy back then. The bad days hadn't started yet. I can still remember the first time Dad hit me. I was eight, and I was confused, and he told me it would never happen again, and I believed him.

I don't realize my fists are clenched under the table until Mom places her hand over mine. She massages my skin with her thumb until slowly, I relax my hands. She doesn't like it when I get mad, but she knows that sometimes I can't control it. That's another similarity that Dad and I share: our short temper.

"Do what makes you feel better," Mom whispers, and she slides something into my hand and closes my fingers around it. When I look at her, feeling more somber than angry, she gives me a small, sad smile. She stands up and places her hand on my shoulder, kisses my temple, and then walks away, giving me the space I need.

I glance down and open my hand. In my palm, there's a lighter.

When I was fifteen, my rage had been manifesting for three years and it had become so unbearable that I needed to find a release that was more satisfying than just getting high. I wanted to wipe away all of the memories I had of Dad, even the good ones. I wanted him completely out of my life. Mom would have done anything to make me feel better. She still would. That's why we went up into the attic together and pulled out all of the old photo albums from my childhood. As much as it hurt her, she let me set up a fire in our backyard and burn all of the photos of Dad and me. It felt good at the time, but even that wasn't enough to let me move on. I still think about him every day.

I get to my feet and grab the photograph in front of me. I take the lighter with me too as I walk over to the patio doors, sliding them open and stepping outside into the warm, fresh air. The slight breeze feels nice and refreshing. I sit down on the lawn by the edge of the pool and I pull my knees up to my chest, holding up the photograph again and dangling it from my fingertips.

I look at my smile again. Then at Dad's, and I think, *Fuck him*. Fuck Dad for ruining my life.

I hold up the lighter to the bottom corner of the photograph, and I don't even hesitate to light it, watching numbly as the flame latches onto the photo. It spreads fast, turning a younger version of me to a blackened crisp first, and then Dad. His face is disappearing into ash, and I let the photo fall into the pool, feeling relief as it begins to disintegrate in the water.

I wish the pain could disappear too.

———————————

My mood is even lower than it was this morning. None of Declan's crew are allowed to swing by Rachael's party tonight, and if Rachael knew I was involved too, I wouldn't be allowed either. It's frustrating, because tonight of all nights, I'm craving a high that's stronger than weed. And if I can't find that at the party, then I'll get it on my own. That's why I'm meeting Declan in a couple hours before I head over to Rachael's.

It's just after seven and I have the house to myself, but it's still too early to get ready so I leave my room, about to head downstairs to watch TV for a while, when I catch Eden climbing the stairs with a dress over her arm. "Looks like it's just you and me," I inform her with a teasing smirk. Tyler Bruce is never in a bad mood. Tyler Bruce doesn't have anything to feel down about. "They're at the Dodgers game. The Angels are totally gonna lose," I add, just in case she's wondering where our parents are. They've abandoned us again, but whatever. I wouldn't have gone to the game with them even if they'd asked.

"I know," Eden says, staring evenly back at me. She doesn't smile, so I figure she's still not all that happy to see me, despite the fact that we haven't crossed paths in what feels like forever. We seem to come and go at different times. "Can you move, please?"

"Sure," I say, moving over to allow her to pass. I don't have the energy to be a complete asshole to her yet, probably because the real me feels like crap. I'm too fed up to pull off a good performance right now. Eden brushes past me, but before she disappears into her room, she pauses and looks at me. "What?"

"You're coming to Rachael's tonight, right?" she asks, her expression curious, her tone gentle.

"Yeah." Why does she ask? Does she *want* me there or something? Probably not. I bet she had her fingers crossed that I was going to say no. Still, that doesn't mean I'm not curious too. I wonder if *she's* going. "You're gonna be there too, right?"

"Yeah."

"Cool," I say as nonchalantly as I can. I'm sort of happy she's going too, despite what happened at the last party. She questioned me, I got furious and smashed my damn beer, but at least she cared. I think. And if she does care, then it's more than anyone else ever has. "What time are we heading over there?"

"What do you mean *we*?" Eden asks, rolling her eyes. She turns around and pushes open her bedroom door. "I'm walking across the street on my own. Not with you. You can head on over there, Tyler, any time you want," she murmurs.

"Chill," I say under my breath, narrowing my eyes at her.

Why is she like this? I'm not even being a jerk to her right now, yet it seems like she *still* hates me. Which is so damn confusing because sometimes, when she's pushing so hard to figure me out, I think she may just be interested in what I have to say.

Wait. That's not what I want though. I *want* her to hate me. I need her to keep her distance.

I quickly shake my head as she walks into her room, and I continue downstairs to the living room. I spread out across the couch, turn on the TV, and pretty much snooze for an hour and a half while Eden is upstairs getting ready. I didn't take my pills this morning, so I've done nothing but mope around all day and all evening. I would happily skip this party entirely and just sleep off the rest of this shitty day, but Tyler Bruce doesn't miss out on parties, especially his friends' parties, so I force myself to head upstairs at eight thirty to shower. If I am to survive this party, I need a buzz.

I shower, work some gel into my hair, pull on some black jeans and a black leather jacket, then spray some cologne. I would have a beer or two before I head across to the party, but I need to drive to Declan's place first, so I hold off for now. I fire him a quick text:

Can you hook me up now?

A minute later, he replies with a thumbs-up and a wink.

Grabbing my car keys, I slide my phone into my jacket pocket and turn off the lights in my room, then open my door. I step out into the upstairs hall at the exact same moment Eden does, and we come face-to-face with one another again.

"I'm about to go over there," she reluctantly tells me, and it sounds like she's fighting back a sigh. She frowns, and despite telling me earlier that we weren't heading over to the party together, she asks, "Are you coming with me?"

I can't help myself from staring at her. She looks different again, almost like she did at Austin's party a couple weekends ago, but better. Her dark hair flows down her back in waves and her eyes sparkle with silver, her lashes thick, her eyebrows dark and defined. My eyes travel down her body, taking her in. She's short, but her heeled shoes make her legs look longer, and this time she's wearing a dress that suits her. It's sort of peach, neatly fitted but not too clingy, and my gaze rests a little too long on the cleavage that's showing through its keyhole design. "I actually gotta head out real quick," I force out. Suddenly, my mouth has gone dry.

Eden looks down at the ground and anxiously folds her arms across her chest as though she knows I'm looking. When she glances back up, she asks, "Where?"

"Just somewhere." Shit, I hope she's not about to interrogate me over this too. I don't want to get mad at her. I never want to see that flash of fear in her eyes again, even if it was only for a fleeting moment. "Just go over," I tell her, and I am mentally pleading that for once, just *once*, she listens to me. "I'll be there in twenty minutes."

"But where are you going?"

So, she's really doing this again. She's really going to question me until I explode. I refuse to break though. She's looking at me from beneath those thick, dark eyelashes of hers, and I know that she is genuinely concerned. Her glossy pink lips are parted slightly as she waits for my answer. "Damn, Eden." I throw my hand up into the air and turn away from her, retreating back into the safety of my room, but of course she follows me. She's so fucking stubborn.

"Why are you getting mad?" she asks quietly through the darkness of my room. When I look at her, I can see the glistening of her eyes as she stares straight back at me. She is slowly coming into focus. "I'm just asking where you're going."

"I'm going to meet someone, alright?" I shoot back at her, my voice raised, my tone hard. I'm snapping already way quicker than usual, and I can feel my temper rising up through me. She needs to stop now. "I've got shit to pick up and you gotta back off about it." And right now, I need that shit more than ever.

Eden goes quiet. I'm watching her expression: a blank canvas that slowly fills with disappointment. "You're meeting Declan," she says into the dark silence. It's a statement. "He's not going to the party so you're going out to meet him instead. Right?" She talks slowly, her voice kept low.

I close my eyes and take a deep breath. She knows. She fucking knows, and now that she does, she is going to fight against me. I love that she cares, that she challenges me, but right now, I really need her not to. I am desperate. "Just go to the fucking party already," I hiss at her once I open my eyes again.

"No," she says, her voice raised now. Her features sharpen with determination as she takes a step closer to me. "I'm not letting you go out to meet him."

"Eden." I say her name gently, firmly. Then, I step closer to her too, closing that distance between us. I lean down toward her, my face inches from hers, and I lock my eyes on hers. I fix her with the most threatening of glares I can possibly pull off, my eyes sharply narrowed, my anger held captive within them. "You can't do anything about it."

"You're right," she states, but her voice is laced with fury and exasperation. She shakes her head at me, her glossy hazel eyes a mixture of everything that I have learned to hate. Disappointment, worry, disapproval, and most of all, pity. She feels sorry for me, and that is the worst feeling in the world.

"I can't do anything about it, because you don't care. You don't care about the fact that I'm worried that you're going to overdose one night or have a bad reaction or end up dead. You don't care about the fact that you're seventeen and hooked on coke. You don't, do you?" She pauses for a second, but I'm not giving her an answer, because she already knows that she's right. "You only care about looking cool at parties, trying to impress people with this whole badass image you're trying to pull off. It's pathetic."

There's that word again. It's true though. I *am* pathetic. She's right about that, but she isn't right about everything. I'm not trying to impress anyone. I'm only trying to cope; I'm only trying to survive. "That's not why I do it," I tell her quietly, shaking my head.

"Then why?" she desperately pleads. She's so close to me that the only thing I can focus on is that fucking pity in her gaze, and I can feel the weight of it pressing down on me. "Is it because you're trying to fit in with those loser friends of yo—"

"Because it's a distraction!" I yell at her, cutting her off. Fuck, I said it. I close my eyes so that I don't have to look at her, so that I don't have to see that pity for a guy who depends on distractions in order to live another day. I take a minute to console myself, breathing deeply. "It's a fucking distraction," I murmur under my breath. I feel like sometimes I have to admit it to myself too.

Slowly, I open my eyes again and find Eden watching me silently. I'm furious now. Not just at her, but also at myself. I'm mad at myself for being such an idiot, and I'm mad that she knows it. I'm mad that she sees straight through me. I'm mad that my facade doesn't work around her. I'm mad that, for a split second, I see understanding in her hazel eyes.

"And right now," I admit, "I could really do with a goddamn distraction."

Suddenly, Eden's hands are reaching out for my jaw as she slams her body into mine. Her lips crash down against mine so fast that I become paralyzed from the shock. I can feel the warmth of her and all of her energy radiating between us, and I close my eyes, absorbing the sensation of her mouth on mine. That fire in my chest fades away, replaced by something new that I can't quite comprehend. Relief? No, it can't be. But suddenly I am not thinking about anything else but her. I'm kissing those lips. Those plump, pouty lips that have weakened me for weeks now. I didn't realize why they had such an effect on me, but I do now—it's because I wanted to feel those lips against mine. I am just about to reach out to touch her face, to *really* kiss her, when slowly I feel her pulling away from me.

My eyes flicker open and meet hers. I stare at her, bewildered, as she retreats away from me. Her gaze has flooded with fear and alarm, and I can see her hands trembling. Did she really just do that? Did she really just kiss me?

Something changes then. A realization hits me hard.

It *is* relief I felt. I have spent weeks asking myself what it is about Eden that gets to me so much, asking myself why I like the fact she cares, asking myself why I can't just be Tyler Bruce around her like I can with everyone else. And now I finally understand. It's because I *like* the damn girl. I like that she gets under my skin. I like that she makes me uncomfortable, that she tests me, that she pushes my boundaries. I like that she cares when no one else does. I like that I don't have to put on an act around her even though the real me is pathetic and tragic. And I like her husky voice and her full lips and her hazel eyes.

"That wasn't me. I don't—I don't know what that was," she begins to babble, her voice fragile and husky, just the way I like it as she splutters her words. It's like she *wants* to give me an explanation, but she doesn't have one. I'm staring at her mouth in a daze as her lips move. I am craving their touch again. "I—I don't—I'm—I'm sorry. I was trying to—to distract you—I—"

It's me who reaches out this time. I step forward and cup her face with both hands, pressing my lips down against hers. I'm so desperate to feel them again, and I kiss her as hard as I can, weaving my fingers into her thick hair. My body is against hers again, and I don't realize I'm pushing into her until we hit my bedroom wall. I kiss her for real this time, properly, like the way I should have a second ago. Deeply and intensely, quickly and desperately. She is kissing me back. Our lips are capturing one another's, her hands are on my chest, she is quivering. I drop my hand to the small of her back and bring her even closer against me, fighting for more, but then I freeze.

Eden is my stepsister. I'm kissing my stepsister.

Quickly, I break off the kiss and as much as I don't want to, I force myself to pull away from her. I stop touching her body. I step back. We both stare at each other with the same exact look in our eyes as we breathe heavily through the silence. It's a look of despair, of guilt.

She's realized it too. We are stepsiblings.

31

I KNOW SOMETHING IS wrong from the moment I wake up the next morning. My wrist is swollen and throbbing, and I'm flinching in pain every time I so much as flex a finger. I'm in agony as I get dressed, and I feel sick at the thought of heading downstairs for breakfast. There is no possible way to hide the Band-Aid on my forehead from Mom, so as I force my battered body down the stairs one step at a time, I begin to rack my brain for a new excuse, one that I've never used before. I can't tell her I fell down the stairs again, because there's no way I'm *that* clumsy.

My teeth chatter as I stand in the hall, not because it's cold, but because I'm scared to walk into the kitchen. I can hear Dad's voice now, gentle and soft as he talks to Mom. Chase is laughing. Why do they all get to be so happy?

With bated breath, I muster up the courage to enter the kitchen. Mom has her back to me, raiding the silverware drawer, and my brothers and Dad are sitting at the table. None of them knew how angry he was last night, how uncontrollable he was. He's so calm now, slouched back in his chair with a content smile on his lips and a cup of coffee in his hand. When I walk in, his verdant eyes flash over to meet mine, and that smile disappears. I stop breathing as he runs his eyes over me, and as he looks at that Band-Aid on my forehead, I can see the muscle in his jaw twitch. His eyes pool with guilt, and he drops his gaze to his lap.

"What have you done now, Tyler?" Mom asks as she turns around. I glance over at her, my breath still caught in my throat, and she is frowning with a hand on her hip as she points a spoon at my forehead.

"I slipped getting out of the shower last night," I tell her. I'm lying straight through my teeth, and I've learned that I'm an incredible actor, because even my own mom can't tell. "I hit my head on the sink. No big deal," I mumble. Dad still has his head down, his eyes on the floor. I sit down at the table next to Jamie.

"I've never known anyone to have such bad luck as you do, Tyler," Mom comments with the hopeless roll of her eyes. She sets some toast down on the table and runs her hand through my hair. She always does that.

"When did your wrist get so fat?" Jamie asks. I glance sideways at him, and he's staring wide-eyed at my swollen wrist with morbid curiosity.

Dad's eyes flicker up to look at me. His expression slowly floods with horror, and he sits up in his chair. I'm just about to hide my wrist under the table when Mom grabs my shoulder, leaning over me.

"Oh my God!" she gasps, her lips parting. She stares down at my wrist in alarm, and her eyes dilate with worry. "What have you done?"

"It's fine," I say. Quickly, I shove my arm under the table, out of sight from my parents, but the sudden movement sends a new shock wave of pain cutting through my arm. I flinch in agony and glance down. The more I look at my wrist, the more it *does* look funny. It looks almost bent, but it can't be broken. Not again.

"No, it's clearly not fine, Tyler," Mom says, and she swivels around and grabs her phone from the countertop, frantically pressing numbers. "I'm calling Dr. Coleman" she states, her eyes on her phone. "We're getting that checked out. No school for you today." She holds her phone up to her ear as it rings, anxiously chewing her lip as she looks at me again. "It looks so inflamed! Did it get infected or something?"

"I want to see it!" Chase says. Excitedly, he slides off his chair and walks around the table, leaning in against me as he tries to peer down at my wrist under the table. Reluctantly, I hold it up a little, and he stares at it in fascination. I don't think he would be so amazed if he knew it was Dad who caused it.

"Don't you have a court case this morning?" I hear Dad quietly ask Mom. With both Jamie and Chase checking out my wrist, I steal a look at him. His elbows are propped on the table now as he leans forward, his hands interlocked. His voice is softer than usual, but he's also guiltier than usual.

"Shoot. I do," Mom breathes. With her phone still to her ear, still ringing, she rubs her temple with her free hand.

"I'll take him," Dad tells her. "Don't worry. It's a slow day at the office anyway. They'll manage without me."

Mom's shoulders sink with relief, and they share a nod of agreement. Someone seems to answer the call then, because Mom says, "Dr. Coleman's office, please," and leaves the kitchen to get some silence.

I don't know why Dad is offering to be the one to take me to see Dr. Coleman. I think it's the guilt, but I really don't want to be alone with him today after everything that happened last night. I'm more afraid of him than ever, and now I'm worried that he's going to be mad at me again for drawing attention. I try to meet his eyes, to figure out if it's going to be another one of his bad days, but he already has his face buried in his hands.

32

"SHIT," I BREATHE. MY chest is rising and falling fast from the erratic thumping of my heart. There is no way that this just happened. There is no way I just kissed Eden, and there is no way she just kissed me *first*.

I stare at her, absolutely stunned, trying to make sense of the past few minutes. Eden's wide eyes are locked on me and she looks paralyzed, almost terrified, but also just as confused as I am. Does she understand what just happened? Does she realize what we've just done? Not only is she my *stepsister*, I also have a girlfriend. Who is waiting for me right now across the street. *I am such an idiot.* I am furious at myself for being so stupid.

"I'm going to Rachael's," I blurt out quickly. I zip up my jacket and turn for the door.

I need to get away from here, from Eden. I need some space to really process this and to figure out whether or not the realization I just had is, in fact, true or not. Because right now, I am seriously praying that it isn't.

I am so desperate to get out of this house. I find myself sprinting downstairs, two steps at a time, and I burst out through the front door, inhaling several gulps of fresh air. I stand on the front lawn for a minute with my hands in the pockets of my jacket and my head tilted back to the darkening sky. Just when I thought my life couldn't get anymore messed up, I have to go ahead and commit a moral fucking sin. *Way to go, you moron.* Eden isn't my *actual* sister, but it's still so weird. It's making me feel nauseous, and I know that the only way I am getting through this is if I do what I do best: distract myself with a whole lot of alcohol. Forget Declan. I don't have time to head across town. I need something *now*, and if alcohol is all I can get my hands on, then I'll take it.

I tilt my head back down from the sky and look directly across the street instead. All of the lights in Rachael's house are on and I can hear the very faint pulsing of music, but from the outside, it doesn't look like there's a party going on. Tiffani did tell me they were keeping it small, probably so that Rachael's parents don't kill her.

I walk straight across the street, my pace quick, and when I reach Rachael's porch, I stop to compose myself. *Be Tyler Bruce. Be cool. Be happy.* Tyler Bruce didn't just kiss his stepsister. I did. I almost gag right there and then, so I throw open the front door and step into the house, plastering a crappy smile onto my face. I need beer. Lots of it.

It's not busy yet. It's still early, but people are beginning to arrive, so Rachael is lingering around by the front door to greet everyone. She struts over to me, already wasted with a gaze that can't stay focused, and she glares at me as though I've insulted her just by turning up.

"*Where* is Eden?" she immediately asks. Not even a *hey*. "*She's supposed to be here by now!*"

"I don't know," I lie, then briskly push straight past her. I am *not* talking about Eden. I am not discussing her, nor saying her name, nor even so much as thinking about her. I stride into the kitchen and scan the mountain of drinks that cover the table. I'm an asshole who hasn't brought my own booze, but whatever. There's enough to go around. There's a box of beer already opened in front of me, so I start by plucking out a can.

Suddenly, someone presses up against me from behind. She rests her chin on my shoulder and runs her hand down my chest, sliding it under my jacket. "Mmm," Tiffani murmurs, and I can hear the seduction in her voice. "You're here."

"Oh," I say, turning around to face her. She is the last person I want to see. "Hey."

Tiffani looks up at me as she slings her arms around the back of my neck, pressing her body close against mine. I can see straight through her teasing smirk though. She's really just mad at me because I haven't seen her much over the past week. I've got too much stuff going on right now.

"Have you missed me?" she asks, and I can't help but place one hand on her hip out of habit. She would instantly figure out that something is up if I didn't go along with the script. I brush my fingers over the white, silky material of her dress. She *does* look amazing, but my head is spinning so much that I can't appreciate it right now.

"You know I have," I tell her. *I haven't.* She smiles wide and pulls my lips down to meet hers, and I kiss her only for a second. It makes me stomach twist. Ten minutes ago, my lips were against Eden's. I retreat from Tiffani, holding up the can of beer in my hand, using it to separate us. "Can I at least get a drink in? I can't do this party sober."

Tiffani's glistening blue eyes and playful smile immediately transform as she presses her glossy lips together. She unhooks her arms from around my neck and steps back. "When do you ever?" she mutters.

"You," I say, pointing my beer at Kyle Harrison as he walks into the kitchen. He freezes, almost as though he's afraid I'm about to pummel him or something. We don't talk, but he was in my history class last year. He'll do. "Get outside. Time to shotgun some beers. A lot of beers, actually."

Tiffani's cool hand reaches for my elbow. She tugs me back a step, narrowing her eyes at me in disapproval. "Tyler… C'mon."

"Not now, Tiff." I shake her grip off me and scoop the box of beer into my arms. I walk over to Kyle, and although he doesn't look too comfortable about the idea of chugging all these beers with me, he also doesn't have the courage to say no. Tyler Bruce doesn't let people say no anyway. I nudge his shoulder, and he follows me out into the backyard.

"Here," I say, setting the box of beer down on the grass and tossing him the can in my hand. I grab myself another, then pull out my car keys from my pocket. "We're finishing this box. Alright? No breaks in between."

"Man… Are you sure?" Kyle says as he stares doubtfully down at the can in his hand. Anxiously, he rotates it around and around, furrowing his thick eyebrows. "I don't wanna throw up."

I roll my eyes. "Shut up. Now go." As soon as the words leave my lips, I stab my keys into the can and press the new opening to my mouth, tilting my head straight back and chugging the entire can in seconds. I shotgun beers a lot. I've found it's the quickest way to get me drunk, numb, and, therefore, distracted.

"*Número dos*," I say, crushing the empty can in my hand and tossing it onto the grass. Kyle finishes a few seconds later, gasping for a breath of air, and I immediately toss him another can. I can feel Tiffani's intense stare piercing straight through me from the kitchen, so I turn my back to the window and try my best to tune her out as Kyle and I chug our way through two, three, four, five beers.

The speed at which we are consuming them is too fast, and I can feel the beer in my stomach, and Kyle has staggered over to the corner of the backyard and is shoving his fingers down his throat. I lean back against the wall for a few minutes, breathing deeply, letting the alcohol soak into my bloodstream. When I glance inside the kitchen through the window, Tiffani isn't there anymore, so I leave Kyle throwing up in the backyard and make my way back inside.

More people have arrived. People from school. People I would only occasionally talk to if I felt like it. Usually, I stick to my own circle. Is Eden here yet?

Stop thinking about her.

I ignore everyone, weaving my way around the girls that are doing shots of tequila by the sink, and I grab a bottle of vodka, fill more than half a cup with it, then top it off with some Coke. And I slam the damn thing. The strength of the drink burns my throat, but I don't *care*. I have every intention of obliterating myself tonight. That's why as soon as I finish the first, I pour myself a second.

"Living up to your reckless reputation?" I hear someone remark, and when I glance over, Jake is approaching. He has a bottle of beer in his hand, and he presses his hip against the countertop and takes a sip, eyeing me with his shitty, devious smirk.

"Don't fucking talk to me," I spit, turning my back to him. It's the first time I've seen him since he took Eden home last weekend, and although I *do* need to talk to him about that, I can't do it tonight. I can't talk about her.

Jake steps around me, smiling wider. He's such an asshole. "Is it because your sister slept at my place?" he says, his voice innocent, his eyes full of sadistic pleasure. He just *loves* to get under my skin.

I press my hand to his chest and shove him back a step. "She's not my sister, you moron." If he comes any closer, I won't hesitate to floor him. "Get out of my face, Jake. I swear."

"Whatever. Drink yourself to death and see if I care," he mutters, turning away and strolling out of the kitchen, probably off to pounce on whatever female he sees first. I can't believe we used to be best friends when we were kids. He's such a fucking freak.

I chug the drink in my hand again and remain in the kitchen for the next hour, because the kitchen is where the alcohol is. I join the girls by the sink and take a shot of tequila with them. I do shots of vodka with everyone who is unfortunate enough to so much as walk into the kitchen. No one is getting a choice. Even Rachael takes one with me, but I figure it's only because she's already drunk. Tiffani, on the other hand, isn't impressed when she walks into the kitchen and lays eyes on me.

"C'mon, Tiff," I call out to her over the music, holding out the near-empty bottle of vodka to her. I am wasted at this point. I can barely even remain upright, and I almost topple straight off the countertop. I've been engaging in conversation with everyone in the kitchen, and we have all been laughing hysterically, with everyone being *at least* tipsy.

Except for Tiffani. Her expression is thunderous as she glares sharply across the kitchen at me, her blue eyes like cool, cool ice. She struts over and snatches the bottle of vodka straight out of my hand, holding it as far away from me as possible. She presses her other hand to my chest and holds me upright. "You're embarrassing us," she whispers as she leans in close to me, glaring from beneath her fake eyelashes. "Stop it."

"Ohhh. Who cares?" I laugh and stretch forward, grabbing back the bottle from her, and I am just about to tilt it against my lips to take another swig when she steals it back again. We fight over it for a few seconds before I reluctantly let go, and she is quick to pass it off to whoever is closest to us.

"*Tyler*," she hisses, pressing her body against my legs, her hands on my thighs. "You look like an idiot. Please. Stop drinking. Or at least slow down." Has she even *had* a drink? Why is she being a buzzkill? Everyone in this kitchen right now is having a good time. She's ruining it.

"Baaaby," I murmur, pursing my lips innocently at her. I can't hide my smile though. I am *so* drunk, and luckily, I am the good kind of drunk tonight. Sometimes I swing the other way. I cup Tiffani's face with both hands and I lean down to kiss her, pressing my mouth to hers, but she immediately pulls away and shoves me back. The indignant look she gives me is almost laughable. Do I taste like one too many beers?

"Rejectiooon!" someone from the other side of the kitchen calls out, and everyone cracks into more laughter, even me.

Tiffani shakes her head and spins around, storming straight out of the kitchen with her arms folded across her chest. Whatever. Now that she's gone, I can continue to drink even more, and that is exactly what I do. More beers, more vodka, more tequila, more rum. I drink until I can no longer open my eyes, until I am no longer in control of my senses. And in danger of losing control of my bladder.

Awkwardly, I slide down from the countertop, landing on the floor, and when I get up, I have to fumble my way across the kitchen. My eyes are half-closed, my feet are moving on their own. I am grabbing people and furniture to guide me. I've been in Rachael's house many times before, but I don't know where the bathroom is. I am stumbling my way across the house, until suddenly I collapse down onto my hands and knees, disorientated. I don't know where I am. The music is pounding in my ears and voices are muffled, yet somehow, I am still able to hear it.

My name. Quiet and gentle. Husky.

My head feels too heavy to lift, but I fight hard to look up. The room is fuzzy. *She* is fuzzy. I try to peel open my eyes wider, but Eden is blurring in front of me. I try to bring her into focus, to see her glistening hazel eyes and plump lips, but I just can't do it. She is staring down at me, and I so wish I could read her expression right now.

"Baby," Tiffani's voice echoes around me. Everything sounds distorted, like I'm under water. My eyes close again, and I can feel Tiffani's hands around my body as she uses all her might to haul me up from the floor. I try to stand, but my legs are like jelly, and I simply fall straight back over, smacking my face into the wall. I'm too drunk to feel it. "Tyler," Tiffani says, but it doesn't sound as nice as when Eden says my name. I am being pulled somewhere, guided, and suddenly I am sitting at the foot of the stairs. "Sober up," Tiffani orders as she slaps her palm straight across my face. I don't feel the sting of it. "You're a nightmare."

My head falls forward. It's too heavy to hold up now, but Tiffani is grabbing my jaw, supporting me, and I hear her fuzzy, distant voice say, "Ella will kill him if he goes back over there like this." *Is Eden still here? Is that who she's talking to?* I try to ask, but my tongue won't form words. "I'll take him home with me for the night."

Ohhh. I am passing out. I can feel this wave crashing over me, like a black shadow arriving, and my entire body is going numb. I slump off the stairs, my eyes closed, my face pressed against into the floor. I could sleep here, but Tiffani isn't letting me. She is by my side again, forcing me upright against the wall, and we are sitting on the floor together. I am drunk and, therefore, I am feeling frisky. I pull at her dress, at her

263

hands, at her face. She is pushing me away. My head is in her lap. She is talking, but I can't hear what she is saying.

Is Eden still here?

———————————

The hangover I endure the following day is one of the worst I have ever suffered through. It's why I spend the entire Sunday in Tiffani's bed, sweating buckets, gulping down water, popping painkillers, and cursing at myself for being such a fucking moron.

It's early evening and I am still wrapped up in Tiffani's sheets, massaging my head and staring at the ceiling. I've showered now, so I do feel *slightly* better. More refreshed, at least. My head, however, is still pounding. I don't even feel sorry for myself. I'm angry. I passed out at the party, which, honestly, is just embarrassing. Tyler Bruce is supposed to be able to handle his alcohol, not pass out and get dragged home by his girlfriend.

"Are you hungry?" Tiffani asks as she walks into her room, a smile on her face. She's been checking in on me every half an hour, waltzing into her room in a pair of silk shorts and a tank top. At 8:00 a.m., she woke me up to yell at me for embarrassing her last night, for getting too drunk, for acting like a loser. At noon, she was being passive aggressive. By 4:00 p.m., she was acting relatively normal. And now, she is being nice. Too nice.

"No," I say. I think I'll throw up if I eat.

"How are you feeling?" she asks with a sympathetic frown as she joins me on her bed. She sits down next to me on her knees and reaches forward, placing her cool palm to my forehead. Her frown deepens. "Are you feeling better?"

"Not really," I admit. Her cool skin feels nice against my face, so I press my forehead harder into her hand. I'm burning up.

"I bet I could make you feel better," she murmurs, and she drops her hand to my chest as she leans in closer to me, pressing her lips to the corner of my jaw. She kisses the corner of my mouth too. Then my neck. Her lips trail along my skin, planting a row of soft, light kisses. She even climbs on top of me, sitting on my stomach with her legs cradling my hips and her hands pressed to my bare chest. She is kissing my collarbone now, and shit, it feels nice.

"Your...your mom, Tiffani," I mumble, my eyes closed, my hands on her waist. I throw my head back into the pillows, enjoying the sensation of her mouth exploring my body. There are not many things I love about Tiffani, but this is an exception. She always knows exactly where to kiss me.

"She just left," Tiffani says, and she moves her lips to mine. I wrap one of my hands into her hair, holding her closer to me, and I kiss her deeply and fast, biting her lower lip. Tiffani and I never do slow or gentle. We are always fast, always rough, probably because we don't actually care about one another. It's exhilarating though. We are fighting for dominance, and as I am kissing her, she is grinding against my hips. She tears away from me for only a brief second to pull off her tank top, then her mouth is immediately back on mine. She is kissing me faster now, her fingers intertwining through my hair. My hands are roaming down her body, her breasts, her waist, her hips, her ass. She kisses a path down my chest, all the way down to the waistband of my boxers. She glances up at me and runs her tongue along her lower lip. But then I remember something.

Yesterday was a blackout. I can't remember anything from the party, apart from making Kyle Harrison sick, but I remember *everything* that came before it.

I remember Eden. I remember arguing with her in the house. I remember admitting that I rely on distractions. I remember her lips against mine.

"Tiffani," I say abruptly, snapping back into the current moment. I grab her wrists, firmly holding them away from my body. I am breathing heavily, and my eyes are wide with panic. "I can't do this right now."

"Are you kidding me?" Tiffani says in disbelief, parting her lips. She aggressively yanks her hands free from mine and climbs off me. She is glaring at me with sharp, narrow eyes. "We *finally* get a free house and you're telling me *not right now*? Fuck you, Tyler. Go home." She grits her teeth and slides off the bed, turning her back on me as she pulls her tank top back on. She heads for the door, muttering something under her breath, probably calling me an asshole.

"Tiffani," I say quietly, sitting up. I pull the sheets up to my waist and stare at her in silence as she turns around. I am looking at my girlfriend, but I am not looking at a girl I even remotely like, let alone love. When I kiss her, I don't feel that same adrenaline rush that I felt last night when I kissed Eden. "What is this? Us," I clarify. "What is it?"

"What the hell, Tyler?" Tiffani says as her expression twists, full of confusion. She looks taken aback that I've even asked.

"Just tell me," I plead desperately. It's always been at the back of my mind, I guess. "What are we doing? Because I have no idea. We don't even…" I inhale, shaking my head. *We don't even like each other*. I can't say it out loud though, because it sounds almost cruel. "Why are we together?"

I know why. We are together because it benefits us both, because I get the hot, popular girlfriend to make Tyler Bruce's life look pretty nice, and she gets the guy who she knows will do anything she asks of him. A guy whose every move she can control. She must know that deep down

I'm weak. That's why it's so easy for her. I'm just a prop in her life, the same way she is in mine. But we are bad for each other. We *shouldn't* be together. "We're not talking about this," Tiffani states. She is clenching her jaw, and I know I'm taking a huge risk here. Tiffani doesn't like it when I step out of line and do something that goes against her wishes. She *always* retaliates. "Don't bring it up again."

"Maybe we should…I don't know." I shrug. "You know as well as I do that this is stupid. Maybe we should just take a break or something."

"How's selling weed going?" she cuts in quickly, her voice seething. She folds her arms across her chest and raises an eyebrow at me, her eyes piercing straight into mine.

My heart stops for a second. "What?" I say, feigning surprise as though I have no idea what she's talking about. *How does she know?*

"You thought I wouldn't find out? You think I'm that stupid?" she says, rolling her eyes, but her tone is venomous, and she is becoming the Tiffani I really, really don't like. The one that is devious and controlling. "Last night, while you were too drunk to function, Greg asked me if I knew where you were, because he was just *dying* for a smoke." Slowly, she walks back over to the bed, a twisted smile on her face. She *knows* she's caught me. "Rumor has it, you can hook people up these days."

"Tiffani…"

"Yeah, that's what I thought. You're a liar." She sits down on the bed, crosses her legs, and then grins at me. She is loving the power she has over me right now. It's almost sadistic. "So, new plan," she says, her voice sickeningly sweet. "We're not discussing *us* again until graduation. Or, you know, I'm not sure if I'll be able to keep your secret." She gives me a small shrug and a frown, then she leans in close and presses her lips to mine again. "I love you, Ty. And you love me too. Remember that." I am paralyzed as I watch her leave the room, swinging her hips and humming. I feel sick, but it's not because of the amount of alcohol I consumed last night. No, it's a reason much worse than that.

Tiffani is blackmailing me.

33

"BROKEN," DR. COLEMAN SAYS as he angles his computer screen around to face us. I stare at the X-ray of my hand as he points out a bone. "It's the lunate again," he explains with a frown. "Of course, it was already weak, so it's no surprise it has fractured so easily again." He turns the screen back around and pushes his glasses up on the bridge of his nose as he begins to type something up.

The small office goes quiet. My wrist is throbbing in my lap. Dad is sitting on the edge of his seat next to me, fumbling with his hands, his foot anxiously tapping against the floor. It's late morning, and instead of being at school and at work, we are here.

"It'll heal though, right?" Dad asks Dr. Coleman. Even his breathing is shallow.

"Luckily, it's not severe," Dr. Coleman says, glancing up from his screen. "Back into a cast for three weeks, but there's a lot of swelling right now, so we'll stick to a splint over the weekend. Bring him back on Monday, and we'll get a cast on. Expect it to take a couple of months to fully heal." He flashes me a teasing smile, but I can tell there's a seriousness to his words as he says, "That's if you don't break it again first, Tyler!"

Dad looks at the ground again. He feels real bad today, way more than usual. Is it because he can't ignore the pain he's inflicted this time? Is it because he has to look at me and see the Band-Aid on my forehead and the swelling of my wrist?

"Peter," Dr. Coleman says as he continues to type away at his computer, glancing sideways at Dad, "how's your father doing these days? I haven't seen him around lately."

Dad swallows as he forces his gaze back up. There's a wave of relief that comes over him, like he's eternally grateful for the change in subject. "Oh, he's doing just fine. Keeping himself busy with that damn Corvette!"

"Remind him that he owes me a drink sometime," Dr. Coleman says with a hearty chuckle. "And a ride!"

Dad joins in the laughter, and suddenly I feel so alone again. They banter back and forth while Dr. Coleman puts a splint on my wrist, and it's like the frequency of my broken bones has been forgotten already.

As we walk back to Dad's car in silence, I trail slightly behind, kicking at the ground and staring at the black splint that I have to wear over the weekend until I can get my cast. I should be frustrated that it's only been a month since I got my last cast off, but at this point, I just don't even care anymore. It's all just so…*whatever*. I guess I've accepted it now. This fracture will heal, and then there'll be a new one.

The thing that's really on my mind is that I don't want to go home. I can see Dad's Mercedes just ahead, but I want to turn around and run away, run back into Dr. Coleman's office and ask him to help me, that my wrist is broken again not because I'm clumsy, but because Dad is cruel. I know I can't do that though. I know I can't tell anyone. Ever. I know that all of this is so wrong, but I don't want to be the one to tear my family apart. I don't want to ruin Dad's life. He's my *dad*.

That's why I do as I should and climb into the car. Awkwardly, I one-handedly pull on my seatbelt and fix my eyes on the dashboard. I'm waiting for Dad to turn on the engine, to drive us home, but he's not doing anything. I wonder if he's mad at me, if he can't keep his anger at bay until we get home, if he's going to grab me right here and now in the hospital parking lot. Mustering up an ounce of bravery, I look over at him.

He's sitting paralyzed with his hands on the steering wheel. He is completely frozen, staring off into nowhere, and I can hear his shallow breathing again. His chest rises and falls, his lower lip quivers. A long minute passes, and then he slowly angles his head to look at me. The expression in his eyes is foreign to me. They are brimming with emotion, wide and heartbroken, full of remorse, of guilt, of regret. He stares at the Band-Aid on my forehead, and then at my wrist, and his green eyes glisten as they fill with tears.

"Never, ever, ever again," he whispers as he chokes up. He presses his hand over his mouth as tears break free, his features twisting, his head shaking fast. He can't even look at me as his voice breaks. "I promise, Tyler. I'm never going to hurt you again." He huddles over the steering wheel, muffling sobs as he covers his face with his hands, his body shaking. "I'm sorry. I am. I really am," he splutters, but he's breaking down so quickly that his words are almost unintelligible.

I've never seen Dad cry before. Not once in my twelve years of living. He once told me only weak men cry. Does that mean he's weak now? Does that mean he's not strong enough to hurt me anymore? He says sorry a lot, but not like this, not with so much meaning.

That's why I believe him.

34

MONDAY IS A BAD day. It's the afternoon, but I'm still in bed. Staring at my ceiling. Listening to the silence. Overthinking.

After I got home from Tiffani's last night, I went straight to my room and climbed into bed. I'm still grateful that neither Mom nor Dave came upstairs to question my whereabouts over the weekend. They know by now that if I don't come home, it's usually because I'm staying at Tiffani's place. Tiffani, my girlfriend, who is currently blackmailing me.

I can't stop thinking about it. I was stupid to promise her that I wouldn't get involved with Declan Portwood and his crew, because now that I have, she is using it against me. If I even so much as *talk* about breaking up again, she will completely ruin me. She's done things like this before. It's how she gets her way, how she keeps me in check, so I don't even know why I'm so surprised by it.

I groan and roll out of bed. It's too hot to lie there any longer. I begin to pace instead, pulling at my hair while I try to piece my thoughts together.

Everything has just gotten so much worse in one damn week. I thought my life was a mess before, but now it's falling apart. I'm working for Declan Portwood. My girlfriend is blackmailing me. I kissed my stepsister.

For a split second when I woke up this morning, I wondered if I had dreamed it. It was two days ago and I haven't seen Eden since the party. I reach up and brush my fingertips over my lips. It wasn't a dream though. I can still feel her mouth against mine. It was real. We need to talk about it, but what is there to say? It was wrong, but I...I don't know. It didn't feel all that wrong when my lips were capturing hers. Do I really like the girl or was I just impulsive in the heat of the moment? I sigh and head into my bathroom, careful not to lock myself in. I busted the lock once when I punched the door, and now I can't close it unless I want to trap myself in. I grab my antidepressants and take two. Today, I *do* need them. I am feeling low.

Sometimes, I wonder just how different everything would have been if Dad hadn't put me through the pain that he did. Our family would still be together. There would be no Dave, no Eden. We would still be living in our old house, most likely, a couple streets away from where we are now. Dad would probably talk to me about girls and tell me not to drink anything more than a beer or two whenever I go to a party. We'd watch football together and he'd help me with my college applications, and he'd give me advice when I needed it. And Mom would still be smiling her wide, dazzling grin that I grew up adoring, but she never smiles like that anymore.

And what about me? How different would I have been if things had taken a different path? If my own father hadn't turned on me? I would be happier; I would be better. I wouldn't need to resort to alcohol and drugs. I wouldn't have such a short temper or so much anger inside of me. I wouldn't have to put on a performance every damn day to hide all of my secrets. I wouldn't be so reckless, so careless. I wouldn't be on antidepressants. I wouldn't be the Tyler Bruce that I pretend to be. I would just be me, just Tyler, a guy who is happy and living life to the fullest, with friends who actually like him, and a girlfriend who isn't Tiffani.

But Dad took all of that away from me. Dad has ruined me. I need Mom right now. She always makes me feel better. No matter how much I let her down, no matter how upset I make her, she is always there for me. She understands me more than anyone else ever could, and when I get myself into these dark moods, I rely on her. I don't think even she realizes just how badly I need her sometimes.

I leave my room and head downstairs in search of her. I'm not sure if she's even in the house right now, so it is a relief when I find her tidying up in the kitchen. She hears me walk in. "You're awake," Mom says, spinning around to face me. She gives me a small smile. She is always so hopeful, always smiling at me, always wishing that maybe I will be okay that day. "Happy Fourth of July."

"Mom…" I whisper as I meet her gaze, but my voice cracks and tears pool in my eyes. My lips tremble, my shoulders sink. I am defeated.

"Oh, Tyler," Mom says as she rushes over. She knows me so well. She can see the pain in my eyes, the same way I can suddenly see it in hers too. It was always there, but now she's not trying to hide it behind a brave face. She immediately wraps her arms around me, pulling me in close, surrounding me with her warmth and love.

"I can't…I can't do this anymore," I tell her, but my voice is too weak and too fragile and too broken. The words cut my throat. I bury my face into her shoulder as she clings onto me even tighter, and I'm not even trying to fight back the tears. I break down every couple months, but it never gets any easier. Mom holds me. She is crying too. I can feel her chest heaving against me as she sniffs. She doesn't say anything for a while, but I don't need her to. Just hugging her is enough. Sometimes, I think the only reason I'm still here is because I'm trying my best to stay strong for her. I can't break her more than I already have.

"I get it," she finally murmurs, but her voice is full of heartache. She has to force the words out, one by one. "You're allowed to feel like this, Tyler. You have every right to," she says, and she buries her face further into the crook of my neck. "It can all become too much sometimes."

Suddenly, I hear the echo of the front door closing, and Dave is cheerily calling down the hall, "Guess whose work let out early?"

It's almost a reflex to immediately pull away from Mom despite how tightly she's holding onto me. She is the only one I will ever allow myself to be vulnerable around. Quickly, I wipe away the tears from my eyes as I walk across the kitchen, taking a deep breath, filling my lungs. I can feel Mom staring after me, but she knows I can't stick around. I pull open the patio door and step out into the backyard. I collapse down onto the grass by the pool, squeezing my eyes shut and burying my face into my hands as I cry.

Hours later, I am crammed into the backseat of Mom's Range Rover. We're heading to Culver City to watch their Fourth of July fireworks display, but I am in no mood to celebrate the occasion. And it gets worse: Eden is pressed up against me. I can't bring myself to look at her. Not after what happened on Saturday. I stare out of the window instead, ignoring the feeling of her arm against mine, trying to tune out her touch. I think she is trying to ignore me too. Even before we got in the car, we pivoted around one another and kept our heads down. "I didn't know you wore Converse," I hear her quietly note halfway through the drive. Mom and Dave are talking up front, but neither of us is partaking in that conversation. I'm surprised to even hear Eden speak.

I angle my head away from the window and glance sideways at her, meeting her warm, curious gaze. She looks nice today, but I guess she always does. My eyes fall to her lips for only a split second, and I have to swallow the lump in my throat in order to force out a quick, "Yeah."

I turn back to the window, and I don't even know why, but my pulse has sped up. I try to focus on slowing it back down again, but it's hard. I keep thinking about her, about the way she looked at me on Saturday night, about the way her mouth felt, about the way she tasted, about her hands on my body. I even close my eyes, squeezing them tightly shut and fighting to force her out of my mind, but it's impossible, especially when her skin is already touching mine.

I don't even like Culver City, but I am so relieved when we finally pull up into the local high school's parking lot. The fireworks display is being held here. Santa Monica hasn't hosted its own display in years. Apparently, it's too dangerous to set them off by the pier or some other bullshit like that. It means that every July Fourth, we have to head somewhere else. This year, we are here in Culver City, and we are definitely not the only people with this idea. There are crowds of people flooding through the parking lot, and as soon as Mom has put the car in park, my seatbelt is off and I am almost throwing myself out of the vehicle. Being around Eden is too unbearable, and I think it will continue to be awkward until we actually talk about what went down between us over the weekend. That's why I walk slightly ahead of the "family" as we follow the crowds across the campus. The fireworks, I think, are being held out beyond the football field, and access is only available by following a series of confusing signs through the school building.

"If any of your friends are here, you can go find them," Mom says, glancing between Eden and me. Jamie and Chase aren't old enough to disappear on their own yet. "We'll call you at the end if we can't find you again, okay?"

"And behave yourself," Dave adds in quickly, fixing me with a stern look as though it's even *possible* for me to somehow create trouble among this crowd. It's just a damn fireworks display. How much damage is he expecting me to do?

"Yeah, yeah, we will," I say, shrugging them off. With the go-ahead to leave, I don't waste anymore time. I don't even know if any of my friends are here—Tiffani definitely isn't, thankfully—but it doesn't matter. I refuse to be seen hanging out with my brothers on July Fourth, so I push my way into the crowd, trying my hardest to disappear out of sight. I don't mind being on my own. Sometimes, I prefer it.

When I get back outside into the cool, fresh air, I am reminded of why I hate the Fourth of July so much. The music, the marching band, the voices. There are thousands of people here, crammed in across the football field and piled up in the stands, illuminated by the floodlights as the sky darkens. All I can smell is the grease from the food trucks. *Gross*. People are brushing against my shoulders as they push past me, but I don't even know where to go, so I just remain in place.

Until, out of the corner of my eye, I spot Eden. She is frozen in place exactly like I am, only a few feet ahead of me, lost among the crowd. Her gaze is wide as she analyzes the scene in front of her, and she has the same look of frustration as I do. It's too busy here, and she looks almost worried. I should talk to her. I'm alone. She's alone. Now is the perfect time to just get it over with. If I don't talk to her about that kiss right now, then I most likely never will. It's nerve-wracking, but I take a deep breath and filter my way through the crowd toward her. "I didn't think you were the type to go off on your own," I say gently as I reach her. I have to raise my voice slightly over the noise around us. Eden glances over at me, and she looks so out of place and so uncomfortable that it's almost cute. "We can talk now."

"Now?" Eden says, surprised. Her eyes flicker around the crowd again, at the commotion out on the field.

"I didn't mean right here," I say. The conversation we are about to have is definitely not one that can be done in public. We need to be alone; we need privacy. "Come on." I'm about to reach for her elbow to pull her along with me to someplace quieter, but I refrain from touching her and keep my head down instead. I'm not sure how she feels about that kiss yet, so until I find out, it's best not to make any moves on her. But it's tough not to.

I turn back toward the school building and push against the flow of people, edging my way through the crowd. All the while, I am praying that Eden is following me. The worst case scenario would be if she couldn't care less, but I think I can sense her behind me, so I'm reassured that she cares enough about that kiss to want to talk to me about it.

Inside the school, I have no choice but to ignore all of the "NO ENTRY" signs taped to the walls of the hallways that are shut off to the public. I need to talk to Eden, and it definitely can't wait. I need a classroom or something. Somewhere that's quiet and still, somewhere away from these Fourth of July celebrations. So, despite the signs, I head on down the first hallway I come across. I can hear Eden's footsteps behind me, but she doesn't say anything. Maybe she didn't notice. It's a long hallway, and I walk all the way to the end of it, and suddenly we are in tense silence. Very faintly, I can hear the music from outside, but it feels so distant. It's dark up here, and I stare at the wall for a minute, trying to gather my thoughts.

Slowly, I turn around to face Eden. She is looking at me with those wide, anxious hazel eyes of hers, and I don't think I've ever seen anyone look so terrified. God, how do I even begin? A lump forms in my throat, and I decide that there is no good in tiptoeing around the subject. I have to just say it: "What the hell happened on Saturday?"

"I don't know," Eden splutters quickly. Maybe she's been as desperate to talk about this as I have, because all at once, she begins to babble a string of words even faster than she did on Saturday night. "I'm sorry. You were just—you were annoying me and I didn't want you to buy more drugs and I just—I just did it. I didn't mean to." She pauses to take a breath, and she needs it. Her voice is husky and ragged, and none of her words sound right. "I'm sorry, okay? It's really weird and it's making me feel sick, and we just need to pretend it didn't happen."

Pretend it didn't happen? Ouch. I should have known it was only a mistake. I should have known a girl like Eden wouldn't be even remotely interested in a guy like me, and not just because we're stepsiblings. Her apology stings. "I wish I could say the same about me," I say, stuffing my hands into my pockets.

"What?"

"I kissed you back," I remind her. I kissed her back because I never knew how much I had wanted to. I kissed her back because I couldn't get enough of it, of her. I kissed her back because I *like* her. She may have kissed me by mistake, but on my end, I kissed her entirely on purpose. "I'm not going to apologize for that."

Eden is staring at me with her lips parted. "Why?"

I take a moment to take in her expression as confusion captures her nervous gaze. In this light, with the final hue of the sunset shining in through the windows and hitting her face at just the right angle, she looks so pure. Do I tell her why? I don't have anything to lose. She should know, because if I don't tell her, then perhaps I will regret it later. I may not get the chance to tell her again. "Because I knew exactly what I was doing," I finally say.

"Why did you do it?" she asks quietly through bated breath, but her voice is almost a squeak. She is on edge. I can tell by the way she isn't breathing, or blinking.

"Because I've wanted to do it so fucking badly." I spit the words out almost as fast as I can so that I don't have the chance to overthink them. I turn away from her and press my hand to the wall for support, exhaling. It's true. I did want to kiss her; I just didn't realize it until her lips were pressed to mine. That's why I felt so weird whenever I caught myself studying her features for too long. It's why I've been curious about her.

"You've wanted to?" Eden repeats, her voice echoing down the still hallway. It feels like we are so far away from everything else that is going on around us. "What the hell are you saying?"

"You want the honest truth? I'm saying I'm fucking attracted to you, alright, Eden?" I spin around to face her again, to read her expression as her eyes widen, and I am getting so heated over the situation that I can't help but feel angry at her. "And I know I shouldn't be, because you're my damn stepsister, but I just can't help it. It's stupid as hell, and I know you don't feel the same way, because you're fucking apologizing for Saturday." Why did it have to be a mistake? It's *still* stinging, and I really wish it wouldn't hurt as much. Hell, Tyler Bruce doesn't know the meaning of rejection. But I guess that right now, I am just me. And *I* care. "I really wish you hadn't said sorry for it," I say quietly, not quite meeting her eyes, "because apologizing means regretting."

Eden is quiet. I don't know what she's thinking, but I'm not sure if I even want to know. If she didn't like me before, then she probably thinks even less of me now. Now I'm the creepy older stepbrother who is attracted to her, and she'll probably never talk to me again. "I thought you hated me," she says after a while. It's not exactly what I was expecting.

"I hate a lot of people, but you're not one of them," I reassure her. Tyler Bruce did a good job of being an asshole, then. "I hate the fact that you turn me on. Like, a lot."

"Stop," Eden says. She shakes her head, closing her eyes for a second, and she even moves away from me. She is several feet away, but I wish she was closer. "You're my stepbrother. You can't say that."

"Who makes up these bullshit rules, huh?" I glance out of the window, at the crowds across from the football field below, and everyone there is as much a stranger to me as Eden is. I look back at her as the frustration of the situation sets in, and she is still staring at me in fear. "Three weeks ago I didn't even know who you were. I don't see you as a sister, okay? You're just some girl I've met. How the hell is it fair to label us as siblings?"

"You have a girlfriend," she whispers. She takes even more steps away from me, her face paling. She looks as though she really is going to be sick. "Tiffani's your girlfriend."

"But I don't want her to be!" I don't mean to yell at her, but she just doesn't get it. I have no *choice* but to be with Tiffani, especially at this current moment in time. I'm not mad at Eden. I'm mad at Tiffani, at myself, at this situation. "I don't want to be with Tiffani, okay? Don't you get that? She's just another distraction."

"What the hell is up with you and distractions?" Eden asks, throwing up her hands. She suddenly seems exasperated too, and now we are both yelling across the hallway at each other.

"Nothing." I take a moment to inhale, to catch my breath, and then I try to stay calm, lowering my voice. This is stupid. I am wasting my time standing here and discussing this with her. Honestly, I'm *embarrassed*, and I just want to get away from Eden now. I can't believe I thought there was even an ounce of hope that she would feel the same way as I do about that kiss. I'm trying to be honest for once, but it's backfired completely and now I regret it. Keeping secrets is so much easier than this. "I've said what I've needed to say, you know what I think of you, you've made it clear you think differently, I'm done." I stride past her, pulling at my hair, and I mutter, "Enjoy the fucking fireworks."

I've humiliated myself, and now I just feel like a damn idiot. I can't even look at her anymore. It's going to be impossible to live in the same house with her over the summer, because we are inevitably going to be around each other. It'll be unbearable from now on. She *knows* I'm attracted to her.

"Wait," Eden says, and I immediately come to a halt as a new sense of hope fills me. *Please, please tell me you didn't regret it.* I can't turn around to look at her, but I am listening closely, begging for her to say something that is worth staying for. And seconds later, her husky voice fills the silence as she says, "You didn't give me the chance to tell you that I find you interesting."

35

FIVE YEARS EARLIER

MY FRIENDS ARE FIGHTING to sign my cast at lunch on Monday when I return to school from the hospital. We're in the cafeteria, huddled around our usual table, and a black Sharpie is being passed around as I hold my wrist out. Meghan is bent over my arm, her tongue out as she focuses on surrounding her name with black, squiggly flowers. I almost beg her not to because it's sort of dumb, but I keep quiet and let her do her thing. Flowers are at least better than the self-portrait Rachael has attempted to draw.

"My turn," Jake says, reaching over to pluck the Sharpie out of Meghan's hand. He's sitting cross-legged up on the table and he bends forward, grabbing my arm.

"Nothing stupid," I warn him. Last time, he drew a pair of boobs, and Mom scribbled over it when I got home. The design of my cast ended up looking like crap after that, and this time, I want it to look pretty cool. It could be the last cast I ever wear.

It's been three nights since Dad last laid a hand on me. He hasn't hurt me since the moment he promised me he never would ever again. I've been watching him closely over the weekend, noticing the way he never comes too close to me and always thinks first before opening his mouth. He still expects me to work hard, which I do, and even when he got frustrated at me last night, he only walked away.

I think this is really it this time. I think the bad nights, the worst nights…I think they might be done for good. I think it might be over. Maybe this time, his apology really is the last. We can go back to the way we used to be, the way we should be, when he would help me out with my homework, when we would watch TV together, when we would play out in the backyard…when he would actually act like a real father who loves his son.

I feel hopeful. I feel almost…happy. Not entirely, but happier than I've felt in a while.

"There you go," Jake says. There's a mischievous smirk on his lips as he sits back. I glance down at my cast, and honestly, I have no idea what he's even drawn. It looks like some sort of satanic devil, and underneath, he's scrawled: *Remember Jake is cooler than you.* It's not even surprising, and it's not enough to ruin my good mood.

"Sweet," I say, grinning back at him. His smirk falters, as though he's disappointed I'm not throwing my lunch at him. I take the pen from him and offer it to Dean. "You wanna sign it?"

"Yeah," Dean says. He shuffles in closer to me, takes the pen, then picks out an empty spot on my cast. As he writes, he asks, "How did you even break it *again*?"

"You do know it's Tyler you're talking to, right?" Rachael cuts in, rolling her eyes at Dean. "Accident-prone."

"Yeah, basically," I agree with a laugh. Little do they know; I'm no longer going to be clumsy. No more bumps and bruises. No more excuses. No more lies.

Dean finishes signing my cast. He's written his name and then underneath, he tells me to get better soon. No boobs or Satan. Dean is too nice for that. I glance around the table, and everyone has signed my cast except for one, and that's the new girl, Tiffani. Although, she's not really new anymore, and she's been joining us at lunch for the past couple weeks.

She's sitting at the end of the table, quietly watching the rest of us in silence, chewing her lip.

I look straight at her, hold up my wrist, and give her a small smile. "Can you sign it?"

"You want me to?" Tiffani asks, widening her eyes in surprise as though she hadn't been expecting me to ask. I figure she considers us as her friends, so it would be rude not to.

"Yep." I grab the pen from Dean and stretch across the table, offering it to her, and she takes it from me as she gets to her feet. She grabs her bag and walks around the table, then sits down on the corner of it as she reaches me. Her hair falls over her face as she scribbles her name, just *Tiff* with a small heart next to it. Then, she tosses the pen down onto the table, reaches into her bag, and pulls out a lipstick. We are all watching her in silence as she paints her lips a dark pink, then she gently reaches for my wrist with both hands and lifts my cast up. She kisses it, right above her name, her blue eyes looking back at me.

"Unique," she says with a smile as she lowers my arm back down. "Like me."

"Hey," Jake calls out across the table. "I think my lips are broken. Do you wanna sign them too?"

36

THE SKY OUTSIDE EXPLODES into colors of pink and blue, green and yellow. The fireworks have begun. In our silence, Eden and I turn to the large windows overlooking the football field, the crowds, the celebrations, the commotion. The colors light up the hallway, streaks of light flashing in our eyes, but I can't focus on the display. No, I can only focus on Eden. Her hazel eyes, lit with red, glistening through the darkness. Did I really hear what she just said correctly?

"Interesting?" I say. The word sounds strange on my tongue. I've never considered myself interesting, and it definitely wasn't what I was hoping to hear. My heart sinks. "That's all you can say?"

"We're missing the fireworks," Eden pathetically mumbles. She can't look at me. She only stares out of the window, watching the world carry on without us.

"I don't care about the fireworks," I snap. How can she even notice those? There are more important things going on right now, like figuring out what exactly she means when she said she found me interesting. "Are you fucking kidding me right now? Interesting?" It's such a letdown. I was desperate for something more.

"Your walls," she says, but her voice is shaking. Is she scared of me again? Is it because I'm angry? Or is she scared of herself? "Your walls interest me."

My heart skips a beat. *Oh, shit.* "I don't know what you're talking about," I lie, but it is nowhere near convincing.

"I didn't realize it until now," she continues. She is anxiously chewing at the inside of her mouth as she looks down at the floor. It's almost like she's thinking it through in her head, gathering her thoughts. Her eyes flick back up to meet mine. "You've got walls up and they interest me."

"You know what? I don't care," I say defensively. She *can't* figure me out. I have gone all these years without anyone breaking me down into pieces and analyzing me, and the thought of Eden noticing the cracks in my life is almost too much to bear. "Think whatever you want about me."

"Think whatever I want?" she repeats, and her voice gets stronger, like she is shifting back into the Eden I've thought was pretty cool over the past few weeks. The Eden who doesn't back down, the Eden who challenges me, the Eden who isn't afraid to tell me the truth. "I think that you infuriate me," she begins, narrowing her eyes. "I think that you are an arrogant jackass who can never simply be nice to someone, because it doesn't fit in with the act you're putting on."

Clearly, I have slipped up on my Tyler Bruce performance one too many times, because she can see straight through it all. She knows it's all just an act. She knows it isn't me, but I *want* her to think that it is. I don't want her to ever figure out that I'm really just fragile and broken. "You have no idea what you're saying," I tell her. *She's wrong.*

"Let me finish," she says, and she inhales a breath of air. "I also think that you're a jerk. Your ego is too big for your own head and you think that you look cool by being a badass. But really, Tyler? You just look pathetic."

Stop fucking saying that! I almost scream it at her, but I bite my tongue and fight to keep my anger from exploding. I tell her I'm attracted to her, and she turns around and throws it in my face like this. It hurts. I should have left while I had the chance. "Alright, now I just look like a moron coming up here and telling you that I'm attracted to you," I say. "You could've let me down easier."

Her lips press together, her eyes twitch as they narrow. "I thought someone as badass as you could handle it."

She is challenging me again. I shove my hands into my pockets and think about her words for a minute, turning back to the window. The fireworks are still lighting up the sky and I watch them in silence, listening to the popping and the crackling. Maybe there is a very small part of me that *likes* the idea of Eden figuring me out. It's a terrifying thought, having someone know my darkest secrets, but a tiny fraction of my being is almost begging for it. I try to fight against it, to push people away, but deep within me, all I really want is for *someone* to finally understand me. Someone who will tell me that everything will be okay one day. Someone who will tell me that *I'll* be okay. I glance over my shoulder at Eden. "And I thought you'd figured out that I'm not really a badass," I whisper. This is me. This is Tyler.

Eden's eyes are locked on me. There are several feet between us, but she stares across the hallway at me through the silence. The bright, neon colors of the fireworks are still flashing in her eyes. So many different emotions are flickering in her gaze. At first, confusion. Then surprise. And finally, a fear that I recognize all too well. It's the same fear I felt on Saturday night after I realized that not only did I just kiss my stepsister, but that I also liked her.

"I think," she whispers, "that I'm attracted to you too."

What? My heart really does stop this time. I turn away from the windows, angling my body back toward Eden. Surprise fills me, but so does doubt. "You are?" I ask, but my voice doesn't even sound like mine.

"I am," she says. She squeezes her eyes shut for a moment, and I can see her swallow hard. "I'm sorry."

"Stop apologizing," I tell her. *Why is she saying sorry?* This is exactly what I wanted to hear, but she looks absolutely terrified. It's a heavy realization to swallow, I know, but it's one I am willing to accept. I hope she is too. Slowly, I move near her, only stopping when I am standing a mere inch or two away from her. "Don't regret anything."

Her gaze flicks up from the ground to meet mine. I am looking down into her eyes, at all of the colors shining within them, but I only see hazel. I want to kiss her again. I am *dying* to. I want to feel her lips pressed to mine again. I want to feel her skin against my own. I reach out to touch her elbow, lightly brushing my fingertips all the way down her arm to her wrist. Then, I move my hand to her waist.

"What's happening?" Eden whispers. She is quivering under my touch. She is tense; she isn't breathing again. She can't even look at me; she is watching the fireworks. I trace circles on her hip with my thumb, and my eyes never leave her face. I can feel our adrenaline radiating between us. She wants this too. I move my mouth to her jaw and brush my lips against her soft, soft skin. She is warm and comforting, and I kiss every inch of her skin from her jaw to her mouth. I hover by the corner of her lips.

The silence feels too fragile to break, but I dare myself to whisper, "Let me kiss you."

"But you're my stepbrother." Her voice is barely audible as she forces the words out through a breath of air, and she is frozen in place, my mouth so, so close to hers.

"Just don't think about it," I murmur, and I can't bear it any longer, so I take her lips in my own.

They are so plump and so perfect, and I kiss her in a way I've never kissed anyone else before. I kiss her so softly, so gently, taking in the sensation of her mouth against mine once more, and I don't think I will ever get enough of it. I tune out everything else around me. I tune out the fireworks. I tune out a distant voice that is calling. I am focusing on only this moment, on my heartbeat rocketing against my chest, on Eden. I pull her closer against me, deepening the kiss, quickening the pace. I want to explore every inch of her, and I can't stop my hands from moving. My fingers are wrapped in her hair, I am touching the small of her back, and I am pulling her against me until her body is molded into mine. My pulse is racing with the electricity and my head is spinning. She is giving me full control, working in sync with my movements, and I slow the kiss back down again. Moving my fingertips to her chin, I tilt her head up so that I can kiss her even deeper. And God, it's amazing.

"Alright, wrap it up," the distant voice is calling out, tearing through the bubble I'm in and bursting it completely. Even Eden has suddenly gone rigid. "Cut it out already!"

"Dammit," I mutter as I reluctantly pull away from Eden. The moment is ruined now anyway. I drop my hands from her body and throw them back through my hair as I turn around to face the jackass who has interrupted us. It's a cop. A Culver City police officer is staring at me, glaring sharply at us, and I fold my arms across my chest as I glare evenly back at him. It's so instant, so subtle, that I barely even realize I have switched straight back into my Tyler Bruce facade until I hear myself growling, "You got a problem?"

"You are trespassing," the officer states, his voice firm. He looks me up and down suspiciously, eyeballing the hell out of me, and then Eden.

"Trespassing?" I repeat. Is he kidding me? Is he on a power trip or something? "Don't you have better things to do? Like sorting out those drunk fights out there on the field?" I nod to the windows, to the masses outside as the fireworks continue to shower the black sky in an array of colors. It's July Fourth. I am pretty sure there are more serious matters to be dealing with.

"Enough with the attitude," the officer barks at me. He places his hands on his hips, resting on his duty belt. "This school is closed apart from the designated hallways. You are trespassing and I am giving you the chance to leave by yourself before I have to make you."

"Make me?" I almost laugh out loud. Is he threatening to drag me out of here? It's really not that serious. "Can't you just give us a second? We'll get out of here, but you kind of interrupted something."

"Tyler, just come on," Eden is mumbling. She is tugging at the hem of my shirt, begging me to drop it and just leave, but Tyler Bruce doesn't back down. I stand my ground, refusing to let her pull me away.

"Yes, I figured I interrupted something," the officer replies, his voice dripping with sarcasm, and he fires us both a disgusted glance. Was he watching us the entire time? What a creep. "I'm not asking to reason with you," he says. "I'm asking you to leave, and I expect you to do it. Don't try to waste my time, son."

"It's a goddamn hallway," I remind him, throwing up my hands. This is bullshit. I'll leave, but not until I get to finish what I started with Eden, not until I get to kiss her again without interruptions. "It's not like we're sneaking around the White House. Just give us five minutes."

"Can't you take no for an answer?" the officer snaps, growing agitated with my defiance. "Didn't your old man ever teach you how to obey orders?"

And there it goes: my temper. "Are you a fucking asshole or what?" I hiss at him as I step toward him, my fists balled by my sides. If he wasn't a cop, I would swing at him. Who the hell does he think he is? Orders are the only fucking thing my dad ever gave me.

"Alright, that's it," the officer says, and he plucks his pair of cuffs from his belt. "I have asked you to leave but you are refusing orders and your attitude is downright inappropriate, so I am arresting you under Section 602."

Shit. This can't be happening. I'm supposed to be laying low, staying off the radar, keeping my name out of their mouths. Out of the corner of my eye, I see Eden's lips part as her jaw falls open in shock, and at the same time, I hear the officer add, "Both of you."

37

FIVE YEARS EARLIER

WHEN HUGH DROPS ME off after school on Friday, I walk into the house to find Dad sitting at the kitchen table. Usually, when he takes the afternoons off from the office, he doesn't actually bring his work home. But today, the kitchen table is covered in binders and sheets of paper, pens, and a cup of coffee. Dad is hunched over the table, his tie loose, one hand in his hair, one hand holding up a sheet of paper in front of him that he's intensely studying.

The house is silent. Jamie and Chase will be upstairs. Ever since Dad moved the PlayStation 2 into their room, they have become hooked on video games.

I pull out a chair and sit down at the table across from Dad. It's been a week now since he made his promise, and he hasn't broken it. That's the only reason I sit down, because I am slowly trying to trust him again, just like I used to before it all went wrong. I rest my cast on the table and smile at him. "You're working from home?"

"Not working," Dad says as he quickly glances up at me without lifting his head. His smile mirrors mine, but I can see that it's forced. There are stress wrinkles on his forehead. "Figuring stuff out."

"What do you need to figure out?"

"You wouldn't understand. At least not yet. You will one day," he says. Sighing, he sets down the sheet of paper in his hand and rubs his temples. "Why does everything have to go wrong at the same time? Why do I have accounts missing the same week that *two* of my guys quit?" he mumbles, though I think he's talking to himself. Dad's company, Grayson's, used to run smoothly, from what I can tell. Structural engineering or something. Offices all up and down the West Coast. Successful. Or at least it used to be. The past few years…not so much. The pressure is stressful for him, and I've always figured that it's the stress that has led to his short temper.

"You'll fix it," I tell him. It's what Mom would say if she was here, but she's not, so I'll do the reassuring for her. I'm trying to stay on Dad's good side, and I don't want him to get stressed. I don't want him to get mad. "That's why you went to college. To be able to know how to fix things."

"No," he says. He lifts his head. "I went to college so that I could provide for you." He pushes the papers in front of him away and then rests his hands on the table, interlocking them as he edges forward. "Tyler, let me tell you something. When I was a teenager, I was an idiot. I didn't care. School? Whatever. I almost got kept back a grade in high school, not because I wasn't smart enough, but because I didn't put in the effort. Oh, your grandma… I drove her insane." He stifles a laugh as he rolls his eyes. "I was sixteen and in love with your mom. I'd steal my dad's truck and sneak out to see her. We'd drink cheap beer together. And then… Well, you know the story of the birds and the bees. We got a little surprise with you."

"Yuck," I mutter, wrinkling my nose at him in disgust. I already know Mom and Dad were young when they had me, that they were seventeen and still in school, and I really don't need to know anything more. It's gross.

"You won't be grimacing like that when you're sixteen, let me tell you that," Dad jokes, but then quickly raises an eyebrow at me and more seriously adds, "Or at least eighteen, please."

"*Dad*," I plead. My cheeks are burning hot.

"Okay, okay!" Dad laughs as he holds up his hands in surrender, then he focuses his soft gaze back on me again. "The point is: we cut the crap. We weren't going to be the parents that were high school dropouts, living in some cheap house and struggling to get by. We wanted better than that for you. That's why we stayed in school, graduated, and went to college." He stops for a moment as his expression becomes solemn again. "Tyler, your mom did seven damn years of college with three kids. Law school. With three kids. Do you understand how hard that was?" I nod. I still remember all of the late nights Mom spent working on assignments. "Well, that's how much she loved you. And me too. Because now you have everything you need, don't you?" I nod again, and Dad sighs. He gets to his feet and walks around the table, sitting back down on the chair next to me, his hands intertwining between his knees.

"This is why I push you so hard, Tyler," he explains, and now I finally understand the point of this story. "Not because I'm being a jackass, but because I don't want you to make the same mistakes I did. I want you to be successful. I want you to focus in school and get into a real good college. One of the best. We'll even pay those Ivy League tuition fees."

I furrow my eyebrows at him. "You expect me to get into an Ivy League school?"

"Well, why can't you?" he asks, and my expression is blank. "Exactly.

And then once you get your degree—in engineering, remember—I need you to run this company much better than I currently am. Okay?"

I don't have the nerve to tell him that maybe I don't want to get into engineering; maybe I don't want to run his company. So I just smile and say, "Okay."

And as his face lights up with pride, Dad pulls me into a hug full of warmth and love.

38

PRESENT DAY

"YOU COULDN'T HAVE JUST kept your mouth shut?" Eden is whispering into my ear from beside me. She is rubbing her forehead, massaging her temples.

We are currently sitting in a holding cell at the Culver City Police Department. Our parents have been called, and the longer we wait for them to turn up, the more visibly anxious Eden becomes. Clearly, she has never been arrested before. The process is unsettling for her, and if we were alone right now, then maybe I would, like, put my arm around her or something. But we're not. We have companions in here, such as the wasted woman in heels who is throwing herself to the floor in protest, wailing and yelling.

"Cop was a prick," I mutter back to Eden. I hate cops, or at least these cops. I sink back against the wall, watching all of the officers as they mill around the station. Phones are ringing, words are being said. "They all are." This is a lie. There *is* one officer who I will make an exception for, and only one, and that is Officer Gonzalez from the Santa Monica department. I like him.

"We wouldn't even be here if you'd just walked away," Eden says, sighing. She's mad at me again, because the only reason she is even sitting in this cell right now is because of me. I dragged her into it with me, and although I do feel guilty about it, I also know that she has nothing to worry about.

I groan and lean forward, resting my elbows on my knees as I stare at the floor. "My mom will get us out of it," I tell her, stealing a glance up at her. She is sitting next to me, but there are inches that separate us. We aren't touching. We can't. Not when there are people around.

Eden rolls her eyes, but she still doesn't look at ease. "What? Because she's an attorney?"

"Because she's done it before," I admit, sitting back up. There are always benefits to having a mom who is a lawyer. A civil attorney, sure, but she still knows her way around criminal law too. She hates it when I get myself into trouble like this, so she will always do anything she can to get me off lightly. She has been on a break from work for the past five years while we have dealt with the mess that we found our lives in, but she has never lost her skill. "She always gets me out of it."

"Before," Eden repeats. She looks at me, her eyes narrowing with curiosity. "How many times have you been arrested?"

"Once. Twice." I shrug as my lips curve into a playful smirk. "Maybe a couple more than that."

"What for?"

"Um. Stupid stuff," I admit. I have to think about it for a moment though. It's been a while since I last got arrested, and it *was* always stupid stuff. I stand up and pace in a small circle in front of Eden, cracking my knuckles. "Fighting, vandalism, disrupting the peace," I say, letting the words roll nonchalantly off my tongue. It's not like I've ever robbed a convenience store or anything, so I'm not too ashamed to tell her. I throw her a look, unable to stifle my laugh. "And trespassing."

"At least you haven't killed anybody," she says, and she *almost* smiles.

"Not yet," I say. I can picture Dad's face so clearly…"I've got someone in mind." My tone must be too solemn, probably because I *am* mostly being serious, and Eden's entire expression contorts with horror. She really believes me. "Eden," I say, cracking up into laughter, and I shake my head at her.

"I haven't figured out your sense of humor yet," she states as she crosses her arms over her chest, defensively pouting. Then, teasingly, she adds, "I didn't even know that you had one."

I smile at her, nodding in surrender. I like it when we're like this. I never act like this around anyone except my brothers. I feel like I *can* be playful around her. "Good one."

"Bruce. Munro." A voice suddenly calls out, catching us off guard, and I spin around to find Officer Greene scrutinizing us from the other side of the bars of the holding cell. He isn't the officer that arrested us, but he has been the one dealing with us while we've been here at the station. He's not *as* much of an asshole as the first guy. "Your parents are here," he states.

"We're going to die," Eden is spluttering under her breath as she gets to her feet. "Oh my God. We're actually going to die."

"Shut up," I tell her. I fire her a warning glance. She needs to relax. "Let me do the talking."

"Follow me." Officer Greene says as he unlocks the door of the holding cell.

Eden is close behind me as we follow Officer Greene through the station, and I can hear her deep breathing. Sure, Mom and Dave aren't going to be impressed, but we haven't *actually* had any charges pressed against us. At least not yet. I guess that's what we're about to find out.

Officer Greene leads us into a smaller, private office where our parents are waiting for us.

I look at Mom first. She knows I'm having a bad day, but right now, she can't afford to show her sympathy. She has her professional mask on—the taut expression she used to wear whenever she had important cases to work on. Her features are hard, her lips pressed tightly together, and she narrows her eyes straight at me. Every time I do something like this, I don't anger her as much as I sadden her. It reminds her that I'm not okay, that I'm off the rails, that I'm losing this war. Dave has enough fury for the both of them though. With his hands on his hips and his body rigid, he glares at Eden and me. His chest is puffed out and his cheeks are flushed red.

"What the hell are you two playing at?" he snaps at us, but Mom quickly steps in front of him. She'll handle this better than he can.

"Officer…" she says, looking at Officer Greene. She dramatically squints to read his badge, even though I know her eyesight is perfect.

"Greene," he says.

"Officer Greene," Mom begins, clearing her throat. She is about to get serious with him now, and she shakes his hand. "Can you explain to me why they have been arrested for trespassing? By the way, I'm an attorney." There is a small, innocent smile playing on her lips as she raises her eyebrow at him. She knows what she's doing, and I love it when I get to see this side of her. So in control, so strong. These days, I don't often get to see that.

"Trespassing under Penal Code 602 within Culver City High School," Officer Greene informs her, but his discomfort is evident. He is shifting his footing. "Only specified areas of the campus were open to the public for this evening's celebrations, and they were found in a hallway in a closed block."

Mom nearly rolls her eyes. It seems she was expecting something more arrest-worthy. "Really? They stumble into the wrong hallway and you arrest them?"

"Ma'am, I was not the arresting officer," Officer Greene tells her, holding up his hand. "Officer Sullivan doesn't have much patience, and your son here was showing a bit of attitude when asked to leave." He glances over at me. "They were given several chances to do so."

I almost laugh out loud. Officer Sullivan not having *much* patience is the understatement of the year. The guy couldn't even give us five minutes to leave. Mom flashes me a threatening glance, so I bite back my laughter and look down at the ground.

"I was in that school tonight and I do recall seeing 'NO ENTRY' signs," Mom says, her voice strong and firm. She is narrowing her eyes challengingly at Officer Greene. "But 'NO ENTRY' signs are not the same as signs warning that trespassing is an infraction and, therefore, neither of them were properly informed that they were committing an offense. They cannot be arrested on the grounds of your colleague's short temper."

I am still trying not to laugh. I lift my head to look at Eden, but her expression is still so dominated by fear and anxiety that I can't help but laugh even harder. I'm trying to hold it in, so I press my hand to my mouth in an effort to stifle it.

"How about," Officer Greene says as he extends his hand to Mom again, "we save both of us the paperwork and I let this one slide?" He gives her a tight, knowing smile.

"Respectable decision, Officer," Mom says, and she shakes his hand. She shoots Dave a look that I can't quite register, and he nods. She needs to stay behind to deal with this.

"Alright," Dave says, clapping his hands together. I can hear the seething anger in his tone as he orders, "You two, out to the car. Right now." Then, he pushes his way through Eden and me.

"Someone's mad as hell," I mutter. Dave will probably have his say once we get outside. He will tell me I'm grounded for another ten years, and then he'll probably give Eden a hug and tell her it's all okay.

I nudge Eden forward and we follow Dave out of the station and into the parking lot. I don't know what time it is, but it's dark and a cool breeze has picked up. I seriously doubt we'll be continuing the Fourth of July celebrations now. We head over to Mom's Range Rover, and when Eden and I pull open the back doors, we find that Chase is already asleep across the backseat. It's ironic, really, that our parents are mad at us for getting arrested for trespassing when they are illegally cramming four of us into this backseat.

"What'd you do this time?" Jamie asks, studying me curiously.

My eyes flicker to meet Eden's, and I can't fight the smirk that toys at my lips. "Something I shouldn't have."

We climb in and I move Chase out of the way, and the four of us are squeezed in side by side again, and I honestly don't know how I am to survive this drive back home. It was unbearable on the way here, and that was when Eden and I hadn't even spoken yet. Now, it is going to be even worse having my body pressed against hers after kissing her an hour ago.

I am waiting for Dave to start yelling at me, but he is only silently sitting in the driver's seat, gripping the steering wheel a little too tightly. Maybe he is keeping quiet because his daughter is here. Even if he is planning on saying something, he doesn't get the chance to, because Mom turns up. She pulls herself up into the passenger seat and slams the door shut behind her again, then crosses her arms over her chest as she stares out of the windshield.

"Nice going, Mom," I say in an effort to lighten the mood. I even sit forward and place my hand on her shoulder, trying to catch her eye. "You're killing 'em."

"Don't even talk to me, Tyler," she says, shaking my hand off her. She doesn't turn around, or even so much as glance at me. She only continues to stare ahead out of the window at nothing. "One of these days I'm just not going to turn up. I'm so disappointed in you."

"I'm disappointed in you too, Eden," Dave finally speaks up. His voice isn't as sharp or as acidic as it usually is, but it's still coarse. He switches on the engine and begins to drive, navigating our way out of the parking lot. "What the hell were you doing inside in the first place? I'm pretty sure the event was outside."

"No. The event was definitely inside," I remark. I am looking at Eden out of the corner of my eye, absolutely loving the alarm that crosses her features when I say this. The fact that this is so wrong is almost...fun. Our parents can't ever find out we were making out in that hallway. The secrecy is exhilarating, and I want to see just how much I can get away with. In the darkness of the backseat, I run my finger down Eden's thigh.

"Cut it out with the attitude," Mom snaps at me, and I realize that she really is mad at me tonight. "I just had to sign for both of you to get out of there when I could have easily just left you all night, okay? So here's an idea, Tyler: just sit there and be quiet for once in your life."

Damn. It's rare that Mom talks to me like that. I don't really take it to heart though. I know I drive her insane, and I know she is allowed to get mad at me sometimes. I take her advice and keep quiet for the entire drive back home. I focus on Eden instead, on touching her inconspicuously whenever I get the opportunity. I brush my hand against hers, press my knee to hers. She is staring out of the window and her face is illuminated orange from the streetlights as we pass under them, lighting her up and letting her glow. It makes the drive go quicker than it did earlier, and it is nearing midnight by the time we are all spilling in through the front door. Dave has Chase in his arms, still fast asleep.

"I don't even know what to say to you, Tyler," Mom is murmuring as she locks the front door behind us. Dave is carrying Chase upstairs, and Jamie is following. "I've just—I've had enough." She turns around to face me as she takes a deep breath. In her eyes, I can see how tired she is. "Eden, just go to your room. Get some sleep," she says, and she gives her a tight smile, politely hinting for her to leave us alone for a second. Eden gets the memo, because she doesn't even hesitate, only nods and heads upstairs.

I am left alone in the hall with Mom, and she walks through to the kitchen, so I follow her. I'm sort of embarrassed now. I *hate* doing this to her, so I keep my head low, too ashamed to meet her eyes.

"I know you're having one of your bad days, Tyler," she says quietly, her tone softening. She sighs and leans back against the countertop, pressing a hand to her face. "But...but please. Stop doing this. I'm worried you're going to get yourself into more serious trouble one day."

Like selling weed? I frown and give her a single, clipped nod to let her know I'm listening carefully. "I'm sorry, Mom," I say. I am. I'm sorry that I am *always* going to let her down.

"I know you are," she says as she stares back across the kitchen at me. The smile she gives me is sad again. I tear her apart sometimes, and I really wish I didn't. "Goodnight, Tyler."

"Night," I mumble, and I turn around and leave the kitchen. I head upstairs for my room, but before I get there, I spot Eden disappearing into hers. We didn't exactly cover everything we talked about tonight, like: What happens now? Before she closes her door, I quickly step into her room. She spins around and flinches at my sudden appearance.

"Hey," I whisper. I study her room for a minute, not exactly sure what I'm even going to say.

"Hi," she says blankly. "What'd your mom say?"

"Nothing," I say. I think Eden's still mad at me for getting her arrested, so I decide to start by apologizing. "Sorry for taking you down with me. I should have just left when the cop told us to."

She frowns. "It's fine."

I am about to say something more, to ask her about what happens between us now, but my ringtone cuts through the silence. My phone is vibrating in my jeans, and I quickly pull it out to find Tiffani's name flashing on my screen. *Please not now.* She always calls me if it gets to midnight and we haven't talked that day yet.

"Tiffani," I tell Eden. Sometimes I just ignore her calls, but I really can't afford to do that right now. Not when she is currently blackmailing me. Right now, I need to keep her happy, because when Tiffani isn't, she makes it known. "Sorry, I gotta talk to her. She'll get mad if I ignore her. I'm sorry," I say, glancing back at Eden. She is staring at me with wide eyes, and she looks almost pale again. I feel like such an asshole. I tell Eden I'm attracted to her and I kiss her, then I ditch her to answer a call from my girlfriend? My phone is still buzzing in my hand. "I'm really sorry. I have to," I whisper. I feel so guilty. I wish I could explain. I wish she knew that it's complicated.

The call will end if I don't answer it, and Eden's crushed expression is too much to bear, so I quickly turn around and leave. As I'm walking into my own room and closing the door behind me, I answer the call and press my phone to my ear. There is no emotion or enthusiasm in my voice when I say, "Hey, what's up?"

"Happy Fourth of July, baby!" Tiffani squeals down the line, and I almost hurl my phone straight across my room.

39

FIVE YEARS EARLIER

MY BROTHERS AND I race downstairs first thing on Saturday morning, elbowing each other out of the way as we fight to be the first to burst into Mom and Dad's bedroom. In unison, we sing out, "Happy birthday, Dad!"

They're both already awake. Mom is sitting in front of her dresser, applying her makeup, and Dad is pulling on a T-shirt. It's the weekend, so neither of them have work today. The sun is streaming into the room, and the smell of coffee is in the air. "You guys are up early!" he says as he turns around to look at us with a beaming smile on his face. Chase runs over to give him a hug, and Dad crouches down to draw him into his arms. Jamie joins them, but I don't. I linger by the door instead, watching their embrace.

"Are you going to turn gray now?" Chase asks.

"I sure hope not for another twenty years!" Dad says, running both his hands through his thick, black hair as he straightens back up again.

"I hope not too!" Mom jokes. She gets up from her dresser and walks over, squeezing Dad's shoulder as he flashes her an indignant look. "I'm just kidding, Peter. I'm sure you'll look just as charming when you're gray." She kisses his jaw, and then throws her arms around Jamie and Chase's shoulders. "Now who's hungry? There's bacon! Dad's favorite."

As she guides them out of the room and toward the kitchen, they all brush past me, but I don't follow. I stay with Dad instead as silence falls over us. "*Feliz cumpleaños*," I tell him. *Happy birthday*. I know he'll appreciate that, and I smile at him too. It's been two weeks now since he made his promise. It's been two weeks now since he's kept it.

His gaze meets mine, gentle and happy. "*Gracias*," he murmurs as a grin lights up his face. He loves it when I speak Spanish without him having to prompt me first. He's been trying to teach Jamie and Chase too, but they just aren't picking it up as quickly as I did. "You don't think I'm old, right?" Dad asks, teasingly raising an eyebrow as he walks over.

"No," I say. "Not yet."

"But I'm now officially halfway to sixty!"

We both laugh and he spins me around, places both his hands on my shoulders, and walks me through to the kitchen. Mom has the TV on and there's bacon cooking in a skillet, and she is swinging her hips back and forth, humming as she pours two cups of coffee. Chase is drumming at the table with two spoons, and Jamie is chugging milk from the carton. Gross.

"Open up your cards," Mom says as she turns around and slides a cup of coffee into Dad's hand. She takes a sip of her own and watches all of us with a sparkle in her eye as Dad and I sit down at the table, her hand resting on the back of Dad's chair.

There's a stack of cards on the table from us, from relatives, from friends. There's also some gifts. Mom picked them out on our behalf, and she picked out the cards too. We signed them late last night.

"Open mine first," Chase says eagerly, swiping one of the envelopes from the pile and thrusting it into Dad's hands, almost knocking his coffee over.

"Sure," Dad says, rolling his eyes. He sets the cup down on the table and opens Chase's card, then Jamie's, then mine. I watch him closely as his eyes run over the message I wrote. It's short and it's simple and it's in Spanish.

I wrote: *Feliz cumpleaños! Te amo, Papá.*

Dad glances up from the card. The smile he gives me is wide and sincere, reaching his eyes, lighting them. My cheeks flush with color, and I don't know why I'm embarrassed. Maybe it's because I mean it for once. Maybe I'm not just saying it to keep him happy. I can't look at him now, so I reach for the orange juice and pour myself a glass.

"I have something to tell you," Mom tells Dad as he begins to open her card. He pauses, the envelope half torn in his hands, and glances curiously up at her. She leans over his shoulder, wrapping her arms around him from behind, and she buries her face into the crook of his neck. "We," she murmurs, "are going to Vegas. Next weekend. Just us two, baby. Happy birthday." She plants a kiss just below his ear.

"Vegas?" Dad repeats, his eyes widening. The pitch of his voice always increases when he's surprised, and he reaches for Mom's hands as he tilts his head back to look up at her. She's still leaning over him, still grinning. Dad is blinking fast. "Ella, really? You didn't...you didn't need to do that." He puckers his lips at her and she leans down to kiss him again, upside down, and he squeezes her hands. "You're amazing."

"Why can't we come?" Jamie asks. He glares across the table at Mom and Dad, but they're too busy smiling back at one another that I don't even think they notice. I love how deeply they love each other.

"Because Vegas is very much twenty-one and over," Mom tells him with a laugh, finally tearing her eyes away from Dad. She glances at

Jamie, then me, then Chase. "Sorry, guys, but you'll be staying with your grandparents next weekend."

"How about," Dad says, "we all do something fun today first? Starting with ice cream."

Chase releases a gasp of excitement and he looks at me, his smile young and innocent, half of his teeth missing. I smile back at him. Dad hasn't taken us out for ice cream in forever. It means he's happy. We're happy. *I'm* happy.

40

I LIKE MY GYM sessions with Dean. Working out is one of the rare things I do to distract myself that is actually *good* for me. It clears my head for a couple hours, and honestly, I like getting to hang with Dean alone a couple times a week. Out of all my friends, he's the one I'm most comfortable around. We used to sneak into his garage when we were fourteen and use his dad's equipment, but over a year ago we upgraded to a gym downtown. I'm trying to bulk up. When I was a kid, I was weak and never had the strength to fight back. That's different now. These days, I can protect myself if I need to. It puts my mind at ease, I guess.

"Can I ask you something?" Dean says. He's currently spotting me while I bench press, his hands under the barbell, gently supporting the extra weight he's added so that I don't end up crushing myself. I need the extra help, anyway, because my left wrist still plays up sometimes and is forever weaker than my right.

I look up at him, watching his concerned expression upside down, but I am straining too hard to even reply. My jaw is clenched too tight, so I only manage to give him a tiny nod as I push the weight up, my biceps tight and my skin sticky with sweat.

JUST DON'T MENTION IT

"What even happened to you at Rachael's party?" Dean asks. "You totally blacked out. You weren't..." He pauses to glance around the bustling gym, but there is no one within earshot of us. He lowers his voice anyway as he looks back down at me again, his eyes meeting mine. "You weren't on anything, were you?"

His question annoys me, and it gives me the final burst of energy I need to raise the barbell back up into the rack above me. The metal clatters together as I blow out a breath of air and sit up, relaxing my arms. "No," I say. Usually, I would lie to him, but this time I don't need to. I'm telling him the truth. "I just drank too much."

"Yeah, but waaay more than usual," Dean says. "You passed out before it was even midnight. And you nearly sent Kyle Harrison to the hospital."

"What? He couldn't handle five beers?" I chuckle as I grab my towel from the floor and press it to my face, drying my forehead and my hair. My breathing is still heavy.

"Five beers in, like, three minutes," Dean corrects. He tosses me my water, and I catch it with one hand. He leans back against the wall and folds his arms across his chest, staring down at me in disapproval. "Not many people *can* handle that. Not even you, apparently. Did you sleep at Tiffani's place?"

I roll my eyes and take a swig of my water. "Unfortunately."

"That doesn't sound too good," Dean says. He narrows his eyes at me, full of curiosity but also concern. He always looks at me like that. I think that a lot of the time, he's still just trying to figure me out even after all these years. Sometimes, I wonder if he doesn't really know who I am anymore. "Are you guys on bad terms or something?"

I almost laugh. Tiffani and I are on bad terms with one another *a lot*, so I get to my feet and simply tell him, "No. Just Tiffani being Tiffani.

C'mon, let's get out of here." I don't want to get into the details, so I head for the lockers.

"Have you talked to Jake yet?" Dean asks as he follows me. I hate when he does this, when he begins to question me about everything and anything. I love the guy, but he's infuriating sometimes.

I glance sideways at him as I pull open my locker door. "About what?"

"About Eden," he clarifies. He looks away from me and shoves his head into his own locker, grabbing a towel and his car keys. "Is he seriously interested in her or is he just messing around?" he asks, and his voice echoes around inside his locker. I slam my locker door shut and turn toward him.

"Why don't *you* ask him?" Fuck Jake. The thought of him and Eden... It pisses me off. I *will* talk to him about Eden eventually, but not now, and I don't need Dean to keep bringing it up.

"No. I'm not... I mean, I don't care," Dean murmurs quickly as he closes his locker and shrugs at me. "I guess I was just wondering. Let's go."

We leave the gym and head back to Dean's car. Sometimes, we grab food or stop for coffee on our way home, but today I can't. I have commitments to stick to, like all of the promises I've made to people asking for a hookup. I need to make some drop-offs before I do anything else today. That's why I'm quiet during the ride home, because I can't keep my head out of my phone. I have messages from Declan asking me when I'm dropping by his place, and Tiffani won't stop texting me ten times every hour to ask what I'm doing. Over the past few days, she has become even more clingy than she usually is. I reply to her most recent message, telling her I'm heading to the beach with Dean for the afternoon, then I slide my phone back into the pocket of my shorts.

"If Tiffani asks," I say, angling my jaw toward Dean, "we're at the beach. All afternoon. Then we grabbed food. Okay?"

Dean makes a face as he glances at me out of the corner of his eye. The lights turn red, so we slow to a stop at the intersection. "What are you *really* doing today?"

I'm about to roll my eyes and ask him if he seriously thinks I will answer that, but my attention is distracted when a girl runs past the car. My head flips around so fast that my neck cracks, and I immediately sit upright and squint out of the window. She disappears across the street and down the sidewalk, blending into those around her as I stare after her. Her ponytail swings around her shoulders and her bare legs glisten in the sun. I have checked Eden out enough times to know that it's her. And I also know that she likes to run.

Our light turns green again. We continue ahead and my eyes are scanning the sidewalk until we catch up with her again. She is easy to spot. She is the only person running, carefully weaving her way around everyone.

"Slow down a little," I tell Dean, pressing my hand to the dashboard. My face is nearly pressed into the window. "That's Eden. Pull up." There is no way I am letting Dean just drive on by. Not when Eden looks so good.

Dean does as I tell him, and as we pull over to the right, he also lays on the horn. Eden has her earphones in, but she must hear the horn over the sound of her music, because suddenly her pace slows and she turns around. She is out of breath, her chest heaving, and she pulls out one earphone and takes a few cautious steps closer to the car. I'm not sure if she knows who we are yet since Dean's windows are tinted, so I quickly roll down my window and flash her a smile. She looks even better without the filter.

"I knew it was you," I tell her. I think I could recognize her anywhere now. All I've been thinking about is her.

"What gave it away?" Eden asks through her ragged breaths. She pulls out her other earphone and rests her hands on the door, leaning forward to look at me with a challenging smirk toying at her mouth. Not only am I in a good mood today, so is she.

I can't answer her question though. Not in front of Dean, so I only laugh and glance away from her for a second. "We just got outta the gym," I say, changing the subject. Teasingly, I add, "We're heading back to my place and you look like you're about to die, so you may as well just get in the car."

"I am not dying," she argues, narrowing her eyes at me. Loose strands of hair frame her face, and I catch her exchanging a glance with Dean before she sets her gaze back on me again. "I can run for miles, okay?"

"Okay," I echo, raising the pitch of my voice in an effort to mimic her. I like messing with her, and even though I have places to be and people to see, I want to hang out with her. I push open the car door and she quickly steps back from the vehicle as I get out and join her on the sidewalk. "I'll jog back with you."

"But I like to run on my ow—" she tries to say, but I'm not giving her a choice.

Before she can finish, I step in front of her and lean back in through the window to grab my bag from inside the car. "Bro, you don't mind, right?" I ask Dean.

He is watching me with what seems to be confusion, but then he shakes his head no and says, "Another session on Wednesday?"

"Yeah. See you then, man," I say, stepping away from the car. Dean rolls the window back up and then heads off down the street. I stare after the car until he is completely gone, and then I turn back to Eden as we begin to walk. "Just so you know," I say, smirking, "it was your ass that gave it away."

Eden's eyes widen and she looks herself up and down. "Um," she says, and I realize that perhaps we don't share the *exact* same level of humor.

Quickening my pace, I change the subject in case I've offended her and instead tease her by saying, "I can probably walk faster than you can run."

"I highly doubt it," she says, not quite looking at me as she places one earphone back in and swigs her water. She keeps her gaze focused straight ahead as she matches her pace to mine.

"I bet I can beat you back to the house," I challenge. I haven't showered yet, so I don't mind working up a sweat again, and besides, she will probably speed back up into a run any second now anyway. "Are you game?"

She rolls her eyes as she looks over at me. "I'm totally game." As soon as she says it, she doesn't wait to give us both a fair start. No, she sets off, exploding into a sprint and darting off down the sidewalk in front of me. I don't mind though. I like watching her as she runs, as she dashes along in wide strides, her chin held high.

I can't stare after her forever though, so I break out into my own sprint, slinging my bag over my shoulder and bounding down the street after her. I'm fast, but I don't have the stamina like she does. It takes all of my energy just to catch up to her, and when I do, I race straight past her, playfully calling out, "Sucker." I hear her laughter echo out around me, breathy and light, and suddenly she is by my side again, our footsteps in sync, thundering down the sidewalk. Already I have pushed myself too hard and I am struggling to breathe, so I slow myself down to a brisk jog. I expect Eden to continue without me, but I'm glad when she slows down too, sticking with me.

"You sure do run a hell of a lot," I comment, but I am panting like a dog. I really, really don't do this running thing. Eden, however, is good at it. "Do you do cross-country or something?"

"No. I just like running," she says. Her gaze is focused on the route ahead, and her breathing is quiet and steady. "It's the best way to work out."

"Personally, I prefer lifting," I say, glancing down at my arms. I even flex a little. The workout Dean and I just put ourselves through is most likely going to leave us aching later. "Alright," I say, bringing myself to a halt and holding a hand up to Eden. "I give up. I'm not a runner. You win." My breathing is ragged and heavy, so I press my hand to the wall of a building for support while it calms down.

Eden stops too and turns to face me as she places her hands on her hips. She is grinning, basking in the joy of my surrender. "You're damn right I won."

"That sounds like something I would say." I laugh and lift my gaze to meet hers, and her hazel eyes are already boring into mine, glistening as the sunlight hits them. Slowly, she takes her lower lip between her teeth, and whether or not she's aware that she's doing it, she is driving me crazy. "We're hanging out tonight," I tell her. It's not a question. I *need* to spend more time with this girl, not just because I am dying to kiss her again, but because I actually like being around someone who I don't feel so pressured to put on a performance around, someone who challenges me, and someone who finds me as interesting as I find her. "Let me take you out. Have you been to the pier yet? Pacific Park?"

She tilts her head down a little as her cheeks flush with color, and it's definitely not from the running. "No," she says quietly.

"Then we'll go to the pier," I say with a smile that I can't quite fight. Did I just ask her on a date? Also, how has she *not* been to the pier yet?

"Okay. We'll go to the pier," she agrees. Her eyes light with enthusiasm and her mouth forms a perfect, intoxicating smirk, but I only witness it for a fraction of a second before she turns around and bursts back into a jog. She disappears in front of me, shrinking into the distance until she is gone entirely, leaving me wanting more.

My smile never falters, and I don't even mind the walk home.

41

FIVE YEARS EARLIER

WE LOVE STAYING AT our grandparents' house. Grampa always lets us stay up late to watch TV, even on school nights, and Grandma cooks amazing food and enough to feed an army. We're staying here for the next three nights, my brothers and me, and we are whizzing through the front door with our luggage. They are the only grandparents we have. We've never met Mom's parents.

"Slow down! Slow down!" Grandma Maria tells us as she emerges from the kitchen to greet us in the hall. We almost crash straight into her, but I'm the first to wrap my arms around her. It feels like we haven't visited in months, even though they only live ten minutes away, and Grandma gives the *best* hugs.

"I can hear you rascals from the backyard!" Grampa says. He walks into the hall, sliding a pair of his glasses onto his nose. He's always been as blind as a bat, and that's why he tells us never to stare at computer screens for too long unless we want to end up like him. Jamie and Chase fight to hug him. Dad and Mom walk in through the front door with an air of excitement surrounding them. The entire morning, the pair of them have been acting like kids, rushing around the house and throwing last-minute items into their suitcases. Mom was even drinking champagne at 8:00 a.m., so I'm pretty sure the celebrations this weekend are going to be big.

"Your flight. What time?" Grandma asks them. She is from Mexico, and although she's lived here for over thirty years now, her accent is still thick and her English is still a little broken sometimes. Her skin is tan, her hair is thick and dark, and she has passed those genes down to Dad and me. She still has her arm around my shoulders, soothingly rubbing my arm.

"Noon, so we better get going!" Dad says. He lets go of Mom's hand and walks down the hall, wrapping his arm around Grandma and kissing her cheek. "Any problems, call us."

"Pete," Mom says, fixing Grampa with a stern look, "please don't take them out in the car. You ran straight through a stop sign last time!"

"Oh, Ella," Grampa says, rolling his eyes, "you *know* I will." He looks over at me and winks. Grampa still owns the red Corvette he had when he was a teenager, and he likes to drive it way too fast. It's old, but it's still cool. We love it when he takes us with him, when we fly down the Pacific Coast Highway with all of the windows rolled down.

"Tyler gets his cast off on Monday morning, so please remember to take him to the appointment," Dad tells his parents, glancing between the two of them, mostly looking at Grandma. She's more likely to be the one to take me, and I glance down at my cast, covered in drawings and names and dirt. It's been three weeks, and I can't wait to finally have it removed for the last time. "And make sure Tyler gets his work done," Dad adds. I quickly glance back up at him to find that he is already staring at me, his eyes narrowed. He doesn't like it when he's not able to keep an eye on me. It's like he doesn't trust me to study unless he's here, so I give him a silent nod of agreement.

"Oh, c'mon, Peter, it's the weekend!" Grampa says with a chuckle. Dad is named after him, though Grampa goes by Pete now. He runs his hand through his graying dark hair and steps closer to Dad, squeezing his shoulder. "Lighten up. If you guys are getting to Vegas, then there's no way the kids are *studying*. That's unfair. Am I right?" He grins at Mom, and she just shakes her head at him, smiling.

Dad doesn't laugh though. He cranes his neck to look at Grampa, who is still standing by his side, still resting his hand on his shoulder. "Dad," he says firmly, his features hardening. His voice is almost threatening as he quietly demands, "Make sure he studies."

"Peter," Mom says, clearing her throat. When Dad looks over at her, she nods at the clock on the wall. "We should make a move. Now," she says, turning her attention to my brothers and me, "you guys need to behave, okay? Come here!" She crouches down and extends her arms out to us, and we all hug her tight, and she kisses each of us, and she asks us to be good, and we promise her that we will be.

"And *you* guys behave too!" Grampa says, pointing a finger at Mom and Dad, wiggling his eyebrows at them.

"*Sí,*" Grandma agrees, stepping forward. She places her hands on Mom's shoulders, kisses both her cheeks, then frowns. She glances at Dad, then back at Mom. "Alcohol…not too much. No casinos. So stupid."

"*Sí, sí. Te amo, Madre,*" Dad says with the roll of his eyes, and I get the feeling he and Mom aren't going to listen to her advice. "Bye, Dad."

We watch them from the porch as they climb back into Dad's Mercedes and drive off, waving goodbye to us until they are out of sight down the street.

"So…" Grampa says, turning to face us. He is smirking. "Who wants to go for a drive?"

42

I'M SO HUNGRY AFTER running around all afternoon that I don't even care that we are all sitting in the kitchen eating dinner together for once. Mom, my brothers, Dave...even Eden. We are all here, all sitting around the table, all facing each other as I shovel lasagna down my throat. The best part about being vegetarian is that Mom always makes separate dishes for me, and therefore, I get more. I'll stick to the four cheeses, and they can all fight over the meat dish.

"So, Eden," I hear Dave say, and I curiously glance up from my plate to listen in. I look across the table at Eden, and she must have already been staring at me because she instantly drops her gaze down to her food and grabs her silverware, clattering it against her plate. "You're being so quiet tonight. What are you thinking about?" Dave asks teasingly, and for once, he's actually being okay. For the first time, I almost see him smile at her.

"I was—um—I was just—I—uhhh," Eden babbles, and I suspiciously raise an eyebrow at her. What is up with her? She scoops up a tiny forkful of food and bites into it, but she's hardly eaten anything so far. She never really does.

"How's the lasagna?" Mom asks. Her gaze travels around the table, studying each of us one by one, her smile content. I can tell that having all of us eat dinner together means a lot to her. It's something normal, something that real families do.

"It's great, Mom," I say, mirroring her warm expression. Even though we *aren't* a real family, I like that she seems happy tonight, so I'm not going to ruin that. Besides, I'm happy today too. I'm taking Eden to the pier after this. "It tastes so great that..." I sit up and pull my plate toward me, forking a huge mouthful of what's left, and I shove it into my mouth. As I do so, I spill half the lasagna on the table, but I just laugh and wipe my mouth as I swallow. "It tastes so great that now I'm totally full."

"You're in a good mood tonight, Tyler," Dave comments. I fold my arms and rest them on the table as I look at him. Dave can be alright when he wants to be. I don't hate the guy or anything. We have just never seemed to click, and it doesn't help that I'm not searching for a new father figure either. Little does he know, however, that I am in a good mood because of his daughter. My eyes flick over to meet Eden's, and it is so hard not to smirk at her. "I guess I am," I say in reply to Dave. I can't wait to hang out with her, so instead of dithering around at the table any longer, I clear my throat and get to my feet, carrying my plate over to the dishwasher. "I'm gonna head out," I announce when I turn back around to the table. Jamie and Chase are still eating with their mouths open.

"Where?" Mom asks. She locks up at me as her smile falters. Instead, concern takes over her expression. "You're grounded."

"But I'm seeing Tiffani," I lie. Even though I'm permanently grounded, Mom usually doesn't mind me heading out if it's to see my girlfriend. Even though she knows it's meaningless, she still thinks maintaining relationships with people is good for me—much better than cutting myself off from the world completely—but she has no idea how toxic this one is. "Didn't you say you're hanging out with Meghan, Eden?" Immediately, I fire Eden a look, one that tells her to say yes.

I'm pretty certain that out of the two of us, I am the better liar. "Yeah," Eden says. She is still sitting at the table, and I catch her glancing at her dad.

"I can give you a ride there," I tell her. I'm keeping my voice loud and clear to ensure that our parents hear us. They'll think I'm with Tiffani and they'll think Eden is with Meghan, and they will never know that, actually, we are going to be together. I suppose they wouldn't bat an eyelid anyway. Maybe they would just think I'm being nice for once and showing my stepsister around town. As if. It's way more than that.

"Thanks," Eden says, and she is getting the hang of this now. She is trying to play along, but the goofy smile on her face would be enough to raise suspicion. Suddenly, she seems way too happy to receive a ride from me. However, I don't think our parents are even paying attention, which is good, because I am smiling back at her.

"Ten minutes?"

"Ten minutes is fine," she says.

"I'll just meet you at the car," I say, and like a complete douche bag, I *wink* at her. It's gross, but I can't help it. I leave the kitchen and head upstairs to my room, rubbing at the back of my neck as the nerves roll in. *Are you really taking Eden on a date?* No, I'm not. *You can't take your stepsister on a date.* We're just…hanging out.

But you also don't kiss her either.

I should have told Eden twenty minutes, because ten is nowhere near enough. I'm in my bathroom, freshening up and spraying more cologne than usual and playing with my hair for too long. I even throw some gel into it before I raid my closet. I pull on a blue flannel shirt on top of the white T-shirt I'm wearing, and then a red one, and then the blue again. I settle on the red, but I am fumbling around with the buttons on my shirt, deciding whether or not I am closing the shirt or leaving it open, and I end up just telling myself to *chill the fuck out*. I leave the shirt open, grab my wallet and my keys, then head downstairs again and make my way outside to my car. I'm so busy overthinking all of this that I forget to say goodbye to Mom.

I sit in the car for a few minutes while I wait for Eden, but with every second that passes, the more anxious I get. I know Eden and I shouldn't be doing this. Tiffani would kill me if she knew I was blowing her off tonight to hang with another girl, and although I still don't really know *why* exactly I'm doing this, I know that I'm not doing it to hurt her. I just need to know, I guess. I have kissed other girls before, but that's all it ever was. With Eden…I don't want to just forget about it and move on, but do I ever want anything more than that?

As I slip on my sunglasses and look over at the house, I spot Dave peering outside from the living room window. The front door opens and Eden emerges, running across the lawn toward me, and I roll down the passenger window as she nears. I lean forward to look up at her as I joke, "I'd open the door for you, but I think your dad would have something to say about it."

Eden casts a glance over her shoulder at the house. She spots Dave too, and she throws her hand up into the air and waves across the lawn at him. Quickly, he disappears from the window after having been caught, and Eden pulls open the car door and joins me inside. "Yeah. I think he'd wonder where your new manners suddenly came from," she says with a grin.

"Hey!" Defensively, I throw my hands up while she rolls up the window and pulls on her seatbelt. She angles her body to face me, and when her eyes meet mine, all of my nerves disappear entirely. "I'll have you know I'm a true gentleman."

She arches a brow at me. "Really?"

"Really," I say. I look away from her as I switch on the engine and turn up the AC, then I pull down my sun visor and take off my shades so that I can see her without the sepia filter. My gaze shifts back to hers and I crack a smile. "Alright, I'm not," I admit. I'm a jerk most of the time. Never a gentleman. "I've just heard that that's what you're supposed to do. Always get out of the car and open the door. Right?"

"Something like that," she says quietly, but she is looking at my mouth.

And I would kiss her right there if I could, but I have to refrain myself. I shake my head and turn my attention to the road, slamming my foot to the floor out of habit and feeling the growl of my engine as we head off. It's a nice drive down to the beach, mostly because it's a perfectly average summer evening here in Santa Monica, with the sky becoming a golden haze as the evening sets in. I roll down the windows, letting the breeze hit our faces, and I even turn up the radio. Usually, I hate mainstream pop, but tonight, I nod my head in sync with the music.

"Why did you lie to your mom?" Eden asks. "Why didn't you just say we're going to the pier?"

Oh, she's so innocent. "C'mon, Eden, keep up," I say with a laugh. "We don't want them to get suspicious."

She chews at her lower lip, not quite smiling at me anymore. "What about Tiffani?"

"I've got it covered," I reassure her, though I have to look away again, staring ahead at the traffic waiting to enter the pier. "She thinks I'm hanging out with the guys." My tone is such a monotone as I say this, but I just can't think about Tiffani right now. Not when she's black-mailing me, not when I'm going behind her back. I swallow the lump in my throat.

The pier is packed, but it always is, so once we are finally parked and heading down the boardwalk, we have to weave our way around the crowds. Eden sticks close by my side and her arm brushes against mine, and for a second, I almost slip my hand into hers like I would if it were Tiffani by my side instead. It's a habit, and tonight I make sure to break it. I *cannot* slip up and touch her tonight, at least not while we're down here on the pier, so open and so public, practically begging to bump into someone I know.

"Alright," I say, clearing my throat. I raise my voice and pull off the most official tone I can as I nod down to the amusement park. "So this is Pacific Park. And I am going to show you Pacific Park because I used to love this place when I was a kid and I want to be the one to introduce you to it." I still can't believe she hasn't come down here yet. Our pier is world famous and most definitely the city's best feature.

Eden doesn't say anything at first, only tilts her head up at me and smiles warmly as we walk, almost like she is waiting for me to say something more. After a minute, she asks, "Why is the roller coaster yellow?"

I look down at her. She is several inches shorter than me, and as we walk side by side, she is eye level with my shoulder. I shrug at her. "Honestly? No idea."

She asks me more questions that I don't know the answers to. Silly questions, like whether or not the food from the food trucks is garbage, and why all the benches are positioned the way they are. I wonder if she's spluttering out random, pointless questions because she's nervous.

"This guy right here used to scare the shit out of me," I tell her as we reach the amusement park entrance. I point up to the Pacific Park sign and the giant, freakish purple octopus that wraps around it. I don't know why, but I hate the damn thing. "It still kind of does," I admit, and I shove my hands into my pockets as we head on inside.

"Ahhh," Eden says with a teasing edge to her voice. "Not so badass anymore, are you?"

"Well," I say, "would a badass tell you that he's in love with cotton candy?" I grab my wallet and lead her over to the nearest food stall that is selling a wide array of amusement park favorites including, of course, cotton candy. When I was younger, way back when things with Dad were good, he would take my brothers and me down to the pier every once in a while, and he'd buy us cotton candy once we got bored of messing around in the arcade. It's one of the few memories I actually like, so it doesn't bring my mood down as I buy Eden and me some.

"Are you sure you *used* to love this place?" she asks me as I pass her the stick of cotton candy. Her hazel eyes are sparkling as she watches my expression, and I realize that maybe I am smiling too wide. Even though Pacific Park is for kids, I do still like it. I'll never admit to it though.

"We need to go on the coaster," I say as I shove a wad of cotton candy into my mouth, changing the subject. It melts on my tongue, and I set off again, searching for someplace to sit down while Eden follows close behind me.

I love the sound of the roller coaster clattering around its track above us, the ocean breeze that whistles around us, the laughter that fills the air. There's something so...*happy* about the pier. The street performers over on the boardwalk. The sun setting behind the mountains. It's real nice just sitting here on a bench in the middle of it all, eating cotton candy with Eden right next to me. We're quiet as we eat, and I realize that although we are relaxed and playful, there is also a more serious matter at hand.

"Eden," I say quietly, angling my jaw toward her. She places the final piece of cotton candy on her tongue, and she stares back at me, her expression calm. I frown. "I wouldn't mention this to anyone. It's just easier if we, um…keep this whole thing a secret for now. God, please say you're good at keeping secrets."

Her expression changes slightly, like she is realizing too that what we're doing here isn't exactly right, and in more ways than one. "I am," she says after a moment of silence. She offers me a small smile. "And I know that you're good at keeping secrets, because you clearly have a lot of them."

Oh, she does know me so well. I *do* have many secrets, and no matter how desperately she tries to crack them, most of them will remain that way. All I can do is smirk back at her, *daring* her to even attempt to figure me out, and I toss the remainder of my cotton candy into my mouth, then get to my feet. "It's time for these guys," I tell her, then point out the rides around us.

And so we set off again, working our way around the park over the course of the evening, getting tokens for rides and standing in line and murmuring our thoughts at one another. At one point or another, I just stop caring entirely about the crowds around us, and I focus solely on Eden at every moment. We are carefree and laughing, and it seriously feels good just to chill out for once and be myself. I don't want the night to end, but eventually, we leave the park and make our way along the boardwalk toward the parking lot. I love the pier at night when it's dark. Everything is lit up and you can hear the soft roll of the waves below.

When we get back to my car, there are a couple people snapping pictures of it, but when they see us approaching, they quickly walk away. I roll my eyes and unlock the car, and both Eden and I slide inside. I'm used to the attention. It's why I bought the damn thing in the first place. *The guy with the nice car has his life figured out.*

"It happens all the time," I tell Eden as I run my finger around the Audi badge on my steering wheel, frowning. *The guy with the nice car is happy.* "I don't know why. It's LA. There's, like, Lambos and shit on every corner in Beverly Hills."

"How did you even get this car?" she asks, narrowing her eyes curiously at me, and it's a fair question. People ask it all the time, and usually, I just shrug and tell them the truth. Or at least half of it.

"Because I got my trust fund early," I finally say. I'm still staring at my steering wheel, slumped back in my seat and running my hands around its edge. "And when you suddenly have all this money, you're not really going to be rational about it, are you? I'm a teenager, of course I'm gonna go out and blow it all on a sports car." *And it was a stupid idea.*

"Why'd you get it early?"

"Because apparently money can make you feel better," I mutter without thinking, and I immediately freeze. I shouldn't be talking about this to anyone, but...she asked. And maybe, for once, I should be a little more honest. Bottling everything up hasn't done many favors for me, and Eden at least seems genuinely interested, like she actually *cares.* "It's a big trust fund," I say after a minute. "I mean, my mom's an attorney and my dad... My dad had his own company. Structural engineering. All up and down the West Coast." I swallow the lump in my throat as I look sideways at her. I feel sick just talking about it, but I need to at least *try* the honest route. Mom always says talking about it would help, but I've never believed her.

"What was it called?"

"Grayson's," I say slowly, my tone hardening. Hearing that name... our name... It breaks me. It brings back too many memories of him, of the family that we used to be. "Because we were the Graysons."

Eden must sense that I'm uncomfortable, because she angles her body to face me as she pulls her legs up onto the seat and crosses them. Her gaze never leaves mine and she offers me a few moments of silence before she asks, "Before the divorce?"

"Before the divorce," I repeat. Before everything went wrong. I look away from her again, out to the thinning crowd of people mulling around the parking lot, and I slide further down in my seat and pull at my hair. It's a habit I have learned from Dad. "I used to be Tyler Grayson. Mom didn't want us to keep his name."

Eden goes quiet. I don't think she knows what to say, but I don't need her to say anything at all. Just being able to talk about these things while knowing that someone is listening is enough. I can't tell her anything more though. At least not now. I don't do this whole opening-up thing, so it's hard enough as it is just talking about the basic, factual stuff like my previous damn surname, let alone my secrets. I don't know if I'll ever be able to share them, and I still haven't figured out whether or not I even want to. It would make me vulnerable, and when Dad was arrested five years ago, I promised myself that I would never again allow myself to become vulnerable.

Eden is staring at me intensely, her gaze on my mouth. Silence surrounds us. Slowly, I sit up and lean toward her, moving my hand to her knee. I have been dying to touch her again all night, and now I am staring at her mouth too, and I can't help but lick my lips. My eyes drift back to hers, and I dare myself to murmur, "Can I kiss you again?"

Suddenly, Eden gets up and climbs across the center console, swinging her body on top of mine. She straddles my lap, pressed between my body and my steering wheel, and she looks down at me with those wide, glistening hazel eyes of hers, and her plump lips are innocently parted. Her hands are pressed to my chest, and I don't know where all of this confidence has come from, but it is the most attractive thing in the world.

I move my hands to her face, cupping her cheeks and winding my fingers into her hair as I press my lips to hers. Every time feels even more amazing than the last, and I just can't get enough of her. I kiss her fast again, as best I can, showing her absolutely everything that I've got. My hands are in her hair, around her back, over her waist. After a minute, I tear my lips away from her mouth and tilt her chin up, moving her hair to one side as I move to her neck instead. I leave a path of kisses across her skin, breathing her in.

She is pressing her body into mine and running her hands through my hair, and then suddenly she reaches for my jaw and lifts my head back up as she leans in closer, her mouth hovering by my ear. Her breath is hot against my skin as she whispers, "You don't even need to ask."

43

DAD AND I ARE wearing matching personalized 49ers jerseys that say *Grayson* on the back. He got them for us as a surprise, presenting me with them right before the game, and now we are sporting them proudly at the stadium. The game is well underway, and the 49ers have the lead with the Chargers trailing behind. It's my first ever football game and the atmosphere is amazing. The crowd is chanting, the stadium is rumbling. There are thousands upon thousands of people here, all packed in and cheering, and I'm on my feet with Dean by my side, both of us peering down at the field. Hugh takes him to games all the time. I wish my dad did the same.

"Did you see that?" I ask Dean, nudging him eagerly with my elbow. The players down on the field look tiny, so we are mostly watching the game on the screens, running our own personal live commentary. Dean understands football a little better than I do—Hugh lets him play, after all, and he wants to play football in high school—so he keeps explaining different plays to me.

"Yeah! That throw was *insane!*" Dean replies, his mouth wide open as his eyes flit around the field, never leaving the game. "Those are the type of throws I want to be able to catch." I lean forward a little and look past him, over to Dad and Hugh, who are sitting talking to one another, laughing and chugging beer out of cheap plastic cups. I'm not even sure if they're watching the game. I think they're just enjoying hanging out.

Dad catches my eye, and he smiles wide at me and asks, "Enjoying the game?"

"Uh-huh. Where's the…the restrooms?"

"I'll be back in a minute," Dad tells Hugh, and he presses his cup of beer to his lips and chugs the remainder of it before getting to his feet. He squeezes past Dean, places his hand on my back, and guides me along the row. There's so many people, so I'm glad he is coming with me, because there is no way I'd ever find my way back to my seat without him. It is *way* more hectic than a baseball game.

"Can we do this again?" I ask Dad as we swiftly navigate our way through the flow of people. I got my cast off at the beginning of the week, so it feels great not to be lugging around the extra weight on my arm anymore. My wrist is still stiff and it's still weak, but at least it's getting closer to recovery.

"It's fun, huh?" Dad says, grinning down at me as we walk. "We never hang out just the two of us, not without your brothers trying to get involved, so let's do this more often. How does that sound?" When I glance up at him, he is holding out his hand to me, so I high-five him with my strong hand. I like hanging out with Dad when it's just the two of us. We get to the restrooms, and when we meet again by the sinks, I study Dad curiously as I'm running the water over my hands. It's been a month now. We're happy. Things are different now, and I don't think they are ever going to go back to the way they were. I think Dad has really changed. He is smiling a lot, and when he *does* get stressed, he keeps his distance from me. That's why I figure it's safe to ask him a question that I've been dying to ask for a while now, because if his behavior is different, then maybe his mindset is too. "Dad?"

He glances sideways at me. "Yeah?"

I don't know why I feel anxious to ask, but I stare down at my hands anyway, watching the water cascade over my skin. "Do you think... Do you think that maybe I could play football sometimes?" I slowly mumble, forcing my words out. I know Dad doesn't like the idea of me playing football. He says it's too dangerous and that I could get hurt. "With Dean and Jake? We want to join the team in high school."

Dad immediately turns off the water and spins around to face me. "What did you just say?" he asks, but his tone is abrupt. I think he already knows what I said.

"Football..." I say again anyway, slowly. There is a sinking feeling in my stomach that I can't quite explain. My nerves begin to heighten. "Can I play it?"

"Drop it, Tyler. I swear. You're not playing football," he says with a certain degree of finality to his words. He looks away, drying his hands on his jeans. There are a couple more guys in here, but they are leaving.

"But, Dad! Dean gets to!" I whine, folding my arms across my chest. Why can't he just let me play? It's only football. It's not going to take over my entire life.

Dad's green eyes flash up to me, and the smile he was wearing five minutes ago definitely isn't returning anytime soon. He narrows his eyes, his jaw clenching as he points his finger at me. "Dean isn't my son; you are. And you're not playing, so don't bring it up again."

I turn back to the sink, staring at my reflection in the mirror, grinding my teeth together. "You can't stop me," I mutter under my breath. I love Dad, I do, and I forgive him, I think, but I wish he would just let me do this *one* thing. I do everything else he asks of me. Why can't he give me a break? Suddenly, Dad grabs a fistful of my jersey and yanks me toward him. It's so quick that my breath catches in my throat. He lowers his forehead to mine until our eyes are level, and he is glaring at me in such a way that brings back so many memories of all of those bad nights from before, all of those nights that I thought were over for good. "You don't have *time* for football," he hisses, and he is so close that I can smell the beer on his breath. "Not now, and especially not in high school. Mention it to me *one* more time… One more fucking time, Tyler!"

"Dad…" I swallow hard as I glance down at his fist. His knuckles are paling as his grip on my jersey tightens. Does he realize what he's doing? Does he realize that he's breaking his promise? My eyes flick around the restroom, but the only person here is a guy at the opposite corner, pacing back and forth while talking on his cell phone. He doesn't even notice. It's up to me to say, "Stop." My voice sounds just as weak as it used to.

With his fist still wrapped up in my jersey, Dad shoves me back against the sinks, hard. He shakes his head at me, and for the first time in a month, he is looking at me with disappointment and aggravation. It is the most terrifying thing in the world. He runs his hands through his hair, the veins in his arms emboldened, and he turns and storms straight out of the restroom without me.

He promised…he promised he wouldn't lay a hand on me ever again. And he just did.

He's a liar.

And I'm an idiot for believing him.

———————————

I don't enjoy the rest of the game. I can't focus. I sit numbly on my seat, staring off into nowhere, my mind awhirl. There is sickness in my stomach that I am fighting hard to keep down. At one point, Dean even asks if I'm okay. And I tell him that, yeah, I'm fine, just tired. I don't meet Dad's eyes again. I hear him laughing with Hugh though. I see him get up for more beers.

Does he realize that the small amount of trust I had in him that has taken weeks to build is now completely shattered again? How can I ever trust him again now? I really, really believed him. I really thought things were different, that things had changed. But they haven't. Not at all, and now I don't know how safe I am with him. We're staying in San Francisco tonight, but I want to go home. I want to see Mom. I miss her. When I'm with her, I'm safe.

As we are leaving the stadium, the crowd is electric, the energy explosive. The 49ers won the game, but I couldn't care less now. Dean is talking my ear off about his favorite plays as we follow Dad and Hugh outside, speed walking to keep up so as not to lose them among the crowd, and I don't think he realizes that I'm not listening.

"Wait," I hear Hugh say, and he abruptly stops walking, grabbing Dad's shoulder. He glances back at Dean and me, and then at the stadium behind us. "We should get a picture, or else the wife won't be happy. She does love her photographs! Isn't that right, Dean?"

"Yep!" Dean grabs my elbow and tugs me over to our dads. Dean and Hugh get photos at games all the time—they have the photographs displayed all over their garage as mementos, so I figure it's a tradition.

Hugh flags down the first guy who passes by and hands him his phone, and then the four of us awkwardly huddle in close together with the stadium behind us. I steal a sideways glance at Dean. He is grinning wide for the photo, his arm over my shoulder, and next to him, Hugh's smile is identical. On the other side of Hugh, Dad has his back to the camera, pointing his thumbs to the back of his jersey, to *Grayson*.

"Tyler!" he calls over to me, his voice light and cheerful. "Turn around!"

I ignore the sound of his voice. I refuse to turn around and show our name. I refuse to smile.

Inside, I am breaking.

44

WHEN DEAN AND I get out of the gym the next morning, I drive him back to his place, and we end up in his garage because he wants to show me the new exhaust system his dad added to his car last night. Dean sits half in the car, the door open, and he is revving up the engine with a beaming grin on his face as we listen to the new throaty rumble of his engine.

But I can't focus. I'm leaning against shelves full of alcohol, my arms folded across my chest, my eyes roaming the walls of the garage. Dean and his dad have always been huge 49ers fans, but I never realized they had such…such a display. The garage is covered in memorabilia, from framed jerseys to miniature helmets to flags, and dotted around the walls are photographs. Mostly, they are all just photos of Dean and his dad at every football game they went to, but there is one photo in particular that I am being drawn to. I squint across the roof of Dean's car, tuning out his engine as I focus, but I can't see the photo clearly enough. I push myself off the shelves and walk around Dean's car to get a closer look, and immediately my stomach knots.

I knew it.

It's a picture from years ago when Dean and I were younger. It was taken after a 49ers game up in San Francisco, with the stadium behind us, and we are not alone. Our dads are with us. Dean's dad, Hugh, and mine, the asshole. I can remember that night so well. I went to that game feeling excited. Happy. It was a time when everything was back on track for a while, but that night…that night, everything went wrong all over again. The memory of Dad grabbing me in the restrooms and yelling at me is so vivid in my mind; I can almost *feel* his hand on me and hear his voice ringing in my ears.

And he's there now, in that photograph, in front of me. Dean and Hugh are smiling at the camera. Dad has his back turned, showing off the personalized *Grayson* jerseys we were wearing that night, and then there's me. I'm staring at the ground, and I definitely couldn't fake a smile that night. The picture was taken only a month before Dad was arrested.

"Why the hell do you have this picture up?" I yell at Dean over the noise in the garage. I crane my neck to look at him, and my jaw aches from how hard I am grinding my teeth together. I didn't know Dean had this picture on display alongside all his happy fucking memories with his father.

Dean stops revving his engine and furrows his eyebrows at me. He glances around the garage. "Uh, because look around you. Dad put up pictures from *every* game," he says, then steps on the gas again. "What do you think of the new exhaust?"

"Yeah, it's sweet," I say quickly, then point at the photograph in front of me again. "Can you take this down?" Sometimes, I wish I was brave enough to tell my friends the truth. They would understand me so much better if they know *why* I get so angry so easily, and they would understand why memories, such as the one facing me, are too much to handle. But it's just easier to let them think I'm okay.

Dean sighs at my lack of interest in his car, and so he kills the engine and gets out. "It's just a picture, man."

And I am about to lose my shit, about to hurl my fist into the photo frame and smash the damn thing to pieces, when the door that connects Dean's garage with his house swings open and Hugh steps out. He folds his arms across his chest and leans back against the door.

"I can hear all that revving from the kitchen," he says with a laugh. He glances over at me and goes quiet for a second, his eyes meeting mine. The smile that he gives me is tight and uncomfortable. "Hey, Tyler, how are you doing?"

I hate the way he looks at me. Every time, every damn time, I see the hint of pity that flashes in his eyes for a fleeting moment. Like he's wondering: What happened to this kid? How did he get so far off the rails?

And the truth is, the truth that Hugh will never know, is that a lot happened. To this day, I am still suffering from it all. And now I'm just some fucking loser, some pathetic kid who drinks too much and drives too fast and gets high too often. It's weird, but I almost feel as though I have let Hugh down. I used to look up to him as a father figure when I was a kid. I was so jealous of Dean.

I shove my balled-up fists into my pockets and turn my eyes down to the ground. "Hey," I mumble. How am I doing? I don't even have an answer for that.

"Dad, you can get out of here now," Dean says, and I can just picture him rolling his eyes. Ever since we were young, he has always gotten embarrassed whenever any of us are around his parents.

"Okay, okay," Hugh says, and I catch him holding up his hands in surrender. "I'll leave you guys alone." He chuckles as he heads back inside the house, and after he's gone, I exchange a look with Dean.

"Do you wanna grab coffee at the Refinery?" he asks as he slams his car door shut. He rests his elbow on the roof of the car and stares across at me.

"No, I'm good. I need to head to Malibu," I say, and instantly, I know I shouldn't have said it. I'm going to Malibu because I have to drop something off at some house on Declan's behalf, and that *something* isn't legal. The past two weeks, *none* of my afternoon activities have been legal. I'm growing more confident at it, more comfortable, but it's still risky. Tiffani already knows what I'm up to, but I can't afford to have anyone else find out.

Confusion crosses Dean's face. "Why?"

"To get my car waxed," I lie on the spot. I don't want him to doubt me or question me further, so I muster up a smile and pull out my car keys. "See you later," I say, and I leave the garage perhaps a little too fast.

My car is parked outside by the sidewalk, so I slide inside and check my phone. It's as I expect: messages from Declan, messages from strangers, messages from Tiffani, and even worse, *missed calls* from Tiffani. I have been ignoring her since last night, and I know I am playing with fire, but I just can't bring myself to talk to her. I have muted my phone entirely. It's not even on vibrate anymore, so I throw it onto my passenger seat and head off to Malibu with peace of mind that Tiffani will not be bothering me.

It's noon by the time I get back to the house, and all of the color drains from my face when I spot Tiffani's car parked on our driveway. I should have known that if I ignored her calls long enough she would end up hunting me down. Last night, I told her I was with Dean and Jake.

Today, I haven't even spoken to her, let alone had the chance to lie about my whereabouts. She'll be furious. She hates it when she feels as though she's losing her grip on my life.

Groaning, I park and head into the house. The first thing I see when I push open the front door is Tiffani herself.

She is standing in the hall, hovering by the living room door, a hand on her hip. I stride straight over to her, murmuring, "What are you doing here?"

Immediately, Tiffani turns to look at me with such speed that her hair whips around her face. Her cool blue eyes are like stone as she sets them on me. "Where were you last night?"

"I told you. I was with the guys," I say quickly. I have learned not to hesitate. Trepidation is the biggest giveaway, and I have *a lot* of experience when it comes to lying straight to her face.

"Tyler," Mom's voice snaps suddenly out of nowhere, and I nearly yell "Fuck!" out loud. Over Tiffani's shoulder, Mom walks over, and behind her, Eden is watching all of us from the couch. "You told me you were with her," Mom says, folding her arms over her chest. "Where did you go last night?"

Mom hates it when I lie. I can already tell that she's thinking I was off on another damn bender last night or something, and I really hate that I'm being ambushed by both her and Tiffani right now. "Oh my God," I say, exhaling. "What does it matter?"

Mom turns her back on us. "Eden, where did he go?"

Instantly, I lock my eyes on Eden. She is sitting rigid on the edge of the couch, staring back at the three of us. The expression in my eyes is full of desperation. I am mentally *begging* her to think of something, to not crack under the pressure, to lie for me.

"Um, he dropped me off at Meghan's and then he changed his plans," she finally says, racing through her words. She can't look at me as she lies. "He hung out with the guys instead."

My shoulders sink with relief, and I think it'll be enough to calm Tiffani's anger, so I reach out to touch her arm as I step closer to her. I'll need to kiss her ass for a while. "See?"

"Don't talk to me," Tiffani growls, pulling her arm free and shoving me away from her. My eyes widen in surprise. *Why is she still mad?* "Eden, come with me," she orders. "We need to talk to Rachael and Meghan. Right now."

I watch in disbelief as Eden jumps up from the couch and Tiffani grabs her wrist, pulling her out into the hall and toward the front door. Tiffani rams her shoulder into my chest as she passes, and she refuses to so much as glance at me as they leave the house. What the hell is her problem? I have an alibi—a fake one, sure—so she has no reason to still be angry at me. Is it because I've been ignoring her calls? And what the fuck does she need Eden for? Now *I'm* furious too.

They disappear out the front door and it slams shut behind them, leaving me breathing heavily with rage in the hall. Silence fills the house until Mom places her hand on my shoulder and says, "Oh, Tyler."

I snap my eyes over to hers. "What?"

"I hope you don't drive that girl insane," she says with a frown. She glances at the front door, then back at me. Is she seriously taking Tiffani's side right now? "It seems she's always getting upset with you. I hope you're not the type to play with a girl's head, Tyler."

"Oh, shut the fuck up, Mom," I spit at her, aggressively shaking her hand off my shoulder. She has no idea what sort of hell Tiffani has put me through for years. Tiffani is far, far from innocent.

Mom's face falls. "Wow," she says. Her expression is blank and she blinks at me, stunned that I've cursed at her like that. I couldn't help it. My temper is way too short.

"I'm sorry," I apologize quickly. "I didn't mean—"

"I'm going grocery shopping, then picking up Chase," she interrupts, walking away from me. She won't meet my eyes now either. She only grabs her purse and her car keys from the hall table and heads for the front door. She maintains a hardened expression, despite how much I know I've just hurt her. "If you need me, then too bad," she calls over her shoulder, then slams the front door behind her.

"Fuck!" I finally yell out loud. Why can't I control myself? Mom doesn't deserve the way I just spoke to her. I shove my hand back through my hair and sink down at the foot of the stairs, grinding my teeth as I grab my phone from my pocket. I'm so pissed off that my hands are trembling with rage as I pull up Declan's number, and I send him a message that I have sent so many times before: *Today is getting messy. Keep the good stuff on standby for me.*

45

I ALMOST FORGOT JUST how much bruises can hurt. They decorate my skin in shades of blue and purple, running around my shoulders and my arms, and there's a large cut along my ribs from falling into the corner of the desk in my bedroom two nights ago. It has started again. Dad is always mad now. I think he always has been but was just able to keep his temper in check for a month. It was amazing while it lasted, but I should have known it was too good to be true. He is back to his old ways now. I think it's even worse, actually. Every single night for almost a week now, Dad has thrown me around. I have taught myself to zone out again, because every night it seems to get worse. It's like Dad has a month's worth of pent-up rage that is finally exploding.

I haven't been focusing in classes this week. I've been acting out again, and Mr. Hayes has already called me back to his office for another talk later this afternoon. I feel sick with nerves at the thought of it. What do I tell him this time? That the only reason I straightened up over the past month is because I was happy for once? And I was hopeful? And I felt safe? And now I'm not happy, nor hopeful, nor safe?

It's lunch on Thursday, and we are back at our usual table in the cafeteria, and I am back to being the quiet one sitting at the end of the bench. My friends are talking, they are laughing, but I am tuning them out. My gaze is locked on a random spot on the table, my shoulders are slumped low, my breathing is deep.

I've decided: I hate Dad.

I trusted him when I shouldn't have. I believed him, but that was a mistake. If he really loved me, he wouldn't have broken that promise. Hell, if he loved me, he wouldn't have ever needed to make such a promise in the first place. He doesn't love me enough not to hurt me.

So why am I protecting him?

Why am I covering up his mistakes on his behalf? Why do I tell people that I tripped, that I fell down the stairs, that I got hurt playing in the yard with Dean and Jake? Why am I accepting these bruises? These cuts? These scars? Why am I living with them when I can get it all to stop by just *telling* someone? Anyone. But would they even believe me? Dad's the respected business guy, the one in the shirt and the tie. The one with the Mercedes and the charming smile. Would anyone believe me over him? I'm just a kid, but I've been lying for so long that I wonder if maybe it's too late to turn it all around.

My head is a mess. My thoughts are all over the place, but slowly, a new realization sinks in. It's not Dad that I'm protecting. It's Mom, and it's my brothers. I don't want to tear our family apart, to break us when they are all so happy. Would Mom ever forgive me for that? I don't want her to get mad at me too.

Mr. Hayes told me that I could talk to him about anything. Would *he* believe me? Maybe I could tell him that I'm scared to go home after school. Maybe he could figure out why. Maybe that way, I'm not telling.

"Tyler," someone says, elbowing me hard in the ribs, right into that cut. I immediately flinch away, tearing my eyes up from the table and glancing sideways at Dean. "Did you hear what Blake said? Are you coming or not?"

"What?" I blink fast, my cheeks heating with humiliation as I glance around the table at everyone's gazes on me. Tiffani even rolls her eyes and exchanges a look with Rachael. I really need to stop zoning out around my friends before they decide that there's something wrong with me. I look up at Blake Montgomery, hovering by our table with one hand on the strap of his backpack and his eyes boring into mine. "Coming where?" I ask him. When did he even approach us? Crap, I really *have* been staring off into nowhere.

"Some of us are getting together after school to play ball out on the field," Blake explains. He's a friendly giant, and even though he's an eighth grader, he always says hey to us in the hallways. I think he's friends with Jake. "So are you in?" he asks with a smile, but then it quickly falters. He makes a face, glancing at Dean and Jake with uncertainty and then back to me again. "Oh…wait," he backtracks. "Your dad doesn't let you play. Forget it. Sorry."

Instead of disappointment at the reminder, a new emotion floods through my veins. It's anger, and I can feel it bubbling inside of me, not at Blake but at Dad. I grind my teeth together, but it isn't enough to stop my fists from balling together, trembling from the intensity. It's only a split second, a fleeting moment where everything inside of me snaps like an elastic band that can't take the pressure any longer, but it's enough. I rise up out of my seat and swing my fist straight into Blake's face.

"Tyler!" the table gasps at once.

Blake falls back onto the ground, staring up at me through bewildered, stunned eyes as he reaches up to rub his jaw, but I am enraged now. I am seeing red. I am seeing Dad's smile in my head, feeling his bruises, feeling his hands on my shoulders. It's like a fire lights me up all at once, and I just can't take it anymore. I throw myself at Blake on the ground, slamming my fists into him over and over again, my eyes squeezed shut.

I hate Dad. I fucking hate him.

I can hear the commotion around me. I can feel my friends pulling at me, touching all of those bruises hidden beneath my clothes, yanking at my arms, screaming my name. Blake hits me back, his fist hurling straight into my mouth as he tries to shove me off him, but I don't even feel it. I am numb to pain. I am used to pain.

"Hey!" a deep male voice yells out, and suddenly a new set of hands are around me, firm ones that remind me of Dad's, and in one swift tug, I am pulled straight off Blake. I stumble back, falling into the man behind me, and when I open my eyes, I see Blake on the floor. I see the cafeteria surrounding us in a tight circle, people pushing through one another to get a better view. I see my friends, Dean mostly, staring at me with their mouths hung wide open, their expressions pale with disbelief. And when I crane my neck to see who is behind me, to see who is holding me firmly and dragging me away, my heart pounds even faster than it already is when I discover that it's our campus police officer.

46

I PACE BACK AND forth across the hall for the entire hour that Eden is gone. I have the house to myself, and it is so very tempting to hurl my fist into the wall, but I manage to keep both my temper *and* the house in order. Something is up, I know it. Tiffani is angry at me and I need to fix it. I have tried calling her numerous times, but it keeps going straight to her voice mail. I doubt she'll reply to any of my texts either. The longer I am pacing, the more panicked I'm growing. I should have made more effort with her the past couple days. I can't afford to upset her right now. Not when she has every control over me.

That's why, when the front door slowly creaks open and Eden steps foot inside the house, I am desperately begging for information from her. I march straight over to her with my fists already clenched.

"What'd she say?" I ask, my voice demanding. I don't mean to talk to Eden in such a bitter tone, but I can't help it right now. Tiffani brings out the worst in me, and I hate it. "What did you say?"

There is no color in Eden's face. She is white, her gaze dominated by fear, and she shakes her head as she steals a glance into the living room. "Where's your mom?"

"Picking up Chase," I answer quickly. I just need to know what is going on. "Now what the hell happened?"

Eden is quiet as she deeply inhales, locking her terrified eyes on mine. "Someone saw us last night," she says, and her lower lip quivers as she glances down at the ground. "Austin Cameron... He told Tiffani."

God, no. Austin can't have seen us. My windows are tinted for a fucking reason. "Are you kidding me?" Who the hell does Austin think he is? Now I understand why Tiffani is so livid at me, and she most definitely won't let this go easily. Is that why she took Eden with her? To confront her? I feel sick at the thought of just how quickly this news will spread. *Tyler Bruce and his stepsister...* I throw a punch now, but only at my own palm. What has Austin done? "I will floor that motherfu—"

"They don't know it was me," Eden interrupts, offering at least *some* sort of reassurance. So Tiffani knows I was with another girl last night, but she doesn't know *who*. That's if the guilt in Eden's eyes hasn't already given the game away. "She's devastated, Tyler," she says quietly.

I fall silent as I think. This has happened before. I have kissed other girls, and Tiffani has heard the rumors, but she has never really believed them. This time...I don't know. She seems to believe it, and the weight of the situation feels much heavier. Those other girls before... Those kisses were meaningless. This time is different, and I know that if Tiffani discovers this information, then she will make my life hell.

"I'll fix this," I finally tell Eden. My gaze meets hers, and I really hate how uncomfortable and worried she looks right now. With Tiffani in my life, I should have known that I would inevitably drag Eden into a situation like this. "Look, she's pissed off. I get it, but I can make it up to her. I'll tell her I made a mistake, I'll buy her something nice, and then she'll forget about it and everything will be fine again," I say. At least that's how I *usually* win Tiffani's forgiveness. "And then we can figure the rest out."

Suddenly, Eden's entire demeanor changes and now she is furious at me too. "Everything won't be fine," she spits, glaring back up at me as though this is all *my* fault now. I guess it is. "Nothing is fine, Tyler! This needs to stop."

I furrow my eyebrows at her. "What needs to stop?"

"This." She throws up her hands and motions back and forth between the two of us. She looks exasperated as she exhales and weaves her fingers into her hair. "You have a girlfriend, Tyler. I refuse to be a cheater."

"You won't be," I reassure her. If anything, the only cheater here is me. I like that Eden is the kind of girl to be concerned about this though. The kind of girl who wants to do the right thing. The kind of girl who doesn't want to hurt anyone. It's so attractive to me, and I can't help but step closer to her, reaching out to touch her elbow. When she raises her voice at me, when she narrows her hazel eyes at me like that, she becomes irresistible. I pull her toward me, leaning in closer, desperate to press my lips to hers.

But before I get there, she pulls her arm free and jerks away from me. My eyes flash open and she is retreating from me, her hands on her hips as she stares at me in disbelief. I figure that, okay, sure, maybe it was bad timing. But oh my God, the things she does to me.

"Are you serious?" she asks. "Now really isn't the time. Even if you could completely guarantee that she wouldn't find out—which she will—I still wouldn't do this anyway." She takes yet another step back, increasing the distance between us, shaking her head at me. "I am not doing this," she states firmly.

"C'mon," I murmur, smoldering my eyes at her in an attempt to win her over. It's such a Tyler Bruce thing to do, and I hate myself for doing it, because she can clearly see straight through me. She wrinkles her nose at me and then storms upstairs. I turn around and watch her, but before she can disappear out of sight, I tell her, "We can figure this out." I'm being serious. I *will* figure this out.

"How, Tyler?" she asks, her voice laced with skepticism as she promptly spins back around, stopping halfway up the stairs. She stares back down at me, her hands resting on the banister. "We only have two options."

"Only two?"

"Two," she says, and presses her lips into a firm line. "You have to break up with her."

"No," I say quickly, shaking my head. "I can't." Tiffani plays too big a role in my life. She's toxic and controlling, but she's also my safety net. It's reassuring to know that she isn't going anywhere, that she'll always be there to keep my mind occupied when life gets a little too hard. I guess I just like that security even though I know being with Tiffani is wrong. I think maybe I *could* survive without her, but breaking up with her isn't an option. Not when she is using my involvement with Declan to blackmail me. Right now I'm just not in a strong enough mental state to challenge that.

"Why not?" Eden questions.

Do I tell her? I don't think I can, at least not without explaining that I am more involved with Declan Portwood than everyone thinks I am, and it is a long, long story anyway. My relationship with Tiffani is a three-year-long mess. "Because it's more complicated than you think it is, alright? Tiffani's... Look, don't push it." I narrow my eyes at her, something I always do when I need someone to realize that I am being *deadly serious*, then I sigh. "What's the other option?"

"We ignore whatever we have between us," Eden answers, and her shoulders sink. I hate the sound of that option, and I think she does too. She is coming from the right place though, and her honesty makes me want her even more.

"So basically," I say, leaning back against the wall and crossing my arms over my chest, "I get to be with you if I break up with Tiffani? It's you or her, right?" I look softly up at Eden on the stairs, wishing she was closer to me. I hate that we're having this conversation. This situation *sucks*. I am being blackmailed to stay in a toxic relationship that I *do* actually enjoy being in sometimes, but I also really think there's something different about Eden that I want to explore.

"Why are you acting surprised?" Eden asks. "That ultimatum is pretty obvious. You should have known that it was going to come to this."

I tilt my head back to the ceiling and run both my hands back through my hair. "Fuck," I mutter. I can't talk about this for a second longer, because I will only end up losing my temper over it all, so I decide to leave while I'm still calm. I head into the kitchen, and a few seconds later, I hear Eden slamming a door upstairs.

Now I am torn. There is no way I am breaking up with Tiffani, but now I'm worried Eden is going to distance herself from me if I don't. And right now, I can't even begin to think about which would be worse: breaking up with Tiffani and having her expose all of my secrets or never getting to figure out what more could have happened between Eden and me. My head is spinning, and I know that either way, I can't win. I'm feeling hopeless and defeated, but also frustrated with a desire to just relax. I will definitely be meeting Declan tonight. I just need *something*.

I fetch myself a glass of water, send Declan another message, then head upstairs to my room. Eden is in hers, but I decide not to bother her. I think we both need some space right now. Instead, I pace in my room and try calling Tiffani again. I listen to the monotonous dial tone on repeat for half an hour, calling and calling, begging her to answer so that I can at least try to explain myself. My heart stops beating for a second when she does finally pick up my calls, but only to promptly hang up again before I can get a word in.

I give up at that point and hurl my phone across my room, only angering myself more when I hear my screen smash. As I'm reaching down to pick it back up to examine the damage, I hear my door open, and I'm disappointed when Mom walks into my room and not Eden. She must have heard the thud, because she leans against my doorframe and frowns at my phone in my hands. She's still holding her car keys, so she must have just gotten back.

"Tyler," she says.

"What?" I snap. Yeah, I've added another crack to my phone. I am always smashing the damn thing, but it always feels *so* good just to throw something. Sometimes, I wonder if Dad felt the same satisfaction when he threw *me* around. I hate him, but there are moments where I think that maybe I might understand him.

"Okay, so you're still in a bad mood," Mom states, releasing a tired sigh.

"I'm not in a bad mood," I argue, turning to face her directly. I throw my phone down onto my bed and fold my arms across my chest, staring evenly back at her.

"Yeah, sure." She purses her lips at me and her eyes grow sad. She lowers her voice and softly asks, "Why did you curse at me like you did earlier?"

"Because I'm an idiot, Mom!" I yell at her. I am craving a buzz more than ever right now, and I am quickly losing my patience. I still feel bad about the way I spoke to her earlier, but I really can't deal with her questioning me about it. I'm already dealing with enough as it is.

We argue back and forth, growing more and more exasperated with each other, until finally, Mom gives up and leaves my room, most likely feeling even more disheartened than she did when she first entered. I do feel bad, and I contemplate heading out right there and then to meet Declan, but dinner is soon, so I decide to hold off. It's only for a couple hours. I can cope until then.

Even when dinner does roll around, my mood hasn't improved. Mom was right, I *am* in a bad mood, and I can't even hide the disgruntled expression I'm wearing as we all sit around the kitchen table. Minus Jamie. He's at his friend's house for dinner, which leaves us as only a family of five tonight. Mom is trying to keep the conversation happy and light, and Dave is talking about some meeting he had at work today, but I am totally tuned out.

I am staring across the table at Eden, my gaze never leaving her. I watch as her mouth curves when she speaks, as she glances down at her lap every so often, as she frowns uncertainly when Mom sets a dish of barbecue ribs down on the table. She doesn't ever really look at me. I think she is still waiting for me to choose which option I am taking in regards to Tiffani, but the truth is I'm not taking either option.

"I can't sit here," I announce, pushing my chair back from the table and getting to my feet. The smell of those ribs is making me feel sick, but that's not the only reason I refuse to stay. My desire for a hit is growing stronger every minute. "I'm heading back upstairs."

Mom immediately looks at me. She is standing behind Dave, her hands on his shoulders, her smile faltering. "But yours is just comin—"

"I've got some stuff to do," I cut in. Nothing will make me stay at this table, not when I can sense Eden's anger at me. As I leave the kitchen, I call over my shoulder, "I'll heat it up later." *Yeah, when the munchies kick in.*

I head up to my room, taking two steps at a time, and I fire Declan another message asking if he can hook me up as soon as he possibly can. I am desperate now, but he isn't replying. I try to call Tiffani again instead, but it's yet another failed attempt. If she doesn't talk to me tonight, I will have no other choice but to turn up at her house tomorrow. That's most likely what she wants me to do anyway. She'll want to see me beg.

As I impatiently wait for Declan to get back in touch with me, I sit down on the edge of my bed and interlock my hands between my legs, focusing on nothing in particular as I try to calm my breathing. I listen to the silence in my room, inhaling, exhaling. It is quickly interrupted when Eden walks straight in without even knocking first.

"We're watching Chase," she casually informs me, her voice back to its usual husky tone. "Jamie's maybe broken his wrist."

My eyes immediately flick up to meet hers as my heart misses a beat. It is such a sensitive subject, and I am so protective that I am instantly on my feet and walking toward her. I am ready to kill someone. "What happened? Where is he? Who?" I ask, and already I can find my body heating up from the panic that is flooding through me. Dad used to break my wrist all the time.

Confusion crosses Eden's calm features. "What?"

I shouldn't have asked *who* did it. That was my subconscious asking that, a question that is so ingrained in me from my childhood. There was always someone behind my injuries. I clear my throat and swallow hard. "I mean, how?"

"I think he fell on it," Eden says with a small shrug. She is still analyzing me, confused by my questions, and I know I slipped up there. I just hope she doesn't think too deeply about it. "I heard you've broken yours, tough guy," she adds in a lighter tone, a small smirk on her face.

What the hell? How does she know that? And why is she *joking* about it? I broke my wrist three damn times in one year, because my father was out of control. "Who told you that?" I demand.

"Um, Chase," Eden says quietly. Clearly, she didn't realize just what exactly she is reminding me of. She bites down on her lower lip and searches my eyes for answers. "What's wrong?"

Oh, Chase. He can't have told Eden the truth about Dad because even *he* doesn't know the truth. He only knows that growing up, his big brother always seemed so clumsy. "What else did the kid tell you?" I ask. I have to make sure. There are so many things his young, innocent self could say.

"Nothing," Eden breathes.

I step closer to her, my eyes never leaving hers. "Are you sure?"

"Stop freaking out," she tells me, though she looks uncomfortable with my reaction. "I'm sure."

I should be trying harder to hide my emotions right now, but for some reason, when it comes to Eden, I don't care if she sees. I'm alarmed at the thought of her knowing about my past, and she can most likely see the panic and the fear in my eyes.

"You know what?" I say, finally releasing all of my emotions in the only way I know how: as anger. "I can't deal with this. I can't deal with you, and I can't deal with Tiffani. I can't deal with your dumb questions, and I can't deal with Tiffani's whining. I can't deal with any of it right now." I walk away from her, striding into my bathroom and resting my hands on my sink. I keep my head low, focusing on my breathing again. I was trying so hard to keep it steady before Eden walked in on me. I need Declan to answer me. I need him to give me something that will allow me to forget about today for a few hours.

"You're getting so worked up," Eden says. She has followed me into my bathroom, and I can sense her hovering by my side.

"Watch the door. The lock is fucked," I tell her through gritted teeth. I am growing more frustrated with each second that passes. The bathroom seems to be getting smaller and smaller. I feel like I am suffocating. When Eden tries to place her hand on my arm, I can't handle her touch. I flinch away from her.

"I need a hit," I admit, my voice seething as I reach up to open my cabinet above my sink. I see my antidepressants, the bottle knocked over on its side. Did I take them today? I reach up to the top shelf and desperately fumble around until I find the cash I have stored up there. It's some of the cash I've made from selling Declan's shit, and lucky for him, it gets sent straight back his way. I'm a loyal client, I guess. I slam the cabinet door shut again, but when I try to turn around to leave, I find that Eden has thrown herself in between the door and me.

"Don't even think about it," she threatens, pressing into my chest. She has her chin tilted up, her jaw clenched, her eyes set solely on mine. She is being serious.

"Eden," I whisper. I lean forward, moving my lips to her ear so that she can hear and understand me perfectly clearly, and I growl, "I. Need. A. Hit. Right. Now." If only she knew just how desperately.

She glances down at the cash in my hand, then back up at me. "Because coke is totally going to fix everything, right?"

"Eden," I say, this time more firmly. Right now, she really shouldn't try and stop me. I am meeting Declan and getting the high I need whether she likes it or not. "Move your cute ass out of my way before you really piss me off. I gotta meet Declan."

"I'm not letting you," she says, pushing closer up against me, her chest against mine. Her gaze is fierce and unrelenting.

"It's not fucking up to you!" I yell, slamming my hand into the wall behind her, right by her ear. As soon as I do it, I regret it. I don't want her to see me like this, so angry and so desperate and so pathetic. I don't want her to see my violent side, because violence is never, ever necessary. I learned that at a young age.

Suddenly, Eden slides out from in front of me and throws herself against my bathroom door. It closes and she presses hard against it until it clicks into place. All of the color drains from my face as my jaw hangs open. No fucking way did Eden just do that. We are now both trapped in here, in this tiny bathroom, just the two of us with no possible way out, and if I wasn't suffocating before, then I definitely will now.

47

FIVE YEARS EARLIER

PRINCIPAL CASTILLO ROCKS SLOWLY back and forth in his chair, his hands interlocked over his stomach, his eyes never leaving me. His lips are pressed together into a thin line of both disapproval *and* disappointment. I've never been in his office before. There was never any reason to be here until now. We are sitting in silence, listening to the clock on the wall tick on by, and I am sitting on the opposite side of the desk. Principal Castillo is usually nice, but everyone knows that he can be strict, and he doesn't tolerate bad behavior, especially fighting, within his school. That's how I know I'm in a lot trouble, and both my parents have been called. It's just a matter of which one shows up first, and I am praying with everything in me that it won't be Dad.

I glance down at the ice pack in my hand. My lip is cut open and my jaw ever-so-slightly aches, but it's nothing too new to me. That's why, instead of holding the ice pack to my mouth, I only turn it over in my hands repeatedly, trying to distract myself from the tension in this office. I'm not only going to be in trouble at school, but at home too.

"I'm...I'm sorry, Principal Castillo," I mumble, glancing up at him again. We have already been over this. "I don't know what I was thinking."

"You don't just do something like that for no reason," Principal Castillo says. His eyes search mine, but I quickly look down at my lap and shrug. There's no way I can tell him that I threw a punch at Blake Montgomery because I was really imagining him to be my dad.

"Blake said something I didn't like," I lie. "I overreacted. It won't happen again, Principal Castillo. I'm really sorry."

As soon as the words leave my lips, there is a quick knock at the door before it swings open. I crane my neck, looking back over my shoulder. Officer Brown steps into the office first, followed by Dad. My heart sinks into my stomach and I swear that for a second, I stop breathing entirely. He doesn't look at me.

"Thanks for getting here so quickly," Principal Castillo says. He stands up and stretches over the desk, shaking Dad's hand firmly while nodding to Officer Brown, who leaves the room again, clicking the door shut behind him. "Please, take a seat."

Principal Castillo sits back down, and Dad sinks into the chair next to me. He sits forward, his foot anxiously tapping the floor, his knee shaking. "What is this about?" he asks, but I can hear the quaver in his voice. He's nervous. Not mad. Not yet. He doesn't know why he's been called here. Does he think...does he think they know? Does he think I've told them the truth? The truth about him?

"Tyler was involved in a fist fight during lunch period," Principal Castillo states. He fires me another scolding glance. He probably didn't even know my name until today. I've always been a good kid, always flown under the radar.

Dad inhales a sharp intake of breath. I think he is relieved at first, but only for the briefest of moments. Then, the outrage sets in and he abruptly straightens up in his chair, narrowing his eyes across the desk at Principal Castillo. He still doesn't look at me. "A fight? Tyler was fighting?" he asks in disbelief. I've never hit anyone in my entire life before. Except maybe my brothers when we were younger and would fight over action figures and the Game Boy. But that doesn't count. This is the first time I've hit someone with every intention of hurting them, and I still don't know why I did it. I lost control, just like Dad does. Blake Montgomery just happened to be in the wrong place at the wrong time. It wasn't his fault, but it's never mine either.

"Unfortunately so, Mr. Grayson," Principal Castillo says. The wrinkles around his eyes are deep-rooted and his expression is so solemn that it makes him look even older. "During lunch period in the cafeteria. Officer Brown stepped in and pulled Tyler away before it got any worse, but there's no place for any violence whatsoever on this campus. I have no choice but to suspend Tyler for the rest of today, tomorrow, *and* next week."

Dad's jaw hits the floor. "Suspended?" he splutters, his eyes bulging straight out of their sockets I thought I was only going to get detention, not a suspension… There's no going back from this now. Dad is going to lose it. "Is the other kid getting suspended too?"

Principal Castillo shakes his head. He sits forward, resting his elbows on his desk as his thick eyebrows knit together. "When I say that Tyler was involved in a fight, Mr. Grayson, what I really mean is that he beat up one of our eighth-grade students. It was completely unprovoked, so no, Blake Montgomery won't be suspended. Tyler, you'll talk about this with Mr. Hayes when you return to school."

Dad stares blankly at Principal Castillo. Then, so slowly, he turns his head toward me. His fierce green eyes lock onto mine and I can see the rage brimming in them. He doesn't even blink. His jaw is clenched tight, his nostrils are flaring. "Thank you, Principal Castillo. Let's go, Tyler," he says through stiff lips. He stands up and I don't dare hesitate, so I quickly scramble to my feet.

"I'll be in touch," Principal Castillo calls after us, but Dad has already guided me through the door and into the hallway. Didn't he see? Didn't he notice the anger in Dad's eyes and the fear in mine? Maybe only I can see it because maybe I'm the only one who knows what to look for.

It's fifth period and everyone is in class, so the hallways are empty and silent as Dad marches toward the main entrance. He is speed walking, his strides wide, and I have to almost break out into a jog in order to keep up with him. He isn't saying anything. That's how I can tell that his anger is growing within him, building and building, because he can't even open his mouth to say anything. His hand is balled into a fist by his side and his breathing deepens until we are outside and off campus.

"What the fuck were you thinking, Tyler?" Dad yells, his voice a rumbling growl, and he throws me against his car. There go those bruises again. A sharp pain flares up where my body bashes against the metal. He grabs me, both hands pulling at my hoodie, dragging me closer toward him. "You just got suspended! Suspended!" He shakes, throws me back against the car again. I can see the veins in his forehead, defined and popping, his eyes engulfed by the fury that he can't control. "You beat up a kid!"

"You do that too," I whisper.

And I shouldn't have said it. I shouldn't have challenged him, because a new anger explodes inside of him as his glare becomes venomous. He stares at me in silence for a few seconds, registering my words, his chest heaving.

"Get in the car, Tyler," he orders, his voice low and seething. He barges me out of the way as he walks around the car to the driver's side, and as he opens the door and steps one foot inside, his glare sharpens across the roof of the vehicle at me when he realizes I haven't moved yet. "Get in the fucking car!" he yells.

I've accepted my fate at this point. It is too late now to change the outcome. There is no going back from this, no calming Dad's rage. Not after fighting, not after getting suspended, not after that remark. As I swallow hard and slide into the passenger seat, I am already trying to focus on something else. I am willing the numbness to set in, to save me, but it doesn't arrive soon enough.

As soon as I pull the car door shut, Dad's fist pummels my face, and I feel every ounce of pain that comes with it.

48

IN THE CONFINES OF my bathroom, Eden and I are staring back at one another in silence. I can't quite process what she has just done. I am trapped, and I know she has done this on purpose. It's almost brave of her, and if I wasn't so desperate for a high right now, then I would most likely appreciate the effort. This morning, I would have loved nothing more than to be locked in here alone with her, but right now, in this frame of mind, I just can't see the positive side.

"Are you kidding me?" I splutter, narrowing my eyes at her. I *need* a distraction, and she has stolen that chance from me. I glance around the room, but there is no way out. I almost reach into my pocket for my phone, but it's in my room.

"No," Eden says. There is a smug sort of smile pulling at her lips, a challenging, devious one. One that says she doesn't give a shit that we are trapped. She knows she has gotten the better of me right now, and she can't even begin to hide her satisfaction. I step around her, nudging her out of the way so that I can at least attempt to escape. I grab the handle and I shake it, pushing and pulling, even pressing my weight against the door, begging for it to open. The lock has been broken for over a year now, and I once got locked in here last summer and had to wait it out for four hours until Dave got home to get me the hell out.

"Just give up," Eden says. She is watching me as I fight for my freedom, and I groan under my breath and step back from the door. It's not going to open.

I can feel my heart racing from the panic arising at the thought of *not* meeting Declan. It pounds in my chest and my body feels tense and rigid. My mouth feels too dry. I place my hands behind my head and tilt my face up to the ceiling. I need to accept that I am stuck here, that I will not be getting the buzz I so desperately need. I close my eyes, breathing deeply, exhaling all of my negative energy. Or at least some of it. I open my eyes again and fix them on Eden. I still can't believe she has done this.

"I'm sorry that I actually care," she says, folding her arms across her chest. She isn't backing down today. "You're just going to have to find another way to distract yourself. An alternative. One that won't kill you."

My eyes are darting all over the room, and they finally settle on my reflection in the cabinet mirror. I hate how furious I look, so I drop my gaze to the floor instead. I don't want to get angry at Eden. She is only trying to help me, and that is a lot more than anyone else has ever done. She *does* care, and I love that, despite how aggravating it can be. Today can be written off as a complete disaster, and the only reason I am craving something stronger than just alcohol right now is because my head is such a mess from the thought of Eden cutting me off. "You were becoming my distraction," I admit, lowering my voice. I can't look at her. "But apparently I can't have you."

Eden doesn't say anything at first. She is quiet as she registers this new information, and I hear her inhale a breath of air. "Why am I a distraction?" she quietly asks.

I look up from the floor to meet her curious gaze. Eden doesn't know it, but I don't have to be Tyler Bruce around her, and that's something so new and refreshing that it is almost addictive to me. "Because you make things a little easier," I finally tell her. This is the truth, and the truth is not something I am usually great at dealing with. "Because I get to focus on you instead of everything else."

"Then don't stop," Eden says, but her voice is laced with nerves now. Slowly, she moves a step closer to me and I stare at her, my gaze never leaving hers. I am trying so hard not to think about a nice clean line of coke right now, but it's still there in the back of my mind, still calling for me. Eden reaches up and places her hand on my jaw, her skin cool. "Focus on me," she whispers.

"Then distract me," I say. I reach for her hand on my jaw and move it away. I need distracting right now more than ever, but something more than Eden's touch.

"We can talk. We've never once just talked," she says quietly, her voice almost a whisper. A new silence has formed around us in this tiny bathroom, and we are afraid to break it.

"Okay. Let's talk," I say. I move around her and lean back against my shower door, sliding down the glass until I'm sitting on the cold floor. I stretch my legs out in front of me and then close my eyes, still focusing on my erratic breathing. I don't really do the talking thing, but with Eden, I'm willing to give it a chance. I like listening to her voice. It's soothing to me.

"Can we talk about Tiffani?" I hear Eden gently ask, as though she's afraid to mention her name. "Calmly this time."

My eyes flash open to look at her again. She is still hovering by the sink, looking down at me with a wary gaze. Tiffani is the *last* person I want to talk about right now. Reluctantly, I mutter, "Fine."

Eden steps around my body and sits down on the floor next to me, hugging her knees to her chest and leaning back against the door. She frowns. "Why won't you break up with her? You don't even like her. You said so yourself."

My eyes roam Eden's body, searching her eyes first, then her lips, then her hands. She wants an answer, but I don't know what to tell her. She wouldn't understand. "I can't break up with her," I tell her again for the second time today. Breaking up with Tiffani just isn't going to happen.

"But why?"

I shake my head, ready to object to answering, but then I realize that Eden will most likely only continue to press me about the matter. I cover my face with my hand and rub at my eyes while I consider what exactly I will say. It is such a long, complicated story and the thought of having to explain it all is enough to make me groan out loud. I decide to simplify it. "Tiffani's really good at acting like she's the nicest girl around. But she's not," I tell Eden. "The second you do something wrong to her, she turns into a psychopath. She knows too much about me. I can't risk it. At least not right now."

"Psychopath?" Eden repeats. She seems surprised, which only means that Tiffani *does* do a good job at acting. We are almost as bad as each other when it comes to putting up a front. "What does she know?"

"It's..." I don't even know what to say. There are so many things Tiffani has done over the years, so I shift on the floor, getting more comfortable. "Okay. Example: back in January, she heard I'd been hanging out with this girl during lunch period every Tuesday, which I totally hadn't, and she went crazy. I slaved over an essay for English lit for two weeks straight because I had to get my grades up, and she told my teacher that she wrote it. My entire grade dropped, and I got suspended for cheating, which is so dumb. The same day she used her mom's email to email my mom, telling her that she was concerned for my well-being because I was smoking joints in the school basement. That part is true, and Tiffani's the only one who knew. Mom didn't talk to me for almost a month. I would have dumped Tiffani back then, but she made it clear that I shouldn't ever go there. So I never have. Breaking up isn't an option. There are so many more things she can do, because she has the upper hand in all of this." I'm nearly out of breath by the time I finish.

Eden listens carefully to each word I say, and she stays quiet as she slowly absorbs them. "What else does she know, Tyler?" I should just tell her the truth, or at least *some* of it, and I definitely can't look at her while I do. I don't want to see her look disappointed in me.

"Do you remember the first day of summer?" I ask.

"Yeah," she says. "Dad was annoying and the barbecue sucked and you rudely stormed into it."

"Yeah, that." I am picking at the rips in my jeans, trying to muster up the courage to keep on talking. It feels weird to me, discussing things like this. "I was super pissed off."

"Why?"

"I was mad at Tiffani," I admit. "I'd been thinking about getting involved in something for a while, and she found out that night. She said she won't tell anyone as long as I stay with her until graduation. That's why I was sucking up to her for a while at the start of the summer. You know, in American Apparel and stuff…" Oh, God, I'm still embarrassed about that. I wonder what Eden must have thought of me back then. Did she think I was a jerk? Does she still think that now? "As long as she's happy and I don't break up with her, she won't tell, because that's what she does, Eden. She likes to blackmail people into doing what she wants, so that she can look cool and stay on top of the rest of us. She told me she used to get bullied when she was younger, so I guess when she started at our school, after she moved here with her mom after the divorce, she wanted to make sure no one stepped over her. She wants to be better than everyone, cooler than all of them. Having me by her side helps to boost her ego. That's why I'm stuck in this mess." Saying it all out loud makes me realize *just* how messy it actually is, and I run my hand through my hair as I let out a groan. "I hate this."

"Wow," Eden says once I'm done. "I don't know what to say."

"I'm not breaking up with her," I tell her as I glance back up from the floor. She is blinking at me, wide-eyed and completely invested in my words. I still don't expect her to understand my situation with Tiffani fully, but I hope she understands it more than she did a minute ago. "Not yet, at least. I can't risk it right now."

Eden leans forward and rests her chin on her knees, staring across the silent bathroom at me from beneath her eyelashes. "Then what are we going to do?"

Is she talking about us? I hope that she is, because if she is searching for an answer to what is going on between us, then that means she is still interested in pursuing something. "I just don't want to make anyone suspicious," I say. I'm not really sure what answer to give her, because I have no idea either.

"Suspicious about what?"

"Us," I clarify. We are really talking about this right now, the possibility of *us*, whatever the hell that means. "We need to just act normal for now until we figure this out. That's another reason I can't break up with her. People would wonder why. So for now, she has to stay in the picture, because Tiffani is my normality."

"But it's wrong to do this to her," Eden says under her breath, and there she goes again, doing that cute thing where she *cares* about people. And not just me, but everyone else too. She is chewing anxiously on her lower lip.

"Eden," I say. I tilt my head to one side as I analyze her. I could kiss her right now. I really could, but I'm trying my best not to ruin this moment. I'm being honest with her while she listens, and that's important to me, but I also want to hear *her*. "Talk about something else. Talk about Portland."

Eden lifts her head from on top of her knees and straightens up, crossing her legs instead as she furrows her eyebrows at me. "You want me to talk about Portland?"

"I want you to talk about yourself," I say. I am calm and no longer thinking about meeting Declan. Instead, all I can focus on is Eden; all I can think about is her. Our eye contact never breaks. "Tell me something that no one else knows."

Eden hesitates. She seems to think it through first before she speaks, but eventually she decides to open up to me like I have just opened up to her. "I love Portland," she starts, and she glances away for a second as her mouth forms a sad, wistful smile. "It was an amazing city to grow up in. I had three really close friends. Amelia, Alyssa, and Holly."

"Had?"

"Had," she confirms. "When my parents got divorced I was thirteen, it hit me really hard. I used to cry myself to sleep, because my mom would be crying, and my dad wouldn't be there, and I didn't know how to make her feel better, and it just sucked. It really, really sucked." She stops and glances down at her lap, intertwining her fingers. She takes a deep breath. "I started to eat a lot because I was so upset, and I put on a lot of weight during freshman year. Alyssa and Holly had a lot to say about it."

Is she seriously telling me what I think she is telling me? I run my gaze over her body, which I have already studied so many times. I like the small dip in her back, the curve of her hips. There's absolutely no way. "You're not fat," I state firmly. Who the hell are these girls?

"That's because I run, Tyler," she says with a small shrug. She's not really looking at me now, but I can see a new sadness lurking in her eyes that I really, really dont want to be there. Slowly, I press my hands to the cold floor and move myself closer to her. I sit in front of her, holding her gaze, resting my hands on her knees.

"Keep talking," I say quietly. I want her to know that I'm here, that I'm listening.

She bites down on her lower lip again and presses a hand to her cheek. She doesn't push my hands away from her knees. "They made me feel like shit," she tells me, and I try not to show the anger that fills me. Eden doesn't deserve to feel so sad over something that is complete bullshit. She's stronger than that. She's deserves better. "I had two of my supposed best friends calling me fat every day, so I started running. We don't talk anymore, but they still bitch about me on the low. It's just hard, because Amelia…Amelia's still friends with them. She stuck by my side the whole time though."

"Eden," I say. I like the way her name sounds, and I want her to look at me. I have noticed a lot of details about her over the past few weeks, and there have been moments where she has rejected food, pushed away plates, and never once actually finished dinner. Now I think I know why. "That's why you always say you're never hungry, isn't it?"

Eden's eyes widen and she parts those plump lips of hers, taken aback. "You noticed that?"

"Only just now," I admit, swallowing the lump in my throat as I drop my eyes to her bare legs. I can't help but touch her, tracing a pattern

ESTELLE MASKAME

with my fingers from her knees up to her thighs. I know my opinion probably doesn't mean much to her, but I think she looks just perfect. "Just so you know, I completely disagree with those girls. I'm sorry for what they did." I glance up at her from beneath my eyelashes, running my fingertips in soft circles over her smooth skin, and our eyes lock.

Eden is looking at me in a way I have never seen her look at me before. There is warmth in her eyes, and she exhales a small breath of relief, her body relaxing, her gaze never tearing away from mine. I can't take it anymore. I need to kiss her, and I need to kiss her right now. Grabbing her thighs, I lean forward and crash my lips to hers.

I kiss her deeply, as though it's the first time I am feeling her mouth against mine. She hooks her arms around my neck and leans back against the door, letting me hover over her body. Her lips curve into a smile against mine as I kiss her, and I don't want to ever stop. I can't get enough of this girl, and no matter how many times I have kissed her now, it's always just as exhilarating as the last. Adrenaline is flooding through my veins. I run my hands from her thighs to her waist, and I am about to slide my hand under her shirt when I pause, slowing the kiss down and playing with the material of her shirt instead. I'm giving her the chance to say no, to push me away, but she locks her arms around my neck and pulls me hard against her. She takes control and I let her kiss me however she wants, as rough as she wants, as fast as she wants.

My hands slip under her shirt, feeling the warmth of her smooth skin under my fingertips, and I clasp her waist with one hand, my other exploring her body, my skin rubbing against the soft lace material of her bra. I slide my hand inside, gently grabbing her breast, and I tear my lips from her mouth and lean back for a second to meet her eyes. She is breathing hard, and her full lips are driving me insane. God, I could kiss her all night. I lean back in and leave a row of kisses all the way along her jaw and down to her neck, and she tilts her head back against the door, running her hands into my hair and tugging on the ends. Both my hands are on her breasts now, rubbing soft circles on her skin with my thumbs, and I exhale against her neck.

Eden lets go of my hair and grabs my jaw with her hands, drawing my lips back to hers. We pause for a moment first, our gazes locking. We are both breathing heavily, out of breath from the adrenaline rush, and my mouth curves into a smirk before I lean forward and kiss her again.

We both know we shouldn't be doing this right now. My hands shouldn't be on her body, her lips shouldn't be against mine, but we just can't fight it. She is too desirable to me. She is everything that I want. She is absolutely and completely irresistible.

49

"THIS IS UNBELIEVABLE," MOM is muttering under her breath for the fifth time already this evening. "A complete disgrace." We are in the kitchen and I am sitting at the table while Mom presses damp cloths and ice packs to my face, her hand in my hair, massaging my head. She tilts my chin up, inspecting my face, and she lets out a small, muffled groan.

She moves the ice pack in her hand to my eye.

It's bad. I know. There is no hiding it this time. No covering it up.

My eye is busted, painted black and purple, and I can't open it fully. My mouth is swollen and cut. My cheeks are bruised. My face seems to have blown up to twice its normal size, and every time I so much as speak or blink, it hurts. That's why I've been keeping quiet, sitting at the kitchen table, staring at the wall as Mom nurses my injuries. I'll never forget the gasp she let out when she got home from work and laid her eyes on me.

"How can you only suspend one of them?" she continues to vent to herself, her voice bitter. I don't see Mom get angry often, but tonight, she is. There is exasperation in her eyes. "Two kids get into a fight and beat each other up, and you don't suspend *both* of them? It's injustice! You know what? I'm calling Principal Castillo first thing in the morning."

Dad is over in the corner of the kitchen, slumped back against the countertop with his head hung low. He's been staring at the ground the entire time, motionless. "Ella…" he says quietly without looking up. "Just drop it. Tyler is still suspended no matter what."

"Drop it? Are you kidding me, Peter?" Mom barks at him, turning to face Dad directly. The mascara around her eyes has smudged, and she isn't even bothering to fix the strands of hair that have fallen from her updo. She's *really* mad. "Look at what that kid has done! Look." Mom angles my head toward him, exposing all of the damage.

But Dad still can't look; he's too guilty to look. He only shakes his head slowly at the ground, and I fight against Mom's hold on my chin to turn away again. I don't want to look at him either. I hate him.

"I started it," I mumble to Mom. I want her to drop this too. Blake wasn't the one who did this to my face. "Blake doesn't deserve to get suspended."

"Be quiet, Tyler. I'm furious at you," she snaps at me, moving the ice pack back to my mouth, dabbing my swollen, plump lips. I flinch at the coolness. Her blue eyes meet mine, full of confusion and disappointment. Mostly disappointment. It's the first time I've seen her look at me like that, and my chest constricts. "Why would you even do such a thing?"

"I'm sorry, Mom," I say quietly. I *am* sorry. I don't know what happened. I got angry and I needed to release it, and I felt better after it. Is that how it is with Dad too? Does he feel better afterward?

"It's just not you," Mom says. She sighs, rubs her forehead, and moves the ice to my cheek. "What did that kid do?"

"Nothing."

"You don't just beat someone up for no reason, Tyler," she says, echoing Principal Castillo's words, growing frustrated at me now. I can't tell her why I did it. Not without breaking her.

"Some people do," I whisper. I crane my neck to look at Dad again.

He is still leaning back against the countertop, staring at the floor, but he seems to sense me watching him, because his empty gaze flicks up for only a brief moment. I hope he can see the hatred in my eyes. Or eye, since he beat me up so badly that I can't open the other.

"Tyler, you're not only suspended. You're grounded too," Mom tells me as she passes the ice pack into my hand. "Go to your room."

I've never been grounded before, but I guess I expected it. I frown up at her. I'm sorry that I let her down. I wish she knew that I regret it now. That I feel so guilty. I squeeze my fingers tight around the ice pack in my hand and slide off the chair. My shoulders are slumped low as I walk across the kitchen. I can feel Dad's eyes following me, but I hate him, I hate him, I hate him. I keep on walking, straight out of the kitchen, all the way upstairs and into my room. For once, I slam the door behind me. I'm not even worried about the consequences at this point. I'm no longer afraid of Dad, because what more can he do to me that hasn't already been done?

Dad has never hurt me this badly before. It is getting worse and worse each night, and in the four years that this has been going on, he has never been so careless. His mistakes have never been so visible. His anger is uncontrollable, and it is never going to get any better. I am sure of that now.

So why am I letting it happen?

I glance around my room, at the scuffs in the paint on my walls from where Dad has thrown me around, at the dents in my desk. Then, I get down onto my hands and knees and reach under my bed for one of my old backpacks. Why am I protecting Dad when really I should be protecting myself?

I'm going to run away.

50

PRESENT DAY

AT FIRST, WHEN OUR neighborhood handyman, Mr. Forde, finally gets my lock removed, it's almost too awkward to bear. Eden and I slowly shuffle out of my bathroom to meet Mom and Dave's awaiting gazes. Eden told me we were supposed to be babysitting Chase, but we definitely didn't do a good job of that because we've been locked up here the entire time. Little do our parents know that it wasn't exactly hell being trapped in there with Eden for two hours, and her plan did work. I'm calm again, and I definitely don't plan to still meet up with Declan.

"We really need to get that fixed," Mom says with a frown as Mr. Forde hands her the questionable lock. He has removed it completely now so there is no chance I can ever get myself locked in there again.

"Yeah," I say, but I'm keeping my head down. I don't want to meet Dave's eyes right now. Not after kissing his daughter. I glance at Eden out of the corner of my eye, and she is staring at the floor too. "How's Jamie's wrist?"

"A small fracture," Dave says, then he reaches into his pocket and pulls out his wallet, handing Mr. Forde thirty bucks. "Thank you."

Mr. Forde heads off, and Eden disappears off into her own room, and Mom and Dave make their way back downstairs. I'm left alone, so I decide to check up on Jamie. I know all too well just how much a fractured wrist sucks.

I walk across the hall to his room and slowly tap my knuckles against the door before pushing it open anyway. Jamie is sitting on the end of his bed, staring down at the splint on his wrist, rotating his arm. My chest tightens a little. I hate seeing my brothers get hurt.

"Hey," I say gently as I walk into the room. I sit down on the bed next to him and give him a small smile as he looks up at me. I raise an eyebrow. "So I heard you've broken your wrist."

"Yeah," Jamie says, and he lets out a defeated sigh. "I tripped over some bricks in Dylan's backyard and fell on it." Jamie is usually boisterous and lively, but tonight, he is quiet. He stares down at his wrist for a few seconds, then slowly his gaze drifts back up to meet mine. "I don't know how you did this."

"Did what?"

"This," he says, lifting up his arm. "The broken wrists. Everything. It hurts."

"I got used to it," I murmur. Honestly, I'm surprised Jamie is even talking about this. He doesn't like to ever talk about Dad. I think he's still traumatized from it all, from witnessing the father that he adored attacking me. Jamie has never really been the same since, and neither of us ever wants to talk about it even though I know we need to. It's too hard on both of us. "I learned to...I learned to make myself numb," I say through the silence.

I sense Jamie swallow as he stares at the floor. All I can hear is the static of his TV, nothing but white noise to me. "I can't believe Dad was really like that."

"I know." Sometimes, I still can't believe it either.

"But why you?" he asks, looking up. His blue eyes meet mine. We look nothing alike. "Why not me? What did you do wrong that Chase and I didn't?"

"I don't know, Jamie, but I'm glad it wasn't you, and I'm glad it wasn't Chase." I stare at the splint on his wrist, and it brings back so many memories of when I was a kid. His wrist will be in a cast soon, decorated with his friends' names scrawled in Sharpie. "He loved you guys," I tell him, then glance down at my own hands. On the outside, I'm fine. But my wrist still aches sometimes. "I think he may have even loved me too."

Jamie looks at me like I'm crazy. "That doesn't even make sense."

"It doesn't, does it?" I almost smile, because he's right. It *doesn't* make sense. Dad didn't hurt me because he hated me—no, he hurt me because he was out of control. "Even I'm still trying to figure it out."

Suddenly, my phone begins to vibrate in my pocket, and I know that it is most likely Declan calling, wondering whether or not I'm still down to meet up. I pull out my phone, ready to simply reject the call, but I freeze when I see Tiffani's name lighting up my cracked screen instead.

My chest tightens as I look back at Jamie. He glances at my phone in my hand, then at me. I can see in his eyes that he doesn't want me to answer it. He wants me to stay here with him, to talk about Dad. And I want to stay too, but I just… I just can't. I can't reject Tiffani's call, not after I've been trying so hard to talk to her all day. She will never forgive me if I don't give her my time now that she's ready listen.

I swallow hard as I get to my feet, and it hurts seeing the way Jamie's face falls. The call is still ringing and my time to answer is running out fast. "Jamie, I'm sorry," I say, but my throat is so dry that my words sound choked. "I have to take this. I don't have a choice right now. Can we talk another time?"

"Whatever, Tyler," he mumbles, but he's mad at me now too. He flops onto his back and rolls over to face his bedroom wall, leaving me feeling guiltier than ever. But the call is still ringing; my phone is still vibrating in my hand…

I dart back across the hall to my own room, closing the door behind me and inhaling. I still haven't exactly decided which explanation I am going to give her, but I'm skilled at lying on the spot. I accept the call and press my phone to my ear. "Tiffani," I say.

"Tyler," she says. Her voice is bitter and my name brings disgust with it. I can picture her in my head so clearly. I imagine her lips pressed firmly together in a bold line, one hand resting on her hip, her blue eyes sharpening. Luckily, I don't have to face her.

"I've been trying to talk to you all day," I tell her. My shoulders sink with relief. Finally, she is talking to me. I walk over to my bed and collapse down onto my back, staring up at my ceiling. "So you heard what happened last night?"

"Of course I heard," Tiffani snaps back at me. She's furious, and this is going to take a lot of convincing. "Did you think I wouldn't find out? You know me, Tyler. I find out *everything*."

I close my eyes and take a deep breath, running my free hand through my hair. "It was an accidental mistake," I start. *It wasn't.* "It all just happened in the spur of the moment. I really was on my way to meet the guys, but when I drove by the pier, some sophomore from Inglewood wanted to check out my car," I lie, and I open my eyes again and sit up, propping up my pillows and leaning back against them. I feel like such an asshole. "She got in my car and… I don't know. Things just happened. I completely didn't mean to. I swear, Tiffani. You know I'm just… I'm an idiot."

"Tyler," she sharply cuts in, and if I were in front of her right now, she'd be pressing her hand to my chest. "I don't want the details. I just want you to promise me that this will never, ever happen again. You don't want me to lose my patience, do you?"

"I promise," I blurt quickly, and I realize as soon as the words leave my mouth that I definitely shouldn't have said them. There is no way I can promise her that it won't happen again, especially not while Eden is in the picture. Now, if we ever get caught again, Tiffani definitely won't give me another chance. She will completely ruin my life, which means that from this moment on, Eden and I have to be very, very careful.

I've been with Tiffani all morning, forcing myself to be on my best behavior, fighting to keep her happy. That's why, using all of the cash I have made so far and stealing some out of whatever small amount is left in my trust fund, I was downtown bright and early this morning buying a damn purse at 9:00 a.m.. Tiffani is happy with it though, so the dent in my financial status is at least worth it.

She's even got it with her now. We've been at her house for hours, talking everything through until we are both in mutual agreement about what exactly this relationship is—toxic and meaningless but important and necessary—and now I'm driving her to the promenade so that she can meet up with the girls. I'm meeting up with Dean and Jake here too, and we will all most likely end up gathering together at some point.

"Drop me off by Nordstrom," Tiffani demands, though at least her voice is light, cheery, and most definitely fake. She has her sunglasses pushed down over her eyes and she is holding up her phone, taking pictures of herself as I drive, her glossy lips pouting back at her screen. I have both windows rolled down, so the breeze keeps blowing her blond hair around her face.

"Alright, Britney Spears," I say, rolling my eyes. I have one hand on the steering wheel, the other on her thigh. I know she likes that. "I think you've taken enough pictures. Which one would you like to set as your wallpaper?"

"Shut up, Tyler," she says, relaxing her features and lowering her phone. She points up ahead. We are heading down Second Street, nearing the promenade, and for a Thursday afternoon, the streets are filled with people. It *is* hotter than usual today, I guess, and the heat always brings out the crowds. "Pull up over there."

I do as she says and pull over by the sidewalk across the street from Nordstrom. As soon as we come to a stop, Tiffani releases her seatbelt and turns to face me, pushing her sunglasses up into her hair. She smiles at me. "You know, I believe you. I don't think you'll make another mistake. I'd hate for that to happen," she says, but I can hear the threat in her perfectly sweet voice. Her hands move while she speaks. "Now can we get back to acting normal?"

"That's exactly what I want, Tiffani," I tell her, mirroring her smile as I squeeze her thigh. I'm trying my best here, and it's the best damn performance I've ever done.

She leans toward me and presses her lips to mine, kissing me hard, and I almost flinch away from her. It takes a lot of strength to kiss her back, to act normal, to pretend I wasn't just kissing Eden last night. Kissing Tiffani isn't the same. It's always so rough, always so aggressive, always so boring. There's no excitement. No passion. How did I ever enjoy this? I stick with it for a few long seconds just to keep her happy, then I finally pull back from her, slumping against my seat.

"I hope you enjoyed that, because you're getting nothing more until I trust you again," Tiffani states as she reaches for the door, her new purse over her arm, her eyes piercing mine. She laughs and then gets out of the car, slamming the door behind her.

I watch her as she strides across the street, and I realize that Rachael, Meghan, and Eden are waiting for her over on the sidewalk. Have they been there the entire time? Did Eden just see me kiss Tiffani? I only look at her. She is sipping on a cup of coffee, her head tilted down, watching everything from beneath her eyelashes. Her gaze travels to mine. I can only hope she understands why I have to do what I am currently doing, and from across the street, I give her a small smile, one that's apologetic. I wish I was with her and not Tiffani. Eden glances away from me again as Tiffani nears the group. Rachael doesn't look too happy, because she aggressively hurls her cup of coffee into a trash can and throws her hands up. I don't care to wait around and watch. I'm meeting Dean and Jake at the Refinery, so I head off, revving my engine all the way around the corner onto Broadway, leaving the girls behind.

I spend fifteen minutes trying to find parking, and by the time I push open the door to the Refinery, Dean and Jake are already there. They're sitting by the full-length windows, watching the hustle and bustle outside on Santa Monica Boulevard, laughing among themselves as they consume their coffee without me.

"Oh, so you *have* turned up," Jake remarks as I enter, rolling his eyes.

"Jake, did I ever tell you how much I just *love* to hang out with you?" I fire back at him, and I barge my shoulder into his as I head for the counter. We're only messing around right now. My relationship with Jake is volatile, but at least we're on the right side of friendly most of the time.

I order myself an Americano, then head back over to the guys and pull up a chair, sitting down next to them. "So," I say as I take a sip of my coffee. It's so hot that it scalds my tongue. I set it down on the table instead, giving it a minute to cool. "What are we talking about?"

"Honestly, not much," Dean says, leaning forward to look at me past Jake. He gives me a warm, friendly smile, which is a much nicer welcome than Jake's. I know I probably frustrate Dean constantly, but he never lets it show. It's nice to have at least *one* friend who has my back. "Just the beach party on Saturday."

Immediately, I straighten up. I forgot all about that. "That's this weekend?"

"Yeah," Jake says, then he stifles a laugh as he mutters under his breath, "and try not to kill yourself this time." We both hear him.

"Jake," Dean hisses. They exchange a look, and Dean gives him a slow, firm shake of his head in disapproval. Jake only shrugs and props his elbows on the table, gulping down his coffee as he stares out the window.

Every year, there is a party down on the beach. Half of the beach gets cordoned off, and there's a stage where different DJs and bands perform all night. Everyone just turns up wasted and parties for hours as the sun sets over the Pacific. It's real sweet, and although officially no minors are allowed, half our school turns up anyway. I should be looking forward to it, but after last summer, I can't help but feel anxious. Even the thought of it is making my stomach twist.

At the party last year, I enjoyed myself a little too much. I was seriously drunk, and I bought some stuff I shouldn't have from a complete stranger. I thought I would be alright, but I wasn't. I don't know what the hell I took that night, but it was definitely laced with something. It was the one and only bad trip I've ever taken. Luckily, despite my friends being wasted themselves, they managed to drag me back to Tiffani's place where they watched over me for hours to make sure I didn't, like, die. I know they don't always care about me much, but they did that night.

"I was thinking," Dean says, clearing his throat, "we could all have some drinks at my place first before we head down to the beach."

"I shouldn't... Maybe I shouldn't go," I mumble. My mouth has gone dry. I drop my eyes to my lap, fumbling with my hands. The beach party last year was one of my lowest moments. It doesn't exactly hold any good memories for me, and I don't want to end up making any risky mistakes again.

"You think?" Jake mutters. He turns to face me and honestly, I could punch him in the face right here and now. "Is Eden going? I haven't seen her in a while."

"Why the fuck do you care?" I snap at him. He doesn't get to talk about Eden. He's an asshole, and he's going nowhere near her. Sure, she may have slept at his place, but that was weeks ago, and I get the feeling her attention is no longer on him. It's on me. "She's not interested in you."

"Really?" Dean says, shifting forward to the edge of his chair. Curiosity lights up his gaze as he looks at me, his eyebrows raised. "She said that?"

"She didn't need to," I say, clenching my jaw. I am losing it quicker than usual today. I just hate hearing Eden's name on Jake's tongue.

"Tyler, seriously, shut the fuck up," Jake says through laughter. I hate that he can always laugh his way through everything. I like to *pretend* that I don't care about anything, whereas Jake *actually* doesn't give a fuck. Never has, never will. "C'mon. Rachael says they're all at Johnny Rockets, so let's go meet them."

I take my coffee with me and drink it en route to Santa Monica Place, the luxury outdoor shopping plaza at the foot of the promenade where I dropped Tiffani off. Dean walks between Jake and me, most likely to prevent any arguments from breaking out, and we head upstairs to the dining deck and search the tables until we finally spot the girls. We pull over chairs and join them as they eat their sundaes. Or at least only three of them. Eden isn't eating anything.

I set a chair down next to Tiffani and sink down into it. I'm not sure how I feel about being in such close proximity to Eden while my friends surround us. I'm scared to look at her because I'm worried I'll smile without realizing, or our eyes will tell a story that isn't ready to be told.

"Hey," Tiffani whispers, smiling wide at me. She places her hand on my knee.

"So," Jake says, raising his voice as he leans forward on the table and runs his eyes around the circle, looking at each of us in turn. He only receives a glare back from me. "We've decided that we'll go to Dean's before the party on Saturday."

"A party before a party," Dean throws in. He bears an excited grin as he glances around all of us too. Dean isn't a huge fan of parties, but he does always love the annual beach party. "We'll take care of the booze."

"You guys just take care of looking good," Jake finishes. He jokingly shrugs and leans back in his chair, nonchalantly folding his arms across his chest.

"Prick," Rachael says, and she throws her spoon across the table at him. He narrowly avoids it, but I wish it had hit him.

"You know I'm kidding, Rachy baby," he teases, sitting up again and cocking his head to one side. He smirks at her, his expression playful. Ever since middle school, they have been like this.

"Don't call me that!"

They argue back and forth for a few minutes, but I can't focus because Tiffani is running her hand from my knee up to my thigh under the table. A lump is rising in my throat as she scoots her chair

JUST DON'T MENTION IT

closer to me and brushes her fingertips up and down my arm, creating goose bumps. I lock my eyes on the table, paralyzed. I wish she would stop touching me. I'm pretty certain the only reason she's doing this is because we have company. This is her way of letting our friends know that everything is totally fine between her and me, even though it's not. Suddenly, she grabs my jaw and leans in to kiss me, but I just can't do it, not right here, not while Eden is right in front of us. Before Tiffani's lips can meet mine, I jerk my head to one side and her mouth lands on my cheek instead. I expect her to get mad at me, but she only leans her body against mine and continues to touch me.

"Eden," I hear Rachael say, her pitch high and her tone teasing, "you and Jake should go for a walk or something. Off you go, lovebirds."

What the fuck? My eyes flash up from the floor, and I look at Eden for the first time. Tiffani is drawing patterns on my neck with her finger, but I can't even focus on that right now, because all I can do is stare at Eden. She looks uncomfortable with all of the attention suddenly on her, and I'm wondering what Rachael is even talking about. Has Eden still been seeing Jake? I don't think so. He said himself that he hasn't seen her in a while.

Jake gets to his feet and shoves his hands into his pockets, waiting for her. "Eden?"

And to my complete disbelief, she actually gets up. She doesn't quite look at me as she does, and as she walks around the table to meet Jake, she mumbles, "We won't be long."

I stare after the two of them as they walk away, disappearing out of sight down an escalator. My teeth are grinding so hard together that my jaw aches, and now Tiffani is biting at my earlobe, her hand on my chest.

"Okay, no offense," Rachael says loudly, wrinkling her nose at us, "but please stop."

Tiffani laughs, then finally presses her lips to mine. This time, I do kiss her back.

That night, I can't sleep. It's nothing new to me. Often there are nights where my mind is in such an overdrive that I just can't relax enough to get any sleep. I lie awake for hours, listening to the soft purring of the air-conditioning throughout the house, staring up at my ceiling through the darkness of my room. I can't stop thinking about Tiffani, about Mom, about Jamie, but mostly I'm thinking about Eden. By 3:00 a.m., I've had enough. I have been tossing and turning for too long, so I throw back my comforter and leave my bed.

Slowly, I creep out of my room and into the hall, and as silently as ever, I open Eden's bedroom door a few inches. I peer through the darkness, but I can't see anything, so I open the door fully and step into her room. As my eyes adjust, I close the door again behind me and whisper, "Are you awake?"

I can see Eden coming into focus, wrapped up in bed, facing her wall. She doesn't stir, so I figure that she's asleep, but then suddenly I hear her murmur, "Yeah. What time is it?" Her tone is the huskiest I have ever heard it, and there is no chance that I will ever sleep now after hearing that.

"Three," I tell her, my voice still low. Carefully, I move across her room, reaching for her comforter and crawling into her bed. "Can I sleep with you?" I ask. Her bed is warm and I'm sure she is warmer, but I keep several inches between our bodies. "I mean, not like hook up with you, just fall asleep, you know, like, rest."

"I know what you meant," Eden says. It sounds like she is smiling. I don't exactly think straight when I'm tired.

I stare at her ceiling now for a while, basking in the warmth and breathing deeply. I can hear her breathing too, and I finally muster up the courage to roll over toward her, gently pressing my body against hers. I bury my face into the back of her shoulder, squeezing my eyes shut. She is so warm, so comforting.

"I'm sorry about Tiffani," I whisper as I wind my fingers into her hair, holding her close to me. I wish she would turn around. I wish I could see the glistening of her eyes.

"You should be," she mumbles.

"Just let me figure it out," I say. I am begging her to give me a chance, to give me the time to think about all of my options when it comes to handling the situation that we're in. I want the result to be her, but I don't quite know how to do that yet. "I'm trying to figure everything out."

"Like what?"

"Eden, in case you haven't noticed, I'm pretty fucked up," I say. I pull away from her, rolling over to face her door, burying my head into the pillows on her bed. I feel her shift too, finally rolling away from the wall and turning toward me now instead.

"I wouldn't say that," she murmurs. She presses her hand to my shoulder blade and traces a pattern on my skin. I think she is touching my tattoo. "More like lost."

"Lost?" I echo. I'm a mess and my life is in ruins, but am I really *lost*?

"Yeah. I think you're lost," she says. She is still half asleep, her voice still low and raspy.

"What makes you think that?"

She runs her finger all the way down my spine, sending shivers throughout my body, and she moves closer, her body against my bare back. She presses her face into my shoulder and throws her arm over me, getting comfortable. "Because you have no idea what you're doing or where you're going," she whispers.

I am silent for a long time. She's right. I don't know what I'm doing, and I definitely don't know where I'm going, so maybe I am lost. I stare at her door, feeling her heart beating slowly against my back, and I reach for her hand and intertwine our fingers. "Eden?" I whisper, but she is already asleep again.

51

I WALK FOR WHAT feels like forever, but it is really only twenty minutes. I trudge along, a backpack slung over my shoulders and only seventeen dollars to my name. I snuck into Mom and Dad's bedroom and stole all the loose change I could find in the pockets of Dad's jeans. It's enough to catch a bus out of Santa Monica. I don't know where to yet, but I won't be picky.

I need to get to the promenade first. I know there are buses that leave from downtown, but it's miles away, and the sun is slowly beginning to set. There is no turning back now though. I've already snuck out of the house, so if I do return home, I'll be in a lot more trouble than I already am.

I keep on walking, my pace slowing, kicking at the sidewalk and keeping my head down. I zip up my hoodie. Now that it's almost December, the weather is changing. The temperature has been dropping. It's not cold, but I'm missing the hot summer sun, even though the cool breeze on my face is offering some relief to my injuries. I stole a packet of painkillers from the bathroom too.

I'm somewhere over in the next neighborhood, somewhere in

Wilshire, and I think Jake lives here. I'll know his house if I see it, so I speed up my pace again, my head swiveling back and forth as I scan all of the houses around me. Maybe his parents will let me crash at their place for the night. I even pass my school, but it feels weird when the campus is so empty, so I keep on walking straight on by it in search of somewhere more welcoming to stop.

But I don't find Jake's house, nor do I get any closer to catching a bus out of here. At the very least, I am thirty minutes away from home, from Dad, and that's good enough for me. I sigh deeply and come to a stop by a huge oak tree with roots that have begun to crack open the sidewalk's concrete. I throw my backpack down onto the grass and then plonk myself down too. I lean back against the tree, my legs hugged to my chest, watching the passing traffic.

Maybe this is stupid. Maybe I *should* go home. But I'm too scared to do that, so I muster up some courage and stay put. I pull out some painkillers and a bottle of water from my backpack, then I take two of them. Even just sitting here, still and unmoving, everything hurts. So I close my eyes, listening to the cars, feeling the breeze on my skin, my breathing slow and deep. Until I hear a car roll to a stop in front of me.

My eyes flicker open, and there is a police car parked by the sidewalk, its engine still running. My breathing quickens as the window rolls down.

"Hey, buddy," the officer says, propping his arm onto the door. The smile he gives me is friendly but concerned. The same smile that Mr. Hayes and Dr. Coleman give me. "What are you doing out here?"

"Hanging out," I tell him bluntly. *He's going to arrest me for being a delinquent. And then I'm going to be in even more trouble. And then I will need to run away for sure next time.*

"Uh-huh," the officer says slowly, as though he doesn't believe me. He shouldn't. "Which house do you live in?"

"I don't live in this neighborhood," I admit. Quickly, I zip up my backpack and sling it over one shoulder, prepared to leg it down the street if I need to. I stay down on the grass for now though, praying that he will just leave me alone.

"Then what are you doing here?"

"Hanging out," I say again. *I'm running away from my abusive father.*

The officer remains silent for a minute, but I can see the curiosity in his features as he studies my face. "What happened?"

"I got in a fight at school," I say, shrugging. I even pull my hood up over my head to shadow the bruises. "I'm suspended."

"That's not good. You shouldn't fight," he says with a frown. He shuts off his engine and gets out of the car, taking a few steps toward me. He is tall and he towers over me, casting a shadow from the sunset. "What's your name?"

"Tyler," I tell him. I shift a little, getting into a better position for making a quick getaway. Should I have lied? I don't think so. He doesn't seem *that* scary. He doesn't look like he wants to arrest me. At least not yet.

"Alright, Tyler, I'm Officer Gonzalez," he says. To my surprise, he sits down on the grass next to me, a safe distance of several feet between us, and he reaches over and offers his hand out to me. "Nice to meet you."

I stare at his hand for a second, and then at the small, sincere smile he's wearing, and I decide then that he's nice and doesn't seem like he will arrest me. So I shake his hand.

"So," Officer Gonzalez says, pressing his palms down flat against the grass and leaning back a little, "do you want to let me know the real reason why you're out here? It'll be dark soon." He glances up at the sky, then back down to me. "You can tell me. We're friends now, aren't we?"

Maybe. I don't know. He's not giving me trouble or anything, so that's good, I guess. Right now, I could do with having someone to turn to, and a nice cop seems like just the right kind of person. That's why I trust him enough to admit, "I'm running away."

"Now why would you want to run away?" he asks, cocking his head to one side. He narrows his brown eyes at me, analyzing my expression. I try to keep my features as blank as I can, showing no emotion whatsoever so that he can't possibly read them.

"My parents were mad at me for the fight at school," I say. I slide my backpack off my shoulder again and set it back down on the grass, because I definitely don't plan on running from Officer Gonzalez now.

"Hmm. I'd be disappointed too if my son were fighting," Officer Gonzalez says. He speaks in a gentle, quiet voice. One that is making me feel a tiny bit better. "But I'd also be extremely worried if he were to run away. Don't you think we should get you home?"

"I don't know," I mumble. My home isn't safe anymore. It hasn't been for four years. I'm more likely to end up hurt at home than I am out on here on the street, so I think I would rather take my chances.

"You can ride up front in the car with me," Officer Gonzalez says, his smile widening into a grin as he raises an eyebrow at me. He nods to his patrol car, then holds out his hand to me again. "What do you say?"

I glance at the car, then at my backpack that barely holds any clothes or money, then back at Officer Gonzalez and his warm, friendly grin. I like him, and besides, it'll be dark soon, and I don't really want to meet the kind of people who roam the streets after dark. So, I shake his hand once again.

52

ON SATURDAY NIGHT, I am taking it easy at Dean's place. After what happened at the beach party last year, I am determined to stay in control of all of my senses this time. That's why I've been sipping the same can of beer for almost an hour while everyone else is chugging drinks and making fools out of themselves. It's weird being the sober one for once. Is this how they feel whenever they watch me drink too fast? Because damn, it's embarrassing to witness.

Dean has only invited a handful of his friends over. Jake and Meghan are here. Tiffani too, of course. Jackson and TJ from the football team are here, shotgunning beers at the same speed I was last weekend. The only other two people who should be here but aren't yet are Rachael and Eden. I keep glancing at the front door, waiting for them to turn up, but they are clearly running late. Rachael always takes forever to get ready, so it isn't surprising, just annoying.

We're all in the kitchen and I'm leaning back against the countertop, minding my own business and observing everyone else when suddenly Dean throws himself in front of me. The beach party is the only party he ever really lets go for, and he's already drunk. He grins wide at me as a bead of sweat trickles down his forehead. "You're behaving. I like that," he says. He taps his can of beer against mine and then walks away, and I stare blankly after him. Dean gets weird sometimes.

I sigh and straighten up, heading over to Tiffani as she pours herself a drink by the center island. I lean over her shoulder and move my lips to her ear. "I'm going outside for a smoke," I tell her over the sound of the music.

"I'll come with you," she says, spinning around with a smile on her face. She presses the freshly poured drink to her lips and knocks it back, closing her eyes as she drinks it all at once. When she's done, she slams the plastic cup down onto the countertop and crushes it beneath her hand. What the hell is wrong with everyone tonight? Is there something new in the air that I'm not quite picking up on?

Frowning, I take Tiffani's hand and we slip outside into Dean's backyard. The early evening sun is still beating down, and it's so bright that I wish I had sunglasses. I lean back against the wall of the house and pull out my lighter and pack of cigarettes. I don't smoke cigarettes all that often, but tonight, I am using them as my distraction since I am staying clear of getting drunk and getting high. I place a cigarette between my lips and light it, inhaling. The smoke burns my lungs.

"You know," Tiffani says as she rakes her hands down my chest, "you're actually *really* hot when you're sober."

"Yeah?" I say, and I exhale a plume of smoke straight into her face in an effort to get her away from me, but she doesn't budge. It was so much easier to put up with her when I didn't like another girl, and now it feels like the benefits of being with Tiffani just aren't worth it anymore.

"Well, maybe not when you do that," she says, wrinkling her nose. When the smoke clears, she moves closer to me, linking her arms around my neck. She looks up at me. "Thank you for being careful tonight. I just don't want you to embarrass me again."

She thinks I'm doing this for her? She thinks I'm being responsible for once so that I don't embarrass *her*? No. I'm doing this for me, for my own damn health so that I don't nearly kill myself again. I'm doing the right thing for once, and for myself, no one else.

I smoke in silence for a few minutes while she buries her face into my chest, and our attention is captured when we hear the door open and close. We both look over, and honestly, I don't expect to see Eden looking back at us. She must have just arrived. She hovers by the door, her posture radiating confidence, and if Tiffani wasn't here right now, I would be all over her. Her dark, thick hair is straight for once, and her eyes are heavily defined, her lashes thick. She's matched a skirt with a pair of Converse. She looks amazing.

"Can you go back inside?" Tiffani immediately snaps at her. She has a nasty streak when she drinks too much, and she's about to take it out on Eden. "And, like, give us some space?"

"Back off," I order, and Tiffani cranes her neck to glare at me. Normally, I wouldn't ever stand up against her, but I refuse to let her speak to Eden like that.

Luckily though, Eden completely ignores her. Instead, she nods at the cigarette in my hand, concern crossing her features. "What are you doing?"

"Relax," I say with a small smile as I place the cigarette back between my lips. "It's just a cigarette."

Her expression hardens and she presses her glossy pink lips into a bold line. "That's all you're gonna smoke tonight, right? Just cigarettes?"

I inhale another drag of the cigarette as I stare at her. If Tiffani wasn't here, I would talk to her about this. I would be myself with her. But

Tiffani *is* here, so I have to stick to being Tyler Bruce, despite how much I hate him. "Go back inside if you're just gonna interrogate me, sis," I say. I narrow my eyes at her for a fraction of a second, praying that she realizes this is all just an act, and then I look away from her and back to Tiffani, pretending I don't care. Tiffani laughs.

"We're about to play shot roulette," Eden states, ignoring me, acting normal. *Good*, I think. *That's what we need to do.* "So if you wanna join in, then you should probably come inside."

"I'm totally game!" Tiffani says, her attitude switching in a heartbeat. Now, she is suddenly beaming wide and skips over to join Eden, as though they are best friends. Even Eden makes a face at the sudden change.

"Are you joining us?" Eden asks me, cocking her head to one side as she watches me take a couple more sips of my beer. I've been holding it for so long that it's warm now. And gross.

"Obviously," I say sharply, rolling my eyes. I hate using this tone with her, but it's my Tyler Bruce voice. Tiffani, drunk or sober, would most definitely pick up on it if I spoke to Eden differently than the way I speak to everyone else.

She shakes her head at me, and then both she and Tiffani disappear back inside. Shot fucking roulette? They're all going to end up wasted in there. I stay outside for a few more minutes, finishing off my smoke and pouring the remainder of my beer into a nearby plant pot, then I finally head inside to join everyone else.

They are all circling the center island where the roulette wheel is set up, cheering each other on, and I awkwardly hang back a little behind Tiffani. I don't really want to get involved, but I have a feeling I'll be asked to take at least one turn. I look at Eden across the kitchen. She is between Dean and Rachael, and Dean has his arm around her shoulders and is yelling something into her ear over the music while Rachael is murmuring something into her other. Suddenly, Rachael grabs her wrist and pulls her away from all of us. The two of them disappear into the living room and then out of sight, and I almost charge after them. Rachael can be a bad influence and I don't trust her with Eden, but if I grow too protective that would be suspicious, so I reluctantly force myself to stay put in the kitchen.

The game of shot roulette gets crazy real fast, with shots being taken and replaced every second as everyone becomes even rowdier. I am firing Tiffani disapproving glances every time she picks up another shot, but for once, she is the one ignoring me. Dean is also drinking way too fast, and I think Meghan may end up passed out before we even get to the damn beach.

"C'mon, you're the pro," Jake slurs at me as he throws his arm around my shoulders and shoves a shot glass into my hand. He spills half the vodka on the floor, and he is grinning at me as though we are suddenly best friends again. "Sober is boring. Drink up."

Honestly, I don't really want to go to this party *completely* sober, so I do give in and knock back several shots. I even crack open another two beers that I swig while everyone else finishes off the game, and by the time we are getting our shit together and heading outside, I am feeling a little tipsy.

Dean's older cousin is giving us a ride to the beach, and his minivan is parked out on the street as he waits for us. As we are all piling out through the front door, my hand in Tiffani's, I suddenly stop. "Wait. Where's Eden and Rachael?" I ask.

"I'll go find them," Dean says, and he turns and heads back inside the house.

Jake and Meghan linger by the front door, but Jackson and TJ are already diving for the van, and Tiffani is squeezing my hand and tugging me across the lawn. We climb into the very back seats, and she is so drunk that she swings her legs over mine, hooking her arms around my neck for support.

"Hey, Dean's cousin, turn the music up!" she yells, and he does as he's told, bumping up the music until it is pounding in our ears. Tiffani begins to grind against me as she dances, but I'm not paying attention to her.

I'm staring back at Dean's house as Eden and Rachael emerge from inside. I don't know what the fuck they've been up to, but they are both absolutely wasted. They can barely keep themselves upright as they stumble their way across the lawn, clinging onto one another, flanked by Dean, Jake, and Meghan. The five of them pile into the van and there aren't enough seats for all of us, so Rachael sits on Eden's lap and Dean squeezes himself into the back seats next to Tiffani and me.

I stare at Eden in disbelief as she laughs out loud. I've never seen her like this, and it's making me really uncomfortable. I don't like the thought of her drinking too much, of losing control and regretting it the next morning like I always do. Getting drunk like this isn't her.

As we set off for the beach, everyone is so lively, jumping around the van and singing out of tune to the music, screaming their words. Tiffani is laughing in my ear. Jackson has the window rolled down and is waving his arm through the air. Jake is filming a video of all of us while he yells out another one of his shitty one-liners.

I grit my teeth and turn to face the window. I really didn't want to go to this party in the first place, and now I'm wondering how long it will be until someone throws up. I can feel someone's eyes boring into me, so I turn back from the window and find that Eden is looking at me over her shoulder among all of the commotion. Our eyes lock, but all she does is flash me a wide, goofy smile. She is *so* drunk, and I'm not sure how she is going to handle tonight. I can't bring myself to smile back at her, because I'm worried. I turn back to look out of the window, tuning everything out.

It's not a long drive down to the beach, and I can see the party raging as we're pulling into the pier parking lot. As soon as Jackson slides open the door, we can hear the music thumping from the stage across the beach. The crowd is thick and energetic, and I have never seen the oceanfront look so busy. There are people milling around absolutely everywhere, and we all pile out of the minivan to join them.

"If any of you morons get us kicked out, I'll personally kick your ass," Jake warns us as we all huddle around one another. The girls are still giggling, and Dean can barely keep his eyes open. "Unless you're a girl. If you're a girl, you'll get the silent treatment."

The nine of us head across the boardwalk and make our way down onto the beach. I feel like I have to keep an eye on everyone as they stumble across the sand, unable to relax in fear that someone will face-plant on the ground. There are a lot of security guards around, but as per usual, they are so distracted by the DJ performing over on the stage that they aren't actually doing their jobs. We sail straight on past them, and that's when we decide to split up. The girls head off in one direction, and us guys head off in another. I'm glad to get away from Tiffani, but I'm anxious about letting Eden out of my sight. She is with her friends though. Or rather *my* friends. And although they are all drunk, I'm sure they will look after her. I doubt they do beach parties like this in Portland, so I hope Eden will be alright.

Jake weaves a path through the crowd, fearlessly elbowing people out of the way while we all flank him. We are fighting our way toward the stage, and Dean is too light on his feet because he keeps swaying into people. I throw my arm around his shoulders, firmly supporting him.

"Woah," he says.

"What, Dean?"

"Woaaah," he says again.

Goddamn. Maybe I *should* have gotten as wasted as the rest of them so that I didn't have to bear this, because I only end up babysitting the guys. TJ disappears from sight after fifteen minutes, and I have to keep apologizing to the strangers Jake keeps knocking into as he jumps around to the music, and I keep having to haul Dean up from the floor and check if he's alright. It is such a drastic change from last year, and although I hate being the sober one, I'm at least proud of myself.

I try to relax into the music, to somewhat enjoy this party, but I just can't get into it. We are in the thick of the crowd and we are being shoved around, and the guys are yelling unintelligible shit into my ear and everyone is laughing but me. I stand with my hands in my pockets, constantly checking the time, but we've only been here for an hour. The sun hasn't even fully set yet, so it's going to be a long night.

I am watching the stage when out of the corner of my eye, I spot Tiffani nearby. She is on her own, weaving her way through the crowd; her head swivels as she searches for something. And I know exactly what she's looking for, and that's me. I really don't want to deal with her right now. I don't need her drunkenly trying to kiss me, so without saying a word to the guys, I turn and throw myself into the crowd in the opposite direction from Tiffani. I quickly make my exit, using my shoulders to nudge by people, desperately trying to put some distance between Tiffani and me. I head away from the stage, toward the back of the crowd where it begins to thin. It's much more chill back here, and just when I think I have escaped Tiffani, I discover I have a new issue at hand.

In front of me, I see Eden. She is alone, still drunk, and in tears. I quickly glance around, but neither Rachael nor Meghan are anywhere in sight. Eden's hair is no longer straight but rather tangled and wavy around her shoulders, and she is hugging her sweater around her while staring down at the sand. Her cheeks are smeared with mascara, and she is barefoot. Her Converse are tied around her fingers by the laces. What the hell has happened?

"Dammit, Eden," I say as I rush over to her aid. Why the hell is she alone and upset? I'm glad I've found her. Who knows how long she has been left like this?

"Tiffani is looking for you," she sniffs through her tears as she looks up at me from the sand. Her eyes are swollen and she dabs at them with the sleeves of her sweater. "Your girlfriend."

I don't care about Tiffani right now. I only care about her. I step closer, tilting my head down so that we are at eye level. "What the hell are you crying for?"

"Everyone left," she says and her lower lip trembles as her shoulders sink. She glances around at the crowd surrounding us, but it only makes her lose her balance "Tiffani, Meghan, Rachael... My phone's gone."

I reach for her arm and hold her still, but she is still swaying slightly, unable to focus on me. "How drunk are you?" I ask her, frowning. I should have stayed with her. I knew she was drunk. This party was such a bad idea.

She cocks her head to one side, her damp cheeks glistening as the strobe lights from the stage hit her face. "Are you drunk?"

"Not anymore," I say, even though I was never drunk in the first place. How the hell do I fix this? I'm never usually the one who has to sober anyone up, because I am usually the one who needs sobering the most. I look down at the sand. There are crushed cans all over the place, and I'm surprised she hasn't cut her feet yet. I reach for her shoes, untangling the laces of her Converse from around her fingers and dropping them down onto the sand in front of her. "Put them back on," I order. My voice adopts a new strict, firm tone. "There's trash everywhere." Eden immediately steps back into her shoes, and she grins up at me despite the fact that she was just in tears a second ago. "Your dad is going to kill you," I mutter under my breath. Dave would have a heart attack if he saw his daughter like this. There is no way I can take Eden home, but I also can't let her stay here.

Suddenly, she darts off, spinning across the sand until she is a small distance away from me. She pauses and turns back to face me again, her expression playful. Oh, God. What is she doing now? I watch her closely, trying to gauge her next movements. When there is a break in the crowd, she clumsily drops herself down onto the sand and somersaults her way toward me, ending up in a giggling heap. The people around us are watching. They're rolling their eyes at her, laughing at her.

"Get off the ground," I snap, reaching down and grabbing her arm. I pull her straight back up onto her feet and fix her with a disapproving look. This isn't funny. "What did I just tell you about the trash?"

"I looove this beach," she slurs, and suddenly, she has gone from crying her eyes out to smiling wide. She must be dizzy because she sways to one side again, and I grab her shoulders with both hands. This time, I don't let go of her; I just keep holding onto her, refusing to let her fall. "I'm going to come back next summer just for this party!"

"Are you coming back next summer?" I ask quickly. It's something I haven't actually thought about too much. I keep forgetting that in a couple weeks, Eden will be heading home. I wish she didn't have to leave.

"I don't know," she says, shrugging beneath my grip on her shoulders. "It depends on if my dad wants me back or not."

"I hope he does," I say. *Please, Dave, invite the damn girl back again.* "I know I do," I add quietly.

Eden's mouth curves back into a smile and she fights against my firm hold, breaking out into what I think may be dance moves. She isn't even in sync with the music, and when I glance around us again, I can still see people laughing. "You're drawing attention to yourself," I hiss into her ear. I drop my hands from her shoulders to her waist, firmly grabbing her body and holding her as tightly as I can, keeping her still. "You're gonna get us kicked out."

"But I'm twenty-one!" she screams through a fit of giggles, and even more heads turn in our direction.

"Oh my God," I whisper, releasing a groan. This is getting bad, and I need to think fast about how I'm going to get her away from here. I close my eyes for a second, thinking through all of my options, and I realize that there aren't many. I inhale as I open my eyes again, then I quickly bend down and slide my hands under her legs, swiftly pulling her onto my back. I straighten up again as I begin to carry her across the beach through the crowd. "You need to sober the fuck up."

Eden rests her head on my shoulder, wrapping her arms around my neck and holding onto me just as tightly as I'm holding onto her. Her legs are locked around my waist, and she is breathing deeply against my neck. I wish she knew that it was turning me on, but I fight hard to keep my mind focused on the situation at hand, which is making sure she is okay.

I don't even know where I'm heading, but I spot TJ among the crowd. He looks even drunker than he did at Dean's place, and I don't even know how that's possible considering none of us have had a drink in hours. He also has two much older, extremely attractive girls on either side of him who he is chatting to. Normally, I wouldn't interrupt, but I know that he has an apartment nearby.

"Troy-James," I call out to get his attention. Quickly, I walk over to him, still carrying Eden on my back. She is nearly strangling me, but I don't mind.

"What's up?" TJ says. He has a hand on the hip of each girl and he smiles at me, his gaze lazy.

"I need your apartment," I say quickly. It's a weird request, I know, but I'm begging him to help me out. "You're still on Ocean Avenue, right?"

"Bro," TJ says uncertainly. He glances at the girls he's with, both of them leaning in close to him, and he seems indecisive. I have a feeling he may want the apartment for himself. "What are your plans, man?"

I nod my head back over my shoulder toward Eden. She hasn't said a word since I picked her up, so I don't even know if she's still awake or passed out. "Sobering her up," I tell TJ, and the expression I give him is pleading, hoping for sympathy. "Her dad'll kill her if she goes home like this."

"Dude, you're kind of messing up my plans," he mutters, widening his eyes at me. He makes a face and subtly nods to the girls by his side.

"My place is free," one of them says, and suddenly, TJ's features relax and he throws me the keys to his apartment without a second thought.

"Leave 'em under the doormat," he says. He gives us no rules, and I manage to quickly thank him before he places his hands on the girls' waists and guides them away.

I think I remember where the apartment is. It's just across the street on the oceanfront, overlooking the beach, and I take a deep breath and begin to head in that direction. I never wanted to come to this party in the first place, so I don't mind leaving with Eden. I need to sober her up as best I can and make sure that she's safe.

"Why are we going to his apartment?" I hear her mumble into my shoulder after I've been walking for a while, leaving the party behind us. She's still alert, which is a good thing. I really don't want her to black out and fall asleep right now. "Why does he even have an apartment?"

"Because you're just embarrassing yourself out here," I tell her with a small laugh. I know the feeling, because I get way too drunk and embarrass myself all the time. That's why I can't get too mad at her. "And his parents are, like, millionaires. They bought him an apartment down here for his sixteenth birthday. Who the hell does that?"

"Millionaires," she says, and we both laugh.

I continue away from the beach, but the music seems to follow us. We can still hear the party continuing without us, and I wonder if anyone will even notice that we left. They are all so drunk that they most likely won't. That's a good thing. The last thing I need right now is Tiffani racing around trying to find me, so I can only hope that she is too preoccupied by the music and the lights.

"You can put me down, you know," Eden says, and she begins to fidget on my back.

"What, so you can get hit by a car? No way," I say. I tighten my hold on her as we cross Ocean Avenue during a break in the traffic.

"You're missing the rest of the party," she murmurs, as though I actually *care* about the damn party.

I don't trust her enough right now not to do anything stupid, so I carry her all the way to TJ's apartment building. When we reach the entrance, I let her down gently, and she seems even more unsteady on her feet than she did back at the beach.

"How are you feeling?" I ask as I shove TJ's key into the lock. It's stiff, so I have to fumble around for a few seconds until I get the door open.

Eden looks down at her shoes and pulls her sweater around her. "Embarrassed."

ESTELLE MASKAME

I reach for her elbow and guide her inside the apartment building, shutting out the music from the party as I close the door behind us again. "We've all been there," I say in an effort to make her feel a little better. We're young. Getting too drunk and making a fool out of yourself is almost a rite of passage.

"Like you last year?" Eden says, and I stop dead in my tracks in the middle of the lobby.

I look back at her, taken aback by the suddenness of that accusation. How does she know? Someone told her what happened last year, about that bad trip I took. I don't think she means to hurt me though, because she guiltily bites down on her lip as though she is wishing she never said it. For that reason, I decide to just move on without talking about it, shaking my head at her and reaching for her wrist. I pull her into the elevator and press the button for the second floor.

"206," I say out loud as I double-check the apartment number on TJ's keys. I never let go of Eden's wrist, and I guide her along the hallway of the second floor and all the way to the door of TJ's apartment. I unlock it and lead her inside. I have been in TJ's apartment before, but only for a party.

It's much different seeing it when I'm sober and when the place isn't trashed. I forgot that he has these amazing floor-to-ceiling windows that surround the living room, overlooking the beach. I can see the lights of the pier, the Pacific Wheel flashing bright as the sun sets in the distance behind it. Eden must appreciate the view because she stands still, her gaze locked on the windows, completely entranced.

I walk over to the kitchen and fill Eden a glass of water, which I carry back over to her. "Here," I say gently, keeping my voice low so that I don't startle her too much. When she turns to face me, I force the glass into her hand. "Drink it. Now."

408

Her smile is thankful as she presses the glass to her lips and gulps down the water. We were on the beach for over an hour in the heat, and I have a feeling she definitely didn't stop by any of the refreshment stands to keep herself hydrated.

"Sit down," I tell her, taking the empty glass away from her. I nod over her shoulder to the couch behind her. I'm not really sure what exactly I'm supposed to be doing, but getting her off her feet seems like a good place to start. I place my hand on her shoulder and lead her over, pushing her down onto the couch.

"It looks so pretty," she murmurs as she focuses her gaze back on the windows again, at the picturesque Santa Monica in front of us. She sinks back against the cushions, and the sunset casts an orange glow across her face. "Doesn't it?"

"Sure it does," I agree as I walk back over to the sink again. I fill her another glass of water from the faucet and bring it back to her, drying my hands on my jeans. She is sitting cross-legged on the couch now, and I don't really know what to do with myself, so I just sit down on the edge of the couch next to her. "You need to sleep this off," I say as I watch her desperately chugging that water again. I'm trying to think of all the things people tell *me* to do when I'm too drunk, and usually, I am forced to drink water and sleep. I don't think it actually works, at least not for me, but I am willing to try anything with Eden. "Come on," I say, gently taking the glass from her again and setting it down on the coffee table. I reach for her hand, interlocking our fingers as I stand up, taking her with me. Just in case she topples over again, I clasp her waist with my other hand. "You good?"

"Good," she confirms.

I take her across the apartment, her hand still in mine, and I guide her into TJ's bedroom. Luckily, he keeps it tidy, and Eden seems desperate to climb into the huge bed in the center of the room; she is already kicking off her shoes. I don't know why, but I find myself sliding my hands under her thighs and lifting her up again. She wraps her legs around me once more, her arms over my shoulders, her chest pressed to mine. I carry her over to the bed and gently set her back down again. I walk around the bed, fumbling with the sheets, pulling them back for her.

"I'll go get your water," I tell her. The silence of the apartment is getting a little awkward now, not because we are uncomfortable, but because we are alone and I still have no idea what I'm doing. I'm just glad it's me who is looking after her and no one else.

I head back to the living room, grab her glass from the coffee table, then top it back up at the sink. I may have been tipsy earlier, but I am completely sober now. I don't think Eden would have had a drink since we left Dean's place, so I'm pretty sure she won't be getting any more intoxicated than she already is. From this point onward, she can only sober up. "Here," I say as I walk back into the bedroom, and Eden flinches at the sound of my voice. She has stuck one of her fake eyelashes onto the bedside table, and I bite back laughter as I set the water down next to it. "Water and sleep: the only way to sober up and minimize your hangover as much as possible," I explain with a laugh. I hope I can lighten the mood a little so that she doesn't end up hating herself for this tomorrow.

"You should take your own advice sometimes," she says as I close the curtains, shutting out all of the bright lights from the pier. "Next time you're drunk, I'm just gonna chant, 'Water and sleep, water and sleep.'"

I smile at her as I turn back around, shaking my head. God, I really do like this girl. "Get some sleep, Eden," I say softly. Eden lets out a warm, gentle laugh as she scrambles under the sheets, fluffing up the pillows and pulling the sheets up to her chin. She lies on her back, getting comfortable, and so I head for the door, ready to give her some privacy to sleep off the alcohol, but I end up lingering longer than I mean to. Does she want me to leave, or does she want me to stay? Should I give her some space or should I watch over her? "Are you going back to the party?" she asks, lifting up her head.

"I don't know," I admit. I look down at the floor. Tyler Bruce doesn't really leave parties early. 'I mean, Tiffani's probably looking everywhere for me."

"Oh," Eden says, and I can almost hear her heart sinking.

"I'll let you sleep," I say as I glance back up at her. I give her a small smile, one that lets her know that I'm here, I'm looking after her, I care about her.

She sinks back down into the pillows and rolls over, hugging the sheets around her. Reluctantly, I leave the room, pulling the door closed behind me. The apartment is quiet and I find myself paralyzed outside the bedroom. I squeeze my eyes shut and rest my forehead against the door, exhaling.

Going back to that party is the cowardly way out. Do I really care about what people think of me? Do I really return to a party just to prove to everyone that I'm there, that I'm happy? I'm stronger than that, I know I am. I don't need approval from anyone. I don't need everyone to think that I'm fine.

Fuck Tyler Bruce. I hate that guy. For the first time, I think I may actually like myself better. I like who I am with Eden, but around Eden, I am only being *me*. The real me, the me who has all of these secrets and all of these insecurities and all of these ups and downs.

Forget the party. I am not going anywhere. I'm staying right here with Eden, because she matters more to me than what my friends think of me.

I push open the door and step back into the dark bedroom. Eden is already asleep, because she doesn't even stir as I walk across the room. I sit down on the floor in front of the window, resting my head back against the wall as I watch her. I wish she knew I was here, that I haven't left. I will sit here and watch her for hours if I need to, just to make sure she is safe.

I think that's the moment I realize I'm in love with her.

53

OFFICER GONZALEZ DOESN'T TAKE me home. He doesn't know where it is. I won't tell him. So he has taken me to someplace even more terrifying: the police station downtown. It makes me regret ever agreeing to get in the car with him in the first place.

There's a phone ringing loudly throughout the office. The air smells of coffee. There are officers drifting back and forth between desks. I am sitting at a row of seats against the back wall, anxiously squeezing the bottle of water that Officer Gonzalez has given me, my gaze darting all over the place, trying to keep tabs on everything. I tried my best. I refused to give them my surname. But one of the lawyers here in the office right now knows my mom and has given away my true identity.

Which means that my parents have now received their second phone call of the day about me. First from Principal Castillo and now from Officer Gonzalez. And if they weren't happy about getting the phone call from school, then they *definitely* aren't going to be happy about answering a phone call from the police. In the space of one day, I have gone entirely off the rails, and even I can't explain what's wrong with me. Mom is going to be so disappointed, and Dad is going to be so furious.

"So," Officer Gonzalez says as he appears again. He sits down next to me with a cup of steaming hot coffee, and he takes a long sip of it. I look sideways at him. "You're lucky. Your parents didn't even realize you were missing, so you *didn't* send them into a spiral of panic for the past hour. They'll be here any minute."

I turn my eyes down to the floor. My stomach hurts from how sick I feel. I shouldn't have stopped by that stupid tree. I should have kept walking. I should have gotten on the bus. I should have really left town.

"Are you alright?" Officer Gonzalez asks when I don't reply.

And the truth is, I'm really not. But how do I tell him that? I feel so weak, my body is aching, my head is spinning, my sight is blurring with the tears that are threatening to fall. I am so, so scared. I lift my head and turn to look at him. My eyes meet his, and I am begging him to really, truly look at me, to see the fear and the pain in my eyes, to tell me everything is going to be okay, that he's going to protect me. I want to tell him the truth, but I can't find the words to explain just how broken I am.

But the truth is in my eyes. I am telling him. I am trying. I am broken, I am in agony, I am scared.

But he doesn't see it. He doesn't say anything at all.

I look away, fighting back the tears, tilting my head back down to the floor again. "I'm fine," I say.

"I'll keep an eye out for your parents," Officer Gonzalez says. He gives me a reassuring pat on the back as he stands, then he walks away again, sipping at his coffee, nodding to fellow colleagues as he disappears back out of the office.

I slump back against my seat, squeezing my eyes shut and pressing my hands to my face. I flinch from the pain, then quickly push my hands back into my hair instead. I pull on the ends in frustration. I'm so exasperated, so lost. How am I supposed to handle this mess now? Every day, my life seems to spiral more out of control. Every day, I feel more helpless. Every day, I grow weaker.

I just want it all to stop. I want Dad to stop.

I'm tired of lying. I'm tired of protecting him. I'm tired of pretending I'm okay.

But I just can't find the words to make it all end.

"Tyler!" I hear Mom's voice echo from somewhere in the distance, but the reality is that she's right next to me, because suddenly her arms are wrapping around me and she's pulling me in close, squeezing me tight as though she's afraid I'll disappear again. "What were you even thinking?"

I open my eyes, suffocating under Mom's hold, and she is planting kisses into my hair. I try to look at her out of the corner of my eye, but it's impossible to see her face when she's clinging onto me so closely, so I remain paralyzed in place. I look up to see Dad's expression instead, but he's not here. My eyes dart all over the office in search of him, but only Mom has come.

Officer Gonzalez is watching us closely, his arms folded loosely across his chest, and he gives me a reassuring nod. "He was over in Wilshire on Twelfth Street," he explains. "Kid posted up by a tree? I thought I better check it out. Turns out he was worried you were mad at him for that fight at school." He lets out a small chuckle. "I didn't realize he was your son."

"Oh, Tyler," Mom says, exhaling a long breath of air. She releases her hold on me now and leans back, delicately cupping my busted-up face in her hands, her fingertips brushing my bruised skin. She looks even worse than she did earlier. More worried, more stressed. Her eyes are wide as they pierce mine. "Don't ever do something so stupid ever again."

I glance down at the floor and give her a small, single nod. I didn't mean to upset her again. Now I feel even guiltier. Today is officially the worst day of the entire year, and I just want Mom to take me home so that I can crawl straight into bed and sleep the rest of the night away.

"Thanks for picking him up," Mom says, straightening up in front of me and turning to face Officer Gonzalez. She shakes his hand, then gently reaches for my shoulder. It's our cue to leave, so I grab my backpack from the floor by my feet and stand up.

"No more fights at school, Tyler, alright?" Officer Gonzalez tells me with a teasing smile. I am staring back up at him, and although he is *still* being nice, I wish he could have been more. I wish he could have helped. I wish I could have told him *how* to help.

Mom guides me through the office, back toward the station's reception. She gives small nods of acknowledgment to some of the officers and detectives that she's acquainted with, but she definitely doesn't stop for any small talk. It's almost like she's embarrassed, because her pace is much faster than usual, and she is quick to lead me through the reception and out the main entrance. As soon as the door closes behind us, Mom comes to a halt and steps in front of me, crouching down so that we're at eye level. She reaches for my hands.

"Tyler," she says sternly, searching my expression for answers. "Why would you even do such a thing? What is wrong with you?"

"You and Dad were mad at me," I admit quietly, staring down at my hands in hers. I try to pull away, but she tightens her hold. I didn't mean to worry her.

"Of course we were mad. You were in a fight, Tyler!" She closes her eyes, tilts her head down, and releases a frustrated sigh. She is quiet for a few seconds, as though she is thinking, and then she opens her eyes again and looks at me with a small smile. "I'm sure as you get older there will be a lot of things I'll get mad at. I'm your mom. It's my job. That doesn't mean I don't love you, and it doesn't mean you should run away. Okay?" She squeezes my hands again.

"Okay," I say. I swallow and dare myself to ask, "Where's Dad?" I'm relieved he hasn't shown up, but also worried that the reason he isn't here is because he is too angry to look at me.

"At home with your brothers." Mom tells me as she lets go of my hands and straightens back up. "He doesn't know, so let's keep this between us. I told him you walked to Dean's, so he's still not pleased with you for sneaking out, but at least he doesn't know *why*. You know how protective he is."

I stare at her. Protective? Dad is the one I need protection *from*. She really has no idea. Which is what I want, I guess. I've tried so hard to keep it all hidden, to keep the truth from surfacing, to protect *her*. I'm doing good, it seems, but it's so, so hard. I am letting myself get hurt in order to protect my family, but if I tell the truth, then I'll hurt *them*. Either way, it feels like I can't win.

"Mom," I say as she's searching through her purse for her car keys. She casts a quick sideways glance at me, raising an eyebrow and listening. But I don't know what to say. Every time I think I might just have the courage to finally tell someone, the words get stuck in my throat. I can't say it. I can't admit it. So, just like I did with Officer Gonzalez, I go for the easy way out. I tell her, "I'm tired."

"Good," Mom says, "because you're going straight to bed when we get home."

My heart sinks. Even my own mom can't hear the pain in my voice, or see the anguish in my eyes, or the bruises all over my body. Even when I want her to.

54

I WATCH OVER EDEN for hours, listening to her soft breathing as she sleeps. I have opened the curtains again and am leaning against the window, watching the party carry on without us. It's the middle of the night, but all of the lights are still flashing, even brighter now through the darkness. I can still see the crowds down on the beach partying by the stage. Very faintly, I can still hear the music.

I hear movement from behind me, and I crane my neck to look over at the bed. Through the darkness, I see Eden stirring. She pushes the sheets away from her and rolls over, desperately reaching out and fumbling for her water on the bedside table. She props herself up on her elbow and chugs it down as though she has been thirsty for weeks. I know how it feels waking up after the night before.

"How are you feeling?" I ask her gently.

Eden stops drinking and tilts her head up, her surprised gaze coming to rest on me in the corner of the room. She stares at me for a few seconds before she finally says, "Better. What time is it?"

"Three," I say. I glance out of the window again and let out a small laugh. "The party's still going strong."

As she comes into focus through the dark, I notice she has her eyebrows furrowed. "Didn't you go back?"

"No," I tell her. Did she think that I would? Did she really think I would leave her here alone? "I was worried that you'd throw up or something," I admit, and my voice grows quiet. "Plus it was probably best that I just stayed away from it all."

Around this time last year, I would have been at Tiffani's place by now, probably suffering through my seizure with no idea what was actually going on. I seemed to totally black out, but from what my friends have told me about that night, it sounds pretty damn terrifying. It's been an entire year, and I still haven't learned from it. I'm *still* hitting Declan up a couple times a week.

"What's wrong?" Eden asks as she sits up.

"Nothing," I lie, pulling my knees up to my chest and resting my elbows on them, interlocking my hands. I have opened up to her about things before, but this is something I really don't want to talk about. I don't even want to imagine what she would think of me.

"I know there's something wrong," she says, and she takes another sip of her water as she studies me over the rim of the glass. Firmly, she asks again "What's wrong, Tyler?"

"It's just…" I try, but I can't get the words out. My shoulders sink with defeat. I don't have the guts to tell her. I'm scared to.

"Just what?" she presses.

"This time last year," I start, but it's all I can say. I can't tell her that I was an idiot, that I almost killed myself because I was searching for a high that would get me through another day.

"You passed out," she says for me, and my eyes flick back up from the floor to meet hers. So, she *does* already know, and she is definitely sober now, because *this* is the Eden I know. The one who tells me the truth straight up. "Rachael told me. You passed out because of the drugs."

I swallow the lump in my throat and get to my feet, stuffing my hands into my pockets as I lean back against the wall. "Just drink your water," I mumble.

She tilts the glass of water to her lips again and quickly finishes it, then puts the glass back on the bedside table before she slides out of the bed and stands up. She takes several wary steps toward me and quietly asks, "Why do you do it?"

Tonight of all nights, I really don't want to go through this again with her. She is always pushing for an answer to that question, but it's an answer I'm just not emotionally strong enough to give her. "Why are you asking me about this again?" I mutter as I throw my hands up out of my pockets. It's such a sensitive subject to me that already my temper is rising.

"Because I want the truth," Eden says.

"I already gave you the goddamn truth," I snap at her, and I end up balling my hands into fists by my sides. I am fighting hard against the anger that is brimming. "I do what I do to distract myself."

"From what?" she asks, but she raises her voice, unable to hide her frustration. I think this is what she has been trying to figure out the entire summer, and she isn't going to stop until she finds out the truth. "That's what I want to know, Tyler. I want to know why you need all these bullshit distractions."

"Distractions make everything easier," I hiss under my breath. I was so calm before, so in control, and I hate that I am now losing that. I'm not angry at her though. I never will be. I only get angry when I'm forced to face the truth.

"Makes what easier?"

I'm grinding my teeth together as I go quiet, and I look her straight in the eye. "Stop, Eden," I say slowly, my voice firm. I hope she can see the plea in my eyes. I really don't want to do this.

"Stop what?" she asks, taking another step toward me.

"Stop trying to figure me out," I say, but my pulse is already racing. I look down into her eyes, and I pray that she will care about me enough to not put me through this. If she figures out the truth about me, she will know that I'm broken inside.

"Tyler," she says, "49ers or Chargers?"

No fucking way did she just change the subject like that. From asking me why I get high to asking me which football team I support... Wow. I will take anything I can get though. "What kind of a dumb question is that? 49ers."

Eden's face falls and she widens her eyes at me, parting her lips. "I saw a photo in Dean's house," she says slowly, her voice low, husky, "of you and him and your dad before a 49ers game. If you're a fan, how come you looked like you didn't want to be there?"

I stare back at her, my expression frozen. I know exactly what photo she is talking about. It's the same photo I spotted in Dean's garage earlier this week, the photo that triggered such a turmoil of painful emotions in me. "Dean was supposed to take that down," I tell her. I don't know what else to say.

"Answer the question," she says, her voice demanding. "What was wrong that day?"

She isn't ever going to let this go. I wonder if she looked closely enough into my eyes in that picture to see the pain I was in. It was a much bigger pain than any injury Dad could ever inflict on me. I was heartbroken that night. I felt worthless. I was breaking down inside.

I can't look at Eden right now, because those same emotions are hitting me all over again at full force. I am breaking down now too. I walk away from her and pick up her empty glass from the bedside table and tighten my hand around it, squeezing it hard to release some of the fury that is taking me over. I pause by the window, looking out again at all of the lights. My life is a mess.

"What is it with you, Eden?" I murmur. I keep my head down, my eyes closed, my back to her. "You're not supposed to figure me out. No one is."

"Tyler," Eden whispers, and my name sounds desperate on her tongue. Slowly, I look back at her over my shoulder, and her eyes are gentle but intense as she stares back at me, her hand pressed to her chest. "Trust me. Please."

I look back down at the floor and close my eyes again. She wants to know so badly, but I am terrified of letting her in to my biggest secrets. I have never told anyone before. I have been holding the weight of this secret for five years, and I just can't let it go. It has become part of me. "Don't make me tell you."

Eden edges her body in between mine and the window. She moves close to me, gently placing her hand on my chest, feeling the erratic thumping of my heart. Her gaze meets mine. "Please," she whispers.

And I can see it in those sparkling hazel eyes of hers that she cares about me, that she is desperate to know the truth so that she can understand me better. I have always kept the truth about my dad a secret from everyone, because I have worried people would never look at me the same. I didn't want pity and I didn't want sympathy. I wanted to move on, to show that I was stronger than everything that I had been through, that Dad wouldn't define me. I don't want to leave myself vulnerable again, but there is something about Eden that is reassuring, like she'll make sure everything is okay, that I'll be okay.

"My dad's an asshole," I whisper and my words cut me. My voice is cracked and my heart is beating so fast that I think I may suffer a heart attack. I'm really about to do this. I'm really about to tell Eden the truth. "I told everyone he's in jail for GTA. That's not true." I can't look at her now, not when I'm about to say the words that will tear me up inside. My jaw is clenched tight and I stare at the wall, blinking fast to stop myself from welling up. Then, so quietly it's almost inaudible, I say, "He's in jail for child abuse."

All of the color drains out of Eden's face, and I close my eyes. My heart is sinking as I hear her sharp intake of breath. "You?" she squeaks. I nod, but I never open my eyes. They are stinging; my throat is tightening. Eden exhales that same breath of air. "Jamie and Chase?"

"Just me," I say. I wouldn't have been able to cope if it had been any other way.

"Tyler, I…" Her voice cracks and grows huskier as she keeps her hand on my chest, reminding me that she is here with me. "I'm so sorry," she whispers.

There it is: *sympathy*. I don't need that.

"I do a pretty good job of keeping it a secret," I mutter as I open my eyes again. Eden is pale, and her eyes are wide and brimming with tears, but this is exactly what I didn't want. I step back from her and she drops her hand. "No one knows. Not Tiffani, not Dean, not anyone."

"Why haven't you told them?"

"Because I don't want pity," I snap. My anger is returning and I can feel it rising all the way up through my chest, tightening around my heart. I walk away from Eden and grab onto the edge of the bedside table for support. "Pity is for pussies. I don't wanna look weak. I'm done with being weak." I hate Dad so much. *Why did he do this to me? Why did he ruin my life?* My rage comes to an explosive head and

I throw a punch, slamming my fist straight into the bedside table. My knuckles should ache, but I don't feel pain that much anymore. "That's all I ever fucking was. Weak."

"You weren't weak," Eden says, shaking her head at me. "You were a kid."

She's wrong. I *was* weak. I should have been stronger, I should have stood up to him, I should have told someone. I storm across the room and lean back against the wall, sliding down onto the floor and inhaling. "You know, I didn't really get it for a while," I admit after a moment, after the anger has subsided. I need to tell her more. I need to open up for once, even if it is only a little. I can't tell her everything, but I can tell her enough. "I never understood what I did wrong."

Eden sits down on the carpet in front of me, crossing her legs and remaining silent. She is listening, and I realize that right now, that's all I really need. Maybe Mom is right. Maybe talking to someone *can* help.

"My mom and my dad…" I begin, but I'm struggling to find the right words. It's a complicated story. It's tough to tell. "They were just teenagers when they had me, so I get that they probably had no clue what they were doing. They both got a little obsessed with building careers. Dad had his dumb company, the one I told you about."

"Grayson's," Eden says quietly. She remembers.

"Grayson's," I confirm. This is going to take some time to explain, so I clear my throat and lean forward, folding my arms over my knees. My heart is still pounding. "It was great to start with. The business really took off for a few years, but when I was, like, eight, some deal fell through. Dad had a shit temper. He came home one night and Mom was at the office working late, and he was super pissed off and he took it out on me. I kind of let that one slide. I thought it was a one-off. But then his employees were all quitting and it stressed him out and he took it out on me again. It kept happening more often. It went from once a week to every single night. He'd tell me I couldn't do anything I wanted to do, because I needed to focus on school instead. Said he wanted me to get into an Ivy League college so that I didn't end up fucking up my career the same way he was. But the truth was, I didn't want to have a big-shot career or get into an Ivy League school, yet I spent every single night locked in my room trying to study so that he wouldn't get mad at me. I thought, I'm trying, right? That's enough, isn't it? But it wasn't. Every night, he still came upstairs and threw me around." For a second, I feel as though I can't breathe. Talking about this is so hard. Memories of Dad are flashing in front of me. The way he used to look at me, the way he used to grab me, the way he used to tell me he was sorry. "Every single night," I whisper. "Four years."

"I'm sorry," Eden says again, still choked up. She doesn't need to apologize.

"Mom was so busy, she seriously had no idea," I continue. "She blames herself for it now. She tries to ground me, but it just doesn't work because she never reinforces it. I think she's terrified of trying to be strict, you know? It's not her fault though. She did notice sometimes. She'd be like, 'Tyler, what have you done to your face this time?' And I just made up some weak excuse each time. I would tell her my face was busted because I was playing football during gym class or that my wrist was broken because I fell down the stairs. When really, I broke my wrist three times one year because Dad just loved to see how far he could bend it back."

"Why didn't you tell someone?" Eden whispers, and it's a reasonable question. Mom has asked me that same question so many times. "Does my dad know?"

"Because I was fucking scared of him," I admit. My voice is so strained. I don't sound like myself. "There was no way I could tell. The only person who doesn't know is Chase. He was too young. Mom didn't want to scare him. The rest of the family hates Dad now."

"When did it stop?"

"When I was twelve," I say. Five years ago. Five years ago, it all ended. Or at least it should have. These past five years have been hell, and my rage returns. Dad's actions have caused a ripple effect through my life. "Jamie came upstairs one night and saw Dad hitting me," I explain as I push myself up from the floor. "Called the cops, even at his age. Dad was arrested that night. It didn't go to trial because he pleaded guilty, so it was never publicized. I got to keep it a secret. I get to pretend that I'm fine." *But I'm not fine.*

I begin to pace around the bedroom, trying to keep my anger at bay before it can manifest even more than it already has. "I really fucking hate him," I spit. "Really, really hate him. After a year or something, I started to believe that there must have been a reason for it all. I thought I deserved it for being a worthless piece of crap. I still do. I can't even move on from it, because it's impossible to forget, which sounds so pathetic, but it's true. I'm supposed to be on antidepressants, but I don't take them because I want to drink and get high instead, and you can't do both. And you know what, Eden? You're right. I'm lost. I'm totally fucking lost in this mess."

Eden gets up from the floor too. She stands still, watching me while I pace, unsure what exactly to say to me. There is nothing anyone *can* say. At this point in my life, I have accepted what happened. My past is a part of me. It has shaped me into who I am today; it has made me the mess that I am. That doesn't mean that I think what happened was okay. It wasn't, and I'm furious.

"I depend on distractions!" I yell across the room to Eden, even though she is only a few feet away. "They make coping easier, because in the hours that I'm drunk or high or both, I forget that my dad fucking hates me!"

I need to release the fury that's running through me, and so I stop pacing and grab the empty glass, hurling it at the wall. I love smashing things. It's satisfying to me, it keeps me calm, and I watch as broken pieces of glass shatter onto the carpet, breathing heavily. Eden gasps.

All of my energy seems to leave my body. I hate what Dad has done to me. I feel so lifeless, so empty. I sink down onto the bed behind me as my pulse continues to race, and I lock my eyes on the dark sky outside. The moon is full and bright. "I hate him," I growl, swallowing hard. *I hate him so much.*

Eden walks over, stepping in front of me. I tilt my head back to look up at her, to meet her eyes, which are full of warmth and reassurance.

Delicately, she reaches out and presses both her hands to my jaw, cupping my face. Her gaze never leaves mine as she sits down on my lap, our bodies pressed together, her skin warm. My breath catches in my throat. She is so close. She brushes her thumbs over my cheeks, then leans forward, moving her lips toward mine. They don't touch though. I don't need them to. It's amazing just having her next to me, feeling her breath on my skin, knowing that in this moment, she is completely mine. I close my eyes, and we remain huddled together like this for a long time. I don't want her to ever let go.

Finally, she breaks the silence, her gorgeous voice whispering, "Thank you for trusting me." Then she kisses me.

And right now, she is everything that I need. She is the only thing I want. My desire to kiss her is overwhelming and I bask in the feeling of her mouth against mine as a new fire rises within me. I have just let her into the darkest parts of my soul, and she is still here with me. She

427

has seen me at my weakest and my most vulnerable. She has seen *me*. And she's still here. She's in front of me, she's kissing me, she's holding me, and I am completely in love with her.

I kiss her desperately as a single tear breaks free from my closed eyes, and I run my hands up her thighs, under her ass. As she presses her chest into mine, I sit up and tighten my hold on her, lifting her up. I never tear my lips from hers, and she is still grasping my jaw in her hands as I lay her down on the bed. I hover over her, kissing her faster, deeper. I need more of her. She is kissing me back with just as much energy and adrenaline, and from beneath me, she manages to shrug off her sweater. Her hands move to my T-shirt, tugging at the material, trying to pull it off. She is struggling, and the only reason the kiss breaks is because I can't hold back my soft laughter.

I sit back, pull off my shirt, and toss it onto the floor while she smiles sheepishly back at me. We are in the dark, but she radiates brightness, color. She takes her lower lip between her teeth as she runs her eyes down my chest, but I can't keep my hands off her for long. I'm back above her, kissing my way along her collarbone. My hand is clasping her waist; the other is traveling up her thigh, under her skirt. She is running her hands through my hair, resting her chin on top of my head. She is trembling a little, but so am I. Maybe I'm nervous too.

I'm exploring her body, touching every inch of her. She is pulling on my hair now, and my face is buried into the crook of her neck as she writhes beneath me, arching her back, grinding her body into mine. She is breathing heavily into my hair, and I can't get enough of her. I place a hand on her cheek, feeling the flushed warmth of her skin.

I am reaching for her top, pulling at it, but I can feel her growing stiff under me. Protectively, she is crossing her arms over her chest whether she realizes it or not, and I remember what she told me the other night.

About what those girls told her. She's insecure about her body, so quickly, I sit back from her to give her some space for a second. I take her hand in mine, interlocking our fingers as I meet her anxious gaze. She glances down at herself and takes a deep breath. When she looks back up at me again, she gives me a small smile and pulls her top off. She reaches for me, drawing me back to her, her mouth against mine.

We are fumbling around one another. She is undoing my belt, I am releasing the clasp of her bra, my fingers are in her hair, her hands are on my chest. My heart is racing. So is hers. I'm breathing deeply. So is she. My clothes are on the floor. Hers are too.

She means so much to me, even if she doesn't know it. I trust her, and I don't trust easily. She is there for me, she cares about me, she wants me to be okay. That is the most anyone has ever done for me in years.

Our hips are rolling together, she is digging her nails into my back, I'm groaning against her ear. It is all so perfect. *She* is perfect, and I wouldn't change any of this for the world, even though it is terrifying.

I may have told Eden my secrets, but now I have a new one.

55

FIVE YEARS EARLIER

MY SUSPENSION FROM SCHOOL over the past week couldn't have come at a worse time. Mom and Dad have been taking turns to work from home to keep an eye on me, but it's mostly been Dad. He has been permanently hunched over the kitchen table, pulling at his hair and tearing up sheets of paper. From what I've gathered through eavesdropping on his conversations with Mom, things are going really, really wrong at work. More of Dad's employees have walked out. Money is missing. One of his biggest projects lined up for next year has been dropped.

Which means that Dad has been stressed this week, and when Dad is stressed, his temper wears thin. I have constantly been around, all day, every day for the past week. The kid who is suspended from school for fighting, the kid who ran away, the kid who has let his parents down. It's easy for Dad to take everything out on me, and that's exactly what he's been doing.

Every day, I have sat at the desk in my bedroom, trying my best to focus on studying without letting my fear distract me while I wait for Dad to storm into my room. I am in a permanent state of numbness. Sometimes, I forget how to breathe and how to blink.

It's Friday afternoon, my final day of suspension, and Dad has stayed home from work again to look after me. It's been a quiet morning. Dad has been pacing the kitchen back and forth in silence, and I've been upstairs studying in silence. The house feels strange being so quiet. Mom is at work, my brothers are at school. They'll be taking the bus home soon, and just like every other day, I count down the hours until they get here, because I like the noise that they bring with them.

I have left my desk though. I'm in the bathroom now, sitting on the cold tiles with my back against the wall, peeling off old Band-Aids from my arms and replacing them with new ones. Dad has been careful not to touch my face this week, so the injuries from before have at least had the opportunity to heal. My eye is still a little bruised, but the rest of the swelling disappeared days ago. The rest of my body, however, looks as though I've been through a war. Dad has been getting more aggressive. He used to throw me around for a minute or two. Now it's much longer. He used to stop when I bled. Now he doesn't.

The bathroom door swings open and I immediately flinch, unable to hide my terror when Dad walks into the small, enclosed room. He doesn't shut the door behind him. That's good.

"What are you doing?" he asks, narrowing his eyes at the box of Band-Aids in my hands and the painkillers on the floor in front of me. He stares at them for a second, then his green eyes meet mine. He hasn't been wearing his shirt and tie this week. He doesn't need to, not when he's working from the kitchen, so he's only been wearing jeans and flannel shirts. It's confusing for me. Usually, I associate Dad's casual attire with his good days, when he's more relaxed. Not anymore. The good days are long gone. "I asked you a question, Tyler," Dad states after a minute when I haven't replied. I am staring up at him from the floor, my eyes wide and full of panic. "What are

431

you doing with those? You're not hurt." He has his hands on his hips, his lips pressed together.

"I need..." I start, but I can't finish. Words fail me. My pulse is racing too fast; my heart is beating too hard.

"You need *what*, Tyler?" he presses, daring me to say it. I think there's something wrong with him. Like, he really believes that if he acts like I'm not a damaged mess, then it'll go away; if he convinces himself that he didn't hurt me, then the pain I'm feeling will somehow disappear.

"I need these," I mumble, holding up the box of Band-Aids. I reach for the painkillers, glancing down at the boxes in my hands, noticing the way I am trembling. "And these. It makes me feel better."

"Listen to me," Dad says suddenly, and he reaches down and grabs my shirt, dragging me straight up off the cold bathroom floor in one swift movement. He pulls me toward him, forcing me to look at him, but it's so hard to look him in the eye. Not when they are so fierce and intense, not when I don't recognize them as Dad's. "You're fine. Alright?" Dad tells me. His voice is firm and threatening. "You are *fine*. Man up a little." With his free hand, he snatches the boxes of Band-Aids and painkillers straight out of my hand and throws them onto the floor. "Now *please* get back to studying. You're suspended. Not on vacation. And last I knew, school doesn't finish for"—he glances at his watch—"another five minutes." He pushes me toward the door.

But I need those Band-Aids. I have scrapes all over my arms, all over my shoulders, all over my chest from where Dad has thrown me into things. They are stinging. So, even though Dad is glaring at me, waiting for me to walk back across the hall to my room, I just can't. I try to be quick. I try to be fast. I try to swoop back down to grab the Band-Aids as quickly as I can, but before I can even turn for the door to leave, Dad has grabbed me again.

"*Tyler*," he spits, his voice coarse, his tone sharper than it was a second ago. His hand is on my shoulder, his grip tightening, his fingers digging into my skin, holding me in place as he plucks those Band-Aids from my grasp again. He squeezes the box in his hand, crushing the cardboard. "Fucking stop it." I don't know this man. This isn't Dad. At least before, he would only hurt me when he lost control, when he would suddenly snap and lash out, but lately, it seems as though he knows exactly what he's doing. He's in control right now. He *knows* he's being cruel. That's the worst part.

"Dad…" I murmur, trying to pull my shoulder free from his painful grip. But in reality I have given up. I gave up a long time ago, actually. That's the only reason I even muster up the courage to ask, "What is wrong with you?" I don't care about the consequences anymore. Dad hurts me no matter what. Even when I try my best, even when I stick to being the hard-working, well-mannered good kid. So screw it. I'm not dealing with this anymore. I'm not suffering through this for a second longer.

"I don't know. You tell me," Dad growls. He grabs me even harder. His nails are tearing into my skin. I focus on his eyes instead, at that rage within them. I don't necessarily think he is angry at *me*. "You fucking tell me why my company is crashing and burning as we speak. Huh? Do you know the answer? No, I didn't think so." He shoves me away again, pushing me hard against the wall, and he runs a hand through his hair, exhaling. He looks at the ceiling, clenching his jaw in frustration. He's mad because of work again. He's mad at himself.

"I know that it's not my fault," I say slowly, staring at him. *Don't stop now. You've already started.* I swallow back the lump in my throat. My hands are still shaking; my heart still feels as though it may explode. "It's not *my* fault things are going wrong, Dad. So stop taking it out on me." I finally said it, and it feels like sweet relief.

Except Dad doesn't like me challenging him. Dad doesn't like it when I talk back. So, that relief disappears entirely, almost as quickly as it arrived, and Dad is reaching for me, his large hands grabbing my arms. He throws me straight out of the bathroom and into the hall. I stumble over my own feet, unable to keep my balance and fall to the ground. I hit my head, but I don't have time for it to register, because Dad is pulling at me again, dragging me back up onto my feet. He starts to haul me toward my room, but with all my might, I fight back against him, pushing my weight backward, desperate to escape from his violent hands. "Stop!" I scream. With everything in me, I slam my hands into Dad's chest, shoving him away. I'm not letting him do this. I don't deserve it. I'm just a kid. I'm good. It's not my fault. None of this is my fault.

He stares at me. There's only a couple feet between us and silence falls over the house again. My breathing is ragged and uneven, and I am fighting back tears that are brimming in my eyes as I look back across at him. His hands are balled into fists by his sides, his knuckles pale from the pressure, and his expression almost goes entirely blank, like he is so stunned by my defiance that he can't even process it. But then, within an instant, it all changes. Hot, burning fury captures his green eyes in a way that I have never, ever seen before. And then he lunges for me.

I am dragged into my bedroom. I am thrown across the floor, into my desk, against the wall. Dad is shaking me. His hands are too tight around me, pressing on all of the bruises that already cover my body. My eyes are squeezed shut, focusing on the darkness, numbing myself to the pain I am feeling. It is bad tonight though. I am bleeding already. Dad's fist slams into my eye again. Into my jaw, my nose, my mouth. I think he's really losing it this time. For the first time in four years, a terrifying realization hits me—one that's new, one that's never crossed my mind before. It never needed to until now. It's never been this bad. I can *feel* his rage in his touch. I can sense the lack of control.

I think Dad might just kill me.

56

I WAKE BEFORE EDEN does. She is fast asleep next to me, hugging the pillow, her lips parted. She is beautiful. I write *te amo* on her bare back with my index finger, then press my lips to her shoulder blade. She looks so peaceful, and I don't want to wake her, so I let her sleep while I slide out of bed and grab our clothes from the floor. I clean up the shards of broken glass that I smashed last night too.

Last summer, I hated the beach party. This year, I have replaced those bad memories with good ones, better ones. Last night was amazing. There is a new weight lifted off my shoulders and I feel lighter somehow, like telling Eden my secrets has taken away some of the pressure pushing down on me.

I shower, pull back on last night's clothes, then fetch myself a glass of water in the kitchen. As I gulp it down, I use the remainder of what is left of my phone's battery to check up on the outside world that I tuned out of last night. I have missed calls from Tiffani and Dean. Messages from them too, asking where I am and if I'm okay and if I'm up to no good. Sure, I was up to no good, but not the kind they're thinking of.

Just then, my phone rings in my hand, and it is TJ calling. I clear my throat and answer it.

"Hey," he says as soon as I pick up. Before even giving me a chance to get a word in, he asks, "Are you still at my apartment?"

"Yeah," I admit. Shit, he knows I've spent the night here now.

"Okay, well, get out," TJ orders with a laugh. "This girl has kicked me out, and I haven't slept, so I really don't want to have guests to entertain when I get there."

"Sure. Thanks, by the way," I say, glancing at the clock on the wall. It's only nine, so it's still early for a Sunday morning. I'll need to wake Eden, but as I'm hanging up the call, I can already hear her muffled voice calling my name.

I grab her clothes that I've folded for her and head back to the bedroom, slowly elbowing the door open. Eden is sitting up in bed with the sheets hugged to her chest, our eyes meeting.

"I was just about to wake you up," I say, smiling at her. I can't help it.

"I thought you left," she says quietly.

She thought I left? She thought I would really disappear after what happened last night? "I'm not that much of an asshole," I reassure her, then glance over to the window. I've never really done this before, the waking up with someone new thing, but I would never leave. "You've got nothing to worry about." When I look back at Eden, I realize she is staring at her clothes in my hands. I walk forward and set them down on the bed. "Here," I say, but I'm feeling... I don't know. Not embarrassed, but more unsure, anxious.

"Are you okay?" Eden asks. Her voice is raspy. Should I have gotten her some more water?

"Sorry. I'm—I'm not really used to, like, this," I admit, but my cheeks are blazing with heat. The only girl I've ever been with is Tiffani, so this is totally new to me. I'm not sure what I'm supposed to be doing. I don't know what she *wants* me to do. I figure that talking would be a good start. "We should probably talk about, uh, last night."

Eden blinks at me, then lowers her voice in the most attractive way possible and asks, "Was I bad?"

"No, no," I say, rolling my eyes as I laugh. God, she's so innocent. She has no idea that spending last night with her has been one of the best moments I've ever experienced. "I meant more along the lines of…you know, where do we stand now?"

She looks at me, and I look at her. Where *do* we stand? This is so much more than just harmless flirting and accidental kisses, but can it even go much further? Can this ever develop into an actual relationship? Even if Tiffani wasn't in my life, it doesn't change the fact that Eden and I are stepsiblings. What we did last night… Maybe it was wrong, but maybe I don't care. Eden matters to me more than what other people think of us.

"I'm not sure," she says after a while. She frowns. "Where do you want us to stand?"

"I'm not sure," I repeat, sighing as I shove my hands into my pockets. Last night meant a lot to me, and I really hope Eden feels the same way. It would destroy me if she didn't. "Answer me this: Do you regret it?"

"No," she answers without missing a beat, and relief fills me. "Do you?"

"You know I don't," I murmur, a smile capturing my lips again. I grab her clothes and bring them to her, placing them in her lap. "We'll figure all of this out. Eventually. But for now, get dressed, because we really need to go," I tell her. We need to be gone before he gets here. "Troy-James just called and he's on his way home."

Eden blushes and pulls the sheets tighter around her, hiding her chest. "Can you, uh, give me a sec?" she mumbles.

"You're acting like I haven't seen you naked," I joke, but I realize that she is clearly uncomfortable, so I nod and head for the door. "Be quick."

I head back through the apartment and tidy up the living room, even plumping up the cushions, and then I call a cab. It's the only way we are getting home today, because there is absolutely no chance of me calling anyone I know for a ride. How damn suspicious would that be? *Hey, can you give me and my stepsister a ride home from someone's apartment first thing on this fine Sunday morning?* No way. People would definitely find that too weird, so I'll stick to the cab. It says it'll be here in five, so I finish cleaning up, tipping all of the broken shards of glass into the trash can just as Eden emerges from the bedroom fully dressed.

"I called us a cab," I tell her, checking my watch. It's nearing ten. "I know it's weird, but I can't exactly ask someone for a ride without having them wonder what the hell we've been doing. We can't look suspicious, remember? The cab driver won't know us. It should be here any second."

"Where are my shoes?" Eden asks, and it's only then that I realize she's barefoot. As she runs her fingers through the ends of her tangled hair, her gaze searches the apartment.

"I don't know," I say. I look around too, but I haven't seen them while I was tidying up. They're just shoes though. It's not the end of the world. "But we need to get outta here."

"But my shoes—"

"I'll buy you a new pair; now come on," I cut in. They were Converse, I remember. I *will* replace them if I need to, if it'll keep her happy. I head over to the door and pull it open while Eden reluctantly joins me, then I lock up and hide the key under the doormat like TJ asked me to.

Eden sprints off into the elevator without me, and I quickly join her inside before the doors close. The floor must be cold, because she is bouncing on her feet. We are about to head home, and I already know that we are going to be in trouble. Our parents wouldn't have wanted us to go to that party, and they wouldn't have wanted us to stay out all night, and they definitely wouldn't have wanted us to sleep together. "I don't think we should mention last night to our parents," I say quietly as the elevator heads down. I can only imagine what would happen if they ever find out. I think we'd be disowned, honestly.

"I don't think we should mention last night to anyone," Eden says with a small laugh, but then she goes silent. The color drains from her face, and she stares at the elevator doors. Is she thinking the same as I am? It's like panic has cut straight through her.

I slip my hand into hers, offering her reassurance. She looks up at me, her frozen gaze meeting mine, and the smile I give her is true and genuine—it's mine. We're in this together. I'm right here. I've got her.

The elevator doors ping open again, and I lead Eden out of the building and into the cab that is waiting for us outside. My hand never leaves hers, and we climb into the backseat together. The cab driver doesn't question us on why Eden is barefoot, or why we look like we've been out all night, or why our clothes most likely stink of booze. I think the driver herself is hungover, and she seems to repeatedly make wrong turns, dragging out the dreaded ride home. Eden and my hands are still intertwined in her lap, and I'm rubbing soft circles on the back of her hand with my thumb. Sure, our parents may kill us, but last night is so worth any punishment.

When we finally get back to the house, we don't go inside immediately. We are mentally preparing ourselves. "Where did you tell them you were going last night?" I ask Eden.

"The movies," she says.

Oh, she *didn't*. Even though I'm anxious about heading inside, I can't fight my laughter. "The movies? Where's your originality?"

Eden purses her lips at me, narrowing her eyes. I love it when she does that. "What was your excuse?"

"They didn't get one," I say. "I left before they could notice."

"Well that doesn't surprise me."

We take a deep breath, muster up some courage, then head into the house together. It is silent apart from the sound of the TV. Cautiously, we enter the living room. Mom is on the couch, intensely studying a bunch of papers in her hands, and Jamie is watching TV while he rests his fractured wrist on a pillow. He turns to look at us, glaring.

At first, I don't think Mom has even noticed us, but then she loudly calls out, "Dave, they're home," in a hard tone without even looking up from whatever the hell it is that she's reading. She's pissed. I can hear it in her voice.

Dave comes storming down the hall and into the living room within seconds. It's early Sunday morning, and he's wearing fucking sweatpants. He throws himself in front of us and barks, "What do you have to say for yourselves?"

"The movie was good?" Eden offers up as an answer. I give her a firm look. She shouldn't even to attempt to lie her way out of this, because that reply was honestly far from believable.

Dave grits his teeth and places his hands on his hips, his stance threatening. Or at least as threatening as it can be in those sweatpants. "You two went to that beach party, didn't you?"

Mom glances up from her papers. I don't even waste my breath answering Dave, because he and Mom aren't oblivious. The entire city would have known about the party, and it's not hard to figure out that we were most likely there.

Suddenly, Eden bursts into tears by my side, and my gaze flicks over to her in surprise. "My friends took me there after the movies," she blurts out through tears, though I know her different tones so well by now that I realize she isn't *really* upset. I don't know what she's doing, but she keeps on going, forcing herself to cry even harder. Is she hoping her dad will take pity on her? "I didn't even know what it was!"

God, she is so bad at this. It's almost embarrassing. I need to stop her from digging herself a deeper hole, so I release the sigh I'm holding and fix my attention back on Dave. "I chose to go," I admit nonchalantly. I shrug at him, narrowing my eyes. When I talk to Dave, I am talking to him as Tyler Bruce. It's second nature. "What are you gonna do? Ground my ass for another five years?"

Dave eyeballs us both as his nostrils flare. Eden is still dramatically sobbing next to me, and Mom watches silently from the couch. She'll be mad at me too, but it seems today, she is choosing to just stay quiet. Maybe she feels as though she's yelled at me enough for one week.

"Where have you been all night?" Dave questions, seemingly letting my remarks slide.

"We all crashed at Dean's place," I answer before Eden can. I don't want her babbling more pitiful excuses. At least mine are believable. "Just chill out. It's summer."

"Oh," Dave says as his eyes widen. He blinks fast for dramatic effect and gives us a smile full of sarcasm. "My bad. I forgot that it's summer, so that means you can do whatever the hell you want. Sincerest apologies." In the background, Jamie is snickering. Dave exhales, shaking his head as his scowl returns. "This isn't the first time you haven't come home, Eden."

"It's just sleepovers," Eden innocently mumbles.

"That's not the point!" he yells.

"Then what is?" she fires back at him.

Dave can't answer her. He only glares at her, his lips moving as though he's trying to find the words to reply, the veins in his forehead popping. He looks at me instead. "You're impossible, so I'm not even going to say anything. Just go upstairs. Get out of here." He shoots Jamie a look too, one that probably asks for privacy, because Jamie gets to his feet.

"Fine by me," I say casually. I don't need Dave yelling at me anyway. Eden is looking at me, her features still tight with worry, and I give her a reassuring smile. She'll be okay. If she can handle me, then she can definitely handle her dad. As Jamie crosses the living room, I throw my arm around his shoulders and leave the room with him. "How's that wrist, kid?"

"Broken," Jamie deadpans, and I laugh as we head upstairs together. I would have answered the exact same way when I was younger. "Can you stop staying out all night? Mom hates it. We don't know if you're alive or dead."

I frown. Sometimes I forget that at the end of the day, I *am* only seventeen. All of this disappearing will send Mom into a mental breakdown eventually. She is staying strong for now, but I hate that I test her patience so much. "I know she does," I say with a sigh, then give Jamie a tight smile as I squeeze his shoulder. I wish I could do better. I wish I could offer them more.

Jamie disappears into his room and slams the door behind him with just enough aggression to get the memo across that even he is growing frustrated with me. My fourteen-year-old fucking brother. Why do I keep doing this to them?

"I'm sorry," I say out loud in the hall, but there is no one around to hear my apologies.

With my head low, I make my way into my own room and collapse down onto my bed. Even though I didn't drink much at all last night, I can feel a pounding headache beginning to form. I check my phone, but the battery is dead. I hook it up to charge and then get to my feet, pulling off my shirt and throwing it to one side as I head into my bathroom. I feel as though I need to shower all over again. I feel...I don't know. Guilty, I guess. Last night was wrong and for more than just one reason.

I step out of my jeans and turn on the water, letting it cascade over me, burning my skin. I squeeze my eyes shut and rest my forehead against the wall, breathing in the steam. So many different thoughts are racing through my head, and I try to gather them, to put them into some sort of order, but everything is just so complicated. I need to get my shit together. All the drinking isn't even worth the few hours of distraction it gives me. The drugs are ruining my life. Declan Portwood and his crew aren't the kind of people I should be surrounded by. I don't want to keep on letting Mom down every single day, and I want to be there for my brothers. I don't have the energy to keep on dealing with Tiffani, to maintain such a bullshit relationship. What am I really doing wasting my time with her? She could ruin my life, I know that, but I think I might just be willing to accept that if it means I can end things for good.

And Eden... I would do anything for her. She's the first girl I've ever found myself thinking seriously about, the first girl I've ever been myself around, the first girl I've ever fallen in love with. I'm not throwing what I have with Eden away. I'm not ruining this like how I've ruined everything else.

It's Monday tomorrow. A new week, a clean slate. I'm going to fix everything.

I sit on the floor of the shower for half an hour, the water pouring over my face, washing away all of the negativity in my life, and when I finally get up and switch it off, I feel rejuvenated. Hopeful. Optimistic.

I am going to do better.

I pull on a fresh pair of jeans, dry my hair with a towel, and am just slipping a clean shirt over my head when I hear footsteps racing upstairs. I expect it to be Mom, or maybe even Eden, but it is neither of them. My bedroom door bursts open at its hinges as Tiffani storms into my room. Does no one ever actually check to see who's at the front door in this house? It seems like Tiffani is forever letting herself in.

"You," she spits. There is a storm forming in her blue eyes as she marches across the room toward me and slams her shoulder into my bicep, pushing me out of her way. She's only wearing sweatpants and a tank top. Her hair is in a ponytail. No makeup. It's rare for me to see her like this, and I get the immediate sense that something is really, really wrong. She's pissed.

"If this is about me disappearing last night..." I say as I watch her cross my room and peer into my bathroom. "I didn't do anything stupid, Tiff. I left, actually. I didn't want to be there after last year."

"Your bed is made," Tiffani points out, nodding behind me as she comes to a standstill directly in front of me. She places her hands on her hips and presses her lips together. "When have you *ever* made your bed? You didn't come home last night. Where is she?"

"What? Where's who?" I splutter, blinking fast. What the hell is going on?

Tiffani has already swiveled around though, striding back out of my room. I'm quick to follow her, desperately chasing her into the hall as she pushes open the door to Eden's room now instead. My heartbeat rockets. Is she... Is she looking for Eden?

"Tiffani," I say, following her into Eden's room. She isn't even here, and Tiffani wildly circles the room in aggravation before she pushes her way past me again and back out into the hall. I reach for her elbow, trying to pull her back so that she can explain to me what the hell she is doing and why she is here, but she suddenly tenses up.

"Oh, here she is," she announces with bitter satisfaction as she shakes my hand off her arm. "You're just in time."

I look up over Tiffani's shoulder and my face immediately pales when I see Eden paused on the stairs, staring back at us with wide eyes full of confusion. She's in her workout gear, and it looks like she's just got back from a run. She is still breathing heavily, and I shake my head slowly at her as I run a hand through my hair. It *is* Eden that Tiffani is searching for. "In time for what?" Eden asks, glancing warily between Tiffani's outraged expression and my panicked gaze. There's no way... There's no way Tiffani knows what went down last night. But then why is she here?

"I need to talk to you both, because in case you can't tell, I am pissed the hell off," Tiffani says, and she spins around to face me. She holds up a clenched fist, her knuckles trembling from the pressure. "I am this close to punching you in the face, Tyler."

"What have I done this time?" I ask, feigning innocence. I already know that it's useless, and I already know that Tiffani *will* swing at me if she gets angry enough, so I step away from her. Better to be safe than sorry.

"What have you done? Are you seriously asking?" she says in disbelief, her mouth open. She looks younger without all the makeup, but right now, I think she might just be the most furious I have ever seen her. She inhales deeply, keeping her cool, and then firmly orders, "Backyard. Now."

She turns away from me, shoving Eden to one side and against the wall as she pushes her way downstairs. Eden narrows her eyes after her, then flashes her gaze back to me, searching for an explanation. And honestly, all I know is that this isn't going to be pretty.

"Fuck," I mouth, burying my face into my hands. I am praying with absolutely everything in me that Tiffani hasn't figured out the truth, that she isn't here to confront me about my relationship with Eden.

Tiffani has paused at the foot of the stairs to look back up at us both. "I can talk to you both outside or I can talk to you right here," she says slowly, placing a hand back on her hip as she casts a quick glance toward the living room. Our parents are in there. She lowers her voice, adding, "And trust me, I think you'd rather I spoke to you outside."

She definitely knows what's going on. There is no hiding from this, no denying it. We have no choice but to face Tiffani *and* the consequences. There is a lump forming in my throat as I reluctantly begin to move, guiding Eden downstairs in front of me as we follow in Tiffani's path down the hall, through the kitchen, and outside into the backyard.

The sun is bright and blinding, and the tense silence between all of us is almost unbearable. Eden locks terrified, and I think she may have realized what's going on too. We both know that we've been caught, and that it is far too late to do anything about it.

"Sooo," Tiffani says. She is facing us both, but she remains several feet away.

"So…" I echo. I'm surprised I can even speak. My throat is so dry, and I'm just waiting for Tiffani to lay the truth out in front of us.

"So I woke up to a text from TJ this morning," she begins, keeping her voice clear and slow. Her fierce eyes are flickering between Eden and me, most likely waiting for one of us to crack. "And you know, I'm getting real sick of other people talking to me about us hooking up, Tyler, because half the fucking time it's not even me."

"What are you talking about?" I ask, making a face. It's another pathetic attempt at digging my way out of this, but I'm only wasting my breath. Tiffani's glare sharpens as she locks her eyes on me, and from beside me, even Eden is looking at me in disbelief as though she can't believe I'm even trying to deny it.

"Don't start, Tyler. Just don't," Tiffani hisses at me, giving me a small shake of her head. Her tone is changing. It's growing harsher, angrier, and her words are becoming faster and ragged. "He made a joke about us hooking up last night, because his room was a total mess, and we both know perfectly fine that it wasn't me."

It's almost a reflex at this point to automatically begin conjuring up excuses for my wrongdoings, and although I know that it is pointless, I can't help but try. "Look, baby, I didn't hook up with anyone," I say quickly, lowering my voice, trying to sound gentle as I step toward her. "I just forgot to tidy the place up after—"

"Shut up!" Tiffani screams at me, and it instantly silences me. She's losing it now, and when Tiffani loses her temper, she is unpredictable. She closes her eyes, takes a deep breath. When she opens them again, her gaze is almost calm, like she is back in control. She angles toward Eden as her mouth forms a cruel smirk. "Eden, didn't you want your shoes?"

The color drains from Eden's face and she parts her lips, searching for words that never arrive. She doesn't know what to say, and neither do I. We're so screwed. Eventually, she manages to whisper, "How did you—"

"Because TJ asked if I'd had a good night and then said I'd left behind my Converse," Tiffani cuts in sharply. The roughness to her voice is back again, and so is the fire in her blue eyes. "Asked me what the words written on them meant. I sure as hell remember you waving yours around the entire night. The ones with the lyrics on them, right?" She cocks her head to one side, her glare almost threatening. "By the way, you're not getting those back. I told him I didn't want them and asked him to toss them in the trash for me."

"But Tyler's my—" Eden tries, but her attempts at denial are as useless as mine were.

"Stepbrother?" Tiffani finishes. She is so angry now that tears are welling in her eyes, and she wipes them away, placing her hands on her hips. "Yeah, I know. I just spent the past half hour arguing with myself. I was like, 'No way, they're totally related.' But I've watched *Clueless* before, okay? You know, when Cher falls for her stepbrother? I'm not stupid."

So, this is it. Tiffani really does know the truth.

We should have been more careful. I should have kept my distance from Eden until I cleared up this mess with Tiffani. I've betrayed her, I've been selfish, and as much as I can't stand Tiffani, I know that this has hurt her. I can see the fury in her eyes, but I can also see the pain. She isn't fighting back her tears now. But did she care when she was controlling my life for the past three years? Did she even care that I didn't want to be with her anyway?

Maybe this is the end of us. I didn't want it to happen like this, but if this is what it takes to finally have Tiffani let go, then I'll take it. She can't be with someone who has gone behind her back like this. She can't be with someone who has cheated on her. We are both better off without one another, and I hope she sees that now.

I glance sideways at Eden, but she is paralyzed. She is staring at Tiffani with wide eyes, barely blinking, her face still white. She is terrified, and I wish I could reach over and take her hand in mine so that she knows I'm here, that we're in this together, that everything will be okay.

"You didn't really hook up with Jake, did you, Eden?" Tiffani asks weakly, breaking the silence.

"No," Eden whispers. She looks down at the ground, starting to blink again now, but I think it's only because she's holding back tears herself. *It's okay; I'm here.*

"It was you that night at the pier," Tiffani says through her sobs. I don't think I've ever really seen Tiffani cry. At least not like this. "You're a liar."

"I know," Eden says, and her husky voice is cracked with guilt. "I'm a liar. I'm a bitch. I'm a terrible friend."

This is really between Tiffani and me. My relationship with Eden would never have come to this if Tiffani had just let me go, if she hadn't blackmailed me into staying with her. I'm not letting her confront Eden like this, not when it is only mine and Tiffani's fault. I want her out of my life.

"You know what, Tiffani?" I say loudly, clearing my throat and stepping in between her and Eden. I narrow my eyes at the girl crying in front of me, at the girl who has controlled my every move for so long, and anger builds within me. It's finally my turn to get my say. It's finally time to end this all for good. "I don't even want to be with you. I've wasted three years because you blackmailed me into staying with you. Do whatever you want. Tell everyone everything you know about me, because having you keep it a secret isn't worth the effort it takes to put up with you," I tell her, and she is staring back at me with wide, swollen eyes and her mouth slightly hung open in shock, but I don't care. She isn't the victim here; neither of us are. We just aren't good together, and all we do is hurt one another. "We're over. Sue me. Report me to the cops. I don't care. I'm done."

"This is all your fault!" Tiffani screams at Eden as she steps around me and throws up her hands. "I don't even care about the fact that you're basically siblings, which I should because it's disgusting, but no, the only thing I care about is that you've ruined everything."

Eden, for some crazy reason or another, actually takes a step closer to her. "Tiffani, I didn't mean for—"

I hold up a hand to stop her. Eden doesn't need to apologize. She tried to convince me not to go through with this, to stay away from her unless I ended things with Tiffani, but I didn't listen. I *couldn't* stay away from her.

I set my gaze back on Tiffani and without even flinching, I firmly state, "It's over, *babe*." And man, it feels like the most satisfying thing in the world. Almost blissful. I step back and jab a finger toward the gate, ordering her to leave. There is nothing more to say.

Tiffani lets out a muffled wail and throws her hands back into her hair. "But you can't break up with me!"

She is so pathetic, it is laughable. And I do laugh. Out loud. She needs to drop this. She needs to move on, to find someone else who she actually *wants* to be with for a more genuine, sincere reason. "Because I won't be there to make you look cool? Because you won't get to control me anymore?"

"Because I'm *pregnant*, Tyler!"

It's like a punch in the gut, knocking the air straight out of me. The entire weight of the world crashes down on me, and my chest tightens while my heart stops beating. I can't hear a single noise. Not the passing cars out front, not even the breeze. Even my sight blurs, putting Tiffani out of focus as she buries her head in her hands and weeps even harder.

"What?" I whisper. I can barely speak. My voice is gone. No... No way. This isn't happening right now.

Tiffani begins retreating from me, backing across the yard toward the gate, her eyes never leaving mine. She is still sobbing, completely and entirely distraught.

"What's all the screaming about?" a voice that sounds like Mom's calls out across the yard, but it isn't clear to me. It's muffled, distorted. I'm not tuned into reality right now. Everything is fuzzy as I stare after Tiffani, watching her disappear in front of me.

She reaches the gate and pulls it open, but then she stops. Her pained gaze flicks away from me, and she takes a deep breath before she opens her mouth and yells, "You should know that he's hooked on coke! And he's started dealing too!" And just like that, all of my senses snap back into function.

My vision clears, my hearing sharpens. Fury overtakes me, and just before Tiffani disappears through the gate, I growl, "You bitch!"

"Tyler," I hear that voice say again, and it *is* Mom's. I glance over to her. She is standing by the patio doors with Dave by her side, both of them staring at me in disbelief. Mom looks pale, her gaze agonizing, a hand pressed to her chest. "Please tell me I misheard that," she says, her voice pleading. "Please, please tell me you're not."

I can't look at anyone. Not Dave, not Mom, not Eden. What do they all think of me now? I'm ashamed of myself. I'm embarrassed. I've let them down. I can't hurt them even more by lying, by denying it all. They deserve honesty from me right now. It's the least I can give them. I tilt my head down to the ground and close my eyes. "I wish I wasn't," I say quietly, and my eyes sting with tears.

The shocked gasp Mom lets out pierces straight through me, and I squeeze my eyes shut even harder. It breaks my heart to put her through this, but letting her down is all I ever do. This time though, it's worse. She already knew I smoked, and although she didn't approve, she knows it wasn't the end of the world. But the coke... She didn't know about that. And she definitely didn't know that I've been dealing for the past few weeks. It's the ultimate low point of my life, and I feel like the absolute worst son in the world right now.

Finally, I force myself to look up from the grass, to face my consequences. I see Eden first. She is staring straight at me, her expression horrified, and I have to look away just as quickly again. I've let her down too, and my guilt only presses down on me even harder. I look at Mom now, but her face is buried into Dave's chest as he holds her tight while she sobs. He is rubbing her back, his intense eyes narrowed at me.

"Mom, don't cry," I murmur, but my voice is cracked and weak. "I'm not, like, addicted or anything. I just—well, it helps," I quietly admit. It's the truth. It does help. It lets me forget about my history, about Dad, for a few hours.

Mom tries to say something, but her voice is muffled against Dave's shirt and she's still crying so hard that her words are unintelligible. She is devastated, and it's all because of me. *I* inflict this on her. I'm the one who keeps hurting her.

"Mom, breathe for a sec," I say gently, and I slowly head across the yard toward her. She's still huddled against Dave, but I place my hand on her shoulder, begging her to look at me. I need her to listen to me. I need her to forgive me.

But Mom only shakes my hand off her shoulder, then finally lifts her head to look at me. Through her tears, her eyes meet mine. "I said," she whispers, "get out."

"What?"

"Get out of this house."

My blood runs cold again, a second punch to the gut. She's… She's kicking me out of the house? We've reached her breaking point. I've finally pushed her too far. She can't handle me anymore, and if only I had been better, if only I had tried harder, then it would have never come to this. My heart is breaking into a million pieces, cutting through my chest. "Are you serious?"

Mom removes herself from Dave's embrace and turns to face me. She is heartbroken. "Tyler, please," she says, but her eyes well up all over again and a new wave of tears flow down her rosy cheeks. It pains me to see Mom cry, and it hurts even more knowing that I'm the reason why. "Just leave. I can't handle this anymore."

I am stunned into silence. Dave draws Mom back to him again, holding her tightly, offering her the support she needs. My gaze travels to Eden. She is still watching everything unfold in front of her and her plump lips are parted wide, her eyes even wider. Does she hate me now? Am I losing her too?

I'm so sorry. I've ruined everything. I've let everyone down.

I can't look at anyone. My shame is too much. That's why I keep my head down as I admit defeat, as I shove my hands anxiously into my pockets and force my frozen limbs to move. I brush past Mom and Dave as I head inside the house, and I am praying with everything in me that Mom will say my name, call me back and tell me that she didn't mean it. That I don't have to leave. That she still loves me despite how many mistakes I've made.

But she doesn't say anything at all. This is really it.

There is bile rising in my stomach as I cross the kitchen, and I feel lightheaded. I can't process any of this. I'm… I'm a fucking drug dealer who has just become homeless and whose girlfriend is pregnant. I am officially at rock bottom. I can't handle this. I don't know how to. I'm so lost. How am I supposed to fix all of this now? How am I going to ever recover from this?

I break into a sprint down the hall and upstairs, but I can hear footsteps behind me. I already know that it's Eden without even glancing over my shoulder. She's the only person who *would* follow me right now, but I wish she wouldn't. I don't know what to say to her. What answers to give.

Jamie and Chase are at the top of the stairs, staring wide-eyed back at me as I push past them. Have they been listening? Have I let them down too? I can't even face my brothers. I want to hide from the world, to completely disappear. If only it were that easy.

Eden follows me into my room, and I close the door behind us. I like that she's here. It gives me hope that *maybe* she still believes in me. I know she'll be disappointed though, so I can't look at her right now either. I am too distracted by the fact that Mom needs me to leave this house. That I'm no longer welcome to live under this roof.

I grab my duffel bag from my closet and stuff it with the first clothes that come to hand. I can't even think straight. Everything feels so numb as I fumble around my closet for shirts. Am I leaving for good? Will Mom ever let me come back? I just don't know. I pack the bag with as many clothes as I can until it's completely full, just in case.

"Where are you going to go?" I hear Eden's husky voice cut through the silence. It's laced with worry, and as I slide the strap of my bag onto my shoulder, I finally glance up. My terrified gaze meets hers. She looks as sick as I feel; even she knows that I've ruined everything. My guilt returns, so I look away again. If I look at her for too long, I think I'll break down, and I am trying so hard not to.

"I have no idea," I say, but my throat is so dry. There's so many thoughts racing through my head as I head into my bathroom. Where am I supposed to go? I'm just a kid. I don't know how to deal with all of this. It's too much. "Dean's. Maybe. I don't know. My head's a mess."

There's a brief silence, and then from behind me, Eden's quiet voice asks, "You've started dealing?"

Now isn't the time for lying. She needs the truth, but it's so hard to admit it. I grip the sink with both hands and release the breath I'm holding. My back is still to her, and I keep my head down, my eyes on the floor. "Only recently."

"Why?" she asks. Her voice is so low, so quiet. It's a simple question, but it holds the weight of the world. I don't even know what the answer really is.

"It's easy to…to get wrapped up in it all," I admit. I don't know how I can still speak at this point. My head is pounding, my stomach is in knots, my hands are beginning to tremble. "Tiffani's so mad. She'll probably try to report me; I just know it."

"I can't believe she's…" Eden murmurs, but even she can't say the word.

"Me either," I say as I reach up to open the cabinet above me, but then the reality of the situation hits me at full force.

Tiffani is *pregnant*. I can't… I can't be a dad. I'm only seventeen. I'm not in a healthy mental state. Dad became a father at seventeen, and look how that turned out. I can't be him. I can't do this. At least Mom and Dad actually loved each other. Tiffani and I are toxic.

I'm going to throw up. Quickly, I spin around and bend over the toilet, heaving. I'm grabbing the wall for support, my stomach burning, but yet nothing comes up. "Fuck," I breathe.

"I don't know what to say, Tyler," Eden admits as she moves closer to me. She soothingly rubs my back as I remain huddled over the toilet, breathing deeply. "Where does this leave us?"

"What?"

"Us," she says again, and I sense her swallow. When she speaks again, her tone has grown cautious, like she is treading deep water. "What's going to happen with us? You and Tiffani?"

I almost hurl again, but still nothing. I exhale and straighten up, but my head is spinning so fast that it's making me dizzy. I think I might just faint at any moment. "I don't know," I say as I turn back to look at Eden. She is full of fear, and so am I. Right now though, I just can't think about my relationship with her. I need to find someplace to stay, and I need to talk to Tiffani. I'll fix the rest later. "I need to figure all of this out first."

"I don't know either," she says, and her shoulders slump low while her eyes fall to the floor.

I move back to the sink, reaching up into the cabinet and shoving my toiletries into my bag. I need to get out of here. I need to leave. It's what Mom wants, and I don't deserve the chance to even beg for her forgiveness.

"Please take them," Eden says, and I see her nodding back at something inside the cabinet. She gives me a small, tight smile that is full of sadness. "You won't feel so down all the time."

I follow her gaze and realize that she is talking about my antidepressants. The bottles of pills are still on the top shelf of the cabinet, untouched for days, and a lump forms in my throat. I rarely ever take them. There are other drugs out there that make me feel much better though they're not the legal kind. I don't think I've ever needed a hit as much as I do right now, but I'm fighting the urge. I can't let my life spiral even more out of control than it already has, so I give in to Eden. I reach for the bottles and tuck them into my bag. I can't guarantee I'll take them, but I'll try. For her, for myself.

I look back at Eden, at the girl that I've fallen in love with. Despite everything that has been revealed, she is still standing in front of me now. She still cares about me, despite how much I've let her down. I wish I could have given her more. She is too good for me, and I don't deserve her.

I wrap my arms around her and pull her in close to me. I squeeze my eyes shut and rest my chin on top of her head, fighting back the tears that are brimming in my eyes. Her body molds so perfectly into mine and I don't know why I've never just hugged her before, because it feels so good embracing someone so tightly, feeling their affection. She buries her face into my chest, wrapping her arms around my back. It's almost like a goodbye. I hold her for a long time, absorbing her warmth, wishing that I didn't have to let go.

I move my lips to her forehead and kiss her skin. "I'll figure it out," I whisper, squeezing her tighter before I finally let go. I don't want to leave her. I wish she knew how sorry I am.

I give her a small, final nod and brush past her. It is almost like torture having to walk over to my door to leave. If I look back at her, I'll break down. I'll collapse. So I keep my head down as I leave my room, my lower lip quivering.

"I really hope you do," I hear Eden whisper after me, and my tears finally break free.

57

FIVE YEARS EARLIER

THE WAVE OF TERROR and panic that fills me is paralyzing, but then a sense of calm quickly follows. Everything within me suddenly goes still. Dad won't be able to hurt me anymore. It will all be over. No more lying. No more excuses. No more pain. And that…that is all I so desperately want.

Suddenly, I long for it. For all of this to be over, for Dad to just hit me harder, to wrap his hands around my throat that little bit tighter, to finally end it once and for all. And I think he will.

It's almost peaceful, the thought of not being here anymore.

The thought of safety.

I hope Mom will be okay. I love her so much. I'll miss her. I really don't want her to cry too much, because I don't like it when she's sad.

And I hope Jamie and Chase won't miss me too much. They can keep the PlayStation 2 in their room forever now. They'll be okay.

And Dad… I hope he's sorry. I hope he suffers for the rest of his life from the guilt and the pain, and I hope he realizes just how much *I* have suffered for the past four years. It's tragic. My dad, the person who always tells me how much he loves me, the person I was supposed to look up to, the person who was supposed to keep me safe, is now the person who will kill me.

I am drifting, following the darkness and all of the peace that comes with it.

I am letting go now.

58

PRESENT DAY

MY PULSE IS RACING as I wait for someone to answer the door, and every second that passes feels like an eternity. It's late. The streetlights are casting an orange glow down the street, breaking through the darkness. The soft breeze in the air cools the skin on my neck, and I tilt my head down, my hand on the strap of the bag that's resting on my shoulder.

It has been a long day. I've been parked down on the oceanfront until now, staring out over the water for hours, trying to get my thoughts in order. It would have been so easy...so, so fucking easy to call up Declan Portwood. My life is in turmoil, and all I wanted was to forget about it, even just for a few hours. But I fought against the urge. Even deleted Declan's number from my phone. I needed to be better than that. I needed to figure out where I was supposed to go. I thought about heading to Dean's place. I'd have been welcome there, for sure. But it slowly became clear to me that there really was only one place I should go, and that's why I'm standing on Tiffani's porch now. Despite how much tension there is between us, we really need to talk. We have gotten ourselves into this mess together, and I'm not going to let her deal with it on her own.

Suddenly, I hear the click of the door unlocking, and slowly the door cracks open a few inches. My gaze flicks up to meet Tiffani's blue eyes as she peers at me through the crack in the door, and she lets out a soft breath of air.

"Tyler," she says.

"Tiff," I whisper, and as she swings the door open fully, I close the distance between us, dropping my bag to the floor and collapsing into her arms. She embraces me, wrapping her arms around me and holding me tight. My head is hung low, buried into the crook of her neck, one hand woven into her hair. I squeeze my eyes shut, grinding my teeth together as I fight to hold myself together. Tyler Bruce is long gone. I am just me these days, and I don't even care if Tiffani sees how broken I am.

"Come upstairs," she murmurs into my ear. "We'll talk."

I nod against her shoulder before I pull away, and she slides her hand into mine. She guides me across the hall and up the marble staircase toward her room, but even my steps are slow and lethargic. All of my energy has been completely drained out of me. I'm not even sure if I'm ready to have this conversation with Tiffani. It's too heavy a subject.

There is tension bubbling between us as we enter her room. The silence is almost making me nauseous, and I don't even know where to begin. There is just so much to say...so much to figure out. I let go of Tiffani's hand and sit down on the edge of her bed, interlocking my hands between my knees. She stands in the center of her room in her shorts and tank top, anxiously touching the ends of her hair, but I just can't look at her.

"My mom kicked me out," I say, breaking the silence. My eyes are still so swollen, and it hurts every time I blink.

"I'm sorry," Tiffani says, but then she sighs. She crosses the room and sits down on the bed next to me, her thigh touching mine. "Actually,

I'm not," she admits, and I can feel her blue eyes boring intensely into me. Yet I *still* can't look up to meet her gaze. "You…You've been cheating on me, Tyler."

"I know," I say, swallowing hard. I think her initial anger has worn off, because right now, she just sounds hurt. The guilt returns, reminding me once more that I handled all of this in the worst way possible. I shouldn't have let Tiffani control me. I should have ended things with her, no matter what the consequences were, and then I wouldn't have had to go behind her back with Eden. I shouldn't have been so selfish either. "I'm sorry," I tell her, and my apology is sincere. Finally, I look at her, and she looks defeated. I've never seen her like this before. Her nasty streak is completely gone, and now all that's left is a heartbroken girl. "I just… I have this thing with Eden," I mumble, fumbling with my hands. "I can't help it. I didn't mean to hurt you, Tiffani."

"I don't want to hear it," she says, shaking her head slowly. She presses her hands to her forehead and runs her fingers back into her hair, taking a deep breath. "We need to put that behind us, because we have… We have a bigger issue."

"Are you…" I can't even say it. It makes my stomach churn, and I even move my hand to my mouth. "Are you really…"

Tiffani drops her hands from her face and turns to look at me. I look up at her too, and finally, our gazes lock. Her features are twisting, her lip is quivering, her blue eyes are glistening with new tears. "I was waiting for the right time to tell you," she whispers, and it's like the moment she first broke the news all over again. It's like everything inside of me is shutting down.

"But how?" I splutter, angling my body toward her, shaking my head fast in disbelief. It's not possible. We're careful. We always have been. "You're on birth control."

"I guess I missed a couple pills. I don't know," Tiffani says, but her words become frantic and full of panic. She gets to her feet, her hands back in her hair, pacing the floor in front of me. "I'm scared out of my fucking mind," she admits, and she bursts into tears.

"It's okay," I say quickly, standing. I reach out for her, grabbing her wrists and moving her hands away from her face. Without letting go, I tilt my head down so that I am at eye level with her. "It's okay," I say again, my voice firm. We are both breathless, both freaking the hell out. Neither of us knows what the hell we're doing, and what I don't tell her is that I am terrified too. "We'll figure it out. Not you, not me. *Us*," I reassure her, blurting out my words too fast. "Okay?"

As the tears roll down her cheeks, she gives me a small nod. Then, I take her in my arms, holding her head to my chest and burying my face into her hair. We have to put our differences aside. I have hurt her, and she has hurt me. But we can't focus on that now. We need to grow up and cut the bullshit. We need to do what's right.

"We have to stay together, Tyler," Tiffani sniffs against my shirt.

"I know," I murmur into her hair, but the harsh reality of the situation is crushing my soul. I want to be with Eden so desperately, but it was already so complicated before, and now it just seems impossible. I have to stay with Tiffani. I can't leave her, not now.

Tiffani leans back from me, but I keep my arms hooked loosely over her shoulders. She wipes away her tears and then locks her gaze on mine. "I'm going to forgive you," she says after a minute, her voice quiet. "Only because I have to."

"And I'll forgive you too."

She furrows her eyebrows. "For what?"

"For telling my mom the truth," I clarify. Tiffani isn't all that innocent here either. She *did* set out to ruin my life this morning, and she achieved everything that she wanted to. I have to look past that now though. There's no more time for games. We have to be responsible, we have to be adults. "Can I...can I stay here?"

"Tyler..." she says, biting down on her lower lip. She shrugs my arms off her shoulders and takes a couple steps back from me. "You know my mom would flip. She always does."

"Please," I beg, reaching out for her elbow. I pull her back toward me until her chest hits mine. "I have nowhere else to go. Just for a couple nights until I can talk to my mom. Please, Tiffani," I say quietly, my voice raspy.

Tiffani's eyes search mine. I don't know what she is looking for, but whatever it is, she must find it. Finally she sighs and gives me a small nod. "Okay, but my mom is gonna kill us both."

Relief fills me. I'm hoping I can lay low here for a couple days while Mom has the chance to think things through. Kicking me out was a decision she made in the heat of the moment, so I can only hope that she'll regret it a couple days from now. "Have you told her yet?" I ask, sitting back down on the edge of Tiffani's bed again. "Your mom?" Tiffani's mom already hates me enough as it is, so I can only imagine how much she will despise me when she finds out I've knocked up her daughter.

"No," Tiffani says abruptly, shaking her head fast. She sits down on my lap, linking her arms over my shoulders and running her fingers into my hair around the nape of my neck. "It's our secret for now, okay?" she murmurs, her eyes locked on mine. She is so close, her mouth only inches from mine, and suddenly I find my body tensing up. The expression in her gaze is changing, gradually transforming into something that is all too familiar. She is confident, she is manipulative, she is in control. "Well, Eden knows too, I guess," she says with a small shrug. She purses her lips and moves her hands to my jaw, tilting my face up to look directly at her. "But she seems to like keeping secrets, so I don't think we have to worry about her," she murmurs, then kisses me.

But her lips aren't enough to distract me from the venom in her voice.

59

THE FIRST THOUGHT THAT goes through my head when I slowly peel open one eye is that heaven looks and feels a lot like real life.

I can smell disinfectant and coffee. There are four pairs of wide eyes looking at me. My body feels broken. I am in a hospital bed, slumped back against a thick stack of pillows, a cup of water sits on the small table to my left. Two of the four pairs of eyes belong to police officers. The other two belong to a man and woman in suits. They hover by the door, watching me closely with saddened gazes.

My right eye refuses to open. My left slowly drifts back to the police officers. One is sitting on a chair in the corner, the other standing by his side. It takes me a minute, but I recognize the one that's sitting down. It's the same officer from last week. The one who picked me up on the street. The one who was nice to me. Officer Gonzalez.

"Tyler," he says quietly, his voice fragile, breaking the silence. The room is tense and suffocating. I don't know what's going on. My head is fuzzy. I try to focus solely on Officer Gonzalez. "Do you remember me? We met last week." I can't even nod. I can't do anything. I am frozen in place, unable to process anything. Officer Gonzalez motions to the other cop. "This is Officer Johnson. And I'd like you to meet Paul and Janice," he says, nodding to the man and woman by the door. "They're social workers. They're going to look after you."

I try to part my lips to say something, to ask what is happening, but my entire face is throbbing. My throat is too dry. I have no words at all. Nothing comes out. I glance down at my arms, but they are black and blue. There's a bandage around one of my hands. There's one around my head too.

I hear Officer Gonzalez quietly murmur, "Please, give us a minute." There are footsteps. The door closes. I look up at him. We are the only two in the room now. He stands up and grabs the chair, setting it down again by the side of my bed. He sits down. Hangs his head low, presses his hands to his face. "Tyler," he says, but his voice breaks. He lifts his head to look at me, but his warm brown eyes are full of sorrow. "I'm so sorry. I should have...I should have known."

"W-what...what happened?" I finally spit out. The words tear my throat apart, but I can't find the energy to reach for the water on the table. I feel so lifeless, so drained.

Officer Gonzalez shakes his head at the floor, his eyes closing for a brief second. He's upset. His lower lip quivers as he looks at me again, but his eyes are crinkling at their corners. "Your brother. Jamie," he says. "You are lucky to have him, because otherwise you might not be here right now. He called us. We got there just in time." He interlocks his hands between his knees and goes quiet for a moment. Slowly, he takes a deep breath and glances back up. "Your father has been arrested, Tyler," he states, and the weight of the world crashes down on me.

He knows. They all know. The secret I have been keeping for four years is now out there in the open. They know about Dad, about what he's capable of. And he...he's been arrested? It's over. It's really, really over.

"And I…" Officer Gonzalez says, but he is choking up. He reaches up and wipes away a tear with his thumb, then edges forward in his chair and locks his eyes on mine. "I absolutely promise you that he will never, ever hurt you again. I will personally guarantee it. You're going to be okay now."

"I am?" I whisper. It doesn't feel like I'm going to be okay. It feels like everything around me is shattering. I expected it all to be over, but I didn't expect to still be alive to witness it.

"You are," Officer Gonzalez confirms with a steady nod. He holds out his hand to me, but he knows I can't shake it, so he gently pats the bandage on my hand instead and gives me a tiny smile. It's full of remorse and sadness, but also hope and reassurance, and I decide that I am going to believe him. I'm going to be okay. No one will ever hurt me again.

The door bursts open and the silence is disrupted when Mom flies into the room, her heels clicking against the floor, flanked by Officer Johnson, who is trying to reach for her elbow to pull her back. She stops dead in her tracks when she lays eyes on me. Horror floods her features and a sickening gasp escapes her lips. Her hands fly to her mouth, her jaw hangs open wide. I don't even have to look at myself to know that I am in a bad state. The pain I am feeling already tells me that.

"What happened?!" Mom screams as she dives toward me, pushing past Officer Gonzalez. She is about to reach for my hand, but she stops herself when she sees just how badly beaten up I am, and she erupts into tears, shaking her head fast, her hand still over her mouth. She has just come from work. She's still in her skirt and blouse, but strands of her hair have escaped from her clasp, falling around her face. I hate that she's crying. I want her to stop, to tell her that it's okay now, that it's over. I'm safe now. She doesn't need to cry.

"Ella," Officer Gonzalez says as he rises from the chair, "can we do this outside?" He steps in between Mom and me, placing a firm hand on her shoulder. He lowers his voice and leans in closer to her, but I still hear him murmur, "Not in front of Tyler. Please."

She is still crying as he leads her out of the room and into the hallway. Officer Johnson goes with them. Paul and Janice enter the room, closing the door behind them, their eyes never leaving me. There is silence again.

I close my eye, returning to the darkness. Are they telling Mom the truth? Are they about to break her heart? I don't know if I can bear it. I am waiting, listening, staring into the dark. My heart is beating slow and heavy in my chest. My breathing is even slower.

And then I hear it: the explosion of Mom's agonizing cries. Her distraught sobbing echoes all throughout the hallways, ringing in my ears, growing louder and louder, laced with the pain that I never wanted her to ever go through. She is screaming, a strangled cry that captures all of the air around me, suffocating both of us.

I never wanted to break her like this.

Mom bursts through the door of my room as she wails. Officer Gonzalez and Officer Johnson scramble in behind her, but I can't look at them. Mom is the only thing I can focus on. Hot tears are streaming down her face and her hands are pressed to her chest, clutching her heart as though to catch all of its broken pieces. Her frantic, pained eyes meet mine, and I break inside too. It's like four years' worth of fear finally comes to a head and the relief is overwhelming, and so I burst into tears too.

"Mom," I whisper. I want her to pull me into her arms, to hold me close against her and promise me that everything will be okay from now on. That she'll be here to protect me. That Dad won't hurt me ever again.

"Tyler," she sobs, and she is shaking her head fast, like *No, no, no, this can't be real.* She pushes her way to me, outstretching her arms, but Janice steps in front of her, holding out a hand.

"Mrs. Grayson, please, he's in a lot of pain. Don't touch hi—"

"Let her," Officer Gonzalez orders, and I don't hear what he says next, but all four of them leave the room—the police officers and the social workers. They're gone, leaving only Mom and me.

Before the door has even clicked shut behind them, Mom drops to her knees on the floor by my bedside. Her lips are quivering as her mascara runs down her cheeks, her wide eyes swollen and red as she looks up at me. "I'm here, baby, I'm here now," she cries, and she gently takes my hand in her own and buries her face into our interlocked hands, weeping against my skin. Her shoulders are heaving and her breathing is ragged, and I wish I could take her pain away the same way she wishes she could take away mine.

I squeeze my hand tightly around hers.

She's here now.

60

IT'S FRIDAY, FIVE DAYS later, and I still haven't heard from Mom. I've been waiting for her to call, or at least send me a text, but she never does check in with me. Does she even know where I'm staying? Does she even know if I'm alright? I figure she's still upset with me. It's not like Mom to cut me off like this; she's constantly checking in on me, making sure I'm okay, letting me know that she's always there for me. On Sunday, I'll make the first move. I'll try to talk to her.

I didn't hear from Eden for the first couple days either. She has every right to be furious at me, so I expected the silence. On Wednesday, I was surprised to see her name flash across my phone. It was a simple message: Was I okay? But even though I knew the answer, I couldn't admit that *no, I'm not.* I didn't reply, and I haven't replied to any of her other messages either. She invited me to meet her for coffee at the Refinery yesterday. Asked if I was staying at Dean's. Warned me to stay away from Declan. Then, she asked if I even remember what happened between us last weekend. I still couldn't reply to her.

Of course I remember what happened. It's been on my mind the entire week. *She's* been on my mind. I wish things could have turned out differently. It felt like everything was finally working out. I was going to fix everything; I was going to be with her and only her. But now it seems like I've lost all of that. I'm suddenly on a different path, and I don't know where Eden fits in my life anymore.

"So you really weren't kidding when you said there'd be no beer, huh?" I hear Jake mutter, and I tear my gaze away from the rain pummeling against the window to look at him. He's sprawled out across the couch opposite me, his head resting on his propped-up arm. He isn't talking to me, but rather to Tiffani.

She's invited our friends over to hang out, but so far, it's pretty damn awkward. Maybe it's because only Jake and Dean have arrived. Meghan is grounded, Rachael hasn't turned up, and Eden isn't invited. It's torrential rain outside too, which is only bringing the general mood down further. The skies are gray; the rain is endless.

"Why can't we just hang out without getting wasted for once?" Tiffani says from beside me, and I can just *sense* the dramatic eye roll. She's sitting crossed-legged by my side, her head resting on my bicep, her hand on my thigh. She tosses the TV remote over to Jake, nearly hurling it straight off his damn head. "Find something good to watch."

My gaze travels to Dean, but he's already staring back across the living room at me with his eyebrows furrowed. He's sitting on the other end of the couch from Jake, but he's bolt upright and clearly uncomfortable. He gives Tiffani's hand on my thigh a pointed glance, then shakes his head in disapproval.

"Can someone text Rachael and ask her where the hell she is?" Tiffani asks, then sighs as she sits up and pushes herself away from me, getting to her feet. "I'll get us some food," she says over her shoulder, crossing over to the kitchen.

As soon as she is out of earshot, Dean seizes his opportunity to ask me the question that he has clearly been dying to ask. "So…you're broken up?" he asks, skeptically raising an eyebrow. "Because it sure doesn't look that way."

"Sort of," I admit. I don't really know *what* Tiffani and I are right now, but we definitely aren't officially back together or anything. I slump back against the cushions, eyeing Dean suspiciously. "Where'd you hear that from anyway?"

"Who do you think? Rachael," Dean says, but I guess I could have figured that out by myself. Tiffani was with Rachael last night, and they're best friends. Of course she'll have brought Rachael up to date on everything that has happened this past week… Did she tell her that I was working for Declan Portwood? Did she tell her about my relationship with Eden? That I've been kicked out of my own house? That she's pregnant? Do our friends know *everything*?

Suddenly, I shoot upright, and I can't help but narrow my eyes at Dean. "What else did you hear?" I ask, my tone threatening. I have too many secrets, and I want to keep them that way.

"God, you're so fucking problematic," Jake remarks as he's flicking through the TV channels. He doesn't even look over at me, but he's probably hoping that my temper will snap. He loves it when I make a fool out of myself. "We heard you broke up with Tiff, but yet you're pretty much living here. Clearly, you two are still a thing. *Shocker*," he dramatically gasps. He sets down the remote and finally turns his head to look at me. "End of story," he says, and he doesn't know it, but his words fill me with relief. So they *don't* know that there is so much more to the story than just that.

Tiffani cheerily calls my name from the kitchen, so I grit my teeth and let this conversation go. I head over to the kitchen to join her as she's filling a bowl of tortilla chips. There's popcorn popping in the microwave, and I lean back against the countertop as I watch Tiffani closely. She's wearing a smile that is almost too happy, a smile that is so forced and so fake. Sometimes I seriously wonder if she may just be a better actor than I am. How can she act so calm? How can she act like we have everything under control when we don't? I've been on edge the entire week, I'm barely sleeping, and I feel sick every time I think about our situation. How can she pretend that everything is fine?

The microwave beeps and she spins around to grab the bowl of popcorn, but it burns her hands and she laughs out loud as she quickly drops the bowl onto the countertop. She looks up at me from beneath her eyelashes, blushing I just can't keep up with this whole performance, but I try my best to at least offer her a smile. Even place my hand over hers.

"Rachael!" she suddenly exclaims as her gaze drifts over my shoulder. She grabs the bowl of popcorn and nudges me out the way. I pinch the bridge of my nose with my thumb and forefinger, closing my eyes and taking a deep breath. But then I hear Tiffani say, "Eden?"

Immediately, I spin around, my heartbeat rocketing…and she's really there. Standing at the door by Rachael's side is Eden, and it is the first time I have seen her since Sunday.

"It took you long enough to notice us!" Rachael says as she wanders into the house.

"Sorry," Tiffani says, but her entire tone has changed. So has her demeanor. Her body has tensed up next to me, and she remains glued to the spot as she stares at Eden.

But Eden is only looking at me. Our eyes meet, and the hazel of her eyes only makes me fall in love with her all over again. God, I miss her. What is she doing here though? She is anxious; I can see it in her expression, in all of her perfect features. Have I ruined everything between us? Does she still care about me? I want to run to her, pull her into my arms, and tell her that I'm sorry. That I want to be with her. That I love her.

"Tiff, can we talk to you for a sec?" Rachael asks as she clears her throat on the staircase.

"Sure," Tiffani says, but her act is slipping. Her eyes are narrowed into a sharp glare, and her tone is bitter as she slams the bowl of popcorn back onto the countertop and walks away from me. She storms past Rachael, all the way upstairs.

I don't know what the hell is going on, but I need to talk to Eden. Quickly, I force my legs to move and I make my way toward her, but I don't even know what I'm supposed to say. I can sense Dean's eyes on us, and my stomach is in knots as I near her. Suddenly, she heads for the staircase after Tiffani and Rachael, but I manage to reach out and grasp her elbow. I pull her back toward me, keeping her close, then move my lips to her ear.

"What are you doing here?" I hiss under my breath. I know Eden can be pretty fearless, but she has some serious nerve turning up here. Tiffani could destroy her entire life if she wanted to. Make it miserable. Turn everyone against her.

"I could ask you the same thing," Eden says, her tone sharp. She pulls her arm free from my grip and steps back, fixing me with a firm look. She is furious but also disappointed. Mostly, she's hurt.

I know how this looks. But I'm not running back to Tiffani. I don't *want* to be with Tiffani. I'm only here because I have no other choice, because I can't just bail on her when she needs me. I couldn't do that. I don't care about much in my life, but I do care about doing the right thing when I can. Dad made too many mistakes, and he never tried hard enough to fix them. I can't be him.

I don't even know what to say to her, at least not now, not here. So I walk away. I head back over to Dean and Jake, and Rachael is yelling Eden's name from upstairs and when I glance over my shoulder a few moments later, Eden has disappeared. I collapse down onto the couch and run my hands into my hair, groaning.

"What's going on?" Dean asks, and I'm glad I'm not the only one who has no idea.

Why is Eden here? Why is she upstairs with Tiffani and Rachael? What the hell are they talking about? It sends my mind into overdrive and the paranoia sets in. Is there something else going on here that I don't know about?

My gaze is fixated on the TV, but I'm entirely tuned out. My heart is still beating too fast. I almost storm upstairs to find out what's going on, but I force myself to stay put. I tell myself I'm overthinking it, that I'm growing anxious over nothing, but I just can't fight the questions that are racing through my mind. I'm too unsettled, and I can't get comfortable.

"Tyler," I hear Eden's voice snap after a number of minutes pass. I crane my neck to look back at her, and she is almost breaking out into a sprint down the stairs. "I need to talk you. Right now. Kitchen," she splutters, and her words are so frantic that I immediately know something is wrong. Has Tiffani said something to her? What's happened?

I leap up off the couch and immediately follow Eden over into the kitchen. She backs away into the corner of the room, as far away from Dean and Jake as we can get, and I stop directly in front of her. My brows are drawn together in confusion as I try to take in the panic in her features. Is she okay?

"Tiffani's not pregnant," Eden hisses under her breath, gritting her teeth. "She's faking it so that you'll get back together with her."

Her words don't quite register with me, so I take a step back, blinking fast at her. "What?"

"She just admitted it to us!"

The world seems to stop for a moment as this new revelation sinks in. Tiffani... She's been lying the entire time? This is all bullshit? God, it stuns me more than it should. I should have known she would never change. She's a Grade A manipulative bitch. How could she even stoop to such a level as pathetic as this? I think about the other night. I think about the tears she shed, the pain in her eyes... It was all so fucking fake. How could she do this to me? How could she muster up such a cruel lie? Is she seriously *that* desperate to be with me? I feel Eden's hand on my arm, the warmth of her skin radiating through me, but then suddenly her touch disappears again. There's footsteps thundering down the stairs, and when I turn around, I see her—I see Tiffani. She is a mess. Tears are flowing down her cheeks, and she runs over to me.

"Baby, please, I'm sorry," she sobs, reaching out to touch me. She is crying even harder than she did on Sunday morning and her chest is heaving. So it's true. She's apologizing. She really did lie. "I'm so, so sorry!"

I dodge her outstretched hand and shake my head at her in disbelief. She is pathetic. "You're a psychopath!" I yell, and the house falls into silence. Dean and Jake are watching from the living room, Rachael from the stairs.

"I hate you!" Tiffani screams, but she isn't talking to me. No, she's talking to Eden, as though this is all her fault. But it's not. Tiffani has brought all of this upon herself, yet the look she gives Eden is full of loathing, and I swear that, just for a second, her expression almost grows threatening.

I realize then that Tiffani has the prime opportunity to share mine and Eden's secret. Why shouldn't she? She hates Eden, and she must know by this point that there is no way in hell I will ever go back to her. Why should she protect us? She has every reason to tell everyone the truth, and I'm waiting for it. Waiting for her to say the words. Waiting for our friends to think I'm out of my fucking mind.

But Tiffani never does say anything. She only lets out a wail and turns her back on us, burying her head in her hands as she runs back upstairs. She even pushes Rachael out of the way so hard that she falls against the wall.

That bitch. Finally, I snap and I slam my hand down against the countertop. I squeeze my eyes shut and breathe deeply.

This is good, I tell myself. Tiffani *isn't* pregnant, which means there is no longer any reason for me to stick around here. I'm finally free of her. It's finally over.

"I'm leaving," I announce as I open my eyes again. "I'm not staying here. She's insane." I feel almost…relieved. Eden is still standing by my side, still staring up at me with those gorgeous eyes of hers. She still looks terrified, but she doesn't need to be. Everything will be okay now. I'll sort my life out just like I was planning to, and I'll get to focus solely on her. *I'll get to be with her.*

I hear Tiffani's bedroom door slam, but I don't care. I have no sympathy for her. She will convince herself that she's the victim, but she isn't. Neither of us are. I just want to get out of this damn house. I grab my car keys from the countertop and make for the door, leaving behind my friends, whose eyes are all fixed on me. I'm sure Rachael can fill Dean and Jake in on what just went down, because right now, I don't have the energy to stick around. I throw open the front door and step out into the pounding rain, inhaling the fresh, cool air.

I'm free. I'm finally fucking free.

The rain is so heavy that it soaks me completely as I sprint across the lawn to my car on the driveway. I slide into the car and slam the door shut behind me, then I release the breath I've been holding. I sit in silence, running a hand through my wet hair and watching the rain flow down my windshield. I like the sound of it, the rain. It relaxes me as I squint through the window, a lump in my throat as I stare at the front door of Tiffani's house. I'm waiting for Eden to follow me. I am *praying* she will follow me.

I start up my engine while I wait for her, ready to make a quick getaway. We'll take off together, we'll get away from here, we'll go home. I'll talk to Mom, I'll fix things, I'll do everything right from now on. I'm ready. I'm ready for change. Finally, the front door opens and Eden steps outside with her hood pulled up over her head. She pulls it tight around her face and runs over to the car, her Converse—a different pair this time—splashing through the puddles that have formed across the driveway. She stops outside my window and knocks against the glass, but she is too blurry through the rain. I don't know what she's doing, but I crack the window open a little and yell, "Get in!"

Eden runs around the car and slides into my passenger seat, bringing the wind and the rain with her. She quickly pulls the door shut behind her, blowing out a breath of air and pushing down her hood. Wet strands of hair frame her pale face and rosy cheeks. She isn't wearing any makeup, but she doesn't need it. Her hazel eyes are so bright, so captivating.

"Ready to go?" I ask, grabbing the steering wheel.

"No, Tyler," she says quietly. "I'm gonna go back inside." Wait. What? She's not coming with me? She's going back inside? For a second, I wonder if she's just being sarcastic, but when I search her expression, I realize she isn't kidding.

"Why the hell did you just come out here?"

"Because," she says, wiping her hand across her face to dry away the drops of rain on her skin, "I need to talk to you first, so listen." Her tone has grown solemn, and as her eyes meet mine, her mouth aligns into a perfect frown. "First things first: please don't ever go back to Tiffani."

I almost laugh. She really thinks I would ever go back to Tiffani after this? "Screw Tiffani," I say, glancing out the window to the rain. Angrily, I roll my eyes and grip the steering wheel even harder. "She's unbelievable."

"Tyler," Eden says, but now her voice has gone quiet, low, husky. Her eyes are intense, and I find myself being drawn into them as I look back over at her. Her frown has deepened. "Please go home and talk to your mom. She's there alone just now, and trust me, she'll let you back into the house. She has something she needs to tell you, and it's really, really important."

If Mom had something she needed to say, she would have called by now. I haven't heard from her at all, which means she still hasn't forgiven me. "I'm not welcome there," I say through stiff lips.

"I'm serious," Eden says. Shifting in her seat, she angles herself toward me, fumbling with her hands in her lap. She's anxious about something and the atmosphere is beginning to grow tense, yet I can't figure out why. "Just hear her out, Tyler. Go home and ask her about New York."

I glance at her. I really don't know what the hell she's talking about. "New York?"

"Talk to your mom, Tyler," she says with a small nod of encouragement.

"Okay," I finally agree. I was planning on talking to Mom anyway. Sighing, I pull at the ends of my hair again, feeling the dampness of the rain.

Eden has suddenly gone silent, and when I look at her, she is staring at me with an expression I've never seen in her features before. Her eyes are crinkling at their corners as they gloss over, and she is biting down hard on her lower lip, but it isn't enough to stop it from quivering. Something is wrong. I've never seen her gaze look so pained before.

"What?" I ask.

"I would kill to be able to kiss you every day," she says so quietly it's almost a whisper. That husky tone... It's so mesmerizing against the sound of the rain hammering against the car.

"You can," I say, sitting up and angling my jaw toward her. My pulse begins to race as I gently smolder my eyes at her, taking her in. I swallow. I could kiss her right now. And tomorrow. And the day after that. I could kiss her forever. "Every single day. I wouldn't mind."

"Me either," she says but then inhales a deep breath of air. Her features twist, her forehead creases with worry. "But that's the problem, Tyler. *We* wouldn't mind," she murmurs. "What about everyone else?"

I take a minute to process her question. What is she saying? She can't be having doubts now. We've already gotten in so deep, already come so far. I know that we're stepsiblings, but it's just a label. We aren't related by blood. It's different, but it's not wrong. We'll deal with it. Is she...is she scared? *Please, no.*

"We can get around everyone else. We can figure this out. They'll understand. Maybe not at first, but they will," I splutter, but my voice cracks from the panic that's flooding through me. It sounds a lot like she doesn't want to do this anymore. It sounds like she's questioning *us.* "Seriously. We'll manage. We'll...we'll do it."

"Tyler," she says, then pauses. I hold my breath as I listen, but suddenly, her eyes begin to well with tears, and she blinks rapidly to keep them at bay. There is a flash of complete and utter devastation in her eyes as she whispers, "We can't be together."

And it's like she's shot me with a loaded gun. My heart explodes into a million different pieces, lodging in my chest. Why is she doing this? I thought that finally, *finally*, things were looking up. We had a real shot. But now… I can't take this. I shake my head in disbelief, pushing her words out of my mind, wishing that she would take them back. My eyes are closed, but I force them open even though they sting.

"You didn't just say that" I manage to mumble, but only barely. My voice is so weak.

When I look at Eden, she is crying. Tears are cascading down her cheeks as she tries to catch them, but there are too many and the stream is endless. She doesn't want to do this. I know she doesn't, so why is she? Why is she throwing it all away?

"We just can't do this" she rasps, and I can see the struggle in her eyes behind all of those tears. My chest heaves.

"Don't do this. I swear to God. Please, Eden," I plead with her, fighting with everything in me. My words are laced with desperation. I can't look at her, not when she's cutting me off like this, so I have to turn my head to the window, taking deep breaths. I watch the rain roll down the glass, and I just wish it would all stop. I wish the rain would stop; I wish Eden would stop. "We've come this far already. You can't give up now."

"We have to."

"Tell me what you want me to do and I'll do it," I say quickly, babbling my words as I twist back around toward her. I tighten my grip on the steering wheel and move one hand to Eden's knee. I will do anything, absolutely anything. "I'll make this work."

Eden's pained gaze lowers to my hand on her knee, and so slowly, she shakes her head. She can't look back up at me again as she whispers, "Don't make this harder."

She can't do this to me. I never thought I'd find someone like her.

Someone who cares about me as much as I care about her. Someone who I can open up to, someone I trust. Someone I want to be better for. I am *in love with her.* "I need to be with you," I whisper, swallowing hard. I grasp her hand and intertwine our fingers, refusing to let go as I lean across the center console toward her. She finally looks back up at me again, but I can see how difficult it is for her. "Don't you get it? You're not my distraction," I tell her. Tiffani was a distraction. The alcohol and the drugs were a distraction. But Eden is so much more than that. She came into my life when I needed her the most, even though I didn't know it at the time. She is my savior. "This is me, Eden. This. Right now," I splutter. I'm crying now too, but I don't even try to fight it. "You're making me a goddamn mess, but I don't care because it's me. I'm a mess. And the thing I love about you is that I'm allowed to be a mess around you, because I trust you. You're the only one who's cared enough to figure me out. I want to be your mess."

"I'm still going to care," Eden says as fresh tears break free. "But as your stepsister."

"Eden," I try again, squeezing her hand. She doesn't need to do this. We're in this together; we'll figure out how to break the news to our parents. And do we really care what anyone else thinks? Because I don't. "What about last weekend? We... Was all of that for nothing? Has the entire summer been for fucking nothing?"

"Not nothing. We've learned a lot," Eden says. She looks down at our interlocked hands and she squeezes mine back. She doesn't let go either.

"This isn't fair!" I yell, slamming my other hand down against the steering wheel. I can't let it all come to this...to nothing. "I told you everything about me. I told you the truth. I broke up with Tiffani, and now she's probably already planning how she's going to ruin my life even more than it already has been, but I don't care because I thought it would be worth it. I thought it would be worth it because I was thinking of you. I was putting you first. You know what the only thing running through my mind was when I walked out of that house right now? *I can finally be with Eden.*" But that's not going to happen now, and it really fucking hurts. Finally, I retract my hand from Eden's and rub my eyes. My expression is blank as I stare out of the windshield at the rain again. "And then you come out here and tell me that you don't want to."

"Do you think I want to do this?" Eden suddenly fires back at me, her voice raised with exasperation. "Because I sure as hell don't, but I'm doing it because it's better for both of us. I don't want to see you get worse if this goes wrong. What are you going to do if our parents find out and absolutely hate us? This isn't the right time. We can't handle this. You need to fix your life as it is because you need to go to New York, and you don't need any of this added on."

"What the hell is in New York?" I question, my voice rising to match hers. We're both still in tears, but we're so frustrated that we're growing angry. Not at each other, but at the situation. "Why can't you just tell me?"

"Because your mom wants to," Eden says, lowering her voice again. She goes quiet, sniffing several times as she wipes away more tears. Seconds pass. We are both silent, and all I can hear is the rain and my shallow breathing. Finally, Eden says, "Whatever there is between us, we have to ignore it from now on. We need to stop this now before we get in too deep."

Eden's mind is made up, and it is clear that there is nothing in this world I can do to change it. This is what she wants. I need to respect her decision, and although it is agonizing, at least she isn't doing this because she doesn't care about me anymore. She is doing this because we are stepsiblings, and things would be too complicated if we were to pursue anything more than that. I've tried my best, but it isn't enough to convince her. I have no choice but to give in. "If that's what you really want," I slowly murmur, my eyes squeezed tightly shut, a lump in my throat. "If you really, really want us to ignore this…then I guess I have to."

I open my eyes and look at Eden one more time. I take her all in, this beautiful girl in front of me. How am I supposed to just forget everything that has happened this summer? How do I pretend that there is nothing between us? I have to… I have to let her go, and I just don't know how I can ever bring myself to do that. My gaze rests on those plump lips of hers that had me weak at the knees from the very first moment I laid eyes on them. I find myself instinctively leaning closer toward her. I am dying to kiss her, just one last time.

Suddenly, Eden climbs over the center console and swings herself onto my lap. I sense her gulp as she places her warm hands against the skin of my neck, and my eyes never leave hers until she gently presses her lips to mine.

If this is going to be the last time I ever get to kiss her, then I'm making it count. My hands are on her waist, pulling her against me so that she's pressed hard against my chest. I kiss her so slowly. I'm scared I'll miss something. I love the way her mouth feels against mine, and I kiss her over and over again until the feeling is ingrained in my mind forever. I never want to let go, and I don't think she does either. Her hands are cupping my face as her thumbs softly skim over my jaw. She kisses me back just as delicately, like the kiss is fragile and sacred. But that's because it is.

I can't hold onto her forever though. It takes everything in me to muster up the strength to pull away from her, and I can't bite back the small groan that escapes me. My eyes are still closed, and Eden's hands are still on my jaw. I sense her move in closer to me again, the soft skin of her cheek brushing against mine. It feels so nice having her in my arms, and we remain entwined in one another for the longest of moments.

"Stepsiblings," she whispers, her breath warm against my ear. "Nothing more."

"Nothing more," I murmur. I tilt my head down as Eden climbs back over into the passenger seat. All I want is to kiss her again, to feel her skin against my own, to tell her that I love her. But I just can't find the words. I am destroyed, and there is nothing I can say to change any of this.

I can't look at her as she leaves either. I rest my hands on my steering wheel and turn to face my window, watching the rain again. It's grown even heavier. When Eden opens the car door, all I can hear is the thundering of the rain hitting the ground. A few seconds later, the door slams shut, and when I look over, she is gone.

My chest aches as I watch her run across the lawn, back toward the house, but I can't stare after her for long. It hurts too much to watch her leave like this, so I yank on my seatbelt and finally leave too. I pull out of Tiffani's driveway, and despite how badly I want to just stomp on the gas and take off, I can't because of the rain. I'm forced to crawl down the street, huddled over my steering wheel, grabbing it so tightly that my knuckles turn pale.

I glance in my rearview mirror, and I know I shouldn't have. I can still see Eden. She is standing on Tiffani's lawn, watching me leave, but she is out of focus amid the rain. She is shrinking and shrinking into the distance behind me. When she disappears completely, I finally break down.

The road ahead is blurry but not because of the rain. My lower lip is trembling; I'm pulling at my hair with one hand, my breathing shallow. Every single piece of my life has been shattered. I thought I was broken before, but now I am unfixable. I feel so lost, so alone. There is only one person I need right now, only one person that I know I can always turn to, and that's Mom.

I drive home for the first time all week, battling the treacherous rain and fighting back my tears. My life is in ruins, and now I've lost the girl who cared about me. The girl who listened to me. The girl who made me believe that maybe I could be okay. The girl I was prepared to be better for. She's gone, and now I don't know what the point is anymore. I was finally making progress, finally willing to make better decisions to fix my life, but now it feels like I am all the way back at square one again. No purpose, no motives, no goals.

Mom's Range Rover is parked on the driveway when I get home. Quickly, I pull up behind her and throw open my door, stepping out into the rain. My chest is rising and falling with each deep breath I take as I squint at the house, letting the rain wash over me, soaking my hair and rolling down my face. I need Mom so much.

I run across the lawn, but she must have already noticed me pulling up because the front door swings open just as I'm reaching it. Mom is blurry through my tears, but she still radiates warmth, love. She means everything to me. She has watched me ruin my life right in front of her eyes, but she has always been there for me, and I have never needed her reassurance that everything will be okay more than I do now. Nothing seems like it ever will be.

"Tyler," she whispers, and I collapse straight into her arms, bringing the rain into the house with me, soaking her.

"Mom," I sob against her shoulder. I'm squeezing her so tight, holding onto her with everything in me. My knees are growing weak. I can't open my eyes; I am crying too hard. I am shaking uncontrollably in her arms, my chest tightening, my heart thumping. "I'm sorry. I'm so sorry," I whisper, and she holds me even tighter, her sobs matching mine.

I'm sorry that I let her down. I'm sorry that I've made so many mistakes. I'm sorry that I couldn't be enough for Eden. I'm sorry for everything.

And in that moment, I make a single promise to myself. To my friends. To my brothers. To Mom. To Eden.

I promise I am going to do better.

ACKNOWLEDGMENTS

Thank you to all of my amazing readers for being such enthusiastic cheerleaders for Tyler and Eden's story and for following their journey for so long. Your support always means the world to me.

Thanks to the team at Black & White Publishing for being my absolute dream publisher. You're the best people to work with, and I'm grateful to all of you. Thank you for being so supportive of my idea to write Tyler's story.

Thank you to Emma Ferrier for being my writerly partner-in-crime and for always listening to my ideas despite how much I ramble on about them. Also thank you to Rachael Lamb, Olivia Matthews, Milly Shimmin, and Jess Cook for your endless support.

And thank you to my mum and dad for continuing to support and encourage me as I live out my dream. I love you both so much.

"I KNOW I CAN'T TELL ANYONE. EVER."

Tyler is the victim of serious physical abuse inflicted by his father. As well as his wounds, Tyler suffers the mental anguish of keeping the abuse secret. Later, in his teenage years, Tyler is still wary of talking through the impact of his father's actions on his own mental health.

We would like readers of *Just Don't Mention It* to know that free, confidential help and advice are always available. Like Tyler, you might not find it easy, but please don't be afraid to ask for help if you are affected by the issues explored in this book.

The following helplines offer free advice, help, and support and will listen to you in confidence.

The Childhelp National Child Abuse Hotline

National hotline is available 24/7 at 1-800-4-A-CHILD (1-800-422-4453)

Crisis Text Line

Crisis Text Line is the free, 24/7, confidential text message service for people in crisis. Text HOME to 741741 in the United States and reach volunteer trained crisis counselors.

National Suicide Prevention Lifeline

1-800-273-TALK (8255)

The National Domestic Violence Helpline

1-800-799-SAFE (7233)

ABOUT THE AUTHOR

Estelle Maskame started writing at the age of thirteen and completed the Did I Mention I Love You? trilogy when she was sixteen. She has built an extensive fan base for her writing by serializing her work on Wattpad. Estelle has amassed followers from all over the world and currently writes full time, working on bringing more stories to her readers. She lives in Scotland. For more, visit estellemaskame.com.